The Graylock

A NOVEL BY T.J. CAHILL

Also by T.J. Cahill

In the Land of the Chalice Maker (2009)

Copyright © 2010 T. J. Cahill
All rights reserved.
COVER DESIGN: Jeffery Etter
COVER ART: Joe Forte

ISBN 1456363409
EAN-139781456363406

ACKNOWLEDGEMENTS

I would never have been able to put this novel (or my first one, for that matter) up on Amazon.com if it were not for the immeasurable help and talents of Jeffery Etter. He designs the book covers, takes my manuscript and works wonderful magic on it so that you can actually read it. He is a delight to work with.

Special thanks to Lori Dillon who volunteered to re-type my manuscript onto a useable electronic format after I learned that the 3" floppy disc where I stored it had become completely corrupted. Now *that's* a friend!

Joe Forte drew the art work for the cover of this novel. He is a naturally gifted and inspiring artist and a joy to know. Check out his work at www.joefortesworld.com.

Eileen Rosenberger has been behind the writing of this novel from its inception and never once lost faith in it or me. It was she who convinced me that I had some creative writing talent. She is a rare breed of friend. Lucky me.

Clear your shelves because I am working on more books!

DEDICATION

My paternal great-grandparents, J.T. and Ellen Cahill, both died in 1937 – a year after the time in which this work of fiction takes place. It was their courageous ocean voyage of emigration from Ireland in 1880 that led them to a new life in a new land. I am the gracious beneficiary of that courage and I honor their legacy by being a very proud Irish-American man. I dedicate this novel to both of their brave young souls who searched for adventure on higher ground and found it.

Chapter One

"Hello, this is Jerome Reed calling."

The wire connection seemed strained for the almost 700 miles the young man's voice had to travel for the administrator of the Jefferson School of Law to hear him clearly.

"Hello. This is Jerome Reed. Can you hear me?"

"Yes, of course I can hear you Mr. Reed," responded Mrs. Myers, the administrator. "You can stop shouting. It's 1936 and we have some very good telephone lines here in Washington, D.C."

Jerome was surprisingly embarrassed at Mrs. Myers' unintended remark about the backward nature of telephone connections in his hometown of Buttermilk Falls, New York – the little dot on the map that he was anxiously about to leave for Washington, D.C. He did not want to appear to be some hick from a small upstate farming town. He was after all a graduate of Cornell University and while he may not have seen too much of the world during his short 21-year life he clearly had abilities way beyond getting up early and helping his father milk cows.

Jerome Reed was going to law school. And he could hardly wait to get there.

"Sorry," he said trying to be charming "I didn't mean to be shouting in your ear. But I am calling about the possibilities of accommodations in Washington while I'm in school. You mentioned in my letter of acceptance that there might be a place for me to stay that was reasonable."

"Certainly, Mr. Reed," replied Mrs. Myers "and quite reasonable it is. It's actually free room and board if you agree to work 20 hours a week. It's quite manageable in your first year."

"Sounds OK to me. Where is it? I mean what is it?"

"It's a small hotel called The Graylock about five or six blocks from the law school. You'll have to work the switchboard, take reservations and do some other small chores. It might work out quite nicely for you – apartments, especially furnished ones are getting very pricey these days."

It couldn't be worse than milking cows at 5:00 am every morning Jerome thought and he was in a pinch anyway. Since his letter of acceptance arrived three days ago he hardly had time to think about a place to live while attending school. He'd spent most of his time trying to convince his father that Washington, D.C. was not on the dark side of the moon and that he was not entering a den of iniquity by heading for the nation's capital.

Jerome worked four hard, long years studying political science at Cornell for this day and spent all summer on the waiting list at three law schools . . . Jefferson was the first to let him in and he wasn't taking any chances by waiting any longer. He was ready.

"OK . . . great . . . I'll take it. What should I do?" he asked.

"Just get down here Mr. Reed. I'll take care of everything else. I'll call the owner of the hotel and let her know you're on your way. School starts next week you know so don't waste any more time."

"No . . . no . . . I'm almost all packed anyway. My train leaves tomorrow morning. I'll be in Washington before nightfall. Now where is it that I go again?"

"The Graylock, Mr. Reed," answered Mrs. Myers. "You go to The Graylock at 17 N Street, NW . . . and take a cab from the train station. It won't cost too much. It's too far to walk with luggage and you'd get lost first time out in our city anyway. Make sure you tell the cab driver that it's in the Northwest section of town . . . you don't want him carting you all over the place and charging you a small fortune. This is your first trip to Washington? Yes?"

Again, Jerome felt like a hick who had never been anywhere.

"Yes, Mrs. Meyers. This will be my first time in Washington," he said trying to be polite. "I'm really looking forward to it and very excited about starting at Jefferson."

"Wonderful. Well, we'll see you at orientation next week and in the meantime, I'll call Mrs. Crickmore and let her know you're coming."

"Who's that?"

"Mrs. Crickmore . . . Hattie Crickmore. She is the owner of The Graylock . . . haven't you been listening? If you're going to be a good lawyer, Mr. Reed, you'd better learn how to be a good listener."

Jerome could barely stifle his laugh. A reprimand already! What was law school going to be like?!

"Sorry Mrs. Meyers . . . it must be the connection. I know it's 1936, but our telephone wires up here in Buttermilk Falls tend to get a little crossed sometimes . . . and I'm a very good listener by the way."

"I certainly hope so. It'll stand you in good stead in your new profession, Mr. Reed. Well, I think you have all the information you need. I'll tell Mrs. Crickmore to be expecting you. Goodbye."

"Goodbye" he replied "and thank you, Mrs. Meyers, for all your help."

After he hung up the telephone he reflected for a moment on her comment about "your new profession, Mr. Reed." New profession indeed . . . more like a new life and he found it almost hard to believe that it was real and just a few short days away. This was the goal of his life about to happen for Jerome. He decided that he wanted to be a lawyer when he was 10 years old and now he was on the threshold of a dream and it made him just a little nervous.

"Everything work out alright with the law school, dear?" Jerome's mother asked from the kitchen.

"Yeah Mom . . . just fine . . . I got a place to live not too far from the school. Free room and board in exchange for 20 hours a week work."

Jerome walked into the kitchen and sat down at the table . . . the place where all the big decisions were always made in the Reed household, including Jerome's decision to get his juris doctorate. His mother was in favor . . . his father was not.

"What kind of work?" his mother asked.

"It's a hotel. I'll have to work at the switchboard and take reservations and some other stuff. Sounds pretty easy."

"20 hours a week . . . that's all?"

"That's it" said Jerome.

"Well, that should seem like nothing to you after working on the farm as many hours as you did all through high school and college. If I didn't know you as well as I do, for a while there I thought maybe you were going to be a farmer."

"Not a chance" smiled Jerome as he hugged his mother "you know how I am when my mind gets made up."

"Don't remind me . . . I haven't got enough time right now to hear the 'I've been wanting to do this since I was 10 years old' argument again!"

Both mother and son laughed at the familial reminder of Jerome's legendary level of determination to do exactly what he set his mind out to do.

"Ok . . . I won't remind you. Speaking of farmers . . . where's Dad?"

"In the barn . . . you two have your chat yet?"

"Nope . . . but I'm going out to talk to him now. Last chance to make him believe that I'm doing the right thing."

As Jerome headed out towards the barn he was struck by the fact that soon he would be leaving the safety net of his family. He loved them and he had always loved living in upstate New York. He thought for sometime that he might even get accepted into Cornell Law School but as of today he was still on their waiting list. The back of the Reed's home (his mother refused to call it a farmhouse) overlooked 210 acres of fertile, rolling farmland that Jerome's father had been working his whole life. It was as pastoral a setting as anyone set on farming could hope for and the land had always provided a good, if sometimes trying, living for the Reed family. Jerome's memories of growing up here on the farm were pleasant, generally happy ones but he knew that those memories alone were insufficient to keep him there. No amount of arguing could make him change his mind. It was time to go.

He was leaving behind a predicable life for one that he was sure would be filled with challenge and excitement. He had a good mind, loved an intellectual challenge and was pretty sure that he'd make a good lawyer. He'd only known a few . . . his grandfather being the most impressive and influential one he could think of. Others he had sort of met in passing while he was studying at Cornell at guest lectures or just through family friends, but his grandfather was the legal icon for Jerome.

Strolling across the expanse of the backyard, Jerome could see into the barn and noticed his father watching over the gray spotted mare due to foal in the next few days. His father did not noticed Jerome walk into the barn.

"How's she doing, Dad?" he asked.

His father turned with a measured step and replied "Anyday now, Jerome . . . seems like you'll wind up missing it if you leave for Washington."

"Yeah . . . I guess I will" he said quietly "but it's not like I haven't seen her do this before."

"True enough" replied Mr. Reed "but it's a miracle every time it happens."

Jerome let a little silence pass before he said anything else. Sometimes he had to let things his father said break out into the air before he could reply.

"Speaking of miracles . . . I just called the law school and they found a place for me to live . . . a hotel not far from the school."

"A hotel!" cried his father "do they think we're made of money up here. Didn't you tell them that you're doing most of this on bank loans?"

"Yes I did. That's how I got this place to live. It's free room and board if I work at the switchboard in the hotel."

"I don't know about this Jerome . . . there's always some kind of catch when somebody offers you something for free. Something always goes wrong."

"Dad, please . . . try to understand . . . I'm going to go to law school. I'm leaving tomorrow morning and you have hardly said anything to me about it."

"I've told you how I feel about this Jerome. I don't expect I'll change my mind anymore than you will change yours. I don't like lawyers. Look what happened to your grandfather. The law sent him to an early grave. I don't want that to happen to you. What's wrong with farming? It's an honest living and your real good at it to boot."

Jerome's frustration level was building fast and he could see the same cyclical argument coming his way yet again.

"No, Dad . . . I'm not good at farming . . . you're the one who's good at it . . . I'm good at helping you at it. I want my own career. And it wasn't the law that killed Grandpa . . . it was shyster lawyers . . . people that had no respect for the law anyway. That's not me and that's not how I'm going to end up."

Jerome's father's own level of frustration was peaking as well and he really did not want to argue with his son the day before he was to leave the farm.

"What's the matter with Cornell, son?" he said thinly disguising the strain in his voice. "Can't you call them and ask them about the status of your application? You always said you liked it there when you were in college and it's close to home. You could stay on the farm."

This is going nowhere Jerome thought. He absently ran his fingers through his wavy brown hair and vocalized his oft repeated response.

"Dad, I've told you . . . law school starts next week and Cornell has not accepted me yet . . . Jefferson has. I have to go where I'm wanted and I don't want to lose my spot."

Jerome's father looked at him dead set in the eyes. "You're wanted here Jerome . . . with us here at home. I need you here to help me."

"Dad . . . you have Jimmy and Alan to help you. They're both good workers."

Jimmy and Alan were the twins in the Reed family. Two of Jerome's younger brothers and just beginning their sophomore year at Cornell University. They were like two peas in a pod . . . never one very far from the other and they'd been that way since they were little kids. Freewheeling 18 year olds who up until this point had always had their older brother to cover for them.

Jerome's father scoffed at the statement. "You must be kidding . . . Jimmy and Alan??! I love them dearly, Jerome. I love all our kids . . . but between the two of those guys there's hardly the sense that God gave a lemon. If they're not watched every minute, nothing gets done. Nothing! You should know that . . . you've been watching over them like a hawk since you were barely old enough to walk . . . Jimmy and Alan . . . no thanks, Jerome. I'd rather take my chances with Stevie."

Stevie, another of Jerome's younger brothers developed asthma and an allergy to hay when he was twelve and could never go in the barn and barely within 200 yards of the wheatfield before he would start wheezing like an 80 year old man instead of the gentle 16 year old that he was.

"Stevie would help you if he could, Dad" Jerome snapped. "It's not his fault he's got asthma. He tries hard to make up for it."

"I know he does, Jerome" his father replied almost apologetically. "He tries harder than Jimmy and Alan combined. He's more like you than any of the kids. I saw him looking at your law school catalogues last week. I walked though the kitchen white as a sheet and told your mother I thought I was having a heart attack! One of our kids a lawyer maybe I can get used to . . . but not two . . . I couldn't take two!"

Jerome smiled at the notion of little Stevie following him to law school in five years. He was a real smart kid with a heart of gold. Smarter than Jerome and not as shy with people.

"Sounds like it might already be too late Dad . . . if he's sneaking peak at law school brochures . . . I mean he's only 16 years old. Maybe we'll wind up starting our own law firm in Buttermilk Falls!!"

"I suppose I could live with that if it brought you both back home where you belong. Christ, they'll be nobody left to run the farm."

"What about Gail??!" Jerome offered. "Don't count her out just because she's a girl Dad . . . I think she likes the farm work."

"Your sister is 13 years old and a barnyard or a wheatfield is no place for a young girl. She should be in the house helping your mother . . . learning a few things about running a house."

"Well I wouldn't want to be the one to tell Gail that. She's pretty strong minded. Besides it's 1936 and women are doing all sorts of things these days . . . flying planes, running businesses and a good number of them go off to law school nowadays, too."

"That's it!! That's enough, Jerome . . . if I wind up with three lawyers in the family I am cutting all of you out of my will. I'll leave what little money is left to your mother and have the State turn the farm into a swimming hole."

Jerome sat back on a bale of hay and roared at the very notion of it.

"A 210 acre swimming hole!!! Dad, that's an awful lot of water."

"I don't care . . . maybe the State will drop a few lawyers into the foundation!"

Jerome knew his father was jesting. It was just his way of avoiding the useless argument over his career choice. Mr. Reed stopped grooming the mare and walked over to his oldest son and carefully clasped his two rough hewn farmer's hands around Jerome's young face. Jerome knew enough about his father to be quiet right now.

"I'm awfully proud of you Jerome. You must know that, but I just don't understand this thing you've always had about being a lawyer. And this law school is so far away . . . you've never been that far from home before . . . you've never wanted to be."

"Nothing's going to happen to me Dad. I'll be just fine and I'll be home for Christmas . . . that's hardly more than three months away."

"It's closer to four. You're talking like a lawyer already!"

"I'm just trying to tell you that I'll be alright."

"A lot can happen in four months . . . there's nothing wrong with being a farmer."

"There is for me. I won't be any good at it on my own. I

want to be a lawyer Dad. I'm excited about going to Washington. There's lots of stuff happening down there. I'm looking forward to this . . . and it all starts next week." Jerome took a deep breath and finished ". . . and I'm leaving tomorrow morning."

Jerome's father looked away from Jerome . . . away from the mare and gazed over the rafters in the barn looking for something to help him through this. Finally, he turned back to Jerome.

"Ok . . . you win. That's what you lawyers are suppose to do isn't it? . . . win your arguments?" He drew closer to his son and grabbed his hands. "But you listen to me, Jerome Reed. If you find out that this law school idea doesn't suit you, or something happens to you or you find those folks down there aren't to your liking . . . you come back here straight away . . . you hear me? Don't you stay down there if you think you might have made the wrong decision . . . you just come back home, you understand? I want you to promise me that."

"I promise Dad. But I know it's the right decision."

"Alright then. I won't say anymore. But you know we'll always be here for you. Now what do you say we go in and get some lunch?"

Relieved, Jerome was beaming. They both headed out of the barn and towards the house arm in arm.

"Great idea. Let's have Gail fix us up something."

"Don't be a wise guy. She can't cook and you know it. The girl's 13 years old and she can't hardly even boil a pot of water. I don't know what's to become of her."

"But she can fix the tractor, Dad."

Mr. Reed wiped his forehead and sighed. "My whole family's coming out backwards."

Jerome hugged his father. "Dad, stop worrying. Lighten up a little. You worry too much. You worry way too much about us."

For the last time in what Jerome knew would be a while, father and son walked across the Reed terra firma. Through the yard where they all grew up, had fights, picnics and celebrated each others birthdays. It was the place where laundry was hung and the Reed kids climbed trees . . . the same place where the unforgiving New York State winters kept them held up inside the expansive home until Mrs. Reed gave the green light to dress up warmly and head outside where they created there own version of the Reed family, relatives and all, in the snow. It was the same backyard where Mr. Reed found his father-in-law lying dead one chilled, frosty October morning nine years earlier. No one in particular was ever found to blame, but Evans Reed, now the family patriarch knew what to blame. He blamed "the law" as he disdainfully called it . . . the messy legal profession and it's scurrilous members. It's was a short walk across the yard, but one long with family memories.

Later that evening when Jerome and his mother were gathering the clothes he would need to carry with him to Washington, Mr. Reed walked into the bedroom that Jerome shared with the twins, Jimmy and Alan.

"I've been up in the attic looking for this, Jerome" he said as he looked at his wife of 23 years . . . pretty as ever. "I thought you might want to take it with you. It belonged to your grandfather."

The suitcase was a weary looking piece of luggage . . . tanned and cracked-worn leather with full length straps and discolored brass catches. He placed it on Jerome's bed and stood back a bit. Mrs. Reed carefully placed the pile of Jerome's just-ironed dress shirts on the bureau and walked over to her husband and gently rubbed his broad shoulders. She smiled as she let her small hands linger over the frame of the old suitcase.

"I remember this one so well, Jerome. My mother told me that she bought it for your grandfather as a Christmas present back in 1902, a month after he was elected as the youngest judge in Cayuga County. She wanted him to have something suitable to put his clothes in while he was riding the circuit . . . that's what they used to call it back then . . . 'riding the circuit.' He brought it with him wherever he went . . . carried it around for over 25 years."

Jerome remembered the suitcase well. He hadn't seen it since his grandfather died and didn't know that it was stored up in the attic. He remembered seeing his grandfather carry it off to the train station every time the tireless judge left Buttermilk Falls to hear a case out of town. Now it was his. He unbuckled the straps and released the catches. When he flipped the top open, barely a scent of musty odor was detectable . . . unusual for something that had been tucked away for nine years.

"Thanks Dad" he said "Looks like everything I have will just about fit in here."

"I'm sure we can get all your clothes in, Jerome" answered his mother. "I'm an old hand at filling this suitcase. I used to help my mother get Grandpa ready for a lot of his trips."

"Well, lets get started then. Morning will be here before you know it" said Mr. Reed.

With that, the three of them busied themselves with packing the present into a bit of the past.

Chapter Two

Jerome was already comfortably situated in his seat by the time the conductor bellowed "All Aboard!!! ALLLLLLL AAAABOOOOARD!!!" The train station goodbyes were compact. Tender, but compact. He had never really had to say goodbye to his family before so he was not too sure how to do it anyway. He lived on the farm all the way through high school and college. Never really been anywhere to speak of before for any time longer than a couple of days. Now was not the time to stage a Hollywood style tear-jerking, heart-stopping goodbye scene. It was not his style to pretend to be someone he was not or to try to pretend that he knew how to do something he had no idea how to do.

They were all looking at it a bit differently than Jerome to start with. While he saw himself heading out of town until Christmas, everyone else was viewing it a departure of extreme proportion. He knew he'd be back, even his family knew he'd be back but they felt like Christmas was forever in the distance. Jerome knew with the amount of work he was going to have to do in the first three and half months of law school before the holiday break that it'd go by like lightning. He promised he'd write often although he knew he might not find the time to. He promised not to forget anybody's birthday. All the Reed kids' birthdays fell between Labor Day and Christmas. The birthday cards he knew he would not forget. The twins assured Jerome that they were going to try to squeeze permission from their parents for a trip to Washington to celebrate their birthday the week before Thanksgiving. He told them he'd be waiting for their arrival but secretly knew that they would never get the permission . . . too much money. It might be fun he thought, but he'd have to get to know the city a little bit better before he could entertain those two wild ponies.

No, this was the time for him to be away from the Reed family for a bit. Time to focus on his new career and make his way in a new place. There was going to be a lot in front of him.

He was daydreaming out the window when the conductor had to tap him twice on the shoulder to ask for his ticket. Jerome reached inside his vest pocket and handed him the most expensive thing he had ever bought for himself, outside of college tuition. The ticket was $12.50 one way. Jerome almost hated to part with it for the little time it took the conductor to rip half of it off.

"Washington, D.C., eh?!" said the conductor.

"Yep," smiled Jerome as he extended his hand "all the way down."

"The nation's capital is quite an exciting place for a young fella nowadays. All the politics and such . . . and our Mr. Roosevelt trying to get himself some more free room and board." The conductor laughed and Jerome was amused at his reference to free room and board . . . exactly what Jerome was going to get at The Graylock. Aside from being a declared Democrat himself, Jerome had never thought anyone might unsuspectingly compare Jerome Evans Reed to Franklin Delano Roosevelt. But Jerome knew full well that FDR was desperately seeking a second term in office and some said (although he could never exactly figure out who *they* were) that his Republican challenger, Alf Landon of Kansas was gaining on the President and might be able to win. The election was nine weeks away. Roosevelt was the Governor of New

York State when he beat President Herbert Hoover in 1932 and it seemed like all New Yorkers were for him then and were for him now. Jerome couldn't imagine that FDR could lose to this guy from Kansas.

"You're going to have to switch trains when we get to Pennsylvania Station in New York City. You know that don't you young man?"

Jerome was surprised that he was not aware of the switch. "No, actually I didn't know that. Thanks for telling me. God only knows where I might have wound up!"

"You'd have wound up in Pennsylvania Station in New York City, that's where" cackled the conductor. "Can't go no further than there on this train. It's the dead last stop."

"What do I do when I get there?" queried Jerome.

"Just follow the crowd upstairs one flight to the main station and look for the big board that posts all the train departures and the track numbers that they're leaving on. Everybody will be looking for the same thing. Make sure you look for the train called the Cardinal Express. That's the one that goes to Washington, D.C. It usually leaves from Track 22 . . . I say "usually" now, so don't take my word as gospel. Make sure you check the big board. The engine switch doesn't take more than 45 minutes or so. Stick to the main station and watch out for pickpockets. We're right on schedule so we'll be pulling into Penn Station around 1:00 this afternoon."

"Thanks for the information and the free advice"

"What brings you all the way down to Washington?"

"Law school" Jerome answered proudly "I start next week."

"You don't say! Law school? Well, that's something. Better enjoy your daydreaming out the window while you can. I hear it's a pretty rough business."

"I'll find out soon enough."

"Well, good luck to you, son."

The conductor handed Jerome his ticket back and headed down the aisle. "Good luck" repeated Jerome to himself. "Maybe I'll need it."

He returned to his daydreaming out the train window and watched as the rolling countryside of New York State passed by him easily. His thoughts were filled with what was ahead. A full schedule of classes, new people to meet, new challenges and all taking place in the legal mecca of the United States. He knew that the first free moment he found he'd get up to see the Supreme Court building behind the Capitol. Maybe he'd even get a glimpse of the President someday . . . whoever it was. Jerome hoped it would be President Roosevelt again and not President Landon. He didn't think the country was ready for a president from Kansas.

He walked leisurely down to the club car to get a snack and wondered where all the rest of the passengers were headed and if the horizon seemed as exciting to them. He passed a group of four men, seemingly in their late thirties or early forties, sitting at a booth in the club car. All were dressed in fancy business suits and frowned while they talked to each other. It was serious business whatever it was they were discussing. So serious that they all had a glass of whiskey in front of them. Bearded and mustached men making big decisions. Jerome eyed them closely and noticed that two of the four were badly balding and overweight. The other two were chomping on smelly cigars. Jerome hoped they were not lawyers because drinking and smoking at 11:00 in the morning was a bad sign . . . not too much to look forward to. Maybe they were accountants he thought.

The older gentleman sitting alone in the next booth closest to the porter's counter was a more comfortable sight. He reminded Jerome of his grandfather. Not so much in attire or looks, but in stature and presence . . . dignified, elderly and wise. And the tactfulness to be drinking club soda before noon. He felt reassured.

"What'll it be sir?" asked the Negro porter. Jerome did not respond.

The porter repeated himself. "Excuse me sir. May I get you something?"

"Oh, I'm sorry I wasn't listening." The real answer was that he was not used to people calling him sir and he did not realize the porter was addressing him.

"I wondered if I could get you something here," the porter politely offered again.

Jerome thought for a second and looked out the corner of his eye at the older gentleman.

"Sure . . . I mean, of course. Yes, I would like something."

They stared at each other a bit uncomfortably until the porter decided to speak again.

"Well then, what'll it be?"

Jerome bent over the counter towards the porter and almost whispered "I'll have what that gentleman is having, a club soda I believe."

The porter shook his head slightly and wondered why Jerome was whispering. "A club soda it is, sir. Would you like a lemon or a lime slice in that?"

Jerome took a quick glance at the gentleman one more time.

"A lime please."

"OK. One club soda with a lime slice coming up. Anything else with that, sir?"

"Oh why not!? How about a bag of those pretzels over there?"

"Alright, sir. A club soda with lime and a bag of pretzels. That'll be 20 cents, please."

Jerome took his snack and turned away from the porter. He was staring out the window before he decided to return to his seat and he noticed that the older gentleman nodded politely to him. Jerome responded with a quiet hello and the man asked if Jerome would like to join him in the booth.

"You shouldn't eat standing up. It's bad for your digestion." said the man.

"I was just heading back to my seat . . . but thanks . . . I can sit for a bit." Jerome was never too good with strangers . . . never seemed to know what to say. He did not have much of an ability for small talk and most of his life he had been taken for being excessively shy. If the man had not reminded Jerome so much of his late grandfather he might not have sat down at all. But he was determined to overcome this handicap and figured that now was as good a time as any.

He slid into the booth and placed his club soda and pretzels on the table directly across from the man. "Thanks for the invitation . . . I'm traveling alone as it is." The man nodded and adjusted his hat slightly. Jerome extended his right hand across the table to his host.

"I'm Jerome Reed, by the way. How do you do?"

"Roberts is my name. Everett Roberts. It's nice to make your acquaintance Mr. Reed." He even spoke like Jerome's grandfather.

"Pleased to meet you," responded Jerome trying to impress and be polite at the same time.

"How is it that you come to be traveling by yourself on this train to New York City?" asked Mr. Roberts as he sipped his own club soda.

"Well, actually Mr. Roberts, I'm on my way to Washington, D.C. New York City is just the stop over point until the engines get switched."

Jerome's snowy haired companion laughed lightly. "You sound like a veteran traveler, Mr. Reed, but my guess is that this just might be your first trip to our nation's capital."

Jerome felt like a real rube and fessed up to his older and obviously wiser fellow traveler. "How'd you guess. Do I really look like that much of a country bumpkin?"

"Oh, my word. Not at all," said Mr. Roberts fearing that he had insulted Jerome. "Please accept my apologies if my comment came across to you that way. No . . . no . . . not at all. In fact, you're dressed very sharply in that suit. I couldn't help but notice, though, when you ordered from the porter that you appeared too pleased to pay the 20 cents for your snack and that you left a 10 cent tip."

"Sorry . . . I don't get it."

"Well most folks who have been traveling on this train for awhile know full well that 20 cents for a club soda and a bag of pretzels is way too much money . . . there's a depression on, you know . . . and then to leave half that amount in a tip . . . well frankly Mr. Reed that was the dead giveaway."

Jerome was too surprised to be embarrassed. "Wow . . . that's pretty good. Yes, in fact this really is my first time on this train. My first time passing through New York City and my first trip to Washington. What are you . . . a detective or something?"

Jerome was getting quite comfortable now in Mr. Roberts' presence and felt very easy when he smiled broadly at Jerome's last question.

"No. I'm not a detective, Mr. Reed."

Jerome interrupted him. "Please call me Jerome. Mr. Reed makes me feel so old." Before he could stop himself, Jerome realized that he may have insulted Mr. Roberts, who clearly appeared to be at least in his seventies.

"I'm sorry . . . I didn't mean anything by that . . . I mean there's nothing wrong with being old."

Mr. Roberts placed his drink down in front of him and set his hands flatly on the table.

"Certainly not. I wholeheartedly agree with you Jerome. There is not one thing wrong with being old or getting older for that matter! I'm quite proud of the fact that I've lived to be 73 years old . . . not too many folks make it to my age nowadays . . . interesting life I've had as well!"

My god, thought Jerome, this guy is a half a century older than me! He shifted very comfortably in his seat and flashed the trademark Jerome Reed smile that his grandfather told him used to light up his life.

"That's great. Wonderful! Well, you certainly must enjoy your work. What was it that you said you do?" asked Jerome.

"Oh . . . pardon me . . . I never answered your question. I'm an observer . . . a political observer to be exact. I've been observing politics for almost 50 years now. My field of expertise is on the national front . . . Presidential races . . . Senatorial campaigns and the like. I follow some local races but not too many."

Jerome was stymied. "I don't mean to be impolite Mr. Roberts, but how do you make a living from that?"

"Please call me Everett. Fair's fair wouldn't you say?"

Jerome agreed but no one Everett's age had ever given him permission to address them by their first name. It seemed a bit odd to him.

Everett went on to explain to Jerome that he made quite a nice living indeed by being a political observer. Roberts said that he had been observing and consulting on presidential politics since 1887 and had a real feel for the national electorate.

"Let me tell you Jerome, I made my first bit of money back in the days when President Grover Cleveland was running for re-election against a relatively unknown Senator from Indiana by the name of Benjamin Harrison. Everybody thought that Cleveland was simply unbeatable! That was back in 1887. I was 23 years old and dying to get on the inside track of politics. I couldn't get near the President at that time . . . too many people around him trying to protect him from the truth as I saw it. So I traveled out to the Republican convention that year and watched this Senator Harrison get the presidential nomination on the eighth ballot. I knew right then and there that Harrison was going to unseat big ol' Grover but nobody believed me."

"I still don't see how you make any money by being an observer."

"Sit tight now and let me finish. You see, Harrison's grandfather was the ninth President of the United States . . . beat President Martin Van Buren right out of the White House way back in 1840 . . . so I figure the Harrisons have a family history sort of in beating the pants off incumbent Presidents . . . and his great-grandfather even signed the Declaration of Independence. I figure that Harrison's got to be thinking that the White House is practically his birthright. And as luck would have it, I bump into Harrison's campaign manager and I run him into a corner with my speech about how President Cleveland is going to get a whipping from the Grand Army who are still madder than hell that ol' Grover vetoed a bill that would have provided pensions for dependents even when the disability had no relation to service during the Civil War. It was a stupid, foolish move by Cleveland. There were lot of vets still around from the Civil War.

"So this guy hired you?

"Well, sort of. I knew that Senator Harrison was a war hero and likely to be well favored by the Grand Army. I also knew that there was a nasty lingering rumor still running about that when ol' Grover was a younger fellow he bought himself a substitute to serve his army duty and that made him a slacker and the story was that he's always had a slacker's vindictiveness towards braver men and that's why he vetoed the pension bill. So I agreed to get some real solid information for Harrison's campaign on that issue and set about talking and interviewing all these war vets. I got paid for my efforts. Harrison won the election just like I knew he would and I became a political observer!

Jerome was awestruck. He could hardly believe that Everett was old enough to remember the presidential election of 1888, much less partake in it.

"That's fascinating, Everett."

"That's politics, Jerome," he chuckled in response. "It's a mighty interesting field. I've been hooked on it all my life."

"Unbelievable" said Jerome shaking his head.

"And now I'm off to Washington to see the current White House resident . . . seems he'd like a bit of my advice on his own electoral battle with Alf Landon."

Jerome was nearly speechless. He was barely two hours outside of Buttermilk Falls on his first real trip away from home and he'd already met a man who was on his way to visit Franklin D. Roosevelt.

"You are actually going to meet President Roosevelt?"

"I've met all of them . . . well everyone since Harrison got in . . . Cleveland, McKinley, Teddy Roosevelt, Taft, Wilson, Harding, Coolidge, Hoover and now Mr. New Deal himself."

"Wow. . . this is almost too much for me to believe. You must feel very important."

"Nonsense, Jerome. I feel like I was lucky enough to find something I love to do and had the stamina to stick with it. It's hardly ever felt like work to me."

"Yeah . . . but FDR . . . he's like a hero to me."

"He's like a hero to most young fellows your age . . . which I guess to be about 21 or 22 . . . am I right?"

"I'm 21 . . . be 22 pretty soon."

"I suspect that you'll be voting in the November election?"

"Absolutely" exclaimed Jerome. "First time, too. I can hardly wait. Who do you think is going to win?"

Mr. Roberts paused for a moment and brushed his silvery handlebar mustache with his index finger. "Well now . . . that's a good question. History tells me that unseating an incumbent president is not unheard of . . . Mr. Roosevelt knows that full well . . . he beat President Hoover four years ago so he understands that there is no guarantee that he'll be re-elected. Right now Mr. Landon is showing some great strengths in big parts of the country . . . running ahead, in fact, in a few places which I think is surprising FDR's advisors."

"You don't actually think he'll lose do you?" asked Jerome.

"It's pretty hard to tell in politics these days . . . there are an awful lot of poor people in this country who thought the Depression would be over by now and they are tired of having to scrape around for a living . . . tired of not having enough money to feed their families. They may just decide to take it on Roosevelt the same way they took it out on Hoover in 1932."

Jerome listened carefully and decided to test out his own powers of political observation on Mr. Roberts.

"Yeah . . . but the President has one big thing working in his favor that Alf Landon clearly does not."

Mr. Roberts raised his bushy eyebrows and cocked his head just a bit to indicate interest in his, young companion's input. He was interested and Jerome knew it.

"And just what might this one big thing be, in your opinion, Mr. Reed?"

"Eleanor."

The sage political observer reared back in the booth and laughed mightily and he slapped his knee with one hand and punched the air with the other.

"Very good, Jerome. That is an excellent observation! Indeed,

THE GRAYLOCK

Landon has no 'Eleanor' in his life or campaign staff. She is a terrific and very strong presence for the President . . . and just a completely lovely woman."

"Now I suppose you're going to tell me that you know her, too!"

"Not well, of course . . . but I was at their wedding. Eleanor's uncle, the President invited me."

"Let me get this straight . . . President Theodore Roosevelt invited you to the wedding of Eleanor and Franklin?" Jerome asked incredulously.

"That is correct. You see Eleanor's father had long since died and so Teddy was to walk Eleanor down the aisle and give her hand to young Franklin. It is a picture etched in mind forever . . . one current president and one future president exchanging a handshake as the bride stood by and waited for Franklin to take her to the altar. She was such a study in grace and presence that day and she looked very beautiful . . . don't ever let anybody tell you differently . . . I was there. I saw it. And she has that same grace and style to this day. . . a woman of vitality and determination."

"I'm almost afraid to ask. . . but how did you know Teddy Roosevelt?"

"I was doing some consulting for him at the request of his chief of staff, whom I had known for some time . . . it was a detailed presentation on tariffs and their impact overseas . . . Teddy was very interested in how what we did as a nation affected other countries . . . especially European ones. It was the kind of work I was getting quite good at and fairly well known for. Well to make a long story short . . . I don't want to bore you . . . ."

Jerome interrupted in an instant. "Believe me, Everett you are not boring me."

"You're very kind. . . most young folks don't want to listen to an old man ramble on these days."

"No . . . please . . . ramble on! Ramble . . . ramble . . . I'm soaking every syllable in."

Mr. Roberts continued with what was quite a tale for Jerome's eager ears.

Well. . . President McKinley had already been assassinated and Teddy hadn't been in the White House for more than a year or so. And like I said, I was doing some work on the tariff issue at the request of his chief of staff, who invited me down to Washington to present it to the President. I was honored of course. . . always am whenever I'm invited to the White House.

"When did you say this was again, Everett?" said Jerome

"Oh, yes. . . I forgot to say . . . it was in July of 1902 . . . it was awfully hot in Washington that summer. My shirt was already sticking to my back by the time I walked over from my hotel across Lafayette Square to the White House. It was a funny day . . . I don't mean in a comical sense but in that way that brings an odd aura to the atmosphere and surroundings. I felt quite confident about the material I was to present to the President but I felt strangely out of sorts for some unknown reason. I couldn't figure it out, I mean I had been to the White House to see presidents before. It wasn't any physical ailment or anything of that nature but I just felt off-beam, if you know what I mean. But proceed I did as I knew I must with the order of the day. I didn't want to keep the President waiting."

Jerome removed his suit jacket and placed it next to him in the booth. "You don't mind do you?" he asked Mr. Roberts as an afterthought.

"No, not at all . . . go ahead and make yourself as comfortable as you please." He paused for a moment as though to collect his thoughts. He motioned to the porter to bring them both another round of club sodas. "After the Pinkertons brought me 'round to the waiting room, I got the sense that all was not well in the

White House that day. And sure enough I was right... my keen powers of observation were right on the money."

"What happened?"

"It seemed as though one of the President's trusted aides had not turned up for work in what was now the second day in a row. One day without an excuse was probably alright with Teddy, but not to show up for work on the second day without telling anyone was unacceptable to him... it also made him rather suspicious, as this was quite a reliable young fellow who rarely missed a day at the office. I had corresponded with him in fact, a Mr. Nathaniel Farley I believe his name was, about the tariff presentation I was going to make to the President. Anyway, Teddy's guts were telling him that something was very wrong and he wanted the matter seen to immediately... and when Teddy Roosevelt said immediately that is exactly what he meant!"

"Did the guy just skip town?" asked Jerome trying to second-guess the story's ending.

"No one knew where he was... that was the odd thing about the whole matter. I don't know if you know this or not, but as a younger man, Teddy was the Police Commissioner of New York City and he had a great instinct for crime solving and he smelled a crime here like it was nobody's business."

"What tipped the President off?"

"Mostly I guess it was logic and common sense. I mean it just didn't make any sense – this young man's disappearance. Here is a well-educated, smart young fellow with a good job working for the President of the United States and he just decides not to show up for work!!?? Without sending a messenger over to the White House or to a fellow colleague?? I don't think so. There had to be some sort of foul play in the air... and the President knew it... and he was most distraught over the matter. I could see it in his face as he whizzed past me about ten minutes after I got situated in the waiting room. I could hear him shouting at the top of his voice from the Oval Office to get all the D.C. police out on a search for this young man . . . he ordered all the available Pinkertons on the hunt right away. He wanted his aide found!

"Did they find him ever?"

"Yes . . . very sadly they did . . . dead."

Jerome gasped. "No . . . really? What happened . . . did he kill himself?"

"Goodness no . . . why would a young man with the world on a string want to kill himself . . . he had a very bright future."

"I thought maybe the pressure of being in the White House might have done him in" offered Jerome. "I read about these new studies going on by doctors recently about how the pressures of a job can affect your mental health."

"Quackery!!! Absolute stuff and nonsense" shouted Mr. Roberts. "What kind of pressure . . . he wasn't the President, Jerome . . . he was an aide to the President and you didn't see Teddy going around trying to kill himself! No . . . No . . . Mr. Farley was murdered and under some horribly violent circumstances judging from the crime scene."

"You actually saw the body?"

"Indeed I did and a gruesome sight it was, too. The poor fellow's face looked like it had been smashed in by a tree trunk. He had been so savagely strangled to death that his tongue was nearly squeezed right out of his head." Mr. Roberts ran his finger along the inside collar of his shirt at the very remembrance of the crime scene. "His killer had obviously been in a hurry to make his getaway because he made only a half-hearted attempt to cover up his vicious crime . . . buried poor young Mr. Farley under a pile of leaves and some dead tree branches. If the President had not been so angry he would have been inconsolable . . . and he was purely livid with anger that someone would dare do this to one of his trusted aides."

"Where did they find him?"

"In a park . . . Rock Creek Park . . . I'm sure you'll discover it's real beauty once you get to Washington."

"How long had he been buried there?"

"Oh the authorities found his body the very same day that I was at the White House . . . Teddy was on a mission to find his boy and he had ordered every available officer, inspector and detective on the hunt and they knew they were NOT to come back empty handed. Apparently, Farley had been murdered only the night before while strolling through the park after dark."

Jerome continued to listen . . . enraptured by the story. "Did they ever find the killer?" He wanted to know as he secretly remembered that no one had ever been charged in his own grandfather's death nine years ago.

"The vagabond was in custody by nightfall," replied Mr. Roberts. "I went out to the crime scene with the President at the behest of his chief of staff. It was a frenzy of activity and the President's presence was beginning to draw a large crowd of onlookers. Simply by looking at Farley's dead, lifeless body I could tell that who ever it was that committed this horrendous act was a very large and strong man, indeed. Such a complete strangulation could only have been executed by someone with tremendous strength and power. The foot imprints left around the area were imbedded into the soft ground indicating to me that the killer was also someone of considerable weight."

"Maybe you should have been a detective, Everett," chirped Jerome.

"It didn't take a detective to see what I saw . . . I was just relying on my powers of observation. Farley was not a big man . . . probably only about 5'6" and looked like he couldn't have weighed more than 140 pounds. He never had a chance against his assailant. Dead and gone from this world for what turned out to be barely $8."

"How'd they catch the guy?"

"Very foolishly he started to spend some of his blood money in one of the local taverns and the barkeep began to get rightly suspicious that someone as tattered looking with such a foul disposition would even have the money for a 5 cent glass of beer much less repeated rounds of it. So, he called for the local beat cops. The minute they walked into the tavern, his guilty conscience got the better of him and he tried to make a quick escape before the cops had even the opportunity to question him. They chased him as he darted out the back door and down the alleyway. As he had already been drinking quite a bit, he was not hard to catch up to and apprehend. By this time word was out all over the city that the whole police force was looking for the murderer of a White House aide and this guy became the number one suspect. The cops gave him a relentless third degree and he finally confessed after three days. The President had already told the local district attorney that he wanted his best prosecutor on the case and they were threatening this thug with a high-profile front page murder trial. If I remember correctly the deal was that they wouldn't hang him if he confessed . . . but he was sure to get convicted if he forced a trial, so confess he did and they sent him off to prison where, as far as I know, he still sits to this day."

"I hope he's rotting in jail," cursed Jerome. "What a horrible thing to do . . . take someone's life like that."

"The world is full of people like that, Jerome . . . you just have to make sure you recognize them for who they are and steer clear of them."

"Well, I'll be sure to watch my step when I get to Washington," Jerome said half jokingly.

"I've been prattling on so here that I never asked you why you

THE GRAYLOCK

are traveling to Washington," said Mr. Roberts apologetically.

"It certainly wasn't prattling, Everett . . . I've enjoyed every minute of it . . . you seem to have had a pretty interesting life. But, to answer your question . . . I'm starting law school next week."

"Oh, now that's just wonderful" exclaimed Mr. Roberts "where are you enrolled?"

"Thomas Jefferson School of Law . . . have you heard of it?"

"No . . . can't say that I have . . . but then again I'm not familiar with a lot of law schools anyway. I'm plenty familiar with lawyers, though and it strikes me as though you'll make a fine one. You're a good listener that's for sure and that is a very important quality in a lawyer . . . it inspires confidence and trust."

"Thank you" replied Jerome accepting the compliment nicely.

"Where will you be staying?"

"I'm going to be living and working part-time at a hotel called The Graylock . . . it's on N Street . . . do you know it?"

"No" answered Mr. Roberts "haven't heard of that either . . . oh, I know where N Street is . . . it's a small, pretty little street as I recall. This hotel must be one of the smaller ones in Washington."

"Where do you stay when you're in town?"

"The Hay-Adams on 16th Street . . . it's on the opposite side of Lafayette Square directly across from the White House. I always stay there . . . been staying there for years whenever I get to Washington. It's a beautiful hotel."

"I don't know anything about The Graylock. The law school set it up for me. I hope it works out alright."

"I'm sure it will," Mr. Roberts assured Jerome. "In fact, I'll be in town for a week or so. Let me give you my card. We can get together for dinner and I can bore with some more of my old war stories."

Mr. Roberts reached into the inside pocket of his handsomely tailored suit and pulled out a leather billfold. He handed Jerome a small card that said "Everett L. Roberts – Political Consultant" in gold embossed lettering. Mr. Roberts turned the card over and wrote down the telephone number of the Hay-Adams Hotel. Very impressive thought Jerome as he tucked the card into his shirt pocket wondering if the day would come when he might be handing out cards of his own.

Mr. Roberts explained that he wanted to retire to his car and rest a bit before the train pulled into Pennsylvania Station. He was meeting up with old friends of his in New York City and would not be traveling on to Washington for two days. Jerome thanked him for the card and for the pleasure of his company. He promised to get in touch with Mr. Roberts next week. He watched as the elderly man made his way down the club car towards his private compartment and Jerome thought how lucky he was to stumble into such an interesting character.

This trip is turning out to be alright he mused to himself and began to watch the countryside pass him by again. After a few minutes in the booth by himself he decided to return to his own car and get a bit of rest himself before he arrived in New York City.

When he arrived at his seat, he made sure that his grandfather's suitcase was still safely secured above his seat. He dropped his seat back just enough to make his 5'9" frame comfortable for a quick nap. He closed his eyes and drifted off to the quiet rumbling of the steel train wheels running across the tracks . . . anxious to get to Washington . . . and to The Graylock.

THE GRAYLOCK

Chapter Three

By the time Jerome awoke from his nap, the train was already lumbering into Pennsylvania Station in New York City. Still sleepy-eyed he reached above his seat and pulled his grandfather's suitcase down from the rack above. It was reassuring and somewhat disappointing to him that everything that was essential to him was packed into such a relatively small space. He liked to think that traveling light was the better option, but all things considered it would have been a stretch for him to try and fill another suitcase with his belongings. Still, it would be enough to last him 'till the end of the first semester when he would return to the farm for the holidays.

He stepped into the aisle and joined the long line of passengers waiting to head up stairs to the main terminal. It was an orderly disembarkment until most of the travelers were on the platform. Impatience took over and some people were determined to make headway to the stairs. A little bumping turned into stronger shoving and the polite "excuse me" quickly became an abrupt "coming through . . . coming through." The differential step to the side was replaced with a defensive "watch where you're walking!"

Jerome knew that he had at least 45 minutes before his train to Washington left and he was in no hurry to become part of the fray the was crystallizing on the platform. He stepped to the right and then to the left . . . he lifted his suitcase above his head and rested it there so as not to bump it into anyone's legs. He held it close to his chest when some irate man accused Jerome of knocking his hat off. He finally stopped and leaned against one of the iron posts to allow the throng of passengers to file past him. Then he leisurely followed the crowd up to what was the kind of spectacle he had never seen in Buttermilk Falls.

The main station room was cavernous and fluid with men, women and children of every shape and size . . . different ages and manner of dress . . . young and old . . . on the move and travel weary. The ones who were standing still were usually bumped out of the way by another in a hurry to get to the ticket booth or train gate. The newsstand operators hollered out the names of the eight different New York City papers and their eye-grabbing headlines of the day . . . all competing for the same thin dime from the would be customers flooding the concourse. The afternoon editions now were out with the screamed promise of an extra edition by nightfall. Billfolds came out and purses were opened . . . coins returned in exchange for the offered paper money and the newspaper was tucked under an arm or put into the travel bag . . . enough world and local news to occupy the traveler to the final destination. What was a source of information for one traveler soon enough became a source of warmth or comfort upon discard to the unfortunates struggling against the unforgiving financial arrows of the Great Depression.

Jerome soaked the entirety of the busy, overcrowded room in with a sharp eye while at the same time protecting his suitcase from snatchers and his person from the train conductor's forewarned pickpockets. He stepped carefully through the people maze in what felt like slow motion . . . heading towards the big board and its confusing display of arrivals, departures, connections and engine switches . . . of gate numbers and train names

. . . familiar city names and foreign destinations. He scanned the board several times looking for the departure time for Cardinal Express. He did not see it. He scanned the room several times around and thought he might see Mr. Roberts but it was impossible in that crowd. No matter he thought. Everett's card was neatly tucked away and he could telephone him once he got squared away in Washington.

Jerome made his way over to the information booth and stepped up to the counter. He was about to ask the booth operator about the Cardinal Express but before he could get the first syllable out he was rudely shoved aside by a huffing and puffing sweaty man in his fifties who shouted at the booth operator "Where is the 3:10 to Philly!! It's always at Gate 12 . . . what are you idiots trying pull here . . . I've only got three minutes to get to the train . . . if I miss it I'm comin' back here with my lawyers!!"

"It's at Gate 14 today, sir" the operator responded like a chilly wind. 'There's track trouble on 12. You'd know that if you checked the big board." The rude man turned and began to walk away without saying a word of thanks. "And by the way" the operator continued "bring your fucking lawyers next time. I'm sure the lawyers from the train company would love to meet them!"

Jerome wasn't sure where to look. He was embarrassed by the openness of the raw exchange between the strangers and offended that anonymous lawyers were the threatening weapons of choice. He stood still for a moment.

"What do you want?" implored the now angry and frustrated booth operator. Jerome decided quickly to stay one step ahead of her.

"Well," he began very genteelly "I've checked the big board pretty thoroughly and I don't see any current information about the Cardinal Express' departure to Washington. Do you happen to have any?"

THE GRAYLOCK

"Not up yet. Engine trouble" she said as she pushed her stringy bangs back into her matted hair revealing a furrowed brow on a round, tired face. "The information will be up in about ten minutes, but I can tell you that the Cardinal is delayed. 'Bout and hour from now it'll go . . . Track 10. Might as well get a seat over there and get comfortable if you can stand the heat in here 'cause you have to wait like everybody else . . . unless you got lawyers that want to crawl all over me, too."

Jerome almost smiled at her. "Nope . . . not a one. Thanks for the information." He turned and headed for the wooden benches but decided not to wait inside. She was right . . . it was too hot inside the station. Maybe there would be a breeze out on the street. He tightened his grip on his suitcase and made his way up the stairs leading to Eighth Avenue and 34th Street.

Long gone already from the cool September morning breezes of Buttermilk Falls, Jerome was disappointed to discover that it was hardly any cooler outside Pennsylvania Station than inside. His first glimpse of Manhattan above ground made him want to beat a hasty retreat back into the covered protection of the station. The streets were teeming with people, but unlike the hasty forward motions and purposeful gaits of the crowds below these people seemed to be wandering with no purpose. The traffic in the streets provided a suspicious dominance over the apparent atrophied presence of the milling crowds.

Street vendors hawking stands half filled with breads and vegetables yelled competitive prices into the hot air attracting only the few willing to stop long enough for a disapproving look at the discolored fruit and quickly wilting assortment of drying peppers, carrots, squash and unshucked corn.

He walked closer to the corner and realized that a very large part of the gathering crowd was nothing more than late-comers joining in a disheartening long line of mostly men standing, waiting their turn for a free bowl of soup at the local Salvation Army kitchen. Desperately hungry casualties of the country's unemployed workers who stood fast . . . stoned faced and almost embarrassed by a fate not of their making. Women mournfully sliding forward ever so slowly with the sticky pace of the line bringing children closer to them as if to keep them from harm's way. Ragged, tattered, exhausted . . . the silent collective growl of their bellies pleaded for a resolution to this misery.

Jerome was dumbfounded. Is this the reality of the Great Depression he wondered. Slivers of its wake were evidenced back home with the singular thud of a farm foreclosure or the wrenching repossession of the machinery integral to its operation. But, nothing like this torn canvas of hollow eyes and empty souls. Nothing like this resounding death knell for human dignity. It was no wonder that the traffic was moving so quickly . . . spiriting people away from entanglement in a web of poverty so perverse that it numbed the senses. If there was a hell on earth this must be it.

"You lost, son?" Jerome looked gloomily at the police officer.

"I'm sorry. What did you say?" he replied.

"I said are you lost. You've been standing there like you don't know which way to turn." The officer had correctly identified Jerome's exact state of mind.

"No . . . I'm . . . I'm waiting for a train to Washington. It's a little delayed and I thought . . ." he paused wondering how to continue. "I thought I might come up for some air."

"You not gonna find any air on a blistering hot day like today, my friend. You oughta talk to those poor souls over there about getting some air" said the officer pointing briskly in the direction of the soup line.

"How can people live like that?" queried Jerome in a tone so full of bewilderment that the officer felt protective.

"Ask Mr. Franklin Delano Roosevelt that when you get to Washington, why don't ya" he said with a cynical twist. "Tell him that up here the only thing those people have to fear is starvation . . . fear itself, my ass "he continued "that crazy bastard ought to get out more."

Jerome bristled at the direct assault on his hero's character. To his mind, this mess was caused by Hoover, not FDR. But he had never witnessed the depth of the living scars the Depression laid on people until now.

"You'd better head back inside and wait for your train there. You stay out here any longer and some vagabond is likely to come up from behind and try to rip the shirt right off your back."

Jerome headed for the stairway turning his back on the breathing, palpable devastation . . . grateful not to see any more.

He made is way over to Track 10 and hoped that passengers would be able to board the Cardinal Express shortly.

None too soon he mused while thanking his lucky stars that New York City was not his final destination.

Chapter Four

Unaware that he had been drifting in and out of a restorative daydream for quite sometime, Jerome failed to notice, until his senses slowly carried him back to the present, that the frail grandmotherly-looking woman who placed herself in the seat next to his just before the Cardinal Express pulled out of Pennsylvania Station and busied herself with a fine stitched and speedy hand at needlepoint had been replaced by a somber, still faced bespeckeld man. His dozing snores sounded like timber falling and Jerome wondered where the quiet presence of the elderly needlepointer had gone. She must have gotten off in Philadelphia he concluded as that was the last barker of the conductor he could remember. He longed for her easy breathing as the unwelcomed substituted wheezing and in and out labored breaths of the man whose shirt buttons looked as those they would pop off with each exhale was annoying to him.

He rubbed his eyes and tried to stretch out as best he could next to the overcrowding of his seat partner's imposing girth. It was a vain attempt as his taut muscles began to feel more cramped. He tried to guess where exactly he might be on his sojourn to Washington, but someplace past Philadelphia was the best he could offer his still sleepy mind. He thought of bounding over the weighty traveler sitting next to him but worried about waking him from what looked like a much needed rest. Balancing his family-taught concern to be respectful to others and the aching call of his legs to be stretched, Jerome reached up and curled his strong hands around the outside edge of the metal luggage rack above his head and easily lifted himself over the sleeping man and placed himself gently into the aisle of the coach car that had nestled him since leaving New York City.

He peered at the unsuspecting traveler and breathed a simple sigh that his small leap into the aisle had barely cause the man to move a whisker on his unshaven face. Jerome massaged the crook in his own neck and looked to both ends of the train car to see if there was a way he might get a breath of fresh air. He headed back towards the conductor's booth firmly placing his hand on the backs of each seat he passed to steady his steps. Almost all the seat were filled. Some passengers were in various stages of rest or sleep . . . some were contemplating whatever ponderous moments that were shielded by glazed, thinking eyes and some were engaged in the time honored banter of nothingness that briefly binds two strangers between points of destination. Not one of them looked to Jerome to be lucky enough to meet up with a man like Everett Roberts. Jerome hoped that Everett had safely met up with his friends in New York and wondered what his "observations" might have been on the desolation he saw outside the train station on Eighth Avenue.

Jerome yawned as he opened the door connecting his car with the next in line. He clenched tightly onto the steel bars framing the outside of the door and stepped very carefully onto the tiny platform. The rumbling of the train was so loud that Jerome could only concentrate on the wind as it packed a full frontal assault on his face, rapidly snapping him awake from his Philadelphia slumber. It felt refreshing. He rubbed his eyes yet again with his free hand to come fully awake only in time to see the conductor stepping quickly towards him, motioning wildly with his hands.

"You can't stand out there, sir!!" yelped the conductor as he threw the door open with one hand and grabbed Jerome's suit lapel with the other. "It's very dangerous. You must come back inside the car!"

"Sorry" apologized Jerome "I didn't mean any harm. I just wanted to get a little air. It's a little stuffy in the car."

The conductor seemed a bit more calm now that he and Jerome were both safely inside and the door was shut. "No harm done, just don't go out there again. If you need to get some air, though, you'll have to go all the way down to the caboose car. There's a proper platform back there for passengers to step out onto. You can stay there as long as you like."

The conductor, a man in his early thirties with a high-pitched voice and a nervous manner, straightened his collar and rubbed the front of his dark blue uniform jacket as though to make certain he had not lost any of its precious brass buttons, much less a passenger. Jerome tried to cover his smile while watching this self designated protector of passengers reassemble his presence and appearance.

"I didn't mean to throw a fright into you" Jerome assured him.

"Well, you just don't know on these trains . . . you'd be surprised at who gets on and off. It's a very odd sort of collection of people some days . . . we have to be on our lookout. Last week a perfectly ordinary man of little consequence got up from his seat in between New York and Philadelphia and went to the edge of a car . . . just like you just done and WHOOSH!!!! . . . hopped right off the train and killed himself! No trouble before hand . . . nothin' of a suspicious nature or anything like that . . . no warning . . . absolutely zero to indicate what was on his mind and BAM . . . there he goes off the back of the train car . . . killed right on the spot."

Jerome realized now why the conductor looked crazed when he was running towards him. He shook his head and declared "I wasn't looking to kill myself . . . just trying to wake up from a nap."

"Oh it's alright now . . . it's over . . . I mean you look normal enough and all . . . but I'll tell ya, you'd be plenty surprised at what fairly normal lookin' folks can be up to . . . some very strange stuff." The conductor adjusted his cap and added in conclusion "I've only been on this run for three years and I've seen a lot of weird goings on."

Jerome felt some unsolicited sordid tales coming on and decided to change the subject.

"Where are we by the way?"

"No more than ten minutes outside of Baltimore" responded his would-be savior. "We'll be pullin' in very shortly. No holdover. Just enough time for passengers to get on and off the train . . . Washington, D.C. right after that."

"Ok, thanks . . . I guess I'll get back to my seat then. I can get some air after we leave Baltimore."

"Good enough, then" the conductor responded "and remember . . . the caboose car is where you get your air!"

Jerome nodded in agreement and walked back to his seat where luckily the snoring man had obviously awakened and removed himself, his girth and all his bags to another part of the train.

"This is great" Jerome said to himself. "Got my space all to myself again." He flopped casually back into his seat and was feeling quite relaxed and wide awake. He laughed again lightly at the sight of the conductor rushing towards him on the outside platform. "Can't imagine why he thought I looked like I wanted to jump" Jerome mused "I can't think of anybody I know who's more looking forward to life right now than me, but then I suppose looks can be deceiving." He could conceive of a criminal mind and someone wanting to take another's life as he recalled Everett Roberts' admonition of just several hours earlier in the day that "the world is full of people like that Jerome . . . you just have to make sure you recognize them for who they are and steer clear of them." He just could not understand why anyone would want to take their own life.

He let his mind wander to more pleasant thoughts, especially the conductor's news that the train was nearly in Baltimore. He grew excited at the thought that Washington would be the next stop after that. His new world was drawing closer with every minute. Jerome noticed that the anxiety about arriving he had when he left Buttermilk Falls in the morning was now replaced with an easier feeling of comfort about jumping into uncharted territory. "I know I've made the right decision" he told himself. "It just feels that way."

He had hardly noticed that the train was leaving Baltimore and a different conductor was already collecting tickets from the new passengers. No one had taken the seat next to him so Jerome decided to pull his grandfather's suitcase down from the luggage rack and placed it in the empty seat for company. He'd had enough newness for this ride and chose the familiar reminder of his deceased grandfather for company on the remainder of the trip.

Family separations, whiskey drinking accountants, warnings about pickpockets in Pennsylvania Station, desolation on Eighth Avenue, stories of a train suicide and the murder of a White House aide all in one long train ride were enough for the blue-eyed farm boy for now. He longed to get off the train and check into The Graylock . . . for some rest.

THE GRAYLOCK

Chapter Five

The holler that all passengers leaving for Washington, D.C. must leave by the rear of the car was all the welcome mat that Jerome was looking for. It was the only one he needed. He was here . . . at last.

He grabbed his suitcase and was almost first in line to get off. Unlike his deference to the pushing crowds leaving the train in Pennsylvania Station, Jerome hurried himself past the dozens of passengers, like himself, who ticketed themselves to D.C. Certain that no one was as glad to have finally arrived as himself, Jerome imitated the hurried bustle he saw in New York City and made a determined headway to the front of the station. No stairway to climb and no real threat to the moving mass, he was all gladness and glee as he, almost victoriously, strode to the front of Washington's Union station.

No soup lines here . . . just the looming presence of the U.S. Capitol Building slightly off in the distance. It was enough of a postcard hallmark to stop Jerome in his tracks. No sight . . . no view from his backyard over the Reed's 210 acres ever compared to the first seen majesty of that oft written about, too photographed white cap over the legislative center of America. The dome. He set his suitcase down without fear from a preying pickpocket, mystically separating himself for a moment from his grandfather and his family . . . almost from himself and set all the blueness of his eyes directly upon a dream. People swirled around him, hailed taxis and met loved ones and friends . . . some headed on their own way unnoticed and others announced their anticipated arrivals with outstretched arms, powerful hellos and kisses.

Only Jerome stood still. Motionless. Staring straight into the home center of New Deal legislation. The main artery of FDR's plan for salvation, Act Two . . . its blue vein.

"I'm here" he mouthed . . . almost unbelievably . . . his lips parting only miserly enough to let the lonesome herald out into the air. No one heard. No one noticed.

A cab driver yelled to him from behind the wheel of his mud splattered moving office. "Hey . . . you there . . . need a cab?"

Jerome looked briefly to his left and right and understood the unsolicited beckoning was directed towards him. He looked at the driver. "Yeah . . . I mean you . . . do you need a ride somewhere?"

Jerome thought of the law school's administrator, Mrs. Meyers, and her advice over the telephone yesterday that The Graylock was too far from the station to walk with luggage. Best to take a cab. He nodded affirmatively to the driver, grabbed his suitcase and waltzed over to the car door. Trying to look as though he was in no great hurry when, in fact, his heart was pounding with excitement, Jerome pretended as though he was used to arriving in the nation's capital. He opened the back door to the cab and tossed his luggage inside first. Plopping himself in directly thereafter, Jerome waited for the driver to speak.

The driver eyed Jerome in his rear view mirror adjusting it slightly, saying nothing. With one arm crooked and resting on the window of the driver's side front door, he lifted his other arm off the steering wheel to remove his cab and scratch his head. After a moment he replaced it covering his thinning gray hair and took a short, slightly exasperated breath. Half turning to Jerome in the back seat he finally spoke . . . hitting the bull's eye right off.

"Never been here before, have ya?"

Foiled again! What is it about me that makes people think that Jerome wondered. He tried to wipe a self-effacing grin from his face as he shifted his position not too uncomfortably. "Well . . . uh . . . not exactly . . . I mean I've seen . . ." The driver interrupted him straight away.

"Didn't think so" he muttered.

Jerome, true to form, decided to give up the short ruse and give in. Now embarrassingly used to being discovered for his untraveled miles, he bent forward to get another clue to unwrap his puzzlement. "Ok" he said spilling it all "this is my first time in Washington, first time on a train trip, almost my first official trip away from home . . . but not my first time in a cab!"

"Coulda fooled me" laughed the driver.

"Why??" he said, mocking shock at the terse observation although he felt better now having told the truth. He always felt better telling the truth. It relaxed him . . . a lesson his grandfather told him as a boy . . . "The truth is something nobody can ever take away from you, Jerome. Don't forget that."

"You stood there staring at the Capitol dome like you seen a band of angels" laughed the driver as he turned his burly frame and set it squarely in front of the steering wheel. "Been livin' here since I was born 48 years ago and drivin' a cab here since '30 . . . only first timers look at it like that . . . like it was some holy shrine. Believe me, kid . . . there ain't no band of angels under that dome . . . politicians, lawyers and country wreckers . . . that's bout all." He continued with more emphasis. "Plus the fact, you didn't say nothin' when ya got inside the cab. I ain't suppose to guess where yer headed . . . yer suppose ta say! I ain't drivin' a tour bus here!" The driver was clearly amused with himself and Jerome took no real offense at his comical delivery.

"What do you say I start over then? Give me a practice run . . . how about it?" Jerome said sincerely winning the driver over with his honesty and charm.

The driver complied feigning readiness by placing both hands firmly on the wheel. "Ok, kiddo . . . shoot. I'm all ears and ready to go! Jake Milden . . . at your service!"

Playing along Jerome announced "All right then Jake. I'd like to go to 17 N Street. It's in the Northwest section of town. A hotel by the name of The Graylock." Jerome smiled again. "I hope it's not too far."

Jerome waited for Jake's snappy local reply but instead watched his thick, stumpy laborer's hand slide off the steering wheel while the playful expression on his face evaporated out the window along with his jovial good nature.

"The Graylock?" Jake repeated unbelievably. "Geezuss H., boy! What the hell are you staying at The Graylock for?" Jerome's face felt like it had no blood in it . . . this was a bad sign . . . washing the glow out of his trip almost in seconds. He was going to give Jake the whole story but instead simply answered "I'm going to live there."

Jake stopped looking at Jerome in the rear view mirror and turned his full-bellied self all the way around. "Live there!!! You mean ta tell me ya came to Washington to actually live at The Graylock!!!"

Jerome's heart was sinking faster with Jake's every syllable, heading for a catastrophic splat on the floor of the cab. "Well . . . I'm not actually living there . . . I mean I sort of am, but not for very long" he sputtered "I'm really here to go to law school. I have a job at The Graylock to help get me through school." By now he was rubbing his forehead nervously with the palm of his right hand . . . clutching onto his dream with the other.

Jake reared back a bit. He had removed his cap, exposing his near-complete baldness and like Jerome was rubbing his forehead. He annunciated slowly dropping any trace of his local accent. "Do you mean to tell me that you are going to live and work at that hotel!!??" "Where you from anyway??" he asked . . . as though it would have made any difference.

Feeling more like he was in the principal's office than in the back of Jake's cab, Jerome responded obediently "Buttermilk Falls" and added "it's a small farm town in upstate New York."

Jake raised his furry brows and shook his head. "I can't believe you gotta live and work at that place. With that kook!!!"

Jerome slumped back into the seat. "What kook? Who are you talking about" he demanded.

"That crazy dame who runs the joint! She's a kook, I tell ya! I know drivers who won't even do pickups there. My dispatcher don't even answer calls to it no more. Too many false calls."

"Good grief Jake . . . I don't need to hear this now. What are you talking about?" Jerome pleaded.

"That old broad use ta call . . . or somebody, I don't know who . . . use ta call for cabs all the time like we had some kinda fleet waitin' for her . . . get to the dump and she give out some horseshit excuse like her party ain't arrived yet an' can we come back later. Use ta drive us nuts . . . so we stopped goin' there. If ya ask me her 'party' left a long time ago . . . if ya know what I mean!"

Jerome wasn't sure what Jake meant at all by his remarks. All he knew was that he'd come all the way down here to attend law school. That was the main thing for him . . . nothing else mattered. "I don't have a choice. I have to go there."

"You can always go home . . . cut your losses . . . train probably ain't even left yet. Do you wanna go home?"

"No!" answered Jerome defiantly. "Just take me to The Graylock, Ok?"

"Ok, yer the boss . . . but I'm lettin' ya off at the corner. I ain't drivin' in front of that place." He turned the key in the ignition and started the engine . . . flipped the flag up on the cab's meter and put the machine into drive. Carefully circling out of the station and heading towards Massachusetts Avenue he offered Jerome one last bit of unneeded advice. "Between law school and that crazy woman at The Graylock, you oughtta be battier 'n hell in no time . . . welcome to Washington, kid!"

Jerome had already tuned him out. He was not going to allow this cab driver to put a damper on his day. He'd see things for himself.

Jake offered no more tales or free advice on the ride through town and Jerome was grateful for that. Instead of having to listen to tales of looniness, Jerome occupied himself with what he could see of his new city from the window of Jake's cab. Night was closing in and the early evening shadows made it difficult to take in Washington's splendor.

He could see, though, that Fall had noticeably set in and the tree colors blended harmoniously with the facades of the townhouses lining both sides of Massachusetts Avenue. Fallen, damp yellow and red leaves inked the sidewalks while the more sturdy orange and fire-hued ones remained affixed to their branches providing whatever sun cover they could before nature loosened their grip as well and floated them to the ground. The streets were not over-crowded like New York, but instead were clear avenues for shoppers, strollers, passers-by and folks just out for the evening air. Jerome noticed it to be an easier pace here and marveled at how the Avenue was repeatedly broken up with one statue-centered, decorous circle after the other . . . Thomas Circle . . . Scott Circle . . . small plots of remembrance to what Jerome guessed to be war heroes, but he was not sure.

Traffic moved moderately fast . . . but not so quickly that Jerome could not see what was passing him by. Jake was not a bad driver at all, keeping his eyes fixed on the road and obviously careful for pedestrians. The roads here seemed as though they were paved with gold compared to some of the single lane, back-road mud pits in Buttermilk Falls.

Passing around the last circle at 16th Street, Jerome very timely turned to his left and caught his first glimpse of the White House, looking to him to be less than five or six blocks down the street. It was just a glimpse, but it was just enough to replenish Jerome's sense of why he was here at all . . . after the battering it took from Jake's cryptic tale up at Union Station. He felt revived.

Jake passed three more blocks down Massachusetts Avenue and waited at the red light at the corner. With his directional signal metronomically ticking out an indicated left hand turn, Jake told Jerome "We're almost there." His immediate thought was not of Jake's warnings about The Graylock, but that he would be living in such proximity to the White House. He felt such a long, long way from home.

Jake made the left hand turn effortlessly and drove two blocks up the right hand side of 17th Street to the corner of N Street. He pulled the cab over to curb side and placed it neatly into park.

"There it is . . . a half a block down the street on N . . . see it there with the little red awnin' sticking out a bit on the left hand side of the street?" Jerome nodded without saying a word. He saw his new home in the short distance. He looked at the meter and saw it's red numbers indicating that he owed Jake $1.50 for the ride. He handed him over $1.75, remembering Everett Roberts' admonition on the train about tipping too heavily. He opened the door and put he and his suitcase at the corner of 17th and N Streets. Jake tipped his cap nicely to Jerome and Jerome thanked him for the ride.

"Good luck to you, my friend" Jake said as he started to pull away. "You are gonna need it in that nut house!"

THE GRAYLOCK

Jerome picked up his suitcase and sauntered with surprising ease down N Street. Good luck is something he'd always had plenty of and he knew it. "What I need now is some strength and courage to make this adventure work" he said aloud as he crossed the street to the front door of The Graylock.

Chapter Six

The hotel seemed small indeed from the outside, not very wide and only about four stories tall by Jerome's guess. The small red awning protruded just to the edge of the second smooth cement step leading to the front door. It served as the overhead protectorate to all comers in whatever weather. The dingy white trim which scalloped its edges in the half circle of the awning's perimeter almost drew attention away from the fading white letters painted in Old English spelling out "The Graylock" on the face of the awning. The two tiny evergreens planted in heavy stone pots on both sides of the entrance way were soft green guards ... silent welcomers ... ever vigilant ... for guests and boarders. The extra wide front door with its ornate brass doorknob was embossed by a twisted configured design of wrought iron ... an affront to the single, thick sheet of plate glass that was shrouded by a sheer white cloak of nylon through which Jerome could almost see movement inside.

Not wanting to appear to be a peering, uninvited trespasser Jerome looked for a knocker and found none. On his right, though, he spotted a white buzzer just above a metal plate on which was etched "All deliveries by side entrance." He pressed the buzzer firmly. Moments later a tall shadowy figure appearing to hover just inside opened the door. With the wrought iron, plate glass and white nylon well out the way now, Jerome got a very clear eyeful of the man . . . tall, broad shouldered, greying at the temples at least from what he could see. The man had his hat and coat on and appeared to be in a hurry to go somewhere. No "hello" . . . no "may I help you?" from this man. He did not return Jerome's smile.

The first time his colorless thin lips parted on his pasty face Jerome heard only a terse, cadence-less "What do you want?"

Surprised by the imposing figure's rudeness, Jerome said nothing in return.

"I'm in a hurry. What do you want?" he repeated. "Deliveries are to be made at the side entrance" he said as he leaned towards and pointed to the metal plate on the door jam.

Jerome was miffed. Tired and miffed . . . and anxious to boot. "Excuse me" he said as politely as could "but I'm not here to make a delivery. I'm supposed to see the owner here, Mrs. Crickmore."

"You can't see her now. She's having her dinner. You will just have to wait."

"Yes, but . . ."

"Never mind" the man said dismissively. "I cannot interrupt her meal. You will have to sit over there and wait." Jerome noticed that the man was directing him to a wooden side bench along the wall and not the more comfortable looking stuffed arm chairs further inside the lobby. "Why do you want to see her anyway?" he demanded.

Jerome did not want to provoke and argument and kept his voice low and even. "I was told by the law school administrator that there would be a place for me to stay here."

The man stopped where he stood. He glared down at Jerome from his full height of 6'4" through practically colorless eyes.

"Did you say you are a law student?" He turned away in disgust and then looked back. "A law student! Another law student.

I wasn't told that there would be another law student living here. I'm the assistant manager of this hotel and nobody told me a thing about having another law student living here!!"

It was the first Jerome had heard about it too except that the news was more welcoming to him . . . he didn't feel quite so alone now. But that hardly took the sting out of the rude greeting he was getting from this assistant manager. Trying to explain, Jerome offered that Mrs. Meyers, the administrator over at Jefferson School of Law had told him that she was going to call Mrs. Crickmore and make the arrangements.

"Well, she didn't tell me!" he barked back "not a damn thing!"

Jerome could not tell whether the man was ranting about the lack of communication from Mrs. Meyers or Mrs. Crickmore but it didn't seem to matter at this point. There was no way Jerome was going to be able to make himself welcomed by this guy. He obviously had something against law students. Jerome watched him stomp off to the back of the hotel muttering something unintelligible under his breath.

Glad to be rid of him, Jerome took a look around the lobby. He was standing on a carpet red enough to welcome royalty. It covered every square inch of the lobby and crawled its way up the winding, sweeping staircase that in another place or time might have guided young Southern belles down to greet their beaus. Ferns potted in stained spittoons covered portions of the white walls. Upon closer inspection, Jerome saw why. Places where the paint was cracked or peeling had obviously been covered up with plants. Two doors were made to look as though they were part of the panel and woodwork, but it was clear to Jerome's well trained workman's eye that they had simply been painted over and shut. There were fading oil portraits of sour and sad looking gentlemen of a bygone era and no name to unveil their anonymity and no obvious signatures to give credit to the artist for memorializing their haunting looks from beyond the grave on stretched canvass. It was posterity paid for and unevenly hung.

The dominant fixture, though, was the nearly floor to ceiling mirror encased in an excessively ornate, gaudy wood-carved, gold painted frame. It might have weighed easily 300 pounds and the craftsmanship of the wood carving would have been more noticeable if its color was not so garish . . . a fourth rate example of what would have been summarily rejected out of hand at Versailles and it reflected all the comings and goings of the small lobby . . . the eye towards which all passers-by turned for a last approval before stepping outside. The ceiling, like its inseparable walls, was white and painted over in spots so it appeared to be in a half state of repair and disrepair. Cleverly, though, if one were simply passing through the lobby, the carpet and the mirror were the obvious eye catchers that made the lobby seemed well maintained . . . until closer inspection, but that was something most guests just did not have time for. The attractive carpet cushioned their weary feet back to their rooms and the mirror re-affirmed what they had already convinced themselves of . . . that they were ready to go out and face the world. Jerome wondered if the assistant manager ever took a good look at himself in it.

Jerome was just about to sit himself down on the wooden bench along the lobby wall, as directed, when he noticed in the huge mirror a woman walking towards him. The measured, easy steps were those of someone very comfortable in these surroundings. Jerome remained standing.

"Mr. Reed?" she questioned.

"Yes, I'm Jerome Reed."

The woman extended her small hand graciously in a welcoming gesture that Jerome had hoped for from the assistant manager.

"How do you do? I'm Hattie Crickmore." Finally.

Jerome was instantly struck, not so much by her diminutive stature, as he was by her immediate pleasantness. Hattie could not have stood more than slightly over five feet tall, but exuded a presence in excess of that. Darting, light blue eyes drew fast attention to a small boned face housed in fair skin nearly free of any makeup. Still-red hair set in the style of another day and only mildly streaked with wisps of gray was the singular indicator that the owner of The Graylock might be a woman in her sixties. Fashionably turned out in a dark brown dress with full length sleeves outlining a frame of not more than a hundred pounds, she was unadorned by jewelry save for a small, barely noticeable pair of baby pearl earrings . . . no necklace . . . no bracelets . . . no watch and no rings. Red nail polish matching her faint touch of lipstick was the only added element of color that was not naturally hers.

Jerome extended his hand in kind. "Very nice to meet you, Mrs. Crickmore. I'm sorry if I interrupted your dinner. I would have been here earlier, but my train was a little delayed in leaving New York City."

"Nonsense" she winked "time's just not that important. The main thing is that you're here safe and sound. I understood from Mrs. Meyers that you'd be coming from all the way up in New York State. You must be wrung out from all that traveling . . . and if my guess is right on young men, probably pretty hungry, too!"

That was the reminder that Jerome needed to recall that he'd not really had much to eat since his snack with Everett Roberts hours earlier. He was very hungry. "Now that you mention it, I didn't eat too much on the train" he replied sheepishly.

"I thought so!" she said clapping her hands together once. "Come back with me and we'll fix you right up." She took Jerome's arm and beckoned him to the back of the lobby, towards her dining room. "Oh . . . don't forget your suitcase, there" she added.

Jerome reached back with his free arm and grabbed his luggage . . . as though he'd forget that important part of him. She waltzed her new, young boarder away from the front of the hotel wedded to his arm, figuratively eloping him officially into The Graylock. Her world. Her only world.

Hattie brought Jerome directly into the hotel's kitchen . . . not the dining room. "First" she said "let's get a tray out from under here." She braced herself on the counter and reached below to a cabinet and pulled out a serving tray and placed it on the long counter. "Now, Jerome, if you'll turn directly around and dig into the second shelf, you'll find a stack of dinner plates. Grab one and bring it right on over here." Jerome complied thinking how much like home this seemed to him . . . getting the Reed family ready for dinner, on a smaller scale, of course . . . and no serving tray . . . definitely no serving tray. She picked up two worn pot holders and made for the oven door. She turned coquettishly to Jerome and laughed "I hope there's something left!! Tim has quite an appetite!"

Jerome kept hearing buzzing sound coming from the front of the hotel, thinking that it might be the front door, except that it kept going off in stacatto measures, then long ones and repeated short tones. This last one was unusually long.

"What's that noise?" he asked Hattie.

"The switchboard" she replied as she lifted a cast iron pan from inside the oven. "You'll get used to it . . . hope so . . . you're going to hear plenty of it when you're not in school!" She paused a minute to look at the remainder of a pork chop and boiled potato dinner still hot in the pan. "Oh, wonderful . . . there's plenty here to fill a young man's stomach. Do you like pork chops, Jerome?" She thought a moment. "You don't mind if I call you Jerome do you? I like to relax my hotel formalities a bit in the evening . . . I hope it's alright with you."

"Oh, sure . . . that's fine with me . . . I mean I prefer Jerome . . . I mean it's better than Mr. Reed."

"Well, I'll be calling you Mr. Reed during the days . . . for the guests sake . . . but at night you'll be Jerome."

He watch her set up a tray for him with napkins, knife, fork a glass of ice . . . she took the plate and centered on the tray.

"Mrs. Crickmore, I certainly do appreciate everything . . ."

She cut him off directly. "Oh, stop now . . . this is nothing . . . and by the way you don't see any sun streaming through that kitchen window do you?"

Jerome smiled and laughed aloud at the silliness of her question. "No, of course I don't."

"Well, then it must be nighttime, mustn't it? Time for me to call you Jerome and you to call me Hattie. Mrs. Crickmore during the day or when the guests are about, but Hattie . . . plain old Hattie at night. Got it?" she said feigning a meek authoritative tone.

Jerome laughed again . . . heartily this time. "Ok. Hattie it is! . . . but Hattie at nighttime only!" he added in wry obedience.

"Terrific. You've got a great smile . . . did anybody ever tell you that Jerome?" He knew his grandfather always did. "And, I might add a lovely laugh . . . so you must have a good sense of humor . . . we're going to get on just fine . . . I can tell things like that . . . Lord knows I seem to have been alive long enough to figure things like that out." She picked up the tray with its plate now heaping full of pork chops and potatoes and started out of the kitchen.

"Let me carry that" said Jerome.

"Nope . . . tonight I'm serving you. It's no trouble at all" answered Hattie.

Jerome followed Hattie out of the kitchen and around the corner to the dining room. She put his tray next to hers on the round table that was out of sight of the corridor.

"Tim" she called "Timothy . . . are you out there?"

"Still here" he replied.

"Well come on back here Timothy." Hattie insisted "I want to make proper introductions. Don't be shy."

A young man appeared in the doorway of the dining room. "Nobody's ever accused me of being shy, Hattie . . . only you" he said jokingly. "By comparison . . . I suppose I am!"

"Always teasing . . . stop it and come right over here" Hattie said stretching out her arm. "I want you to meet Jerome Reed."

Timothy walked over and Hattie put her outstretched arm gently around Tim's waist. "Jerome, this is Timothy Owlster. Tim is also just starting school over at Jefferson."

The other law student thought Jerome instantly. The other one the assistant manager doesn't like. Tim and Jerome shook hands.

"Boy, am I glad to see you . . . I thought I was going to have to work this switchboard by myself all year."

"Well" said Jerome "your help has finally arrived. Nice to meet you Tim."

"This is just wonderful!!" Hattie exclaimed. "Both of you finally here to help us run this place. We'll have a great time, won't we?!"

Tim heard the switchboard buzzer going off again and turned to answer it. "Duty calls. I'll explain everything to you later, Jerome. There's nothing to it."

"Thanks" said Jerome. Relieved that his colleague and he hit it right off.

"Now you sit right next to me" said Hattie pulling out a chair for Jerome. "Eat your dinner before it gets cold . . . and tell me all about yourself." She sat next to him and raised her half empty glass of bourbon and branch water over ice in a sweet toast to him.

T.J. CAHILL

"Welcome to The Graylock" she smiled.
A disguising welcome it was indeed.

THE GRAYLOCK

Chapter Seven

After dinner, Jerome was directed up to the top floor of the hotel . . . four flights up. No elevator. Hattie told him that he'd be in Room 401 . . . a small room on the front side of the building overlooking N Street. He could hardly wait to collapse into bed. It was a minuscule room in comparison to the large bedroom he shared with the twins, Jimmy and Alan whom he had already begun to miss. A single twin bed with two pillows, a four drawer bureau with an attached mirror and a sturdy but spare-looking wooden desk, with one lamp at its edge, and an unmatching chair was all the furniture the little room could hold. The closet was narrow and its door could not be open if the room door itself was ajar at the same time. However, it was more than spacious enough to hold and hang the minimal wardrobe carried with him from home.

He switched on the overhead ceiling light and found is naked glare from three uncovered light bulbs too bright. The amber glow from the single lamp shaded fixture on his desk was sufficient to light the room. After setting his suitcase on the bed, Jerome walked over to the tall three paned double window, folded aside its wooden shutters and looked down four stories to the street. The sill was wide and deep enough for him to sit in and he did . . . resting back to get a feel for his new surroundings. His survey was interrupted by a knock on the door. It was Tim.

"Hi . . . can I come in?"

"Sure" replied Jerome "make yourself comfortable . . . if you can find a spot!"

Tim slid the desk chair out turned it around and straddled it backwards. "It looks a little cramped, doesn't it?"

"Not really . . . I think it'll be fine once I get settled in. It's probably all I'll need in between work and school. Speaking of work . . . are you finished downstairs?"

"Yeah . . . the night guy showed up early so I let him take over after I put Hattie to bed."

Jerome looked bewildered. "What do you mean "put her to bed"?

"Too much bourbon again . . . it doesn't happen every night, but several times since I started and I only got here a little over two weeks ago."

"She's a drunk?!'

"Nah . . . not really" said Tim matter-of-factly. "There's a couple of drinkers in my family so I can tell when somebody's going overboard with the stuff . . . Hattie just seems to forget how little she is and how much she's had or can hold. It's more like she gets a little too tipsy for her own good . . . so when it happens you kind of guide her into her room and let her be. She's fine after that. Never a word of it the next day either."

"And this doesn't bother you?"

"Nope . . . she's not mean or cantankerous when she's like that . . . doesn't get depressed or anything. More jovial like drinking . . . but it's those last two or three sips and then she gets kind of quiet and wistful. It's not really a problem to watch out for her . . . she really a nice old lady . . . a little weird, but nice."

"The cab driver I had on the way over here told me she was a kook" said Jerome.

Tim laughed at the remark. "No . . . I wouldn't call her a kook . . . a little eccentric maybe but that's probably all. The real kook in this place is Maneray, believe me!"

"Who's that?" Jerome wanted to know.

"That nut case that let you in tonight. He's the assistant manager . . . at least that's what he calls himself. Hattie just says he's her assistant. Makes him crazy . . . crazier I should say. Steer clear of him . . . he's just plain nasty. Hasn't given me anything but a hard time since I got here."

"He sure was rude to me. What's his problem?"

"I don't know. Hattie hired him about four months ago and since then three switchboard operators have quit . . . and now I understand why. I think he thinks he can frighten people into doing what he says."

"How do you know all this? I thought you said you just got here?"

"Mr. Duffy fills me in on all the hotel stuff. He's the only full-time switchboard operator here . . . said he started here right after Hattie opened it up full scale back in 1903 or '04 . . . sometime back then. You'll meet him tomorrow. He's a real character. He can't stand Maneray . . . nobody can . . . I don't even think that Hattie likes him . . . but he does all the dull, grunt work of running the hotel and he NEVER gives Hattie so much as a crossed eye, trust me. She runs this place and makes that fact very clear to him."

"I don't know about all this, Tim . . . it all sounds a little odd to me. I'm not used to these kinds of people."

"Oh, relax . . . I mean it's odd alright . . . but it's a funny kind of odd . . . nothing to worry about . . . at least that's how I find it so far . . . but then again I've lived in New York City my whole life . . . I'm used to running into odd people."

Jerome told Tim about what he saw when he briefly passed

through New York earlier. "Eighth Avenue is a horror show." Tim nodded in agreement. "No doubt about it . . . but the whole city's not like that . . . it's really an exciting place to live . . . I miss it already . . . Washington seems like a sleepy village to me in comparison."

"You'd think that Buttermilk Falls was pretty much a graveyard then!"

"Is that where you're from?" Tim asked. Jerome nodded. "I've heard of it . . . Cornell University is up there someplace, isn't it?"

Jerome nodded again. "Sure it's only a five mile drive from our farm . . . that's where I went to school."

"No kidding . . . a couple of my friends went there. I went to Columbia University myself . . . I was really thinking I might get into Columbia Law School but they kept me on their waiting list forever . . . I got my letter from Jefferson last month and decided I'd better jump on it."

The similar tale brought a smile to Jerome's tired face. "Same with me" he said "except I was waiting to get into Cornell Law School and just got the letter from Jefferson three days ago! And here I am."

"Here we both are!" laughed Tim "Living at The Graylock!"

"I hope this doesn't turn into some freak show" worried Jerome.

"Stop worrying, will you? It'll be fun. Hattie's really a lot of fun. Besides, as soon as school starts we probably won't even be here much except to sleep and put in our twenty hours."

"What to we have to do exactly?"

Tim looked at his watch. It was past eleven. "It's getting late . . . I can explain all that to you tomorrow. It'll be pretty busy, too . . . she's got a whole big group from the Delta Theta Phi fraternity checking in."

"A fraternity?"

"It's the national law fraternity, Jerome. They're having their annual convention in Washington this year. Students from all the best law schools in the country will be here. By tomorrow afternoon, this place will be crawling with lawyers and judges and law students. Great day to start working, eh?"

"Yeah . . . I suppose so. Might meet some interesting people" agreed Jerome.

"I can hardly wait to watch Maneray's blood boil over with the thought of having to serve law students breakfast" howled Tim. "That's part of his job . . . carrying the trays from the kitchen during the breakfast shift."

"The less I see of him, the better I think I'll like it" said Jerome.

"I can take you over to the law school, too, if you want . . . it's only about a ten minute walk down New Hampshire Avenue. I've been over a couple of times already . . . just to get used to the place."

Jerome had just enough energy to get excited at the thought of seeing the law school. "Now that's something I can look forward to!!"

"All right, then . . . it's a deal" responded Tim. "We can go over after breakfast . . . maybe walk around town a bit before we start work at 3:00 pm . . . we'll be taking over from Mr. Duffy. He starts at 7:00 am. When you wake up just pick up the phone next to your bed there . . . Duffy'll pick up . . . tell him what you want for breakfast and he'll give the order to Polly the cook. By the time you're showered, shaved and dressed . . . it'll be waiting for you in the kitchen . . . Not too bad a deal, is it?"

Jerome shook his head. "I'm speechless. And I'm tired, too."

"Ok . . . I should let you be, then. The bathroom's right around the corner between my room and yours . . . I'm in Room 405, the next door down the hall. The shower's that door on the right hand side half way down. If you need anything . . . just shout."

"Thanks, Tim . . . you've been a great help."

"Don't mention it. See you tomorrow."

"Night." Jerome closed the door to his room. Once again he knew his good luck had rescued him from a potentially sticky situation. The oddities of The Graylock did not concern him so much not after meeting Tim. He knew they'd get along like brothers. He moved his suitcase from the bed onto the desk and didn't bother to unpack. He was too exhausted. He undressed, threw his suit pants and jacket over the back of the desk chair and crawled under the bed covers. He was sound asleep in seconds.

Chapter Eight

Both Tim and Jerome received a cold almost harsh morning acknowledgement from Mr. Maneray as they stepped into the hotel's kitchen for a quick cup of coffee before heading over to the law school. It was a stark contrast to the cheery, warm greeting offered up by Polly, the hotel's cook and head maid. Jerome felt better after she fussed over him and was concerned that he had a good night's sleep, his first night in the hotel, in the room that she personally made up for him. It would have been nearly impossible for him not to have slept well as completely exhausted as he was last night. When he finally awoke to the aroma of what Polly laughingly referred to as her "world famous coffee" wafting up the open staircase four flights to his room, Jerome felt as though he left Buttermilk Falls a month ago rather than a little more than twenty-four hours. "This adjustment is going to be huge" he acknowledged to himself as he showered and shaved "I'd better get used to it fast." When asking after Hattie in the kitchen, Jerome got a quizzical look from Polly who almost whispered to him "Mrs. Crickmore does not come out into the hotel before eleven o'clock . . . no matter what."

"That's why she needs Maneray here" added Tim with a scoff. "She needs somebody here to take care of business until she's ready to face the day . . . no matter how inept they are." That comment prompted Polly to gently tap Tim on the shoulder while jerking her net wrapped hair towards the kitchen door. "Shhhhh now Timothy . . . you never know where he's standin' . . . he could be right outside the door."

"I take it, Polly, that you're not too fond of Mr. Maneray" said Jerome in a hushed tone.

"Been here in this kitchen since the day the Mrs. opened up the hotel, Jerome" responded Polly as she took his coffee cup and saucer and began rinsing it out in the sink. "Seen all kinds come an' go here . . . an' I mean *all* kinds . . . an' that Mr. Maneray is a very strange fellow. Nobody likes him . . . not even the Mrs. But, she thinks he keeps things in order 'till she comes out of her room when really it's Mr. Duffy."

"Why don't you just tell her who's doing what?"

Polly laughed. "You ain't been here hardly a day . . . I been here 35 years. You will learn that what the Mrs. thinks is exactly what she is gonna think . . . and that's that . . . can't nobody tell her a thing! Some says it's strong-willed and some says it's foolish, but she's been her own boss for so long that she don't know no other way. She runs the show and that's the way she likes it. But like I says . . . I seen 'em come and go 'round here an' soon enough she'll catch on to Mr. Maneray an' he'll be outta here faster 'n summer lightin'. 'Till then, it won't do no good to tell her nothin'."

"I hate him already" interjected Tim as he slurped his last gulp of coffee "and I've haven't even been here three weeks." He handed his cup and saucer over to Polly. "You best watch yourself, Mr. Timothy" she warned him "don't do no good to provoke a strange man like him . . . no tellin' what he might do."

"Polly, I swear to you I try to stay out of his way" Tim implored "but he's always finding something to nag me for. It's like he's just looking for a fight." He put his light coat on and continued "I don't like fighting with anybody . . . just like to go my own way, but if I have to slug him I will."

Polly wiped her hand on her apron and edged closer to Tim with a look of real concern and said emphatically and pointedly "Mr. Timothy . . . I do not want to hear nothin' 'bout nobody sluggin' nobody at The Graylock. You hear me??!! I mean nothin'! You let the Mrs. worry 'bout how to take care of matters here. Yous is both young boys 'spose to be mindin' your schoolin' in the law down here and you can't go 'bout hittin' on no older gentleman . . . no matter if you likes him or not. Even if he don't like you . . . you just let the Mrs. take care of it. I don't want to hear 'bout or see no hittin' . . . you understand?"

"Ok . . . Ok . . . Ok" said Tim as he raised both of his outstretched hands figuratively trying to arrest, but helplessly soaking in another of Polly's unintended scoldings. He'd had a few since he started working. They were all sternly delivered, but not one ever had a vindictive tone to them. They were all in the nature of friendly advice from someone whose vantage point and wisdom Tim had not only learned to respect in his short time there, but actually enjoyed. Their matter-of-fact obviousness was amusing to him. He knew Polly liked him and he knew that Polly knew it, too. He knew that he needed Polly to guide him around some of his missteps while learning the unusual weave of the past and present at The Graylock. Polly knew *that*, too.

Uneducated, but worldly-wise she was the real angel of the morning at the hotel . . . the buffer between Maneray's almost fearsome, ornery directives to the hotel staff. Polly was the one who knew everything about the hotel . . . and almost everything about the Mrs.

Jerome listened carefully to Polly as she reprimanded "Mr. Timothy" as she always called him during these exchanges. He decided then and there that she was right on the money. They were, both he and Tim, in Washington to study the law . . . that was the main thing. Maneray's obstinate demeanor and whatever additional quirks lurked about at the hotel immediately became secondary to him at that moment. He would follow Polly's advice and let "the Mrs." take care of matters at The Graylock and he would go about the business of studying to become a lawyer.

"Now y'all go on an' stop botherin me" she said back in her now familiar motherly tone "I got to finish with the breakfast and get on up to the rooms . . . y'all done had your mornin' coffee . . . now scoot!" Tim wrapped his arm gently around her round, stooped shoulders. "Thanks, Polly . . . great coffee . . . see you this afternoon . . . stay out of trouble, now!!"

"Mr. Timothy, you go on an' git out o' my kitchen!" she mildly snapped" Tim laughed as Polly gently maneuvered him out the door with Jerome in tow. "Alright . . . we're going . . . we're going!"

"Where you boys goin'? . . . I don't want you takin' Jerome into no trouble on his first day here." she demanded to know.

"We are going over to the law school for awhile . . . them maybe around town for a bit to see some sights" explained Tim.

"Well you stay out of trouble or I'll give you what for myself . . . an' go out the side door . . . don't go trackin' through the lobby on the Mrs.' clean rug." She was steering them clear of Maneray and Tim knew it but let it pass as Polly moved them both quickly towards the screen door that led to the hotel's side alleyway. "I'll fix somethin' nice for supper if I get a chance." She turned explicitly towards Jerome as she unhooked the screen door and motioned them out. "Jerome . . . do you like fried chicken 'n gravy?" It was Polly's specialty. Tim had never tasted anything like it.

"Yeah . . . sure . . . I love fried chicken . . . that'd be great, Polly" answered Jerome.

Tim stood in the alleyway with his hands stuffed in his pockets and boyishly grinned at her. "I love fried chicken too, Polly . . . mmmm . . . mmmmmm . . . mmmmm" he said continuing his tease "lots of mashed potatoes, too!"

"Git!!" she ordered, waving him off "I ain't makin' nothin' for you . . . I'm mad at you!" Tim could hardly contain his laughter this time. "Go on! Git! . . . an' don't you be late comin' back here for work . . . don't you be gettin' Jerome in trouble with the Mrs. just 'cause you can't tell time proper." She watched as they both headed for the fifteen foot iron gate that separated the side entrance and the back of the hotel from the rest of the world.

She hooked the screen door closed and started to make her way back to the kitchen . . . her daytime domain.

"Do you think they'll be back in time for me to leave by three o'clock?" timidly asked Mr. Duffy from the switchboard station. "I have to leave right at three today."

"Lord knows Mr. Duffy" said Polly shaking her head "Lord knows with Tim." Tim had demonstrated an annoying habit of being just a few minutes late for the beginning of the afternoon shift and the pattern was not lost for a moment on Mr. Maneray. It was the source of several of the curt exchanges between he and Tim in the last couple of weeks.

"I hope he shows up on time today" whispered Mr. Duffy to Polly "I really need to get out of here at three and I don't want to hear it from Maneray if I leave the switchboard unattended 'til those boys get down here."

Polly continued her treck back into the kitchen. "Those boys, Mr. Duffy, are a worry to me . . . especially that Tim." Duffy just shrugged his shoulders. "Jerome seems alright . . . he's very pleasant . . . the guests will take to him right away. Mrs. Crickmore can rest easy with that one."

"They're both charmers" replied Polly "that's what worries me . . . and that Jerome has a real inquisitive nature . . . you can see it in his eyes . . . very bright young man."

"He'll get that worked out of him after a few weeks here"

assured Duffy.

"I hope so" said Polly as she collected the dirty breakfast dishes off the trays "I hope so."

Tim reached out to pull the iron gate open. "That's what that noise is!" said Jerome "that squeak is so loud that I heard it all the way in my room last night . . . couldn't figure out what it was!"

"It was probably Maneray skulking back to the hotel in the middle of the night" said Tim. "He does that."

"Where's he coming from?" asked Jerome.

"Who knows. . . . who cares? Let's get over to the school."

They walked down the tree lined street. It was a glorious, warm Fall September day in Washington. Tim began to immediately point out what was familiar to him in the neighborhood. They cut across Thomas Circle at the end of N Street and darted across to New Hampshire Avenue towards the school . . . leaving The Graylock behind them 'till later.

The schedule of classes had already been posted by the time Jerome and Tim arrived at the law school. School did not officially begin for the Fall semester for four days yet but the offices and hallways were busy with staff making preparations, professors submitting syllabuses and other early arrivals, like Jerome and Tim, walking about, getting a close look at where the balance of their time would be spent and a great part of their lives would be shaped.

Students hovered around the bulletin board outside the Registrar's office all curious to see who's mind was going to be molded by which professor during what course. Jerome noticed his name on the typewritten list right off. Suddenly it became very concrete. People were going to start to teach him a lot about things he knew almost nothing about starting next Monday morning. Torts, Contracts, Real Property, Constitutional Law, Civil Procedure and Criminal Law. He had little idea what any of it was about. Torts? Never heard the word before. Couldn't even guess what it was. Professor Cole . . . never heard of him despite overhearing from another student that "Cole really knows his stuff." Real Property . . . as opposed to what? . . . fake property? . . . stolen property, but that's probably something in Criminal Law he thought. He wondered for a second what kind of property the Reed farm in Buttermilk Falls was and good property did not seem like a lawyer-like answer. Civil Procedure? For what . . . to teach people how to behave? He was starting to feel mighty lost . . . 'till he saw the real reason he decided to follow in his grandfather's footsteps. Criminal Law . . . Monday morning . . . 9:00 am . . . lecture hall number two with Professor David Lucien. Whew! There it was and starting right off the bat too . . . everything else would fall right into place. More incredible Reed luck. His instinctive sense of what was right and wrong was an intuitive trait he inherited from his grandfather and had finely tuned by his parents. Injustice repulsed him. He distained criminals . . . viewed them as nothing more than bullies and street corner punks who never grew up. His indignation was never more self-righteous than when he read of some thug taking advantage of someone. He would find his niche in Criminal Law. It was there he was going to make his mark. He knew it in his bones. He resigned himself to having to learn if somebody's property was real or fake. No big deal.

Tim came out of the Registrar's office sucking on another sour lemon drop he bought from a street vendor on the way over. They were ten for a penny and he only had two left. "See my name up there anywhere, Jerome . . . they don't have any record of me in the Registrar's office."

"No sweat, my friend . . . must just be a misplaced file . . . there you are right there" said Jerome as he pointed Tim to "Owlster" on the list and then noticed after the comma was the name "Samuel

THE GRAYLOCK

N." Hey, can you believe it Tim . . . another Owlster in our class?"

"No" said Tim dourly "I'm the only one. That's my brother. Now I know what the mistake is."

"You've got a brother in law school here?"

Tim shook his head silently. "I used to have a brother. My twin. He's dead. Looks like they forgot to take him off the list."

Jerome felt an unearthly quiet tightly wrapping in all around him. He looked at Tim looking at his dead brother's name. His dead twin brother. "Jesus, I'm sorry, Tim. I didn't know."

"How could you?" answered Tim hollowly "We just met last night. It's not something you tell somebody when you first meet them. It's not something I like to talk about at all, in fact." They both stood there in an awkward moment that took too long to pass until Tim spoke. "Look, I've got to go in there and straighten this out. It might take a while. The book store is open and they've got some of the case books we need for next week. Why don't you pick up the stuff for Monday's and Tuesday's classes and I'll meet you in Lafayette Square in about an hour. Ok? You can't miss it . . . straight down 16th Street across from the White House."

"Ok . . but Tim suppose they . . I mean. . . do you think... what if they ask . . ."

"Ask what" Tim said impatiently.

"Suppose your name is not on the list in the bookstore" answered Jerome emphasizing "your" and hoping he was not being indelicate.

Tim cocked his head back and turned his sturdy jaw line to the right a little and glinted at Tim out of the corner of his eye as he headed back into the Registrar's Office. "Then simply tell them you're picking them up for Sam."

"Tim" Jerome balked "I don't want to . . ."

"C'mon Jerome. Just do this for me alright!? I'll meet you in about an hour." Tim disappeared into the office and Jerome looked for the stairwell to take him to the bookstore in the basement. A dead twin brother. What else was he going to be surprised with? It must have been a horrible experience for Tim . . . recent, too. The administrators hadn't even had the time to take Sam's name off the list of prospective students.

Sitting on a bench in Lafayette Square was a relief to Jerome. It was the first real quiet, waking moment he had to himself in what seemed like days. After a quick stop into the Hay-Adams Hotel across the street to leave a brief note for Everett Roberts, his friend from the train, Jerome grabbed an empty spot on a bench close to Pennsylvania Avenue. He closed his eyes and let the warm, comforting afternoon sun soak through him. The second year student operating the bookstore was accommodating enough to let Jerome pick up the two sets of casebooks for Monday's Criminal Law class and Tuesday's Real Property. Tim's name was on the bookstore's list of first-year students so Jerome did not have to lie about Sam. He hated to lie . . . was terrible at it to boot. He always felt that there was a sign over his head visible to all but himself whenever he played with the truth . . . more likely it was the red blush that came to his face every time he tried. Telling the truth was ingrained in him since birth and he was glad for it, too. He realized at an early age that it help him determine whether other people were being honest with him. It was something he could feel inside . . . a primal instinct that never failed him. His grandfather told him that it was a gift that would work heavily in his favor when dealing with criminals. "They will lie to you boldfaced, Jerome and you will always be able to tell. Not all prosecutors are as lucky. Some try to play the guessing game and it doesn't always work" his grandfather always said. And that was what Jerome Evans Reed was determined to be . . . a prosecutor. Maybe back home . . . maybe not, but he was going to apply his natural skills to that field of law and everything else would be an intellectual exercise. He gazed down at the casebook on Real Property. He was not even curious enough to crack the binding, but he would infuse himself in the casebook on Criminal Law.

He lifted it off the bench and placed it in his lap . . . began to flip through the pages without really reading anything . . . just getting a feel for the book itself. He raised his head towards the sun again and slowly lowered it taking in all the majesty of the White House not more than one hundred yards away. His sense of history rushed through him and he breathed, almost comfortably, with the notion that he was so close to the same ground where his favorite president, Abraham Lincoln, toiled to preserve his beloved country. His musing through the ages was cut short by the sound of a shrill whistle. Jerome opened his eyes from his tiny time travel when he heard the whistle a second time. He looked behind him and saw Tim making his way across the lawn. The friendly wave and quick gait made Jerome think that Tim had straightened difficult matters out over at the school. From behind the bench, with one hand Tim hurdled over and landed in the space next to Jerome barely missing the books. "Nice park, isn't it?' he asked Jerome.

"Beautiful" Jerome replied.

"I spend a lot of time down here when I'm not shackled to that switchboard. I'll be glad next week when school starts and we only have to be at it 20 hours . . . I've got a schedule all worked out with Mr. Duffy."

Jerome was too curious not to ask how things worked out in the Registrar's Office. "I guess then that everthing's ok over at the school?" he said vaguely.

Tim did not reply immediately. Instead he picked up the casebook on Real Property that laid between he and Jerome and toyed with it a bit. Finally he said "Look, let me get most of this out of the way now . . . what I don't say now maybe I'll talk to you about some other time, alright?" It was a rhetorical question and Tim did not wait for an affirmation from Jerome.

"Sam died two months ago. He got scarlet fever after we came back from a camping trip we took up to Bear Mountain to celebrate his acceptance at Jefferson. Columbia Law School had us both on the waiting list and we were anxious to get in someplace. Sam heard from Jefferson before I did, but the school said a place for me was almost a certainty because I was first on their waiting list. We were suppose to be here together. When we got back to New York City he got sick really fast and nobody could stop it. His fever was way too high for doctors to help. It killed him after two weeks. It was misery for him . . . misery for all of us. My mother was a mess as usual and my father stone-faced his way through the whole ordeal. I had to take care of all the funeral arrangements myself . . . they were paralyzed with grief and Sam was buried practically before I knew it. I was just plain numb."

Tim took a moment to exhale and continued. "It was Sam's idea for us to go to law school together . . . well, actually it was my father's idea for Sam to go to law school . . . it was Sam's idea for me to follow and I always did . . . follow him wherever. I adored him and I'll probably never meet anybody like him again as long as I live. It was his plan for us to come down here and make a big adventure for ourselves . . . Sam was a great one for adventures."

"So, I'm down here now on Sam's big adventure and I won't let him down, Jerome. No matter what, I'm going to make these three years fun."

Jerome thought of his grandfather and groped in vain for something personal to say. "You must miss him terribly" was the best he could come up with.

"With every breath I take" declared Tim "but I learned pitifully hard this summer that life goes on. You can try your damnedest to stop it and if you do it'll roll right over you. So, I figured I could let it roll over me or I could roll with it. When we were growing up, Sam always said I was the real survivor but I never believed him. I have chosen to survive his death and I'm going to make the best of it."

Tim was finished. No more details for the time being. He said enough and it was not Jerome's place to ask for additional information. He'd heard enough.

"I'm sorry that your brother died, Tim" Jerome said in conclusion "But I'm glad that you're here."

"Good!" said Tim enthusiastically "that is exactly how I feel."

"I'd hate to have to live in that hotel by myself!" Jerome quipped.

"Ugh . . . don't remind me of Maneray! We'll just have to learn to ignore him . . . speaking of which . . . we'd better head on back . . . it's getting near three and I don't want him jumping on me first thing." Tim stood up and grabbed his copies of the casebooks. "Thanks for getting these, by the way."

"No problem . . . glad to help."

"You are a big help, Jerome . . . things are going to be a lot easier now that you're here."

Jerome smiled with the thought that he was now a part of Sam's intended adventure. "Well, I suppose since there's no sight of the President, we should leave."

Tim looked at him pathetically and laughed. "You'll get awfully hungry sitting here waiting for the sight of him."

"Why?"

Geeze, Jerome . . . have a look at the newspaper once in awhile. FDR's not even in town. He's in Nebraska scanning the drought situation. Farmers are choking on their own dust out there. The land is cracking wide open from lack of rain. You're a farmer's son . . . aren't you up on this stuff?"

"You must be kidding . . . you're not actually going to try and tell me something about farming are you, city boy?" Jerome teased. "I've lived and breathed it for 21 years . . . I know all I want to know about it!"

"Oh yeah . . . ok farm boy" shot back Tim with a wide grin "where's our beloved President headed?"

Jerome pursed his lips for a second and shook his head.

"Yeah . . . I thought so" said Tim. "For your information he's on his way to Des Moines, Iowa to meet with Alf Landon at a big conference on the drought. It's going to be a big showdown between the two Presidential candidates."

"Makes me thirsty just thinking about it!"

"Well, it's serious business. People are dying because of it."

"I know it's serious . . . geeze back off a little will ya? I was just making a joke."

Tim turned around and started walking backwards up 16th Street motioning with his hands at Jerome "I'm just trying to get you prepared for tonight my friend."

"What do you mean?" asked Jerome quizzically

"Hattie . . . that's what I mean."

"What about her?"

Tim spun around on his heels and matched Jerome's gait. "After a couple of glasses of bourbon she starts in with the third degree on current events. You'd better be prepared. She is very up on things . . . and she HATES Roosevelt with unbridled passion!"

"Get out of here!!"

"I am not lying . . . she calls him a son of a bitch at least five times a night!!" Tim protested.

Jerome slumped his broad shoulders in mock dismay. "Oh my God . . . I'm doomed!"

They both howled at the notion of a 62 year old woman, who rarely left the confines of the hotel picking their brains on politics and current events for, at least, the next three months. Their conversation trailed off onto other subjects. Not Sam. Not family. Not Buttermilk Falls. It was laced with dreams of their futures . . . peppered with Tim's pragmatic paens on how to survive the "reign of Maneray" as they absurdly nicknamed it. They bet on who would be gone first . . . Edward VIII who's reign over the British Empire was slipping away over his love for Wallis Simpson or mean, evil Oliver Maneray, who's precipitous early morning grip on the hotel would be cut short, they both thought, by the perceptively wise protectorate, Polly the kitchen maid. Both of them laid their empty pockets on Maneray. Neither thought the King of England would abdicate because he could not carry on without the woman he loved. Nobody's passion could be that strong they agreed, as they headed back to The Graylock. Few outside of Buckingham Palace thought so either. No one knew that in twelve short weeks Edward's reign would be in ruins. Jerome and Tim would soon learn that passion could, with unquestionable force, be just that strong.

Chapter Nine

"Hattie owns this one, too" said Tim as they walked leisurely up N Street. He directed Jerome's attention to a four story town house a few doors up the street, directly across from The Graylock. It was a white stone edifice with three large windows facing the street on each floor, descending in size and presence with each elevated floor. The heavy looking dark black door was sharply different from the entrance to the hotel which guests could almost see through the nylon veil into the lobby. Instead, the town house door was a solid oak, windowless barrier protecting its insides from unwanted, strange intruders. But for a stained brass doorknob and an imposing hook-shaped equally stained knocker that dwarfed the one on the hotel's front entrance way, this door was unaffected with any signs of welcome to visitors. The flat hammer base of the door knocker looked as though it had landed too many times on an ornate, heart shaped plate in the middle of the door. The plate bore some kind of crest that was scratched and worn from too many blows to its center from callers long since past who sought permission to enter. "It's prime real estate going to hell from neglect" added Tim.

Relieved on their walk home from Lafayette Square with Tim's soliloquy on how real estate was going to be his corner of the law to conquer, because he knew he'd need help understanding its archaic principles, Jerome was more confused now than interested in the value of Hattie's apparently vacant and deteriorating property.

"You mean to tell me that she owns this whole house and lives in that little room off the lobby?" ask Jerome incredulously. "Why?"

"I don't know. But I'm going to find out . . . there's a story here and I'm dying to find out what it is. I asked Mr. Duffy one day and he clammed up right off . . . told me it was none of my business and I wasn't to meddle in Hattie's affairs. I asked Polly, too. She gave me some ridiculous explanation that Hattie stays in that clutter nest off the lobby because she can hear all the comings and goings in the lobby from her room."

Jerome said he thought the explanation seemed plausible and didn't see anything unusual about Hattie wanting to be a twenty-four hour a day presence inside the hotel.

"Then why doesn't she sell it?" said Tim "It's got to be worth a fortune." Jerome looked at the house and just shrugged. "Beats me . . . I mean you're the real estate baron here . . . you tell me. I, on the other hand, don't see anything criminal here. It's her house . . . I suppose she can do what she wants with it."

"You don't see anything even the slightest bit curious here? What kind of criminal lawyer are you going to make?"

"I don't have a suspicious nature. When a crime is committed, I'll be able to handle it just fine, but I'm not going to go snooping around where I don't belong."

"Well, if you ask me this whole thing bears a closer look."

"Better watch it Sherlock" joked Jerome "you don't want Maneray after you!"

"I'll handle him . . . no problem" replied Tim with disgust.

The two law students responded swiftly to Polly's beckoned hand waving from the hotel's side door. Tim wondered why she was waving so. It was still fifteen minutes before three. Today he would not be late for work.

"Y'all boys git in here now" she shouted "theys lots of people in the lobby to check in an' poor Mr. Duffy can't go runnin' about an' answer the switchboard, too. He's only one man and a tiny one at that. C'mon now . . . hurry up." It might have resembled more like her friendly greeting in the morning if she didn't almost pull them both up the one step from the alleyway into the tool room that led to the small corridor in between the switchboard station and the dining room. "An' Timothy . . . the Mrs. seen you lollygaggin' in front of her house there . . . you know she don't like nobody hangin' round in front of that place!"

"But, I was just showing Jerome . . ."

"Don't give me no never mind 'bout Jerome, now . . . I told you last week you ain't 'spose to be hangin' 'round there . . . now don't forget what I told you an' go on in there and relieve Mr. Duffy."

Tim complied and walked into the switchboard station. "Hi Mr. Duffy" he said in a friendly manner. He liked Duffy from the first day they met. It was Duffy who showed him how to operate the arcane switchboard with its wire loops, crossed and uncrossed, red lines for incoming calls, gray for outgoing. Two special hooks-ups for long-distance callers . . . white lights for calls from the rooms . . . red lights for calls from the lands beyond the hotel walls . . . and that hawking buzzer to summon whoever was on duty from wherever they were to return to the nest and mind to the questions, needs and eccentricities of The Graylock's family of guests.

Tim took a quick glance at the reservation sheet. It was a mess from cross-outs and erasures and add-ons. "Looks like it's been a busy day so far." Four of the five red lights on the switchboard were lit and twelve of the thirty-seven white lights were simultaneously ringing out impatiently and Duffy's hands were shaking in a feeble attempt to respond to all at one time. He had a naturally nervous disposition that was reacting badly to the onslaught of calls, the gathering crowd of unusually talkative guests in the lobby and Maneray's lurking, ominous presence never far from the switchboard. It was a busy day for Mr. Duffy, indeed.

"Oh ... Tim ... I'm so glad you're here. It's been crazy since noon around here. There've been people showing up here from that law group claiming that they had reservations and we have no record of it ... Mr. Maneray was blaming you for not writing down all the reservations on the sheet when you took them."

"Bullshit" Tim whispered into Duffy's ear "if anybody's to blame it's Maneray ... I don't think he even knows how to take a reservation, that stupid bastard."

Mr. Duffy nervously tugged at the frail wire rims of his spectacles and readjusted them on his small nose. Tugging at the vest to his black suit ... seemingly the same black suit he wore every day he pleaded with Tim not to swear because the guests might here ... worse Hattie might.

"She can swear like a sailor at night when she's of a mind to!"

"That's nighttime" replied Duffy. "It's different. This is the daytime and there are guests all over this place"

"Ok, I'm sorry ... besides I wasn't swearing at you, Mr. Duffy. I would never swear at you." Tim carefully patted Duffy's waif-like back gently and said "Why don't you slip on out of here. I can handle these calls ... go on into the kitchen and grab a cup of your favorite tea ... it'll calm you down."

"I can't handle all these big crowds anymore like I used to Tim. I can't carry that luggage anymore." His chin was beginning to quiver delicately as he pointed to three rows of luggage lined up in the lobby near the front window under the geranium box. "Who's going to take all that luggage upstairs?" Duffy worried.

"Don't worry about it, Mr. Duffy. Jerome can do it while I

watch the board . . . go on in the kitchen and rest up."

"Oh, I have no time to rest today . . . I have to leave right at three o'clock . . . on the dot" he punctuated "I have a meeting to go to."

Tim brought the electric clock on the switchboard closer to his face and feigned shock. "Why . . . that's just two minutes from now . . . good thing I showed up on time, Mr. Duffy! Otherwise you'd be late for your meeting. . . . you know you sure have a lot of meetings to go to . . . what are you in some group or something?"

"I didn't say the meeting was at three" Duffy corrected him "I said I had to leave at three . . . I have to go home and get ready for it . . . and just you stop trying to get into my private affairs. I'm an old man and nothing I do would interest a young fellow like yourself."

"Old my foot . . . why you're probably not . . ." Tim winced trying to guess Duffy's age ". . . probably not a day older than Hattie! C'mon Mr. Duffy . . ." Tim coyly begged "tell me where you're going . . . I won't tell anybody."

In fact, Walter Duffy was 52 years old, but it was hard to tell by looking at him . . . he looked easily fifteen years older. Worry lines cut deeply into his small forehead and age had made his lightweight frame all the more noticeable under his fair, wrinkled skin. The bone structure in his wispy face gave the impression that his cheeks were hallow and he was underfed, but it was simply such a diminutive visage that genetics only could be blamed for condemning him to have such a look that made people feel immediately sorry for him upon meeting. But, it was the singular twinkle in the corner of his right eye, the grey one . . . the other was sometimes grey . . . sometimes green . . . that made everyone like him at the same time. Everyone but Maneray. Duffy was a tiny well-meaning man who did his job well and mostly without serious complaint. He'd done so since he arrived at The Graylock

THE GRAYLOCK

35 years ago at the age of eighteen. He'd never once thought of leaving.

Duffy ignored Tim's plea for private information and slipped past him to get his belongings that he always stashed in the small space behind the switchboard. Jerome walked out of the kitchen with a mouthful of Polly's promised fried chicken and nodded a friendly hello to him. "She's stuffing you already, eh?' he said to Jerome "maybe you'll be the first to squeeze the secret recipe out of her."

Suddenly Maneray appeared in the small corridor blocking Jerome's way. "Where do you think you're going?" he said in a gravel tone.

Duffy stopped what he was doing and looked up at Maneray's towering frame . . . he realized he was speaking to Jerome. "Where did you get that food?" he demanded to know. "That food was cooked for Mrs. Crickmore's dinner . . . for her and her guest not for you."

Jerome backed off a couple of feet and swallowed the last bite hard. "I'm going out to help Tim with the guests . . . and Polly gave me this food . . . I didn't just go in and take it." He tried not to sound defensive as he wiped a bit of grease from his lips.

"You shouldn't be in that kitchen. It's not where you work." Maneray stared at Jerome with an unbalanced sense of loathing. Seething through his every syllable.

"Is there a problem back here, Mr. Maneray?" It was Hattie . . . to the rescue again . . . gliding around the corner, in command, looking for Jerome. Maneray fumbled for a response. "Mr. Reed should have a jacket on, not a sweater, if he's intending to be around guests in the lobby" he said with the lie coming from his dark soul.

"Nonsense. He looks just fine" she replied without looking at him. "Jerome come out here, I want you to meet some of your colleagues . . . they're all from the national law fraternity . . . our whole hotel is almost full with them. Isn't this just a fine thing!" She took Jerome's arm and started walking him towards the crowd in the lobby.

"I'll be off duty now . . . for the day." Maneray whimpered back.

"Yes, of course. Thank you, Mr. Maneray." Hattie replied with an uninterested air . . . again not looking back. Tim and Duffy exchanged glances as Maneray stiffly climbed the back staircase to his own room on the second floor. Duffy had nothing to say as he fitted his black, wide-brimmed fedora on his little head and tilted it, to the side as usual "for style" he told Tim on his first day at the switchboard. "I like to be stylish." Completing his "stylish" look was a three quarter length black, full flowing cape with a huge flat collar that Duffy flung around his shoulders with a flourish. Tim tried to turn away every time Duffy did this to conceal his amusement. Duffy looked anything but stylish. Tim thought he looked like an extra in a Bela Lugosi movie but he could not bear to insult Duffy by telling him. He looked more like someone from the 1920's not 1936.

"You probably won't need your cape this afternoon" Tim suggested "it's really kind of nice outside. Must be at least 75 degrees."

"I always need my cape" Duffy replied, as though Tim did not know. But, Tim just had to turn away from the sight of Mr. Duffy and, all his style. He left by the side door sheathed in an eccentricity that knew no home except The Graylock. "See you tomorrow, Mr. Duffy. Have a good time at your meeting!" said Tim as he easily managed to field all the incoming and outgoing calls that had been giving Duffy tremors. "Goodnight, Tim" he answered back with a slight, airy wave from his right hand before it also disappeared with the rest of Duffy underneath his cape.

Duffy thought he had all the style in the world when, in reality, it was sadly the only style in the world he had. The Graylock had that effect upon him.

Meanwhile, Hattie had been introducing Jerome to all the various members of the Delta Theta Phi national law fraternity that, in Hattie's mind more importantly, instantly became members of her expansive Graylock family as soon as they signed the register. She demanded no special grades, no legal practitioner's field of expertise and no impressive family background. The only connection anyone had to make with Hattie Crickmore was to walk through the door and sign in. She wanted everyone to feel welcome. She was the expert at that. By the time Jerome completed one trip up and down the stairs with someone's set of luggage, Hattie had already endeared herself to the next guest waiting to be escorted to their room. The introduction always preceded the climb to the room.

"Mr. Reed" she would always begin "this is Mr. Taylor. Mr. Taylor is on the board of the law fraternity. He will be in Room 205. Mr. Taylor this is our Mr. Reed. He and our Mr. Owlster at the switchboard whom you've already met are first year law students at Thomas Jefferson School of Law right here in Washington. Isn't that wonderful!" Mr. Reed and Mr. Taylor shook hands. The reply was mostly the same from the seasoned, older members of Delta Theta Phi. "Yes. Very nice" from Mr. Ray Bell who was in Room 202. "Excellent. Good choice of schools" from Mr. Homer McCormick who was in Room 201. "Wonderful, indeed. Good luck to the both of you" from Mrs. Meredith Daubin who was in Room 307. Mr. Taylor was even less effusive. "Good to know" was all he could muster before Jerome led him off to Room 304.

The younger, single male members of the group were checked into rooms in pairs. Some were placed in rooms in the fourth floor . . . a sure sign that the hotel was filled . . . Tim told Jerome that Hattie rarely put guests on the top floor because few of them cared to walk the full four flights up and down every time they went out of their rooms. Besides, Hattie thought Polly was getting too tired to carry breakfast trays up to the fourth floor and back again every time someone wanted breakfast served in their room instead of with others in the dining room. Jerome thought the law students who were attending the fraternity's 1936 annual convention were strong enough to carry their own luggage . . . especially up to the fourth floor, but he understood that Hattie wanted them all treated like guests, not staff. So, by six o'clock that evening, Jerome had carried forty-seven pieces of luggage up to thirty-three different rooms for the forty-two members of the Delta Theta Phi national law fraternity who were staying at The Graylock. It was just a sliver of the 300 delegates who were in town to attend, but it kept everyone at the hotel hopping. The switchboard went wild for awhile, but Tim efficiently handled all calls, never missing a one.

Hattie was sitting in the empty dining room at her round table looking pleased and satisfied that all the guests were safely in their room and all reservation conflicts had been resolved. She was staring out the window into the hotel's pretty back garden at a large patch of ivy covered ground in the far corner of the garden wall. "I'll have to get that ivy watered soon" she said aloud to no one "it's starting to look awfully brown around the edges." Even in the foggy bottomed humid Washington, D.C. summers she was so accustomed to, Hattie realized that the severe drought conditions in the south and southwest parts of the country were having a rippling effect in the nation's capital . . . mostly on FDR's approval ratings in the polls. "That fool Roosevelt doesn't know what he's doing . . . there's water a plenty, he's just doesn't know how to use it. I'm going to water my garden and to hell with him."

"Did you say something, Hattie?" asked Tim as he stuck he

head around from the tool room. "Everything ok.?"

Hattie simply nodded while she tapped her fingers mindlessly on the garden-like flower print of the tablecloth. With no answer Tim returned to his search for a wrench to tighten a leaky bathroom sink faucet up in Room 300.

"Tim?" she called.

"Yes, m'am. Right here."

"I think I'll go rest awhile. You boys have everything under control?"

"Yep . . . everything at The Graylock is under control" he said humorously reassuring her.

"Come here." Tim walked into the dining room with the found wrench in his left hand and approached Hattie's confidential motioning. "How's Jerome doing on the switchboard?" she whispered. Tim put both his hands on his hips and squinted at her. "Hattie . . . I'm surprised at you! . . . I trained him . . . Mr. Duffy trained me . . . Jerome's taking to it like a duck to water . . . don't you worry a bit, the line of excellence continues at The Graylock!" he announced confidently.

This teasing produced a clear smile from Hattie. "Oh, you stop it now . . . you're just being silly" she said again in a whisper. "I just wanted to make sure he was alright."

"He's fine."

Hattie stood up and glanced quickly out the window at the ivy patch again as she used both hands to mat her perfectly coiffed hair in place. "Good enough. Ring me at eight will you, please? Miss Pack from the law fraternity will be joining me for dinner. You and Jerome can set up the trays, can't you?" she winked at Tim as she began to walk away "I think Polly made something special for dinner."

Tim already knew it was fried chicken. "Sure we can. How about her husband?"

"No. Mr. Bergeron will just join us for drinks then he has to go off to some convention dinner . . . oh, that reminds me, Tim, check to see that there is enough bourbon and branch water for us, will you?"

Tim reluctantly answered "I think there's plenty, Hattie."

"Check just the same." She passed the switchboard station and gave a kindly approving nod to Jerome who was busy attending to an outside call. He smiled back.

"It's so good to have my boys here" she told herself as she opened the door to her very private little corner of The Graylock . . . closing herself off for a few hours from even that uneven slice of the real world that she ever allowed in. She could rest easy now, though . . . her boys were here.

THE GRAYLOCK

Chapter Ten

Jerome stayed on the switchboard after all the guests were checked in and Hattie retired. Maneray made his usual dusky departure and Tim went upstairs to read his Real Property materials. By then quiet seemed to have found its way back to the lobby of the hotel . . . the pre-dawn type of solace where haunting memories lingered before the earth's spinning wove reality's forces into a hammer that forcibly awakened, all but the most resistant, to the edge of a new day. Hattie was in her room taking with her in there all the mystique that made The Graylock interesting. Absent her presence, it was just a place to stay. Without her all the magic of a life maddeningly lived was left to be conjured up by weaker, mortal souls with far less to offer. It was her gift to dance with the power of life so easily. She shared it willingly with those who could take to the floor with her. She always led and knew that few could follow . . . or even knew how. It never bothered her that partners could not keep up . . . it bothered her that they did not want to learn to try. So, she learned to dance alone years ago. "Come take my hand if you can" was her implicit invitation . . . "but don't try to stop me." The music was her own composition . . . her life its orchestration. Only she understood it best. Only she could teach the intricate steps. Too often she was the only one who could hear the tune.

THE GRAYLOCK

Like a call from beyond, the white light over Room 100 on the switchboard lit triggering the buzzer into alarm state. It jolted Jerome from a studied focus on the elemental principles of proof for the crime of murder as set forth in his casebook which he had begun to read in earnest after Tim went to his room. It was Hattie.

"Jerome?" she asked softly as he plugged the incoming wire into the socket for Room 100 instantly connecting Hattie.

"Yes m'am."

"Is everything alright out there?"

"Sure is" he said snappily "no problems at all."

"Oh, good." She sounded relieved. "How about Miss Pack, have you heard from her?"

"Yes, I have. She and her husband will be down in the dining room at 8:30 if that's all right with you."

Hattie thought for a second. "That's fine with me. What time is it now?"

"Almost a quarter to eight."

"Good. That gives me enough time to get myself together. Call Tim and ask him to come down and help you set up the drink trays. I'll be out shortly." She disengaged the line without saying good-bye . . . an unusual trait for someone so keen on manners, but she explained to Tim the first time it happened to him that she did not believe in saying good-bye to anyone anymore. She said she had to do it once and it was too much for her to bear. It was too final. She preferred to imagine that all who ever stayed at The Graylock found it, and her, so wonderful that they would always come back. Or at least planned to. It was easier for Hattie to think that everyone could come back . . . it obviated the need to part.

Jerome rang Tim in Room 405. "What are you doing?" he asked.

"Planning how to buy all the real estate on N Street! We can't live here forever."

"That's in your casebook?" Jerome quipped.

"No, my friend . . . it in my head . . . where all the rest of my great ideas are."

Jerome laughed at the idea of Tim scooping up all the real estate on N Street . . . with Hattie's townhouse in the bargain. He's bound and determined to get inside there, he thought.

"I've got a good idea, too . . . why don't you come on down here and help me set up the drink trays for Hattie? I don't know where anything is."

"You'll probably be sorry after I show you. Is she up yet?"

"Yeah . . . she just called . . . said she'd be out shortly."

"Ok" said Tim "I'll be down in a few minutes."

No sooner than had he disconnected Tim did Hattie appear in the lobby. She walked slowly through it, ever the owner and always the overseer. She lifted the draperies on the front window aside as though to monitor who might be looking in . . . wanting to get in . . . while readjusting two small pots of African violets on the window sill. Satisfied that all was well, she turned and walked towards the back, fussing with the ferns on the way.

She stopped at the switchboard and smiled at Jerome. She looked rested . . . ready to start again. "Holding down the fort for me ok, Jerome?" she teased.

"Yes, Hattie" he said feeling very needed "I am successfully protecting your empire!" he teased back.

"A couple of knights . . . that's what you boys are . . . just a couple of knights" Jerome laughed. He did not know how much Hattie meant it. "Any new reservations?" she wanted to know. Jerome handed her the reservation sheet.

"Just one . . . a Mrs. Virginia Claypool Meredith. She said you would know who she was."

Hattie beamed like she had been shot through with sunshine. "Oh, my ... how wonderful!!" she exclaimed. "My dear, dear sweet Virginia is coming back!" She was wholly alive now. "Oh what a treat this will be to see her again!" She clutched the reservation sheet to her chest and grinned from ear to ear. "When is she arriving, Jerome ... tell me!"

Jerome was not at all suspect at Hattie's enraptured enthusiasm ... just a bit taken aback ... he was not used to it ... yet. But he knew it was real. His keen Reed intuition told him that. "It's right there on the sheet" he told her "she'll be here in three weeks."

Hattie quickly reviewed the reservation sheet looking for "Mrs. Meredith. "There it is!" she squealed. "Oh, I can hardly wait ... we'll have to do something very special for her."

"Who is she anyway?"

Hattie looked at him and pretended to huff. "Why Jerome Reed ... I'm surprised at you ... a farmer's son." He shrugged.

"She's the Queen of American Agriculture ... at least that's what I call her ... many others as well and a fellow Mississippian, too." She returned the reservation sheet to the top shelf along side of the switchboard. "And let me add that Mrs. Meredith is the only woman ever to have served on the Board of Trustees of Purdue University" said Hattie proudly. "Don't let anybody ever tell you, Jerome that women can't do things just as well as men ... it just isn't true."

Jerome thought of his 13-year old sister, Gail and her love for farming and got a twinge of homesickness. "Well ... I mean it is 1936 after all" he offered.

"Posh ... 1936 nothing" Hattie declared as she began to unnecessarily straighten things up and shift them about in the dining room. "1930 ... 1918 ... 1900 ... makes no difference ... women have had the ability to do well since the dawn of creation

". . . some just don't believe it, that's all . . . that's what their problem is. Nothing more."

"I guess you're right" agreed Jerome.

"Guess nothing . . . I know I am." Hattie stated definitively. "Why do you know that if I listened to half of the people who told me I couldn't do with my own life the things I wanted to do I'd probably be dead by now . . . I surely would probably have died of boredom . . . can you imagine being bored to death, Jerome?? What a horrible fate."

Jerome kind of shook his head and had no response.

"You have picked a great profession to be in . . . the law, I mean. If you learn it well you'll never be bored."

"I sure hope not."

Hattie leaned forward to open the dining room window and let in the warm, Fall evening air. "Did you know that I have a law degree?"

Jerome was stunned. "Really?"

"Oh, yes sir! . . . and believe me when I was your age there were no women in my law school. I was the only one. Everybody told me I shouldn't go . . . it was no place for a women, they said. They all thought I was this pretty little girl who ought to stay out of a man's profession. But I was determined as hell to make a go of it."

"Did you?" he asked.

"Did I what . . . ?"

"Make a go of it . . . practice law, I mean."

Hattie looked back in time and smiled at the walls. "No, not really . . . I got the degree that's for sure . . . but after I graduated I . . ." she stumbled for the right thing to say "I just never got the chance, that's all. But I was never bored!"

Jerome could not imagine going through three years of law school and not practicing the chosen profession. He began to wonder. "But, if . . ." Hattie cut him off and changed the subject.

"Oh, Jerome there's so many interesting people that come to see me here . . . it's the most wonderful part of running the hotel . . . I just know you're going to love it here!"

The clumping of feet down the wooden back staircase brought Hattie out of the dining room and into the small corridor. "Is that the handsome Mr. Timothy Owlster, I hear?" she shouted. Tim hopped down the remaining two steps to the base of the stairs and fell into a full courtly bow. "At your service, madame."

"You're just a character, Tim . . . that's all you are . . . a silly character." They both laughed.

"You're in fine fettle this evening Hattie" Tim told her.

"Life is so good to me sometimes, Tim . . . it makes me want to burst. Can you boys hurry and get those trays ready before Miss Pack and her husband get down here?"

"We'll be done in no time" said Tim "why don't you go in and sit down?" He motioned for Jerome to join him in the kitchen. He started to pull out the trays and told Jerome that the bourbon was stashed in the back of the cupboard next to the stove. "What's with her . . . she's flying around here like somebody gave her a million dollars . . . not that she probably doesn't have that much already."

"Mrs. Meredith's coming here in a few weeks" answered Jerome dryly.

"Who's Mrs. Meredith?"

Jerome found the bottle and gave it to Tim, hardly looking at it. "Don't you know anything. . . . Sir Timothy?" Tim got a little red in the face. "Shut up and get me some ice."

As Tim and Jerome busied themselves preparing the drink tray and dinner trays for Hattie and her guests, Hattie sat in the dining room and leisurely paged through copies of "The Breeders Gazette," a bible for cattle farmers that Mrs. Meredith had been the editor of . . . first and only woman editor . . . for ten years. Hattie had been a regular subscriber to the magazine for years, but only kept copies edited by her dear friend Virginia on display in the lobby and in the dining room. Mrs. Meredith stopped editing the magazine in 1931. That was of no consequence to Hattie . . . one year was the same as the next to her. Time marched on, but she was not in the parade.

"Hello?" called out a woman's voice from in front of the switchboard. "Is anyone there?" Hattie heard it and put her magazine to the side to respond. "Yes . . . yes . . . I'm in here" she answered. A slightly heavy, round and cheery faced woman in her late thirties walked into the dining room. She wore a lovely red and pink wide cut satin dress with long sleeves and white cuffs. A white and purple orchid corsage decorated the left side of her dress and covering parts of her double strand looping gold chain necklace. "Hello, Mrs. Crickmore. How are you?" she said.

"Why Miss Pack! . . . how nice you look. I'm very well . . . thank you for asking. Please come in a sit with me." Hattie rose and pulled out one of the chairs at her round table. "How pleasant to see you. I apologize for the confusion earlier today over the reservations . . . but I assume that everything is satisfactory now."

"Oh my yes . . . absolutely. It's just a lovely room. Very warm and comforting . . . and such a beautiful bed. Where ever did you get such a find?"

There were very few things Hattie liked better than to hear a compliment on the rooms in her hotel. She reveled in the notion that the odds and ends that she had collected over the years . . . the unmatching pieces of furniture from different periods . . . came together in an ensemble of decoration that seemed as though it had been carefully put together.

"That gorgeous bed, Miss Pack, is an exact copy of the bed in the Lincoln Room at the White House . . . isn't it just a real piece of work?"

"Just lovely" was the response "so sturdy and comfortable."

"I can't even remember when or where I got it . . . seems like I've had it here forever." It may as well have been in the hotel forever . . . or last year. Hattie's concept of the passage of time ran its own line . . . paralleled to no other's. Unparalleled. To her worst critics is was unheard of.

"Now where's your husband, Miss Pack? We can't start without him, can we?" said Hattie.

"Why not!?" joshed Miss Pack. "He's gabbing on the telephone upstairs with one of the directors of the law convention. He'll be down directly."

"Well that's good enough for me. We'll be the devils, then won't we and break that silly tradition of waiting for the man!" Hattie laughed at her response. "I don't think I've ever waited for anyone!" That was almost true. "Mr. Reed! . . . Mr. Reed . . ."

Jerome popped his head into the dining room. "Right here."

"Mr. Reed would you be kind enough to bring the drink tray out for us ladies?"

Jerome went back into the kitchen where Tim had already set the drink tray aside and put up two dinner trays. He started to say something but Tim interrupted him. "Never mind . . . I heard her from here. She's starting without that lady's husband. I'm going back upstairs. Good Luck!"

"Wait a second! Don't leave me down here by myself. What if she . . ."

"Just go along with her . . . she doesn't bite. Turn the oven off in fifteen minutes and let the food stay warm until she calls for it. Bring the drink tray in and leave . . . she'll pour. Just stay close to the switchboard . . . if she starts to get a little nutty call me . . . I'll come down. I'm not going anywhere." Tim bounded up the back staircase, but not before he told Jerome that he'd left the day's edition of *The Washington Post* on his chair at the switchboard. "Better read fast! I got a feeling she's in the mood for a quiz!!!" Jerome picked up the drink tray and walked towards the dining room. However Hattie may be feeling, Jerome was in no mood for a quiz on current events. He wanted to continue reading about the elements of proof for the crime of murder.

"Mr. Reed" he heard again. Not exactly a nightingale's call. Mr. Reed are you . . ." Jerome entered the dining room. "Oh there you are. The tray looks very nice." She knew that Tim had probably set it up. "You can set it right here on my table."

"Thank you." Both the ladies smiled. "Miss Pack, I would like you to meet our Mr. Reed." Jerome nodded. "How do?" said Miss Pack.

"Mr. Reed will be starting his first day of law school on Monday. Isn't he in for just the most interesting time of it?" said Hattie as she began to pour Miss Pack her requested, practically required, bourbon and branch water.

"I should say" replied her guest "a most interesting time indeed. How lucky for you."

"Thank you" said Jerome showing all his good Reed breeding "I'm really looking forward to it."

"What's this I hear . . . another lawyer in the making?" bellowed Miss Pack's husband as he walked into the room. "Hello, dear" said Miss Pack. He walked over to his wife and kissed her on the forehead. "Sorry for the delay, Mildred . . . I'm afraid that Mr. James got somewhat longwinded there on the telephone."

"Another long winded lawyer!" quipped his wife.

Hattie took a sip on her bourbon and laughed as she brushed her knee in animation. "Is there any other kind!" All three laughed heartily. Jerome stepped to the side starting to make his way out of the room. "Darling, this is Mr. Reed about whom you overheard Mrs. Crickmore and I referring" announced Miss Pack.

"Mr. Reed . . . how do you do. I am Joseph Bergerson. We spoke briefly earlier over the phone" he said strongly.

Jerome extended his hand in a firm shake . . . almost a grip. "Jerome Reed, Mr. Bergerson" he said in an equally strong response "Pleased to meet you." Hattie smiled as though a son of her own bloodline was displaying inherited manners. "Mr. Bergerson" she said "come join us, now. You take this seat right here." Hattie directed him to the chair next to his wife. "We've been terrible and started without you" she added with a coquettish flair "I hope you don't mind."

"Not at all" Bergerson replied easily "why stand on ceremony when there's good bourbon on the wing? Shall I pour my own?"

Hattie nodded affirmatively and motioned him with a small, magnetic wave to the drink tray which Jerome had placed next to her . . . her companion for the evening. "You go directly ahead and help yourself as you please, Mr. Bergerson . . . I have plenty."

Jerome returned to his station to field more calls and thought he'd best have a look at the newspaper . . . just in case. There was no telling what kind of turn the evening might take. What might Hattie be interested in, he pondered, as he perused the newsprint? He read that Amelia Earhart Putnam, the heralded pilot, had just completed a solo flight of two hours and fifteen minutes from Cleveland to Long Island. The article stated that Mrs. Putnam was also an entrant in the upcoming Bendix Air Race to be flown from New York to Los Angeles next week. "I wonder if Hattie knows this" he said to himself "sounds like this item is right up her alley . . . maybe I'll decide to quiz her instead." He scanned other articles and learned that Benito Mussolini was in Avellino, Italy with King Victor Emmanuel III to watch 60,000 troops with full war pack march in full review in a demonstration of Italy's preparedness for war. He knew there'd been talk of another war in Europe and that FDR was cautious about alarming the voters that he'd bring the United States into it for fear of losing the election. No one liked the thought of burying more American soldiers. He also saw that the deficit of the U.S. was at an all-time high of two billion dollars. It was no wonder that there were still soup lines in New York City.

There was a small side bar column that reported the Republican candidate for President, Alf Landon was in Springfield, Illinois paying a visit to the grave of Abraham Lincoln. Fond as he was of Lincoln, Jerome couldn't help but think that Abe would be rolling over in his grave at the thought of Landon piously peering down at him in his final resting place.

Further inside the newspaper, on page fifteen, was an article that got Jerome quite interested. It was an interview that Miss Pack had given the paper before she arrived in Washington to attend the national convention of Delta Theta Phi. She was the focus of the article because of her singularly determined approach to being a woman practicing law in Cleveland.

"I don't think any career-woman should worry one minute about this business of whether she is, or isn't a victim of discrimination just because she's a woman. That's one thing I never worried about" she was quoted as saying. "I believe any woman who does will be constantly on a tension, can never do her best in her profession and will antagonize every man with whom she comes in contact." Jerome read on with fascination at Miss Pack's quote in the next paragraph. "A woman in any line of work has a much better chance to succeed if she doesn't insist on anything – particularly her rights. If she proves her ability she won't have to and if she can't prove her ability her rights aren't important so far as her profession is concerned."

It was no surprise now to Jerome why Hattie seemed so fond of Miss Pack. It was almost as though Hattie could have spoken those words herself . . . all except the all important part about actually practicing law. How could she have gone to law school and not "got the chance to practice" as she tried to explain to him earlier. How could that be? he queried himself . . . a woman of such apparent determination? He went into the kitchen to turn the stove off like Tim had suggested. As he made his way back he heard Mr. Bergerson saying goodnight to his wife and Hattie . . . excusing himself as he had to attend a dinner at the convention. Jerome thought to hand him his coat that he had hung on the hooks outside the dining room. "Thank you Mr. Reed" said Bergerson.

"Not at all." replied Jerome. Then he added just loudly enough for Hattie to hear "I couldn't help but read with interest your wife's interview in *The Washington Post* today. You must be very proud of her." Bergerson smiled appreciatively. "Nice of you to say . . . and I'm very proud of Mildred indeed. She is a very fine lawyer."

"What's that you're saying about me, Joseph?"

He turned towards his wife. "I was just telling Mr. Reed here, Mildred, how proud I am of you. He's been reading the interview you gave to *The Washington Post*. He was quite impressed." Miss Pack beamed. "How kind of you to say, Mr. Reed. Thank you."

"Mr. Reed you must bring that paper into me. I haven't even had a chance to read that article for myself" cried Hattie. She turned to Miss Pack. "I meant to get right to it earlier, Miss Pack . . . but I got so distressed over the news on the front page about the President and his handling of the drought situation we find our country in that I just had to put it down and think of more pleasant things."

"Yes" chimed in Bergerson "FDR seems to be all in a knot over what to do doesn't he? One thing one day . . . another the next."

"Isn't he just a son of a bitch!?" declared Hattie. Jerome took three quick steps into the tool room and covered his mouth to stifle his laugh. Tim was right. That was "son of a bitch" number one for the night!

Bergerson and his wife did not seemed bothered by Hattie's comment and chuckled. "There's many a lawyer at our convention that would agree with you, Mrs. Crickmore . . . especially after his attempts to pack the Supreme Court of late."

"Well, I mustn't go on about him must I? But, I tell you . . . he's a real son of a bitch in my book!" Number two.

Unfettered, Bergerson simply said "I won't be too late, Mildred. Probably not much past eleven. You both enjoy yourselves, now." He winked at Jerome on the way out . . . leaned forward and whispered . . . "Interesting woman isn't she . . . that Mrs. Crickmore?"

Jerome did not know whether he was grinning from embarrassment or out of amusement . . . but he shook his head in ready agreement just the same.

"Oh, Mr. Reed?" said Hattie slyly "would you mind coming in here a moment?" Jerome tried to compose himself a bit . . . he was still almost red from laughing . . . then he decided not to bother. "Yes m'am . . . what can I do for you?" he said standing with his hands in his pockets and smiling right at Hattie.

"Would you take the drink tray away for us please? I think we'd like our dinner now." Jerome began to oblige as Miss Pack started to speak. "It's quite a good thing that a prospective lawyer comb the newspaper, you know" she said speaking to Jerome. "I find it keeps you sharp on what's happening, don't you?"

"Oh . . . yes . . . especially the smaller articles inside the newspaper. They give a paper its real local flavor . . . all of the news isn't just the headlines and current events."

"I couldn't agree with you more" said Miss Pack.

Jerome lifted the tray off the table with one hand . . . the other still in his pocket . . . and stood a few steps from Hattie barely able to contain himself. "Will there be anything else Mrs. Crickmore?"

he asked almost impishly.

Hattie was covering a knowing smile with her own hand. "No thank you, Mr. Reed. Just the dinner when it's ready." He walked backwards the few remaining steps out of the dining room grinning at her all the way. She knew he had just beat her to the punch and she loved it.

"Isn't he an awfully charming young man . . . and so handsome, too" remarked Miss Pack.

Hattie did not really have to reply. But she thought to herself that Miss Pack was quite correct. Jerome was clearly a very handsome young man . . . but more than that she mused silently "You're a clever one Jerome Reed. Smart and clever. I like that."

Chapter Eleven

The balance of the evening passed without incident and soon enough Miss Pack and Hattie were finished with Polly's special fried chicken dinner and ready to call it a night. Jerome was in the kitchen putting trays away and stacking quickly rinsed dishes in the sink for Polly to attend to when she arrived at 5:30 am, as she did every day except Sunday for the last 35 years. The one chore Tim and Jerome did not have to do was the dirty dishes. Hattie knew that Polly cleaned them best anyway and that's the way it had always been in The Graylock. Change in the structure of the day was not a welcomed event. Predictability was easier for Hattie to deal with. Predictability was not the same as boredom to her.

He could hear the ladies bidding good-night to each other and realized soon that his shift would be ending. Not a bad night he thought . . . this won't be such a bother at all. He turned the kitchen lights off and closed the door behind him. It was nearly eleven o'clock and he could hear Hattie rummaging about in the dining room by herself. He did not disturb her and returned to his chair at the switchboard. With his back turned, he felt the slight swack . . . more than a tap . . . on his back with the newspaper.

Hattie then sweetly poked him in the ribs with the paper. "So you like the local color this paper has do you Jerome?"

"All right . . . all right . . . I couldn't resist . . . I didn't feel like getting quizzed" he said affectionately. Hattie folded the paper and clasped it in her hands. "Now what made you think I was going to quiz you?" she asked.

"Tim told me I'd better be prepared for the third degree on events of the day" he confessed. Always one for telling the truth. Hattie let out a telling little laugh. "You boys . . . you're something else . . . the both of you. It's not the third degree, Jerome. I try to engage people in lively conversation . . . get their opinion on things. Some folks have some very interesting opinions, Jerome and how are you ever to find out about them unless you ask?"

She looked at him for a moment and folded a revealing comment in without remorse. "I don't go out into the world much anymore, Jerome. The newspaper is just one way for me to have a look at the outside . . . one-dimensional as it is, it's just a small source of information. But people, Jerome, people can keep you alive no matter where you are . . . or what you do. That's why I love running this hotel . . . different people in and out all the time. So many different lives and professions. I've learned that you never can tell what's on person's mind so it's just best to have one of your own. That's why I 'quiz' you boys . . . I want to make sure you're having a mind of your own."

"Well my parents always said that I had a mind of my own" replied Jerome.

"Then they've raised you right" Hattie pronounced. "It's quite sad to watch people go through life not being able to think for themselves . . . always dependant on someone else . . . how are they ever to know who they are?"

Intended or not, Jerome did not like the pontificating tone Hattie seemed to be leading up to. Maybe this mini manifesto was steeped in bourbon but whatever it was it felt like it was bordering on a self-righteous attack on the weak-willed. That was not Jerome, but he knew how retiring he could be at times . . . consciously avoiding focus from invading horizons.

"Not everyone can be like you, Hattie. Some people just are just called to a different kind of life . . . some folks probably just stay in the shadows by choice."

"Shadows have nothing to do with it . . . I'm talking about people who use other people . . . who never have an original thought in their life . . . who make, whether they need it or not, other people prop them up." She paused momentarily to think. "Like that son of a bitch Roosevelt, for example." Number three.

"For God's sake Hattie . . . he's the President of the United States . . . what more do you want from someone!"

"A backbone would be nice to start with!" she snapped. "And I don't mean that just because he's a cripple. He's a greased up politician who lies through his eye teeth and lays it all out with fancy airs . . . and that hideous accent!" She was heading for the dining room's side door. "Just talking about that son of a bitch makes me so mad . . . I'm going out to the garden for a bit" she called back. Number four.

As Hattie walked out the side door, Ali, the night doorman arrived through the front door. Tim said that whenever Ali arrived that meant the shift was over whether it was eleven o'clock or not. Ali stood guard over The Graylock until Mr. Duffy took over at seven in the morning. Jerome introduced himself quickly to Ali who had a guru-like air about him and then picked his criminal law casebook-up and walked around to the back staircase. He almost forgot to reach inside the kitchen on the counter and grab the three left-over pieces of chicken he promised to deliver to Tim. Before he headed up to the fourth floor he mentioned to Ali that Hattie was out in the back garden so he shouldn't lock up just yet. Ali nodded . . . like he knew.

Jerome knocked twice on the door to Room 405. "Enter" was

the lively response. He walked in and stopped after a couple of steps. It was three times the size of his little room . . . with two beds and a fireplace. Tim was slouched in a battered overstuffed easy chair with his feet propped up on one of the beds. "How was it?" he asked Jerome. Jerome was still looking around the room when Tim realized what was probably going through his mind.

"Not to worry, Jerome . . . I'm not getting special treatment or anything . . . this was meant to be a room for two" Tim explained.

Suddenly Jerome understood what he meant. This was supposed to have been the room for Sam and Tim . . . now it was just for Tim. It didn't bother Jerome . . . he did not have a covetous nature.

"Maneray tried to move me into one of the rooms like yours, but when I checked in he was off duty and by the time he found out which room I was in, I had already explained the situation about Sam to Hattie and she offered just to let me stay right here. It's kind of nice, isn't it?"

"I'll say . . . does that fireplace work?" Jerome asked.

"Yeah . . . he tried to get me on Hattie's bad side by telling her I was having roaring fires in here and leaving them unattended. He's such a liar! Hattie just laughed and asked me not to burn her precious hotel down." Jerome handed Tim the chicken and he started to devour it. "Ever taste anything like this?" he said.

Jerome shook his head. "I can't believe we can eat like this here."

"Everything Polly makes is good . . . but this is the best" said Tim with half a mouthful. "You'll probably hear something from Maneray tomorrow about not leaving him any . . . but Polly told me she'd rather feed us than him any day. Did you see him tonight at all?"

"Nah . . . no sign of him at all. Just Hattie and that lady and her husband from the law fraternity."

"How was Hattie . . . alright?"

Jerome shrugged incidentally and walked over to the back window of Tim's room that looked down over the garden. "She was ok most of the time . . . only called Roosevelt a son of a bitch four times."

Tim burst into laughter and nearly choked on his food. "That's all!! . . . must have been a slow news day in the Post . . . did you get that ridiculous third degree quiz on current events?"

"Nope" he said proudly "I beat her to the punch and I think she liked it. She's a curious woman, you know Tim."

"I thought you said you didn't have a suspicious nature."

"I don't . . . I mean I don't go looking for where things are not obviously wrong . . . but you can hardly help but wonder a bit about her can you?"

"You don't have to convince me" said Tim absent mindedly "we just might be the two most normal people working here you know . . . what are you looking at out there anyway?"

Jerome turned to Tim and made sure that he saw him pointing out to the garden. "Is that her out there?"

"Who?" asked Tim as he rose from the chair and looked out over Jerome's shoulder.

"Hattie . . . over there in the back corner of the garden." The half moon hanging low in the starless sky threw just enough pale light for them to watch her moving very slowly. "Why is she picking at that ivy patch?" said Jerome.

"Looks more to me like she's hanging on to the iron fence post for support. I thought you said things were alright tonight. How much bourbon did she have?"

"I didn't know I was supposed to keep track. I just left the drink tray in there and let them be."

"Mmmmm . . . well I've seen her worse . . . I actually had to go out there and get her one night and bring her in . . . she was weeping and kept saying how awful it was for poor Edmund. I think she just let the evening get the better of her."

"Who is Edmund?" asked Jerome while all the time keeping a careful eye on Hattie whose head was hung as low as the moon . . . but more sorrowfully.

"That was the saddest part of it all . . . she couldn't even remember the guy's right name."

What do you mean?"

"She had a few of the guests down for dinner a couple of weeks ago" explained Tim "must have been five or six of them . . . having drinks and dinner and getting kind of loud. This one lady was from London and they all start arguing over whether Edward VIII . . . not Edmund VIII . . . was going to have to give up the throne because he wants to many this American woman who's already been divorced . . . twice I think."

"Yeah . . . I know. . . . Wallis Simpson . . . listen if it made the newspaper in Buttermilk Falls the whole world must know about it."

"That's not the half of it" continued Tim "this lady from London starts to swill the bourbon and Hattie makes the mistake of asking her what her opinion of the whole mess is . . . being that she's living right over there and all."

"I'm getting the sense that is her style . . . she likes to know what other people are thinking" interjected Jerome.

"Yeah . . . well let me tell you she asked for it and she got it . . . full square from this British lady who went on and on about what a disgrace this Mrs. Simpson is and how the whole United States should be ashamed of what she is doing and that if she had any style or breeding or whatever that she'd pack all her sorry bags and never set foot on British soil again . . . and all these other jokers are drinking and nodding and being just a bunch stuffed shirts about the whole thing that I thought they'd all burn that Mrs. Simpson in effigy in the back garden before the sun rose."

Jerome furrowed his brow and said it sounded like they all had their priorities backwards. "Who cares about Edward VIII and Wallis Simpson?" he said with disgust. "I mean really . . . who cares what they do?"

"Well believe me . . . obviously Hattie does because she sat there sipping on her bourbon and branch water and listened to all of them . . . especially that British lady until she couldn't stand it any more and finally went after her like a foaming at the mouth palace guard dog. It was almost shocking the way she ripped into her."

Jerome grinned at the thought of Hattie battling for the King of England. "What did she say?!"

"It was unbelievable." said Tim now very excited about recounting this tale. "Hattie accused them all of being nothing but a pack of know-nothing hypocrites and told them they could all just stop drinking her free bourbon right then and there . . . told them that they were so stupid and pitifully ignorant in 'matters of the heart' she called it that it made her want to spit on the floor in front of all of them!"

"Jesus" responded Jerome with his mouth almost agape.

"Wait" said Tim "it gets better. Hattie got up from her chair and stands right in front of the British woman and told her that she was appalled . . . simply appalled that any grown woman could be as down right ignorant and judgmental as her . . . that she was an embarrassment to women everywhere . . . that she obviously had never been in love before and ought to keep her mouth shut and stop babbling about things she knew nothing about. Then she went on about how Mrs. Simpson has the right to fall in love with anybody she pleases and those who don't like it can go to hell . . . and everybody ought to get off of King Edmund's back and leave him alone 'cause he's just a man. Can you believe it? Just a man? He's the King of England . . . of the whole British Empire and our little Hattie says he's just a man. I couldn't believe what I was hearing. And she's so stewed and excitable at this point that she's messing up his name. She stood in the middle of that dining room after terrorizing her dinner guests shaking her fist and shouting 'I want everyone to leave him alone!!!' And then to top it all off she says 'And by the time I get back from the garden I want all of you out of my dining room . . . and by the time I wake up tomorrow morning I want every single one of you out of my hotel!' Then she absolutely stormed out the side door and slammed it behind her."

"Tim . . . she just got finished telling me not fifteen minutes ago that she likes to hear different opinions on things from people . . . what got into her?"

"She wanted nothing to do with the opinions of *that* crowd . . . trust me . . . at least not so far as it concerned Edward VIII and Mrs. Simpson. And like I told you before. . . it's those last few sips of bourbon that puts her over the edge."

"You said 'wistful' Tim . . . you said the last few sips made her sort of wistful and quiet -- not like some Nazi . . . you told me that she wasn't a drunk."

"She's not Jerome. Believe me, I can tell when a woman's getting drunk. She was fine until that lady started going on about the King and his girlfriend."

Jerome looked out the window again and saw Hattie still out there . . . gazing up into the dark night . . . holding on to the iron posts bordering the ivy patch. "It sounds crazy to me . . . doesn't make any sense. What happened anyway? Did they leave the dining room?"

"It was crazy I tell you. And every single one of them checked out that night . . . I was calling cabs and running luggage all over the place for an hour. I couldn't get a cab from Red Top to get over here at that hour so all of them just picked their stuff up from the lobby and left. Didn't pay a dime for the rooms either."

Jerome immediately thought of his cab driver, Jake.

"When did Hattie come back inside?"

"Are you listening to me at all? I started to tell you that I had to go out and get her. I brought all the stuff into the kitchen from the dining room and I could hear her crying from the kitchen window. I thought she tripped and fell and hurt herself in that state she was in. Turns out that she was making her way back and holding onto the iron posts out there by the ivy patch and just sobbing and in a horrible state."

"Did she talk to you?"

"To be honest with you Jerome . . . I don't think she remembers I was there. I took her arm and told her that she'd better come inside. She kept crying and saying "Poor Edmund . . . Poor Edmund . . . I wish they would just leave him alone . . . just leave him alone . . . it was an awful sight . . . she was all disheveled by this time like she'd been rolling around on the ground."

"What did you do?"

"Took her to her room . . . what a mess it is . . . there's stuff all over the place and not a single clock in the whole room. That's why she calls out all the time . . . just to see what time it is. Drives Duffy crazy."

"This is when you had to put her in bed?"

"Well, I set her down on the side of it and left. Then I went into the kitchen to rinse off the dishes and glasses as usual and I turn to my right and there she is standing in the doorway. Just staring at me. She scared the begeezus out of me. And she said very calmly without crying and in real low voice "Timothy, please don't be offended if I ask you to wash and dry those dishes right now. I cannot bear the thought of their saliva on my glasses and plates while I sleep . . . turns around and walks away like it was nobody's business."

"Whew . . . and you're still trying to tell me that she does not have a drinking problem?"

Tim shook his head and peered out the window standing next to Jerome. There was no one in the garden. Hattie had gone. At the very least she was out of sight. "Listen Jerome . . . my mother has a bit of a drinking problem . . . I know what it's like . . . Sam and I had to take care of her whenever my father was away on one of his many business trips . . . I'm telling you I don't think Hattie is a drinker. I think it's something else entirely."

"Like what?"

"I haven't got a clue. But I can see already that she's too full of life to be laden down with an alcohol problem. It's got to be something else that sets her off so sometimes." Tim changed the subject. "Hey . . . you know we're off the next two days."

"Already" said Jerome with surprise.

"Yeah . . . we're off every Saturday and Sunday . . . free as birds. I arranged it with Duffy and Hattie ok'd it . . . left Maneray out of it altogether. Want to do something? The weather is suppose to be terrific. Maybe we can go canoeing down the Potomac. They rent canoes very cheaply down by the Jefferson Memorial . . . you can swim can't you?

"Of course I can swim . . . I mean I'm not great or anything, but I don't sink in the water."

Tim stood up to his full height of six feet and stretched his arms to the ceiling in mock triumph. "Fear not, Mr. Reed. . . . for I am an excellent swimmer. We'll have a great time."

"Great idea" agreed Jerome ". . . but not too early, I want to get a little extra sleep." He opened Tim's door to leave and turned around for one last question. "Where's Hattie's husband, Tim?"

Tim bit into his last piece of chicken and said "Dead . . . been dead for years and years so Duffy tells me."

"Of what?"

"Don't know, Jerome . . . maybe she scared him to death!"

"Yeah . . . right. Never mind. See you tomorrow."

"Night."

THE GRAYLOCK

Chapter Twelve

Jerome was feeling quite good walking down the cut-through street behind the hotel. It was a rough, brick layed road that resembled more of an alley than a street. It ran straight through from 16th Street to 17th Street parallel to N Street but in back of the hotel. He could see the rear of every building on N Street as well as the backside of some of the embassies that line the beginnings of Massachusetts Avenue. Some of The Graylock's guests who arrived in their own cars parked in a tiny space Hattie provided on the far side of the garden wall right next to the back gate, as long as they left their keys at the front desk. Tim and Jerome often had to jockey the autos around so a guest could get access ... something Jerome never minded doing ... he liked getting behind the wheel, if ever so briefly, of some of the newer model automobiles. He also liked sitting for a bit in the hotel's garden after classes finished for the afternoon. Coming in the back entrance, he found, was a good way to avoid the glares of Mr. Maneray that he always encountered when he came through the hotel's front door. He always felt like Maneray was staring at him all the while he made his way up to the fourth floor. Today, though, Jerome decided that he was going to let none of that bother him as he strolled down the alley.

The first three weeks of school seemed to be going quite well for him . . . and Tim, too. None of the courses was overwhelming him and he liked a couple of them more than he initially thought he might. He had no trouble keeping up with the assigned readings and had already spoken out in class more times than he believed he would. Tim was more vocal, but that was his style. Jerome knew that he was a better listener than a talker and was happy to learn from what some of the other students had to say. Except in Professor Lucien's Criminal Law class . . . he was always the best prepared. He knew the cases better than anyone except Lucien and often questioned him on a layer of criminal law that was not apparent in the case reading . . . at least not to the other students. Lucien was impressed and told Jerome so the other day.

Professor David Lucien was taking his first stab at teaching the law after having practiced it for thirty-six years. He told his class that he thought it was time for him to share some of what he had learned about criminal law over the years and that was why he decided to sign on at Jefferson Law School. Tim told Jerome that he knew a different story about Lucien. Mr. Owlster, Tim's father who was also a lawyer, knew of Lucien back in New York City where he had been practicing since 1902. Lucien had a reputation in the city as one of the fiercest defense lawyers in town. Local prosecutors knew that they had better have a real good case against one of Lucien's clients before proceeding to trial otherwise everyone knew Lucien would gnarl them to bits before the jury. Lucien had the advantage of having already been a prosecutor in Washington . . . his first job right out of law school, before the allure of a big city like New York and more money drew him in. But Tim said that Lucien's wife of thirty-three years recently died and Lucien decided to return to the place where his law career began. Truth was, as Tim told it, Lucien confided to his close colleagues, who in turn confided it inappropriately to others, that he could not stay in New York after his wife died . . . too many memories. Since they had no children he had no real reason to stay. He thought he had learned all there was to know about his special field of practice and didn't want to become stagnant . . . or melancholy for that matter. Lucien determined that teaching would be the best way for him to carry out the remainder of what had been a very interesting and lucrative career in the law. He turned down offers from Columbia Law School and Harvard, choosing instead to back home to Washington after having been away what seemed like a lifetime to him.

Lucien did not seem fierce to Jerome and he was not at all intimidated by him as were some of the other students in the class. Lucien looked to be everything that Jerome was looking for in a criminal law professor. If his grandfather was no longer alive to teach him, Jerome was happy enough to take all the instruction Lucien had to offer. The more he learned the better off he knew he'd be so Jerome never minded when Lucien seemed to push the class to understand the fine hair points of a case. "You must dig deep . . . deep into the facts before you go into court. Know the facts better than you know yourself and research the law completely. Apply the law to the facts and use your skills to the best of your ability" he told the nervous student on the first day of lectures. "The practice of criminal law is much more complex than merely having an instinct to be able to tell right from wrong. If that's all it took all your mothers would be appearing in court. Intuition is just a fraction of what you need to be successful in this particular corner of the law . . . you must understand human nature completely and that can take years." Jerome knew that he had good instincts and a born ability to tell right from wrong . . . if it took him a lifetime of learning to understand human nature it was alright with him. He didn't think he was suppose to understand it all at the age of 21 anyway. He'd learn to understand it eventually . . . and he'd learn the practice criminal law, too. But for the moment, he'd learn what Lucien had to teach him . . . all the rest of the professors as well . . . but most importantly Lucien.

Since it was such a nice day, Jerome decide he'd go upstairs, change clothes, drop his books off and write another letter to his family. He was not on duty today and wanted to take some time to write a longer letter than the first one he mailed after his second day in Washington. He was a bit surprised that he had not gotten a letter in return after almost three weeks, but assumed that things were pretty busy up on the farm . . . especially with him gone . . . he wondered if his father was making it alright with what be knew was the erstwhile help of Jimmy and Alan, the good intentions of Stevie and the well-intentioned intrusions of Gail, whom Jerome knew was never going to be tied to the kitchen no matter what. "He may as well let her help before she tries to get work on somebody else's farm" he thought as he made his way through the back gate.

The garden of The Graylock was Jerome's favorite spot. It was away from the interior bustle of the hotel and set back far enough from N Street so that the occasional passing traffic was sufficiently muffled. Hattie had planted special plots for a large rose bed and a long double row of purple and white irises. Ivy grew everywhere . . . almost uncultured and on its own without tending. It climbed the eight foot high white wooden fence that bordered that garden until it tangled itself all around the intricate lattice work that added another foot in height to the top of the fence all around. It was as thick as meadow grass over in the back corner of the garden and dripped over and around the three foot high iron posts that led down the brick pathway that ended just under the outside of the kitchen window. The most imposing growth in the garden was the 60 foot high spruce tree that was a sight to behold. It was as tall as the hotel itself and shot up to the sky as straight as an arrow. Hattie loved her garden, too, and the spruce was her pride and joy. She brought it back as a seedling from a trip to Atlanta the week before she opened the hotel. It was the first thing she put in the ground. The prettiest, though . . . even prettier than the roses now in glorious late September bloom . . . were the scores of geraniums that were everywhere in the garden . . . growing like wild poppies. There were only red and pink ones . . . no white ones . . . and the red ones were more vibrantly red than any rose in full flower . . . all in Hattie's garden.

Jerome walked around a bit before he went inside and noticed that the garden looked beautiful in the day's afternoon sunshine, but for the first time he noticed that it could use a little gardening. He decided he offer to put his farmer's green thumb to work for Hattie . . . mostly because he truly enjoyed working out of doors and he got great satisfaction out of watching things grow. It would also keep him away from Maneray. Just then he heard a knock on the glass panes of the kitchen window. It was Tim . . . already on duty at the front desk. Jerome had been sauntering so on the way back from the law school that he didn't realize that it must now be at least three o'clock and Tim's shift had already begun. Tim waved and Jerome waved back. Then he shouted out from the kitchen "Where have you been?"

"Nowhere really . . . just walking around" was Jerome's reply as he neared the window. "Do you need help today?"

"Nah . . . there's only one guest checking in tonight . . . everything's pretty quiet. Great lecture this morning wasn't it?" Tim was referring to his favorite course, Real Property and his favorite teacher, Professor Philip De Lange.

"I can't believe you like that guy . . . he's so dry. I can't follow him all the time."

"Might help if you didn't nod off in class . . . I saw you snoozing. How can you not stay awake in the middle of his insights on the Interstate Land Sales Act?! How are you ever going to know

THE GRAYLOCK

how to buy property in another state?"

Jerome hopped up and sat on the edge of the brick wall that jetted out from underneath the window. It was the wall where Polly always set her delicious pies out to cool after she took them out "just in time," she always said, from the oven.

"Need I remind you, Tim . . . we earn 40 cents an hour here . . . that's not enough to buy a pot of geraniums."

"So what . . . that's now . . . we're not going to be earning 40 cents an hour forever. Just you wait and see . . . I'm going to own this whole street by and by."

Jerome smiled but not at Tim's plans to become a real estate baron but at what he could see that Tim could not. Polly was moving slowly up behind Tim as he bent over to make himself heard out the window. She landed her broom dead center on his backside. "Hey . . . what's with you!" he said as he stood up straight brushing his head on the bottom of the window pane on his way up.

"Mr. Timothy" she scolded him "why you jes' hangin' out here at my window? Yous is suppose to be out at the switchboard . . . theys calls comin' in and you ain't doin' your job. Poor Mr. Duffy's tryin' to get hisself out of here . . . he done put in his eight hours and he don't have to do your job too! Mr. Maneray is buzzin' all over everywhere lookin' for you . . . sez he's gonna have the Mrs. fire you."

"Fat chance . . . that fool will be long gone before me. Besides, I was down in the cellar looking for your turkey tub . . . like you asked me to . . . I put it over there."

"I told you before 'bout callin' an older gentleman bad names . . . now you done found my tub. Thank you. Now git! I don't know why you is hangin' 'round in my kitchen when yous 'spose to otherwheres."

"God, Polly . . . I was just talking to Jerome."

"There you go bringin' Jerome into your troubles again. You best git outta here now 'fore I don't know what to do with you." Polly looked closer out the window. "An' Mr. Jerome don't you go be laughin' so hard when I'm tellin' him his bizness . . . he don't take me serious no how . . . and you best be gettin' off that wall 'fore Mr. Maneray sees you there."

Jerome hopped off the wall . . . to please Polly, not Maneray. "And how are you today, Polly?"

"Oh fine I 'spect. How come you didn't come down for your breakfast this mornin' . . . I didn't see you . . . don't you like ol' Polly no more?" she teased.

"Of course I do" he threw her a kiss to reassure her. "I was running a little late for class and I didn't have time to eat."

"Yous is both growin' boys and can't be runnin' off in the mornin' with nothin' in your belly . . . how you 'spect to learn your law if yous is hungry? . . . Tim was down here eatin' enough for the both of yous . . . I can bring breakfast up to you if you got a case of lazy bones in the momin' . . . I don't mind."

Jerome was embarrassed at the thought of Polly climbing four flights of stairs with a full breakfast tray because he wanted a little extra shut eye. "Don't you dare . . . you don't have to serve me breakfast in bed, Polly . . . it's not right."

"Well, then you best git your body down here for mornin' food 'cause the next time I don't see you I'm bringing it up to you so I sees for my own eyes what's holdin' you up, you hear?!"

"I hear you Polly . . . I hear you . . . I won't miss breakfast anymore."

"Good . . . now you go on now an' stop botherin' me . . . I got to finish me this other turkey in the oven 'fore I leaves. I done made one already and cut a little off an' made you a sandwich an' put it in your room . . . I thought you would be hungry when you got back here seeins that you didn't have none o' my fine breakfast."

"Thanks, Polly . . . you're an angel." She waived him off. "Go on now . . . 'fore I has to show both yous boys my bad side!"

It was inconceivable to Jerome that Polly could possibly have a bad side. She took such good care of him . . . she took care of both of them. There were days when Jerome was sure it was Polly running the hotel . . . nobody else. He saw Mr. Duffy in his usual garb making his way through the garden. "Hi Mr. Duffy . . . how's life treating you?" he said as he strode over to talk with the little figure in black. "Oh . . . hi Jerome . . . I'm ok . . . yes I guess I'm alright." Duffy responded in his typically timid fashion. "Yes . . . I suppose I'm fine . . . How are you?"

"Terrific! . . . Isn't it a nice day?"

"Seems so" was Duffy's weak reply. "Oh by the way . . . your friend called again today . . . you know . . . oh I can't remember the name right now . . . let me see . . . you know, Jerome the same one who called last week and left his number . . ."

"Mr. Duffy . . . I didn't get any messages last week . . . are you sure it was me . . . maybe it was for someone else in the hotel."

"Oh no . . . no it was for you . . . same man as last week . . . I know I put the message in your mail slot . . . I always do that."

"I know you do . . . I'm just saying that I didn't get any message last week, that's all."

"I'm sorry Jerome . . . I know I put it there . . . Oh now I remember the name . . . it just took me a bit . . . it was a Mr. Roberts, I believe?"

"Everett Roberts? . . . Everett Roberts called me last week?"

"Yes . . . yes . . . that's the one!" exclaimed Duffy, now happy that his mind was clear of the mystery. "Yes . . . and he seemed surprised when I told him that I was certain that I put the message in your mail slot . . . it was if he wondered why you hadn't called him back."

"Well, I would have called him back if I knew he had tried

to reach me" said Jerome in exasperation. "He's a very important man."

Duffy looked sullen. "Again . . . I'm very sorry, Jerome. I'm just sure as I can be that I left you the message."

"Oh I'm not blaming you Mr. Duffy. C'mon now . . . don't give me that face of yours . . . I'm just saying that I didn't get any messages last week, that's all."

"Well . . . there's one in your mail slot right now. I'm certain of it because it's the last thing I did before I went off duty. You can probably call your friend from the telephone in the lobby. That horrible character Maneray has already gone up to his room . . . I saw him."

"Ok . . . thanks, Mr. Duffy . . . You enjoy the rest of your evening."

"Oh I suppose I can" Duffy replied as he made his way up the three small steps leading to the walk and the back gate.

Jerome headed inside through the side door and walked through the tool room. With Maneray already upstairs and Hattie in her own room for her regular mid-afternoon nap, the hotel seemed unusually quite. He walked around the front desk to the mail slots which were directly to its left. He saw that the days mail had already been delivered and envelopes were partially sticking out of their respective delivery points . . . the hotel's pink message slips were signals of the news from the outside world. But there was nothing in the mail slot for Room 401 . . . Jerome's room. No mail from the outside and no pink message slip to indicate that Everett Roberts had, indeed, called not long ago. Jerome wondered if Mr. Duffy had mistakenly slipped it into another mail slot and he quickly checked the other slips to find it.

Tim has just finished taking a reservation and returned the telephone receiver to its hook when he saw Jerome with a quizzical look on his face. "What are you doing?" he asked.

THE GRAYLOCK

"Did you notice a message in my mail slot when you got on duty?"

"Nope . . . there was nothing there . . . I checked before Duffy left."

"He said he put one in there . . . swore it was the last thing he did before he left."

"Are you sure it's not in another slot by mistake . . . he said Maneray was making him very nervous all day . . . he might have put it in the wrong slot . . . poor guy gets so jittery around that asshole."

"No . . . I checked the other slots . . . there's no message here for me."

"Maybe he put it in his cape by mistake!" laughed Tim.

"Yeah . . . well it's gone for good then" laughed Jerome in return "I'm surprised Mr. Duffy can find his way out of that cape . . . it's almost 70 degrees outside and he's got himself entombed in that thing."

"He thinks it makes him look stylish." They both just looked at each other in wonderment at Mr. Duffy's peculiar notion of fashion.

"Surprising though, you know . . ." said Jerome "he was so adamant about telling me that he was certain he put a message for me in here . . . from a friend of mine who, Duffy said, called last week. I didn't get that message either . . . strange." His voice trailed off in thought. Tim paid it no mind. He had learned over the last six weeks that strange was almost the order of the day at The Graylock.

"Tim, hand me that phone book under the switchboard will you?" Jerome asked. "I think I'll just call Mr. Roberts myself . . . on the odd chance that Mr. Duffy is right . . . wonder what happened to that message slip though."

Tim reached down and handed over the white pages to Jerome.

"Who's Mr. Roberts?" he asked.

"Oh . . . I never told you. He's a very interesting guy I met on the train down to Washington. He was on his way down to see President Roosevelt . . . he's sort of a political consultant . . . he's had quite an interesting career. You should meet him."

"He's not going to stay here is he?"

Jerome laughed at the notion of Everett meeting Hattie and wondered how long Everett could tolerate her constant haranguing of FDR before they went at each other. "God, no" answered Jerome "he told me that he stays at the Hay-Adams on 16th Street. I don't really know where he was calling from since I don't seem to be able to find my message, but I'll try the Hay-Adams as soon as I can find the number in here. I have it on the back of his business card upstairs." Jerome flipped through a few more pages and returned the telephone book to Tim in frustration. "I'll make the call from upstairs . . . you don't mind putting me through, do you?" Tim shook his head. "Just pick up the phone when you're ready. It's pretty quiet. I'm just going to sit here and try to plow through these Civil Procedure cases . . . have you looked at these yet? They are as dull as dirt."

"Mmmmm . . . I suppose compared to the heart-throbbing Interstate Land Sales Act you must find them just dreadful!" Tim gave his friend a frown and Jerome waved him off as he started to climb the four flights of stairs to his room.

He opened the door and saw that Polly had laid the turkey sandwich on his desk, as promised. The sheets were changed and the bed was made and there were clean towels on the back of the door. This was done twice a week for both he and Tim. Hattie was doing everything to make them feel comfortable and at home and Maneray seemed to be doing everything to make them want to leave. Jerome did not see how Polly and Mr. Duffy could stand being around him all day long . . . still did not see how Hattie

THE GRAYLOCK

could deal with him. He propped himself up on the deep window sill and brought his legs up in a crouched position. He like to look out on N Street from four flights up. No matter what The Graylock was like, N Street was beautiful to look at. He finished his sandwich and returned from his daydreaming. He wanted to get out to the back garden before the sun went down to write his family another letter. But first, he'd try to get a hold of Everett Roberts at the Hay-Adams. He slipped down off the window sill and tossed himself flat out on his newly made bed. He picked up the receiver and it took Tim about thirty seconds to answer.

"Where'd you go?" Jerome said.

"Had to take the garbage out to the shed . . . been waiting?" explained Tim.

"Nah . . . thought maybe you fell asleep reading those Civil Procedure cases" Jerome joked.

"Do you want me to hook you up at The Hay-Adams now?"

"Yeah . . . that'd be great." Jerome gave Tim the telephone number off of the back of Everett's business card and the phone began to ring. The operator at the Hay-Adams put Jerome on hold for a moment until he could put him through to Mr. Roberts' room.

"Hello?"

"Hi Everett . . . it's Jerome Reed."

"Jerome, my boy!" shouted Everett "how are you? How nice to hear your voice. I was beginning to think that Washington may not have been to your liking and that you headed home."

"I'm sorry if it appeared that way . . . I just found out a half an hour ago that you called me last week . . . I just didn't get the message, that's all. I apologize . . . but I was so glad to hear that you called today!"

"So you got this message . . . that good to know."

"Well, I couldn't find the actual message slip . . . I think it got lost... but the switchboard operator told me that you had called again."

"Goodness... not getting messages... that would never happen at The Hay-Adams... someone would wind up getting fired."

Jerome rolled into a huge belly laugh. "Believe me Everett, this is not the Hay-Adams... it's as far from the Hay-Adams as you can possibly imagine!"

"I hope it's working out alright for you... sounds a bit odd to me." If he only knew, Jerome thought. If he only knew.

"It'll be just fine for the time being." Jerome assured him... almost trying to reassure himself. "Tell me how you've been. I can hardly wait to see you. Will you be in town long?"

"Well... that's the purpose of my call, my boy... you've caught me on the way out, in fact. I must return to New York City right away. My train departs in less than a half an hour and I'm in a terrible rush... the porters have already taken my luggage down to the cab driver who is waiting for me as we speak... I was just about to leave my room when I got your call." Jerome was disappointed to hear this and thought it was all the more reason for him to have gotten in touch with Everett last week... if he had only received the message. Too late to worry about it now, he thought.

"When are you coming back?" he asked.

"I'll be back here next Wednesday evening. The President is quite keen on seeing me again. Let me give you my schedule quickly... if you have the time perhaps we can have dinner?"

"I can hardly wait!"

"Wonderful. Well, as I said I'll be..." The line went dead.

"Hello... Hello..." said Jerome to no one on the other end of the line. "Everett??... are you still there?" Jerome clicked the receiver several times. What the hell is Tim doing down there?

"Hello . . . Hello" he repeated angrily. He waited a bit more in the hopes that Tim could re-connect him before Everett left his room.

"Yes?" was the response.

"What the hell are you doing down there!" Jerome shouted into the receiver.

"Mr. Reed, you'll find that if you speak to me that way there'll be a price to pay. What do you want? I'm in a hurry." It was Maneray.

Jerome said nothing for a moment trying to calm himself. "I was in the middle of a conversation" he said tersely.

"I'm sure I don't know anything at all about your conversation. Give me the number. I'll try to re-connect you" seethed Maneray into the switchboard receiver. Jerome decided against it. He did not want Maneray knowing anything about any of his private calls. "Never mind. I'll try later." He hung up his phone. He made a note to himself to call Everett on Wednesday evening and put it on his desk so he would not forget. No point in trying now . . . Everett was probably in his cab by now.

Chapter Thirteen

Jerome calmed himself for a bit before he went back downstairs to the lobby. He could only imagine that Everett must have thought something funny was going on ... he couldn't possibly think that Jerome hung up on him purposefully. He said he was in a big rush and Jerome hoped that he didn't give it any more thought than the line got accidentally disconnected. Jerome wanted to think that too but his keen instincts and Maneray's tone of voice made him think otherwise. He came down the front staircase and could see Maneray leaving Hattie's townhouse across the street. The lights in the empty place were now on and Maneray was on his way. Jerome knew that he'd not return to the hotel for the rest of the evening. He walked past Hattie's room and heard no noise and knew that she would not be out for several hours yet. He saw Tim totally preoccupied with his case materials on Real Property. He tapped the side of the front desk to bring him back from his singular focus on the merits of learning how to buy property in other states.

"Hey..."

Tim looked up and removed his glasses. "That was quick ... did you get a hold of your friend at the Hay-Adams?" Jerome nodded.

"What was going on down here?"

THE GRAYLOCK

"What do you mean?" asked Tim innocently.

"With the switchboard . . . where were you . . . I think I got disconnected . . . I tried to get you back and Maneray picked up the line."

Tim had a disgusted look on his face at the mention of it. "Oh . . . I had to take Mr. Reynolds up to his room. He got here just at the time Maneray was getting ready to leave. He was skulking around here like some ghoul and told me flat off that I was supposed to carry all guests luggage up to their room . . . Mr. Reynolds had a small overnight bag and said it wasn't necessary . . . he could manage. Maneray took into one of his moods and I was getting really embarrassed, so I just grabbed the guy's bag and told him to follow me. I tell you, Jerome . . . I have just about had it with that guy treating me the way he does . . . I'm going to have a talk with Hattie when she comes out tonight. If this keeps up, I'm going to leave. I think the guy is crazy."

The look of resignation on Tim's face told Jerome that his friend was serious about leaving.

"You can't leave, Tim . . . what am I going to do here by myself! . . . Besides, if you leave Maneray will have won. I think he's trying to force both of us out and if you leave, he'll be halfway there."

Tim closed his book. "Jerome, I don't like people speaking to me the way he does and I've only been holding back from a real confrontation with him because Polly always says that Hattie will take care of things . . . she can't take care of things if nobody tells her what a real pain this guy is. I'm not used to being treated like this . . . and I have no intention of getting used to it."

"Alright. Listen . . . he doesn't treat me any better. He's obviously got some bug up his ass about lawyers or law students or something . . . I really don't care what it is and I'm not very interested. The guy means nothing to me. I just try to ignore him."

"I don't buy it . . . why do we have to ignore him? He treats everybody around here like they were peasants. I'm through with it."

"Ok . . . when Hattie comes out tonight what do you say we talk to her together. Maybe we can work something out . . . besides I've got a real bone to pick with him now anyways . . . I lost my call to my friend, Mr. Roberts and by the time he answered my buzzer it was too late to get Mr. Roberts back on the line."

Tim's face lost all sense of expression. He blew an exasperated breath and looked at Jerome. "This is exactly the kind of bullshit I am talking about. That bastard disconnected you!"

Jerome did not want to hear that he was the target of such petty vindictiveness. "What are you talking about . . . you mean he did it on purpose?! . . . while I was in the middle of talking to my friend?"

"It had to be . . . He was standing right behind me looking at the reservation sheet when Mr. Reynolds was checking in. You were the only call connected on the whole switchboard and I saw him staring at your line. Then he started to make such a commotion about me walking Reynolds up to his room with the luggage, so I did it just to shut him up . . . I'm halfway up the front staircase and I turned back just to see him yank both the wires out and release them into the well with this stupid grin on his face."

"I can't believe this."

"That's why I said 'that was quick' when you got down here a few minutes ago . . . I thought maybe you were just leaving a message for your friend . . . but I swear to you, Jerome, I saw him with my own eyes pull the wires out of the switchboard. I thought you were through with your call."

Jerome was getting dejected. He hated petty behavior like this . . . always had . . . he never understood it. "Why would he do something like that . . . what's it to him if I talk to a friend?'

"He does it because he's an idiot" Tim said sharply "he probably doesn't have any friends . . . who would want to talk to a nut case like him?"

Jerome thought of the message slip that Duffy protested so strongly that he placed in the mail slot. "I'll bet he took that message slip out of my mailbox, too."

"You're probably right" agreed Tim "Duffy says he's always hanging around the mail slots looking at who gets what mail and who's calling who . . . Hattie never gives it a second thought because she knows he's supposed to distribute the mail every day."

"Yeah, but once it's delivered doesn't she think something of him always checking around the slots."

Tim threw his hands up in utter frustration. "C'mon Jerome . . . wake up . . . this guy's a snake and he'll lie to save his own skin . . . in fact, Duffy told me that last week she even saw him pulling the mail out of people's slots and she asked him what he was doing. Duffy said that Maneray looked right at her and said he got so busy and distracted in the morning that he was just double checking to be sure that he put the mail in all the right slots . . . and she believed him!"

"Mr. Roberts said that he called me last week, too. Duffy told me this afternoon that he took the message and put it in my mail slot."

"Yeah . . . well the miserable old coot probably took that one out, too . . . this guy is trouble Jerome . . . real trouble. I've known it since the day I got here. It was miserable working here alone before you showed up."

"And now you're thinking of leaving me here by myself! Tim . . . I can't afford to go rent an apartment . . . I don't have the money . . . maybe you do . . . but I'm stuck here. If I don't live here I have to leave law school and go back home. I can't let that happen!!"

"Then we talk to Hattie. . . . tonight." Tim said with a very determined look on his face. "No more putting it off . . . I've had enough of this." Jerome agreed. Tonight would be the night. "You know, Jerome . . . living here would not be so bad if it weren't for Maneray . . . I mean things get a little odd sometimes here, but it's nothing I can't live with. But Maneray is just plain evil. I know it now and I don't want to live around that kind of evil."

"Well let's not do anything rash. I think we can settle this all tonight . . . I'm going back upstairs . . . I want to write my parents a letter."

"Are you going to tell them what's going on around here?"

"No . . . all they'd do is worry. Besides, the whole matter could be finished by the time they get the letter, so what's the point of worrying them unnecessarily?"

"I'll call you when she gets up. She's just going to have to listen to us."

By the time Jerome got back upstairs, he was angry all over again about being disconnected from Everett Roberts. He didn't want any of it to show up in his letter . . . they'd be able to tell. Jerome couldn't even disguise his feelings when he was writing a letter . . . especially when he was writing. But he felt terrible that Everett had left town under such rude circumstances. "Wednesday will come 'round soon enough" thought Jerome "I can explain everything to him then." He began to review the extra credit option that Professor Lucien was offering all his students. Jerome didn't think that he was going to need extra credit for a good grade in criminal law . . . real property maybe . . . but he knew he was already the best student in Lucien's class. This term paper that Lucien was suggesting was for those who might want to up their grade a bit . . . Jerome decided that it would be a chance for him to learn something about a point of the law in detail . . . and help him sharpen his research skills at the same time. He had an appointment with Professor Lucien at the end of next week to discuss a topic, but he wanted to have a clear one in mind before he went into Lucien's office.

After the requirements of the paper itself, Lucien listed a few topics on which interested students could write although the professor added in class yesterday that "this list was my no means exclusive. If there are any of you that think you have a more interesting idea, I'll be very happy to listen." Jerome wanted to come up with something on his own to show Lucien that he had initiative . . . he also knew that if he had his own topic his paper could not be compared to another student efforts on the same subject. He wanted to show Lucien that he could go it on his own.

He almost chose to write on one of Lucien's listed suggestions . . . about the use of photographic resemblances only in handing down indictments. He had read of a good New York State case where a woman had been cashing worthless checks in small upstate towns and got indicted in six of the towns where the checks had been cashed on the basis of a single photograph. The authorities put her in jail and while she was awaiting trial, several checks of the type she was accused of passing were reported cashed in lower New York State and Pennsylvania. It turned out that when several of the victims were brought face to face with the woman in jail, they declared her not to be woman who cashed the checks and handwriting experts finally found that the forgeries were not in the woman's handwriting and she was released from jail. The photograph being used by the local authorities was a bad one that did not show features clearly but they were so anxious to catch someone that they arrested the wrong woman whose reputation in her local community was, by then, completely destroyed. Jerome knew the mentality of small upstate towns and understood exactly how this type of thing could have happened. He also knew that the poor woman who was falsely accused and arrested probably had to move . . . guilty or not he knew that too often people from these small towns had little lives and long memories. Initially, he thought it might be fun to dig into the local municipal laws that aided and abetted the innocent woman's arrest but decided that there would be plenty of time for that if he wound up practicing law back home. For now, he wanted to tackle something new.

His interest was peaked mildly by a topic that Lucien emphasized when explaining the nature of the extra credit option to the class. It had to deal generally with confessions in capital offenses and how they might be used to convict. Lucien was telling the class a story about such a matter and tried to stir up a discussion around it. He said that back in May 1928, after Herbert Hoover had been President only a few months he raised the ire of law enforcement officials by, what they called at least, "interference with the process." The very first prison sentence that Hoover commuted was that of a Negro who had been convicted of murdering a woman. No eyewitness was present at the crime and the man's conviction depended solely on his confession which was signed in the presence of police officers. In his 1928 inaugural address, President Hoover had called for a complete overhaul of the American judicial system noting that law enforcement officials, in particularly, must keep their efforts to reduce crime within the confines of the existing laws themselves.

Lucien knew that the man whose sentence was commuted by President Hoover was convicted by his own confession and that there was no need for a trial in that case, but it turned out that the confession was not valid and since there was no additional evidence to point to the man's guilt, he was set free. The students debated that someone killed the woman and someone should pay for it. Jerome thought of his grandfather's murder and knew that no one paid for that crime except the Reed family. They lost their beloved family leader and no one was ever arrested. Lucien seemed to want to one of his student to pick up the gauntlet and produce a term paper on the nature of confessions before trial. He got more than a few students interested in writing a paper on the subject and Jerome figured they'd all wind up arguing over the same cases. Besides, he did not want to deal with a subject that would have that much family emotion involved in it. He was going to find something to write about that Lucien had not suggested. Maybe he could enlighten the professor on something . . . he doubted it . . . but then again he knew he'd never find out if he never tried. He'd have to give the subject of his paper some deeper thought and dozed off on his bed thinking of ways to impress Professor Lucien.

Chapter Fourteen

The three short rings on the phone woke Jerome up. The familiar ring meant it was Tim. Still half asleep, he rolled over and picked the receiver up. "Yeah . . . I'm awake" he said.

"You don't sound it" replied Tim "have you been napping this whole time . . . what about that letter to your parents?"

"I'll write it later . . . what's up?"

"Hattie's up, that's what . . . you coming down so we can talk to her?"

Jerome rubbed his eyes and looked out the window. It was already past dusk. He must have been sleeping for a couple of hours. "Give me a little time to wake up here and throw some water on my face. I'll be down shortly."

"Good. She's in a pretty good mood, too and there won't be any dinner guests tonight so we'll have her full attention."

Jerome sat up in bed and thought he ought to change clothes before going downstairs. Everything he had on was wrinkled from his nap. He must have been sleeping very deeply because he was having difficulty getting fully awake. He opted for a quick shower.

By the time he changed and got down to the lobby he could hear Hattie in an animated telephone conversation from her private office almost directly across from the switchboard station.

He waved to her as he passed and looked for Tim. She certainly seemed like she was in a good mood.

"Oh, now darling I just know you are going to win . . . Well, of course I do . . . I know these things. Don't ask me how . . . I just do. And Louise, honey . . . don't you worry one little bit about that little old Amelia Earhart . . . you're twice . . . no, no, no . . . your three times the pilot she is . . . why you'll be flying circles around her before your halfway across the country . . . you'll do all us women in Washington proud and that Bendix Trophy will be such a nice feather in your cap, won't it just!" Hattie took a small sip of her bourbon that Tim saw her bring out of her room.

"Well, I know you're nervous, honey . . . you always get nervous before you fly . . . shows you're on your toes . . . now who is taking care of those darling two children of yours while you're gone? He is? . . . well good for him . . . isn't he a dear? But they're supposed to do that nowadays anyway . . . oh, my yes . . . I was reading in *The Washington Post* today the most interesting article by that Alice Clarissa Richmond . . . did you see it? Well, let me tell you there is another woman who is breaking some ground . . . she went on and on about how husbands simply must take a greater interest in rearing their children . . . bringing in a means of livelihood just is not enough anymore . . . oh heavens yes . . . it was very interesting to read . . . why what baby do you know that cares about dollars and cents?? None! . . . that's right! They understand human contact, that's all . . . and if the fathers aren't around to give them some they'll have a time of it establishing an easy and happy relationship with the children. Oh me, too Louise . . . I'd love to meet her . . . half the men I know *need* to meet her. Wouldn't she just be able to tell them a thing or two!! Why in a couple of months it'll be 1937 . . . high time they got the message don't you think? I think I'll just find out where she lives and invite her over to The Graylock for dinner one night . . . oh sure, dear . . . I'll wait until you get back from the race . . . I just know you're going to win . . . oh think nothing of it, Louise . . . you just get back here safe and sound . . . all right . . . that's fine with me . . . I'll be here, of course . . . I'm always here, aren't I? Good luck." Hattie hung up, as usual, without saying goodbye.

She left the confines of her office and glided into the dining room where she thought she might find Jerome and Tim. It was empty and silent. Still girlishly giddy from her phone chat she made her way towards the kitchen where she figured the boys were hunting around for signs of another of Polly's impeccably prepared dinners.

"Boys . . . boys" she cried out with an unusual lilt in her voice. "Boys are you in there?" They looked at each other and Tim said "You first . . ." Jerome was surprised, after all he came downstairs to lend support to Tim's tale of woe with Maneray, not pick up the gauntlet himself. He shot Tim a look that said "You must be kidding."

"Hey . . . he's been stealing your messages! Go on . . . go ahead" whispered Tim.

Hattie found them standing side by side near the stove. "Oh there you boys are! I thought you'd been hiding from old Hattie." She waltzed up to Jerome and softly poked him in the shoulder and eyed the both of them. "What are you two up to . . . you've got looks in your eyes that spell trouble. What are you boys doing huddled in here? . . . plotting to take over The Graylock while I'm not looking!!" she teased. This brought an embarrassing laugh from Tim who immediately recalled his declaration to Jerome a few hours ago that he would "own all of N Street by and by" . . . including The Graylock, but most especially Hattie's townhouse across the street. He turned slightly away from Hattie to hide his grinning face. "Timothy . . . don't you try to fool me. Now . . . what's so funny?"

Jerome chirped in getting a dig at Tim. "Yeah, Timothy" he emphasized "what is so funny?" Now Jerome passed his poked from Hattie onto Tim's shoulder. "Boy, Hattie . . ." he continued "I don't think Timothy wants to tell us what is amusing him so."

"Well, whatever it is . . . it is certainly making him blush! But you never mind Tim . . . that little rush of red in your cheeks makes your nice blond hair all the nicer." Jerome stepped aside to allow Hattie closer to the stove. "I don't think I'm blushing!" protested Tim.

"Oh yes you are" informed Jerome. "You are most definitely blushing . . . Timothy!" he added with a twist.

"Now you boys stop fooling around. What are you up to?" she repeated.

Jerome took a more serious tone while Tim tried to rub the red out of his cheeks. "Hattie . . . Tim and I wanted to talk . . ."

She interrupted him, not thinking. "What has Polly cooked up for us tonight?" she said as the grabbed two potholders and opened the oven door. "Oh goodness me . . . that pot's too big for me to lift. Here Tim . . . take these and give me a hand, would you dear?" She handed the potholders over to Tim who obliged and lifted the two-handled blackened cast iron pot out of the oven . . . still warm.

"Um . . . Hattie" Jerome tried again "Like I said . . . Tim and I . . ."

"You what dear . . . ?" she said only half paying attention as she took one of the potholders back from Tim and used it to lift the top of the pot off and set it aside. "Oh good . . . it's beef stew" she said with a heavy approval "Polly can make the best stew ever." She replaced the top onto the pot. "What were you saying Jerome . . . did you and Tim want to eat a little earlier this evening . . . that's fine with me . . . we can stand to warm it up right now, if you like . . . I'm a little hungry myself, if I must tell the truth."

Jerome tried yet again to no avail. "Well, that's not exactly what I was trying to . . ." Just then two buzzers went off on the switchboard . . . one following the other almost in unison. "Better go get those Tim" directed Hattie ". . . you never know . . . could be someone wanting to make a reservation . . . we don't want them to think that we're not on the ball here at The Graylock, now do we?" Tim left the kitchen shaking his head of blond hair to the sky. Jerome continued in Tim's absence and mostly for his sake . . . frustrated, but politely determined. "Hattie . . . if I could take just a minute."

"Mmmm . . ." she murmured absent-mindedly. "Jerome, why don't you set us up three dinner trays . . . we'll eat whenever you want to."

He scratched his head with nowhere to go from here. "Ok . . . but I just wanted to . . ."

"I have to check the reservation sheet" she said. She looked at him standing there with a rather resigned and dejected look on his face. "And then I have to check the newspaper for something." He did not respond, mostly knowing full well that he'd get interrupted again. "I'll be in the dining room, Jerome . . . I'm not going anywhere. We can talk in there" she said with only a mildly reassuring air. Jerome felt like he was going to have a tough time getting a word in edgewise. He was probably right.

Tim had already placed the reservation sheet at Hattie's place on the table. She went humming into the dining room without a care in the world . . . mostly. "Tim bring me the reservation sheet will you please?"

"It's right where you want it . . . on the table" he shouted back as he dashed into the kitchen. "Well . . . ?" he said with much anticipation to Jerome.

"Well . . . nothing" said Jerome as he laid the trays out with a bang. "What do you mean "well . . . nothing . . . did you tell her?"

Jerome reached into the middle drawer and pulled out a handful of silverware . . . more than he needed. He tossed the extras back in and carelessly threw the knives onto the trays. Tim could see that Jerome's good-naturedness was evaporating out the kitchen window into the garden. "What's the matter?" he asked sincerely.

"Look Tim . . . you weren't much help with Hattie . . . I thought we were going to do this together. I couldn't make any headway with her and I want this matter settled as much as you do. I don't feel like Maneray screwing with any more of my calls or messages."

"Alright . . . I'm sorry. I shouldn't have been laughing so hard . . . but I can't help it . . . sometimes she just cracks me up something awful." Jerome continued to set the trays up with a blank stare on his face. "Come on now, Jerome" Tim continued "You'll have to admit that she can be pretty funny sometimes . . . Look we'll try again later. We've got all night. No dinner guests . . . everybody's checked in and Maneray's not due back for hours yet. Alright?"

"Fine" said Jerome "But no fooling around this time . . . this might be more serious than we think." He heard the switchboard and pointed Tim out the door ". . . better not shirk your duties."

Hattie made herself busy with the newspaper peering quickly through the headlines until she could find what she was looking for. She picked the edge of the paper up carefully so as not to get the ink print on her fingers. She read right into the lead story that reported that plans for a great industrial mobilization machine to be directed by FDR and a War Resources Administration were being sent up to Congress. The plan would allow FDR to immediately conscript America's industry and manpower. The plan was also going to allow FDR to regulate the commodity exchanges and give him discretion to close the stock exchanges for the duration of any war emergency . . . that and the power to put a price-fix on war materials and draft into service industrial management personnel. "That son of a bitch won't be happy until he can rule the world... he makes me sick... I hope he never gets re-elected" she said aloud. Jerome walked in at the tail end. "President Roosevelt getting under you skin again, Hattie?"

She turned into the third page. "I'm not even going to let him bother me tonight" she responded as she lifted her head up to Jerome. "Are you going to want a drink tray?" he asked dourly.

"Jerome" she said with a bit of concern "come over here and sit down next to me... why do you have such an unhappy look on your face?... and no I don't think we'll need a drink tray tonight, unless of course you boys want to fix yourselves one... feel free... you know where everything is."

"I'll take one!" said Tim gleefully as he stuck his head in the doorway. Jerome pulled his chair closer into the table and sternly looked an Tim. Then he pointed directly to the chair on the opposite side of Hattie and firmly motioned for Tim to sit there. "Jerome, dear... what is it? You don't seem yourself."

Now that all three of them were at the table, Jerome began. "Hattie, we don't mean to start any trouble... Tim and I... but we've been having some real difficulty... problems, I guess you could say with Mr. Maneray." Hattie set the newspaper aside and folded her hands in her lap.

"You see... we think... or at least it seems to us..."

"Boys" Hattie said with an intonation now equally as somber as Jerome's "I just don't want to talk about unpleasantness this evening, alright?"

Jerome slumped his shoulders and looked away from her for a second. Tim tried to continue "Hattie, I don't think you understand what goes on when you're not around. He can get really nasty, not just to us but to the whole..." She raised her hand to halt his speech.

THE GRAYLOCK

"He's gone" she said without emotion. Jerome quickly looked back and then directly at Tim. "Excuse me . . . but did you say that he's gone?" said Jerome pointedly.

"Yes, that's what I said. He had to leave this afternoon to return home . . . a family emergency he said . . . he won't be back until next Sunday." Tim practically leaped out of his seat and exclaimed "That's more than a week away! That's the best news I've heard since I got here . . . more than a whole week without him stalking around like some kind of ghost . . . I'm going to fix myself a drink . . . Jerome do you want one?"

"No" he answered somberly. Tim spirits almost skipped him into the kitchen. "You don't seemed as buoyed by the news as Tim" said Hattie still matching Jerome somber tone for somber tone.

"But, he's coming back . . . right?"

"Yes . . . he's coming back. And when he returns, Jerome, if you would like to continue this conversation at that time, we will. But, since Mr. Maneray is not here to defend himself against any accusations you and Tim want to make, we won't go any further right now. I just don't want to go into unpleasantries tonight . . . We need proof, now don't we?" she said now teasing him. "You're going to be a criminal lawyer, Jerome . . . you don't want to go about accusing people without proof, do you? And don't you think everyone should have some right to defend themselves against accusations . . . at least that's the way it was when I was in law school."

She just won the argument and Jerome knew it. He started to break into a smile. "Oh wonderful . . . there's that natural Reed smile!" Hattie teased again "I was beginning to think you'd lost it." He smiled even more broadly at her compliment. "Ok . . . no more talk of Mr. Maneray until he gets back . . . it's a deal" he said. Hattie threw her shoulders back in a mock professional posture and jetted her hand out to Jerome. "A deal it is then . . . let's shake on it." Jerome offered his hand almost mildly in defeat and ran his other hand freely through his wavy brown hair wondering how it was that she had so deftly maneuvered them both out of their pact to make her listen to them. "You're something else, Hattie."

"Now what do you say you get that stew ready for us? . . . I'm so excited to tell you boys about my wonderful telephone conversation . . . just as soon as I can find this article I'm looking for." Jerome rose from the table and strode in a more relaxed frame of mind, to join Tim in the kitchen.

He found Tim pouring himself a bourbon and branch water and humming to himself a tune of his own making. "You sure are in a better mood" he acknowledged to Tim. He made a face and pointed to the chilling drink. "How can you stand that stuff?"

"I can't really" said Tim "I don't even really like the smell of it . . . but there's hardly an eyedrop full of it in here . . . just a little bit in celebration . . . are you sure you don't want one?" Jerome shook his head. "He's coming back, you know."

"So what? We have over a week without him lurching around here . . . enjoy it while we can. We can divide and conquer after he gets back . . . I know I'm going to start sleeping better already. C'mon . . . let's go back in and keep her company."

When they sat themselves back in the dining room, they saw Hattie smiling so broadly that if it was possible, the smile would have covered her whole, small face.

"What's the good news in the paper that's got you smiling so, Hattie?" asked Tim "did Roosevelt resign?!"

Hattie looked up from her reading and chuckled. "No such luck, Timothy . . . but I was just talking to my daring young friend, Louise McPhetridge . . . well, she's Louise McPhetridge Thaden now, but I've always known her as Louise McPhetridge. She lives here in Washington . . . just the prettiest lady with all her curly hair. Do you know what's she's doing this week?" They both shook their heads. They had never heard of her. "Well, she's entered the race for Bendix Trophy!"

"What's that?" said Jerome pleading ignorance.

"It's the most prestigious long-distance flying award in the nation, that's all. Every high profile pilot in the country is going to be in it . . . some from other countries as well. It starts in New York and ends in Los Angeles . . . and my little friend is going to win it . . . I just know it!! She has such a pioneering spirit" Hattie beamed.

"Men and women in same race?" inquired Tim in a nonchalant manner.

"Not in the same planes . . . no of course not . . . why should they be . . . no, each pilot will be flying solo across the country" answered Hattie. Tim had a blank stare on his face. "What's the matter Tim . . . do you think a woman should have a man in the plane to help her fly? . . . Surely, you've heard of Amelia Earhart haven't you?"

"I have" declared Jerome "is she in this race, too?"

"She sure is" exclaimed Hattie "but she's not going to win . . . my friend Louise is!" she said confidently.

"You seem pretty sure of that, Hattie" said Tim as he took another small sip of his drink. "Have you got a crystal ball stashed away someplace here we don't know about?"

"Nonsense . . . who needs it . . . crystal balls . . . soothsayers . . . it all craziness . . . no, I just have a feeling that's all. She's such a wonderful woman" Hattie continued with pride "bright . . . educated . . . married . . . two lovely children . . . such a pioneering spirit . . . flying all over the country . . . Why way back in 1929 she was already breaking records! She flew at an altitude of 20,270 feet . . . can you imagine that!? . . . higher than any woman had ever flown before!! I can't wait for you boys to meet her!"

During dinner, Hattie continued on singing the praises of

Louise McPhetridge Thaden and generally the praises of women who were, what she referred to as "breaking the mold." She inquired if there were any women enrolled in classes over at Jefferson and Jerome replied that he knew of only two in the first year class and hadn't really paid too close attention to the second and third year classes. Hattie recalled how some had tried to make it difficult for her when she was attending law school when she was a young woman in her twenties. She recalled with a reflective sense of humor how few professors would call upon her in class because they didn't think her assessment or opinion on legal issues was relevant. "I think they thought they should just have to tolerate my presence when the real truth of the matter was that I was tolerating them and their ridiculous frame of mind that, because I was a woman, I was just not all that bright. Hell, I was one of the smartest students in that class and I knew it!" The passage of the many years had taken the edge off the sting of their offensive behavior and Hattie now could laugh when she retold some of the pathetic answers her classmates would offer certain professors. "Some of them were simply idiots, but got to voice their opinions because their voices were deeper than mine." She let the bows and arrows fly over her head but never backed off her determination to finish the degree. "I hung in there when a lot of other classmates dropped out because they found that law school was too tough." Hattie suggested to both the boys that they make some effort to make the two women in their class feel welcome. "No need to overdo it . . . just treat them as you would any of your other colleagues . . . trust me, it will mean a lot to them . . . even in 1936 there are still some fellows who think women have no place in law school." Jerome told Hattie that he was sure Tim might not have too much trouble putting forth an effort with one of the two as he seemed pretty smitten already.

"Why, Timothy . . . how nice" said Hattie "I tell you what . . .

why don't you invite her over here for dinner one night . . . whenever you feel comfortable, of course . . . no need to rush."

"Yeah, Tim" Jerome chirped in "I think Hattie would like to meet Carolyn, don't you?" Tim grimaced and shrugged in a silent affirmation not knowing what to say to Hattie. He knew what to say to Jerome though, but he had already scurried off with the dinner trays into the kitchen. Jerome sort of knew that Tim would "address the issue" later but couldn't help but tease his friend in the interim. He was still smiling at the thought of it when he returned to the dining room and saw Hattie peering out the window towards the back gate. She turned to Jerome and said "I think I can see the shed door open . . . those alley dogs have probably gotten into the garbage again . . . I see some of it spilled out into the garden. Jerome, would you mind terribly going out and sweeping it up . . . and make sure you close the shed door tightly."

Tim was propped against the door jam and pointing happily to the broom, dustpan and flashlight. "Garbage duty" he whispered "serves you right, blabbermouth!"

Jerome found more garbage spilled that could be seen from the window and propped the shed door wide open while he turned upright one of the cans. He used the flashlight to look inside the shed and saw more garbage strewn in the corner. He moved all four of the cans out into the garden and used the broom to pull the small pile of garbage in the corner up to the front. Not until he dumped the first dustpan full of refuse into one of the cans did a familiar sight catch the corner of his eye. He dropped the dustpan in disbelief and reached for the flashlight again to shed some light on what he hoped in his heart was not true.

There was a letter addressed to him in his mother's immediately recognizable handwriting barely visible in the garbage he had just thrown into the can. The envelope was stained and smeared with grease. His heart began to pound with anger as he retrieved it. It bore a postmark of more than a week ago. Jerome was so angry that he emptied the whole garbage can out onto the cement. He stirred the refuse with the broom handle stick in one hand and the flashlight in the other like a detective wildly searching for clues to a mystery. Sure enough, he found another letter addressed to him . . . this one from his younger brother, Stevie postmarked just three days ago. Jerome was crushed and felt sick to his stomach . . . not from the retching smell of rotting garbage, but with the blasting fact that someone had thrown his mail away. He knew that there was only one person who operated at such a base level of vindictiveness. Maneray.

"That bastard . . . how could he do such a thing? What the hell is wrong with him . . . I've never done anything to him!" Jerome became even more incensed when he thought of his parents and his sick brother harboring the notion that Jerome had forgotten about them . . . or just couldn't find the time to answer their letters. He dropped himself onto the bench next to the back gate and prayed for the strength not to explode with rage. He knew that he had inherited the famous Reed temper and had worked with great success to keep in under control. But now he was on the verge of losing that control. "What is going on here?" was all he could help but think. No more, he decided right there and then, would he ever give Maneray the benefit of any doubt. The Reed dye was cast and as far as he was concerned Maneray was a fool to return to the hotel. He had interfered with Jerome's family and that was an unpardonable, unforgivable error. He carefully wiped the two letters off as best he could and set them on the bench. He finished sweeping up the garbage, returned the four cans to their place in the shed and slammed the door shut with the force of a thousand angry gods.

Tim noticed Jerome come back into the tool room and throw the broom and dustpan into the corner with disgust. He tossed the flashlight onto the shelf with such force that it nearly broke.

"It couldn't have been that bad, Jerome" said Tim "I mean I would have done it." Tim stopped his commentary when he saw the bitter look on Jerome face. It was a look that he had not seen on his friend's face before. "What's the matter?" he said with genuine concern. Jerome did not respond. He took the letters out of his pocket and let them speak for him. Tim took them out of Jerome's hand and realized to whom they were addressed. He knew immediately what was wrong and he understood just as quickly who was responsible. "My god . . ." he said as he stood there with Jerome's letters in his hand. Jerome still had not uttered a word. Tim handed him back the letters. "This is terrible." Jerome walked past him and started to climb the back staircase.

"Where are you going . . . don't you want to show these to Hattie?"

"Upstairs" Jerome said in a depressed monotone "to read my letters."

"Yeah, but . . ."

Jerome interrupted him. "Not a word to Hattie, Tim. I mean it. I'm going to handle this myself." Tim knew that Jerome meant business. "And if that fool Maneray for some reason his stupid enough to return to this hotel tonight . . . you just ring me, understand?" Tim nodded. "Yes, but Hattie said he'd be gone for a week." What Jerome knew to be true did not register with him at the moment. He was burning up with anger inside.

"I don't care what he told Hattie . . . if you see him, call me." He turned and walked out of sight.

Tim returned to the switchboard and felt terrible for Jerome . . . felt sorry for

Maneray whenever he decided to return. He knew that Jerome would not forget this.

"Something awful is going to happen here" he whispered to himself.

THE GRAYLOCK

Chapter Fifteen

Jerome had calmed down considerably by the time his phone rang the next morning with the familiar three rings from Tim.

"What are doing on the switchboard?" he asked Tim.

"Before she went to bed last night, Hattie asked me if I could help Duffy out just a little bit before class this morning... you know... since Maneray isn't here. I've been down here awhile taking breakfast orders... what do you want to eat? Polly is insisting that we both have breakfast before we leave."

Jerome never had much of a stomach in the morning and would have been happy with a cup of coffee, but he knew Polly would nag him until he surrendered his empty belly to her culinary whims. "I don't know... whatever she's got down there. I'll be down in fifteen minutes." Jerome got ready to take a fast shower and took a quick look at the two grease stained letters still on his desk. He was not so much angry anymore over how he discovered the letters... he knew he'd deal with Maneray later... but with some of the news the letters contained. His little brother, Stevie, had been placed in the hospital for three days after a very serious asthma attack on the farm. According to Jerome's mother, Stevie was insistent about trying to lend a hand with some of the chores in the barn when his asthma attack knocked him down so hard that he almost stopped breathing. He had to be rushed to the local hospital and the emergency room doctors performed a tracheotomy on the 16-year old to breathe some life back into his collapsed lungs. His mother suggested to Jerome in her letter that it would help lift his brother's spirits a lot if Jerome wrote a letter addressed just to Stevie "... It would mean the world to him ... he misses you so" she wrote. Jerome knew he would have written right away ... if he had only gotten his mother's letter. He was sure that Stevie must have thought he forgot about him when he read a line in his brother's letter "... I know you're probably awful busy with all your new classes, but I wanted to write and tell you that I miss you ... I've been having a little trouble with my breathing for a bit, but I'm trying to help out as much as I can." Not a word about the tracheotomy. That was Stevie's style. Never complain. He'd been that way since he was a little boy. The thought of Maneray even laying his filthy hands on Stevie's letter, much less throwing it in the garbage, made Jerome want to rip the bastard's skull out. "I'll deal with that later" he said as he dried off "but I'll surprise Stevie with a call this afternoon ... after Hattie goes in for her nap."

It was Jerome's day to be on the switchboard starting at three o'clock and he wanted to have a look at the reservation sheet to see how busy he'd be. But he swept down the back stairs and into the kitchen first.

"Well now ... there's a young man with a hungry look on his face. I suppose you come a runnin' down those stairs like a herd o' who knows what just so you can have some of my fine breakfast?!" Jerome decided to raz Polly a bit just for fun.

"Umm ... well, to tell you the truth, Polly ... I think maybe I'll just get a cup of coffee on my way out if that's all right with you." It worked. Polly got on her high horse with ease.

"It ain't all right with me at all! Don't go talkin' to me 'bout no silly cup o' coffee 'fore yous is 'spose to go off and listen to them smart gentlemen over at your school try to teach you somethin'! You can't learn nothin' if all yous is thinkin' 'bout is yer aching belly. You sure is goin' to have somethin' to eat 'fore I lets you outta my sight this fine mornin' Mr. Jerome . . . I can tells you that."

"Well you know, Polly, I was kind of hungry when I woke up this morning but Tim rang me up and said I'd better steer clear of the breakfast today . . . said you were off your mark."

"He said what!!" she huffed.

"Yeah . . . I'm pretty sure that's what he told me . . . you were off your mark a bit" he replied knowing it would probably send Polly spinning out to the tool room to look for her broom . . . the domestic weapon she relied on when she was on a tear.

No need or time right then. Tim happened to walk into the kitchen with a stack full of empty breakfast trays from guests who apparently had lapped up Polly's breakfast with delight. He barely got his "hello" out to Jerome before Polly laid into to him.

"Mr. Timothy . . . what you mean tellin' Jerome I'm off my mark this morning? Didn't I make a nice stack of wheatcakes for you 'cause you asked me special?! An' didn't you come back here an' beg me to put a few more up for you . . . an' me tryin' to get a regular breakfast out for the payin' guests . . . you know I don't go makin' my wheat cakes for everybody . . . how come you callin' him up in secret an' sayin'. . . ."

"Wait a minute! What are you talking about? Jerome what are you stirring up?"

"Oh there you goes agin tryin' to bring Jerome into your troubles . . . I'll tell you one thing . . . you ain't gettin' no wheat cakes outta this kitchen no more . . . you can beg 'till you is blue in yo' face . . . now you set those trays down an' git 'cause I ain't talkin' to you!"

Jerome was laughing hysterically while he poured himself

a cup of Polly's coffee when she realized that she had just been teased. "Mr. Jerome . . . did you jes tell me a fib?" She started to walk towards him . . . broom or no broom . . . he made a quick confession before she dumped the hot coffee on him. "I'm sorry, Polly . . . really I am . . . I was just kidding . . . you're breakfasts are the best in the world!"

"I jes don't know what I goin' to do with yous boys . . . both of yous is becomin' a worry to me . . . an' I don't need no more worries in my life." Jerome's eyes were tearing from laughing.

"I'm sorry . . . I didn't mean anything by it. I love to watch you go after Tim."

"Well, that Mr. Timothy needs it . . . even when he don't deserve it, he needs it 'cause I know he's actin' up when I can't see him . . . he's jes a little devil, that one. 'An now you . . . don't you go takin' after him . . . I can't deal with both o' yous boys bein' bad."

"Ok . . . ok . . . I'll be good! Can I have some breakfast?"

"You go on now an' git outa here . . . wait in the dining room . . . I make you somethin' good . . . how 'bout some nice eggs over an' crisp bacon an' some toast with marmalade?"

"Whatever you decide, Polly . . . I'll eat it."

"Well you move on outta here then . . . I can't have yous boys in here botherin' me while I'm tryin' to do my morning work . . . an' take your coffee with you" Jerome obeyed and left to find a seat in the dining room. A wave of guests had just left and all the tables were empty. Tim was picking up some empty trays. "What were you doing in there?"

"Oh, come on . . . I was just having a little fun. You know she adores you . . . she'd make you eight meals a day if you asked her to . . . besides it's kind of fun joking around in the morning without Maneray around . . . how's it been down here?"

"You can't believe the difference, Jerome" Tim said. "It's like night and day. I hope he never comes back."

Jerome took another swallow of his coffee. "He's going to be mighty sorry when he does, let me tell you." Polly walked in with Jerome's breakfast and set it in front of him. "Who's gonna be sorry? What are you devils cookin' up?"

"Nothing" said Jerome "thanks for the breakfast, Polly."

"You're welcome . . . but whenever somebody says 'nothin' to me . . . I knows it means 'somethin'. I hopes yous boys ain't gettin' in no trouble."

Tim reassured her that there was nothing going on as he walked back to the kitchen with her with the trays. Mr. Duffy walked into the dining room to say hello to Jerome.

"Good morning, Mr. Duffy. How are you today?"

"Oh. I guess I'll be alright" he replied with little enthusiasm. "Are you coming on duty at three today?" Jerome nodded with a mouthful of toast and marmalade and reminded himself that he still had to ask Tim if he could take the early part of the shift so he could get up to the Library of Congress and do a little preliminary investigation into the subject of his criminal law paper. His meeting with Professor Lucien was Friday morning and he wanted to get a few of his facts straight before telling him what he wanted to write about. He didn't want to confuse Mr. Duffy with details he'd not be interested in. Jerome knew Duffy would just get nervous if he wasn't sure somebody would be here at three to relieve him. So he just assured Duffy that he'd be on time.

"I'm only asking, you know . . . because I have to leave right at three today. I have a meeting to go to."

"Another meeting, Mr. Duffy"?'

"Oh . . . yes and this is a very important one at that. I must attend it." Tim would have tried to pry out of Duffy what all these meeting were about, but Jerome didn't much care. He just thought that it was nice that an older man like Duffy had some things in his life to still keep him interested. "Don't worry, Mr.

Duffy. I'll be here on time."

"Thanks Jerome. I know I can rely on you . . . it's just that . . . you know . . . I don't like to be late for my meetings." Jerome got up and headed for the kitchen to return his breakfast tray. Polly's breakfasts really were terribly good. "Don't know how she does it . . . but she always makes me glad I ate breakfast" he mused to himself. He slid the tray onto the counter and pushed it closer to the sink. "Tim . . . you ready to head over to school?" Tim nodded. "Just let me get my stuff."

"Thanks again for the breakfast, Polly. It was great . . . as usual." said Jerome.

"You are welcome, Jerome. You'll be on tonight won't you? The Mrs. is havin' company, so I'm goin' ta fix somethin' nice. You like roasted chicken with some nice stuffin' in it?" Jerome walked over to her hand gave her a hug and kissed her on the side of her forehead. "I'm going to weigh 300 pounds by the time I get home for Christmas at this rate!" He grabbed his coat and books from the dining room and walked out the front door with Tim. "See you later, Mr. Duffy" they both said. Duffy adjusted his glasses out of habit and watched them walk up the street. "I like them both" he thought to himself. "I hope it works out for them here."

This morning's class, constitutional law, was neither Tim's nor Jerome favorite subject. The professor, Christian Goldenberg, was a retired U.S. Appeals Court judge who seemed as contradictory in his presentation of the law as his name was in a religious vein. One day he'd mandate a steadfast iron-fisted support of the constitution and the next he'd tell the class that it was so poorly written that it needed twice as many amendments to it as already existed. Most of the students thought he was just bitter at never having received a Senate confirmation for his appointment to the U.S. Supreme Court and for years contradicted himself in his appellate opinions just so they'd be taken up the Supreme Court. "It was his way of getting back at them for not supporting his nomination" opined one of the more pompous students, Kevin Mitchell "... he thought it would increase their case load so much that one of the justices would decide to retire and he'd get another shot at being nominated." At 72, most everybody in the class knew that Professor Goldenberg's judicial contributions were now limited to essays and books on constitutional law and the eventual memoir. Still, he did have his good days and on those days he could command attention from even the most disinterested student. It was wisdom from the ages that was resolutely undistilled by the former judge who demanded that the students drink up his constitutional libations . . . not he theirs. When it was clear . . . it was a rare concoction for a young, eager mind.

Before Goldenberg entered the lecture hail, Jerome asked Tim if he could take up the first hour or so of his shift. He wanted to spend a good part of the day up at the Library of Congress starting the background research for his criminal law paper.

"I can't Jerome . . . not today. I'm going to help Carolyn Peretti with some of the Real Property cases . . . and then I'm going to ask her if she wants to go to the movies . . . I can do it for you on Friday if you want."

Jerome shook his head. "My meeting with Lucien is on Friday. I have to have it done by then . . . no problem . . . I'll just go up tomorrow. I can spend all day there."

"And skip the Real Property lecture . . . how could you?!" said Tim in mock surprise. Jerome laughed at the needle from his friend. "Jesus, Tim . . . I think you must know at least as much as Professor Curry by now . . . I'll just look at your notes." He paused just seconds long enough for Tim to soak in the compliment before he added wryly ". . . or maybe I should just get them from Carolyn!"

Tim was not about to fall for the unusual Reed sense of humor twice in one morning. "You just come to the primary source, my friend and you'll be just fine. My notes will be sufficient for you to understand . . . no need to go elsewhere." Tim opened *The Washington Post* to the theater and movie section and asked Jerome what movie he thought would be a good one to ask Carolyn to see. Humphrey Bogart and Pat O'Brien were starring in Warner Brother's "China Clipper" but they decided they'd go see that together . . . too much hero stuff for a first date.

"Hey . . . here's one" said Tim " Norma Shearer and Leslie Howard in 'Romeo and Juliet' . . . not a bad choice?"

"I don't know about that, Tim . . . you sure you want to take her to that? There's an awful lot of fighting and arguing going on in that . . . besides Romeo kills Juliet and then kills himself by the end of the story . . . a little intense for starters, don't you think?" Tim agreed. Then Jerome pointed to the opposite page. "That looks like a good one . . . Fred Astaire and Ginger Rogers in 'Swing Time' . . . probably kind of light and fun."

"Yeah . . . I mean how can you go wrong with Fred Astaire?" wondered Tim. "'Swing Time' it is then!" he decided "now all she has to do is say yes!" How could she resist? "Swing Time" at the National with the handsome swimmer soon-to-be real estate baron? It would be Fred and Ginger dancing straight away into their hearts.

It was just about three o'clock when Jerome dashed through the front door of the hotel lobby in time to relieve Mr. Duffy. He saw Polly carefully backing out of Hattie's room and miming a sign for him to be silent as she gently closed the door. He slowed his pace down to investigate the situation. "What's the matter?" he asked the cook.

"The Mrs. don't feel too good today, Jerome. I think she best take her some rest for a few days. She ain't even been out o' her room today. She got 'em bad this time."

"Got what bad? What do you mean . . . what the matter with her? Why don't you call her a doctor?"

"The Mrs. don't believe in doctors, Jerome . . . don't you know that? No sir . . . she ain't seen no doctor since the Mr. passed on . . . an' that was before I got here . . . goin' on 35 years now."

"Polly" Jerome said with great concern "if Hattie is sick, she should be seen by a doctor."

Polly waived him off without so much as a bother. "Won't do no good to fuss, Jerome . . . ain't no doctors gettin' near the Mrs. . . . she won't allow it an' that's that. 'Sides can't no doctor find no cure for what ails the Mrs. no how . . . ain't no medicine for it."

"Hey, Polly I mean it . . . if she's going to die, I'm calling a doctor. I don't care what she believes in."

Polly smiled to herself and reached for her carpet sweeper. "Boy, you sure is all o' yer 21 years ain't you, Jerome?" She stood fast and took a long look at him. He was four decades younger than Hattie and a lifetime or two removed from her past. He was just beginning his life and he thought she was about to end hers. Polly could see that he cared and tried to explain.

"Jerome, the Mrs. gets like this ev'ry so often. I been takin' care o' her for years now and I seen it come an' go . . . it ain't nothin' to cause no real worry. She got the miseries . . . that's all . . . but I don't 'spect a young boy like you knows anythin' too much 'bout the miseries . . . don't get me wrong . . . I don't mean no disrespect . . . yous is very smart an' all . . . but the miseries don't have nothin' to do with bein' smart." Jerome followed her into the tool room where she placed the carpet sweeper into its familiar place in the corner. "I don't get it, Polly . . . is she sick or not?"

"Oh she's sick alright . . . I'll put it to you this way, Jerome . . . white folks calls it a broken heart . . . she ain't never got over it . . . that's what the miseries is . . . a heart forever broke." Polly left him there with just enough information to confuse him while she returned to the kitchen to straighten up before she went home.

"Jerome . . . Jerome" said Mr. Duffy in a low voice almost as though he did not want to disturb Hattie in her room "I have to leave now. Are you ready to take over here? I have to make my meeting." Duffy was hurriedly throwing his cape over his shoulders and placed his fedora flatly on his head. No time to be stylish today; he was obviously in a big rush. Jerome watched him swirling himself up in all his black attire. "Sure Mr. Duffy . . . go ahead . . . I can take care of things."

"Alright then . . . I'll be going . . . see you tomorrow." He brushed right past Jerome and lit out towards the garden gate. After the screen door slammed behind him, Jerome noticed that a pamphlet had dropped out of Mr. Duffy's cape and he picked it up and tried to holler after him to let him know that he'd mistakenly left it behind. "Mr. Duffy" he yelled "Mr. Duffy . . . you dropped something." Duffy did not turn around . . . only raised one of his hidden arms from the protection of his enveloping cape to respond to what he thought was Jerome's loud farewell for the day.

Jerome did not give it too much thought until he inspected the pamphlet more closely. He was bewildered by its contents and strangely amused at this tiny peek into Walter Duffy's private interests. He read it half aloud to himself, still in the tool room. "The Life Extension Institute, Inc." read the front flap. Jerome scratched his head. "What the hell is the Life Extension Institute?"

He was going to carefully read the pamphlet when he heard Polly walking up the stairs from the cellar. She was changed into her street clothes and Jerome thought how different she looked out of her gray uniform and apron. She had on a light purple dress of no particular cut and flat black walking shoes. She was adjusting her powder blue velvet hat with a pheasant feather in its side and carrying her pretty yellow sweater. "What are doin' Jerome

... mumbling to yo'self?" Jerome folded the pamphlet in half and stuck it in his back pocket.

"Just seeing Mr. Duffy off that's all" he said.

"Well, I made a dinner for the Mrs. earlier an' it's in the oven. She was 'spose to have a guest tonight, a Mr. Lewis in Room 309. You best call him in awhile or leave him a message in his box that she jes ain't up to it. If she calls for somethin' to eat, you jes fix her a tray and bring it in to her, you understand? An' you an Tim jes help yourselves to the meal."

"Ok . . . thanks Polly. You think she'll be alright?"

"The Mrs. will be jes fine . . . but don't you go disturbin' her for no account . . . let her be. I got to go now." Jerome opened the screen door for Polly and eased her down the step to the alleyway.

"Thank you, Jerome. Yous is a gentleman" she smiled at him and began to walk away.

"Polly" he called out politely. She turned back. "Yes, Jerome."

"What was Hattie's husband's name?"

Polly paused in thought and pursed her lower lip out in brief contemplation. "Edmund, I believe . . . yes . . . it was Edmund Crickmore."

THE GRAYLOCK

Chapter Sixteen

With no sight or sound from Hattie, the hotel seemed again to Jerome more like a museum with bad artifacts from unidentifiable, mysterious con men posing as curators at the time of purchase. The odd combination of a long medieval looking black oak table on the side of the front staircase, just in front of the switchboard station, which was splattered with outdated issues of "The Breeders Gazette" and a variety of cheap looking candy dishes filled with oversized looking squirrel nuts was the most bemusing to Jerome. He wondered what the guests thought when they passed by the table to check in at the front desk, although he never bothered to ask. Mr. Duffy explained to Jerome a few weeks ago that the different cut glass and pewter candy dishes were not filled with squirrel nuts at all but tung nuts from a piece of property Hattie owned in Mississippi. The oil extracted from the nuts was believed at one time by Hattie to have a cornucopia of medicinal and healing properties. Polly now used an undiluted form of it now to polish the furniture, hoping to breathe some life back into the dead wood. It smelled like lead paint that had gone bad and looked more like syrup than furniture polish.

But somehow Hattie had an ability to make the eclectic collection of furnishings make sense almost by not explaining them at all. It was the very same ability she used in dealing with her guests, however prominent or eccentric others found them to be. Hattie could keep them at bay or embrace them like family, she could interrogate them or let them chat with her for hours, or she could just accept them and in doing so neutralize their egos and oddities and bring into full flower the special slants of their unique personalities. They were her guests, just like the furniture was hers . . . just like the hotel was hers . . . and the townhouse across the Street. And the garden. Everything that came in or out of The Graylock, permanently placed or passing through, eventually bore her indelible, invisible and irresistible imprimatur. Whether she spun her welcome mat for entertainment value or real education was anyone's guess. But then one of Hattie's specialties was to keep people guessing. Very rarely did any of them guess right. To be correct was not primarily important to Hattie . . . to be at The Graylock was. Miseries or no miseries, the place was all hers.

Jerome made a few handwritten notes to himself about what specific points he wanted to research tomorrow at The Library of Congress as he stood guard at the front desk. It was unseemly quiet and he decided to break the uncomfortable mausoleum air by calling home. He wanted to let Stevie know that he had not forgotten about him. He wanted to hear familiar voices, so he plugged himself into one of the two long distance lines at the switchboard and gave the operator his family's number in Buttermilk Falls. There was no answer. Unusual, he thought for just a second until he looked at the clock on the switchboard. It was only a little past four. Gail and Stevie were probably not back from school yet. His father was, no doubt, out on the farm. His mother could have been in any variety of places in the sprawling home. There was only one telephone in the living room. Maybe he should have let it ring longer to give his mother a chance to get to it in case she was upstairs. No matter. He'd try again closer to the dinner hour when he knew they'd all be there.

The front door bell rang and he could see from the desk that a guest was waiting to be let in. He opened the door with a much more friendly disposition than Maneray had ever showed him and before he could welcome the guest the man stepped right inside and said "Hello. My name is Mr. Lewis. I have a reservation."

Jerome walked Mr. Lewis to the front desk and gave him a card to sign in. Lewis, a man in his late forties, was a good three inches taller than Jerome, standing at a shaky six feet tall. He looked smaller though, because he was almost embarrassingly slight. So slight that, while it would have been anatomically impossible, Mr. Lewis appeared that he might only be half of Jerome's 170 pounds. His thread bare blue suit was most unbecoming and it hung horribly on Lewis' skeletal frame. His orange and red plaid shirt gave no indication to anyone that he had arrived to do business. Jerome checked the reservation sheet and saw that this was the man Polly referred to earlier who was invited to have dinner with Hattie tonight. He was booked into Room 309 . . . it must be the same man, Jerome thought . . . Polly must have mistakenly thought he was already registered. Mr. Lewis handed his business card to Jerome which he read while Mr. Lewis filled out the registration card. "Joseph P. Lewis . . . President of the Freethinkers of America" the card said. The guest noticed that Jerome was looking at the card rather strangely.

"Yes . . . the card is correct . . . I'm a freethinker" he said proudly ". . . are you a freethinker, son?"

Jerome had no response. He hadn't a clue as to what the guy was talking about.

He took the registration card from Mr. Lewis, who with his Ichabod Crane type presence looked more like he should be running from headless horsemen in Sleepy Hollow than running an organization. "He'll fit right in around here, though" said Jerome to himself.

"Well . . . are you?" Lewis repeated.

"Am I what?" Jerome timidly replied trying to avoid the question.

"A freethinker, of course. . . . are you a freethinker?"

"I can't say as I've ever heard of your organization."

"Do you want to join?" Lewis asked with an encouraging tone. "There are more freethinkers around than you think . . . I think you'd be very surprised."

Jerome did not want to join anything . . . especially an organization run by this man. "Well, my schedule it kind of busy these days and I really don't think I'd have time . . . ."

"What do you do, anyway?" Lewis pressed on. "It doesn't take any time at all to be a freethinker . . . really!"

Jerome felt like he was being backed into a corner by a clown. "I'm a law student."

"Oh that's great" said Lewis as he snapped his fingers in the air. "You'll be most interested in what I'm doing then."

Jerome almost dared not ask. "Why do you think that I would be interested?"

"Well, you're going to be a lawyer aren't you?" Jerome nodded almost matter-of-factly. "And I'm down here to file a law suit . . . you see the connection . . . it makes sense doesn't it?" Not to Jerome it didn't. "Yes, indeed. I'm going to sue the Catholic Church . . . and that stupid pope, too. I think he's very rich."

By now Jerome was biting the inside of his cheek and using his considerable stomach muscles to keep from laughing. "Mr. Lewis, I don't really know what your law suit is about, but surely you must know that Pope Pius XI is not an American citizen . . . he's Italian and he lives in Rome not Washington, D.C."

"He's the head of the Roman Catholic Church, isn't he?" Lewis said directly without waiting for a response. "He calls all the shots right there from the Vatican . . . of course he does . . . so I'm blaming him in my law suit."

"Blaming him for what?" asked Jerome incredulously.

"He's using my tax dollars to provide free bus service for parochial school pupils! That's against the law . . . it's unconstitutional, by god!"

Jerome wanted to tell Mr. Lewis that he was very sorry but the hotel was fully booked, except that he'd already signed the registration card. Instead he simply asked him why he was filing suit in Washington. "The United States Supreme Court is here, that's why . . . this is practically a constitutional crisis . . . I think the justices need to know what is going on here!" Jerome could not bear to explain to Lewis how silly filing a law suit directly with the Supreme Court was and decided to humor him instead. "I'll bet the justices will be mighty surprised to see you."

"Me, too" said Lewis with glee. "I don't know if any of them are freethinkers, do you?"

No more decided Jerome. It was past time he took Mr. Lewis and his baggage up to his room. "Mr. Lewis . . . you'll be in Room 309 . . . ."

"Oh yes . . . I know. I always stay in Room 309 . . . been her many times before." Filing crazy lawsuits, no doubt thought Jerome. Lewis picked up his luggage and headed upstairs.

"Do you want me to get that for you?" asked Jerome. "No . . . not at all . . . I know where it is" Lewis said.

"Oh, Mr. Lewis . . . Mrs. Crickmore won't be able to have dinner with you this evening. Something's come up and she can't make it."

"Now that's a disappointment. I always so look forward to seeing her. Well, tell her I can make it tomorrow night, if she has no plans. I'll still be here . . . and, by the way, just let me give you some pamphlets on my organization . . . maybe you'd like to be a freethinker, too . . . or any of your friends!" He reached inside his coat pocket and gave Jerome several small pamphlets about the "Freethinkers of America".

Mr. Lewis walked off towards Room 309 and Jerome returned to the front desk rolling his eyes. "Good grief" he said "pamphlets on the 'Freethinkers of America' and the 'Life Extension Institute' all in the span of 90 minutes. Hardly a dull moment here." He laughed when he thought that Mr. Duffy and Mr. Lewis would run into each other tomorrow. He laughed even harder when he thought of Hattie and Mr. Lewis having dinner and a few bourbons together tomorrow night. "They'll spend all night arguing over who is the bigger son of a bitch . . . Pope Pius XI or President Roosevelt. At least it'll be Tim on duty . . . not me."

Jerome did not realize that almost three hours had passed without a single call coming into or going out of the hotel. He hadn't realized that it had already started to get dark outside. No word from Hattie yet. He wondered if she was alright but remembered Polly's admonition "not to bother her on no account." He thought he'd better heed it. If Hattie wanted anything, she would not be shy about asking for it. He went into the kitchen and decided to heat up the dinner that was supposed to have been for Hattie and Mr. Lewis. Jerome lifted the deep pan out of the oven first to have a look at it. Another feast. A golden brown roasted chicken with cornbread stuffing . . . a pan of homemade giblet gravy on the side and one of Polly's mouth watering cherry pies sitting on the window shelf. The kitchen was the only room in the whole hotel that reminded him of home. He ripped one of the chicken legs off and bit into it. There was nothing like it . . . Polly had some magical way with whatever she cooked that had very little to do with the actual recipe. She cared for the meals and dishes she prepared like a loving head mistress at an orphanage would care for her wards. She watched over them with great caution, almost never leaving them unattended. Every effort was made to make the meals presentable and considerable time was spent in planning. No meal was served before it was ready. She knew what she was doing and it seemed to Jerome that there was nothing in that kitchen she couldn't do. And she asked for nothing in return. Luminescence and grace hiding behind an apron . . . shielded singularly by a recipe for disaster that only The Graylock could have served up.

Jerome had just lit the oven when he heard the front door close and someone whistling through the lobby. He looked for a towel to wipe his hands before going out to the front desk to see who it might be when he heard tapping on the tile floor in the corridor outside the kitchen. When he stuck his head around the corner he saw Tim doing a horrible impersonation of Fred Astaire dancing. He tossed the towel at his friend who deftly caught it in his right hand while pointing to his feet with the other.

"You're a nut" laughed Jerome.

"Yeah . . . maybe so, but who cares? Fred Astaire, though is a genius!" said Tim as he sloppily and terribly tap danced his way into the kitchen. "I'm starved . . . what's on the menu?" Jerome cocked his head in the direction of the roast chicken as he yanked two trays out of the cupboard. "God . . . is this heaven or what? . . . meals cooked every night . . . rooms cleaned twice a week . . . and Maneray out of the picture . . . for now at least . . . this is good living."

"How was your date with Carolyn?" asked Jerome ". . . you think she's home tap dancing too?" he teased.

"Maybe . . . who knows?" replied Tim as he pulled the remaining leg off of the chicken. "I had a good time . . . she's really very nice . . . doesn't know anything about real property though . . . she's worse than you!"

"I know enough to get me through . . . I just don't care about it much" he retorted. "It just doesn't grab me the way criminal law does. Did you both like the movie?"

"It was a hoot. Great suggestion . . . thanks . . . what's going on around here?"

"Not much . . . been real quiet . . . checked one real goofball in. I thought I was going to have to listen to him all night. He was supposed to have dinner with Hattie, but she hasn't been out of her room all day."

"What's the matter with her?"

"Dunno . . . Polly said she has the miseries . . . she'll be back on her feet soon . . . help me get this food out, will you?"

The two leisurely put together two dinner trays heaping with Polly's feast and brought them into the dining room . . . where they found Hattie sitting in silence . . . vacantly staring at the walls.

She turned her head slightly and gave them a half-hearted winsome smile. "Hello, boys" she said almost inaudibly.

"Hattie . . ." said Jerome with quiet surprise "how are you? . . . I thought . . . I mean Polly said that . . . um . . . I didn't think . . ."

"I haven't felt so well today . . . that's all. My stomach has been a bit queazy . . . I'll be alright."

"Can we get you something, Hattie?" asked Tim. "Would you like some dinner?"

"No, thanks dear . . . I'm afraid my stomach might not welcome it with open arms . . . I'll just sip on this seltzer water . . . you boys sit and enjoy your meal . . . looks like Polly's done it again, hasn't she?"

They had never seen Hattie this way before. She was dressed in a floor length dressing gown and slippers with only a white knit shawl held closely around her shoulders. She looked pale and drawn. There appeared to be very little light in her eyes and only a trace of cadence in her voice. They wondered if they should leave her alone and go back to the kitchen to eat.

"No . . . don't be silly . . . I could use the company . . . Timothy, tell me how your date was."

"How did you know I went on a date? Did Jerome . . . ."

She almost smiled again, but the sigh was what they noticed. "I've been sitting here for a little bit . . . I overheard you boys in the kitchen."

"Oh . . ." said Tim. He tried to show some enthusiasm, hoping it might find its way over to her. "Well . . . we had a very nice time . . . I certainly enjoyed myself . . . Carolyn looked like she was having a good time, too."

"That's nice" said Hattie nodding her head, but looking at the tablecloth on her table ". . . what did you do?"

"We just walked around for awhile after class and talked . . . we were going to go see 'Romeo and Juliet' but Jerome talked me out of it . . . said there was too much passion in it for a first date!" Tim said trying to get a rise out of Hattie.

Jerome did not hesitate to correct him in a joint effort to lift Hattie's spirits. "What I really said Hattie was that there was too much arguing and fighting in it . . . too much tragedy . . . not passion."

"Anyhow . . ." added Tim ". . . we decided to see a Fred Astaire and Ginger Rogers movie called 'Swing Time' . . . it was a lot of fun."

Hattie stared at the ceiling and sighed again. "Take it from me, boys . . . passion and tragedy go hand in hand . . . hardly one ever shows up without the other." She fidgeted with her hands mindlessly locking finger in finger. "Ginger Rogers, though . . . that must have been nice to see . . . I hear she's quite the dancer . . . how about you, Jerome . . . what have you been up to . . . guarding the fort for me again?"

"As best I can" he smiled. "Not a whole lot to do this afternoon. I only had to check one guest in . . . a Mr. Lewis. He was supposed to have joined you for dinner, but I told him something had come up and you couldn't make it . . . he said he'd be available tomorrow night if you like."

"Mr. Lewis, oh yes . . . he's something else isn't he? Did he try to get you to join his freethinkers group?"

Jerome almost choked on his food as he began to laugh. "Here sure did! Look at what he gave me!" He reached in his back pocket and gave Hattie the pamphlet he folded in half. In the two steps it took for him to reseat himself he noticed that Tim's look had changed as he watched Hattie unfold the pamphlets. Jerome swerved to the left of his chair and saw that Hattie was not smiling as he thought she might after looking at the "Freethinkers of America" pamphlet. Her face had gone completely gray. Her lips were drawn in a tight, thin line and her brow was furrowed more in shock than anger. But it was clear to both of them that she was not pleased.

"What is this Jerome?"

"It's the stuff Mr. Lewis gave me. I thought . . ."

"No!!" she shouted "this . . ." she said pointing ". . . what is this other thing!! Where did you get this!!?" She was as upset as Jerome had ever seen her. He stepped over to her table again and saw what was creating the fuss.

"Oh that . . ." he said sensing that nothing could be wrong now ". . . that's a different pamphlet. I didn't get that from Mr. Lewis. I forgot that I had that stuffed in my pocket, too. I didn't really look at it too closely when I picked it up off the floor . . . it dropped out of Mr. Duffy's cape as he was leaving work this afternoon in a big rush to go to one of his meetings again" Jerome said innocently.

Hattie was deadly silent at Jerome's explanation. She drew her hand up to cover her mouth and absent her own restraint it seemed as though she was about to scream. Tim got up from his seat and walked over to her table standing beside Jerome.

He picked the pamphlet up from the table and said "'The Life Extension Institute' . . . what's that?" Hattie took the pamphlet out of his hand and held it firmly in hers without looking at it.

She looked Jerome straight in the eyes. "Jerome, are you sure . . . absolutely sure, now . . . that this belongs to Mr. Duffy?"

"Yes m'am . . . I mean I'm certain that it fell out of his cape on his way out the door. Is something wrong?"

Hattie folded the pamphlet in half and put it in the side pocket of her dressing gown. An expressionless countenance replaced her obvious shock as she attempted to compose herself. She rose from her seat and patted Jerome lightly on his forearm. "It's nothing for you boys to concern yourselves with. I'll return this to Mr. Duffy tomorrow. You'll excuse me now . . . I'm going back to my room." She walked away without looking back . . . without stopping at the front desk . . . without saying anything more.

They both stood there dumbfounded. They had no idea why she reacted the way she did. Tim looked at Jerome. "What the hell was that all about? What was in that thing?"

"I don't know . . . I didn't really read it after I picked it up off the floor. I called after Duffy, but I guess he didn't hear me."

"Jesus . . . I'll bet he hears something from Hattie tomorrow. I haven't seen her look like that since she told those people to get out of her hotel the first week I was here. I wonder what's in that thing?"

Jerome just shook his head and sat down.

"This place gets weirder every day" said Tim.

THE GRAYLOCK

Chapter Seventeen

When Ali arrived almost an hour before his shift was to begin at eleven o'clock, Hattie had been retired for almost two hours and Jerome had not heard a sound from her room. Tim had left for the fourth floor after the two finished dinner and rinsed the dishes. Jerome was left in the quiet again to ponder over Hattie's putative reaction to Duffy's pamphlet on The Life Extension Institute. Whatever unexplained connection existed between Duffy and the Institute or Duffy and Hattie or, bizarrely enough thought Jerome, Hattie and the Institute Jerome understood that Hattie had found out something that she didn't like. This unwanted and unwelcome information had pierced her protective shield built by years of living singularly in and for The Graylock. It stuck her like a needle and she winced at its intrusion. It was as though she had been forced to acknowledge a fact that she did not want to know . . . a forced exhumation out of her control. And for a woman so used to painting the directive of her own day, she plainly did not favor the accidental unearthing of a deeply buried past.

Jerome told Ali that Maneray was away on family business so he could lock up any time he wanted. Ali was as pleased as anyone working at the hotel that Maneray was away. "He's a bad person, that man" said Ali in his most non-judgmental Hindi way. "He has a very dark soul that steals life from him every day . . . and so angry is he that he believes he can then steal it from others who walk more easily. He comes in at night when he thinks I am resting in the front, but I know he is full of alcohol once again. He does not understand that it is a thief that steals his mind with every gulp. He is the one who puts it in his body and yet he does not understand that he is the robber and the victim both in one. He will need another life, at least, to figure this out. Yes, this one will be coming back . . . he has many debts to pay, yet . . . many debts . . . but, I for one, will be pleased not to have him cast his troubled shadow in my path for a little while."

Jerome said nothing about the letters he discovered in the garbage, but it was the most he had ever heard Ali talk about Maneray . . . or anyone for that matter. Ali was an observer of the human soul . . . every bit as much an observer of the soul as Everett Roberts was of politics. Jerome paid heed to both of them.

On his own climb up to the fourth floor, Jerome wondered about the guests all safely shut behind the doors to their rooms . . . temporary lodgers here just briefly enough to be what Hattie wanted them to be . . . messengers from the battlefront . . . ideologues who still had to confront opposing forces . . . they saw of her what she wanted them to see . . . she fiddled and they danced. She could take their eyes off the smoke and in doing so they could never report the mystic blaze. It was her trick . . . it was why they almost always came back. It was as though they did not want to see the smoke and she did not want to see the fire. Hattie's guests were her asbestos shield against the world they all knew and the one she was determined to keep away. "She never lets anybody see too much of her" Jerome concluded. "If they get too close to the heart, she can leave . . . or she can tell them to leave." He wondered if the arrow shot by Duffy's pamphlet had found its mark. He wondered if it landed too close to home for Hattie's comfort.

He knocked on Tim's door and did not wait for the customary, jovial "enter". Tim was propped up on his bed writing.

"What are you doing?" asked Jerome

"Making entries in my journal . . . I try to make a note or two in it every day."

Jerome slumped into the battered easy chair next to the fireplace whose hearth cradled a small fire. "Are you keeping track of the nut cases that come in and out of this place?"

"Sort of . . . they're mostly like little letters to Sam."

Jerome was not sure what to say next. Tim did not speak too much of his dead brother and whenever he did, Jerome always let him take the lead. Tim looked at him and smiled a bit as he closed the journal. "Don't worry . . . it's not like I'm trying to conduct a séance or anything. . . . it's just . . . I don't know . . . I guess it's just some days I feel like talking to him and writing in my journal is the only way I know how to do it . . . I get these 'blues for Sam days' every so often and this is a good way to get past them."

Jerome thought of Hattie and her case of the miseries and hoped Tim was not experiencing the same. He spoke about it so easily that Jerome just took his statements at face value. Sometimes there was no reason to delve any further into it. So, he did not comment on the journal entries.

"Can I still get your notes from the Real Property lecture tomorrow?" he said instead.

"Oh, sure . . . you still going to spend the day at the Library of Congress?"

Jerome nodded. "I think I can get all the research done in a few hours and then I'll just need a little bit more time to assemble it in my head for Friday's meeting with Lucien."

Tim rose from the bed and walked over to sit at his desk. "So, I take it you're going to try and get through the meeting with Lucien without any notes in front of you?" Jerome nodded again. "I want to be able to watch him and his reactions while I present the subject and not have my eyes cast on my note pad the whole time."

"What are you going to write your paper about?"

"The third degree" Jerome announced

"Sounds interesting . . . should be plenty of old case law on it."

"Tim" Jerome teased "you surprise me . . . have you actually been reading your criminal law casebook again?"

Tim took the razzing in stride and crossed behind the easy chair to raise the window a bit. "I'm just trying to make sure I'll recognize stolen property along that way if anybody happens to try to sell me some. I don't want to have to call you five years from now and tell you I'm in jail . . . you'd never let me hear the end of it." As he raised the window Jerome heard him breathe a sigh of resignation. "What's the matter?" asked Jerome without looking up.

"She's out there again." Jerome got up from the easy chair and looked out the window as well. They both saw Hattie out in the garden again . . . with no more on than she had in the dining room two hours ago . . . just her dressing gown and the white knit shawl tightly wrapped around her shoulders.

"What is she doing out there?" said Jerome as he tried to focus in on her movements. There was no moonlight to expose her secret sojourn in the garden tonight. Her mission, was protected by the natural cloak of midnight hours as much as Duffy used his cape to cover whatever he was and where ever he went in the light of day.

"Jerome, I am much more interested in why she is out there at this hour in her dressing gown. I can see what she is doing." Jerome could still not make it out.

"She's picking geraniums" said Tim.

"You know Tim . . . tomorrow I bet we don't see any sign of

those geraniums in the hotel and Hattie will act as though not a single thing is awry."

"She doesn't know that we can see her . . . we're the only ones who know that something's not right here."

"I mean with Mr. Duffy and that pamphlet . . . I bet we never hear another word about it."

"The hell . . ." declared Tim. "Something clearly set her off when she saw that . . . I don't care if she talks about it or not . . . I'm going to find out where that place is and go see for myself what goes on . . . and I'm going to find out what these midnight trips into the garden are all about, too."

"Yeah . . . and you're going to own all of N Street, too. I can see your in one of your snooping moods again."

"You are starting to tee me off, Jerome. I'm not a snoop. But we'd both have to be fools not to think that something pretty odd is going on around here, don't you think? I mean . . . look at it carefully. Your messages and letters are being thrown out. Nobody can explain Maneray's continued employment at the hotel. Duffy has these vague 'meetings' he has to go to all the time and flies out of here in that black ensemble he thinks is so stylish . . . Jesus Christ, Jerome . . . the guy's been working here since he was eighteen years old . . . we don't know how long he's been carrying that Life Extension Institute thing around with him. Hattie's a nice woman and all, but I still think it's a little strange that she's got that house across the street that she won't even go into . . . and she wanders in that garden at night like she's looking for something and now she's out there picking geraniums at midnight. Nothing adds up."

"Sorry. I didn't mean to rile you . . . but at the same time we don't know that any of these things are connected. They may all be just a collection of oddities all converged here at the hotel."

"I'm not saying that they're connected either . . . probably not.

But I don't think that a little investigation will hurt . . . it wouldn't do any harm to try and shed a little light on some of this strangeness, would it?"

"I suppose not . . . maybe we can check this Life Extension Institute thing out on Saturday."

"That's the spirit . . . might be fun . . . you never know what we'll find."

"I'm going to bed . . . I'll probably see you sometime in the afternoon."

"Ok . . . see you then." Jerome started to head out the door and quickly turned around.

"Damn . . . I forgot to tell you. I took a reservation after you went upstairs . . . geeze, I think I forgot to write it down, too. I'll call Ali and ask him to add it to the list."

"Who is it?" asked Tim.

"Some guy named James Parrish . . . nothing unusual except that he's in a wheelchair."

"Didn't you tell him that we don't have an elevator here!"

"Yeah . . . but he couldn't get a room anyplace else. Room 205 is vacant tomorrow and it's right at the top of the front staircase." Tim looked at Jerome like he was crazy.

"Are you telling me that I have to pull him up that front staircase in his wheelchair?" Tim yelped ". . . and then bring him down every time he wants to go out?!"

"Well, yeah . . . sort of, I guess . . . he said he'd have a friend along but he wanted to know if there would be anybody at the front desk who would be strong enough to lend a hand . . . I mean, I'd do it except I won't be here when he checks in."

"Let's hope Mr. Duffy isn't on duty when he gets here."

"Actually, I told him that it would be best if he checked in around four o'clock or so . . . that way Mr. Duffy would be gone and Hattie would already be inside for her afternoon nap. I told him to be sure and ask for you."

"Goodnight, Jerome."

"C'mon Tim, be a sport . . . he just needs a little help, that's all. You swim four times a week . . . you could probably pull him up the stairs with one arm."

"Goodnight, Jerome."

"Great . . . I knew you wouldn't mind. See you tomorrow. Take good notes for me!"

"Goodnight, Jerome."

"Night!"

THE GRAYLOCK

Chapter Eighteen

Jerome left by the hotel's front door in the morning. He did not feel like a full breakfast from Polly and did not want to hurt her feelings by refusing one. Neither did he want to run into Mr. Duffy for fear that he might ask why Jerome was calling after him yesterday afternoon.

Whatever transpired between Mr. Duffy and Hattie over the objectionable pamphlet was a private matter and Jerome did not want to be a part of it . . . at least for now. He had more important things on his mind this morning. He hoped he would find what he was looking for on the third degree up at the Library of Congress. He thought the topic was interesting and was pretty sure that if he presented it to Lucien in the right way he would agree.

He could hardly believe that a little bit more than a month had passed since he arrived in Washington and this was his first trip up to Capitol Hill. It was the first sight he saw coming out of the train station upon arrival and he thought for sure it would be one of the first places he would visit. But nothing had really gone according to his plan since his arrival anyway . . . except his obsession with criminal law. Law school was the right place for him and he knew it. For that he was grateful. He was also glad to have Tim at the hotel. He knew he could not bear all the bizarre behavior if he had no one comparably sane to talk to. He remembered his father's admonition that ". . . if those folks down there are just not to your liking, then you come home." Without Tim at the hotel, as much as Jerome did not like to admit it, he may have seriously thought of heading back to Buttermilk Falls and plead with the administrators of Cornell Law School to let him in even if he had to wait a year. He was learning quite a lot in his classes and the rest of his classmates were friendly enough, but none of them had to live at The Graylock. Only Tim understood the unusual existence they both had after the classes were over. Most of the time, they both told their friends that they "had a place a few blocks away on N Street." They never asked anybody from the school to meet them there. Primarily because they did not want anyone to be dismissively insulted by Maneray. Hattie would be intriguing for most anybody to meet, but it had to be on a good night. Without his compatriot on the fourth floor, Jerome would probably have become what his cab driver, Jake, had said ". . . battier 'n hell in no time."

Jerome decided to walk up to Capitol Hill on Pennsylvania Avenue rather than Massachusetts Avenue. The sights were better and he could have a look at parts of the city he'd not seen before. As much as he enjoyed being with Tim, it was relaxing to be out on his own. He had the whole day to enjoy and did not want to rush through it. He sauntered up Pennsylvania Avenue and his mind wandered to what it might be like to work for the government. He stopped in front of the Department of Justice at Pennsylvania Avenue and 10th Street to stare for a bit. He was aware that freshly graduated law students could land jobs in the Criminal Division and thought how that might strike him . . . to be a federal prosecutor for the United States Government. Assuming that he'd get re-elected, FDR would be in the third year of his second term by the time Jerome graduated from law school. Working as a federal prosecutor would be a great job but it also meant that he would essentially be working for FDR under the layers of the Attorney General and several Assistant Attorney Generals. Jerome got a kick out of the notion that working for his hero was such a possibility. The thought of working for Alf Landon left him cold. He didn't think he'd be able to get out of bed in the morning to go to work if that were the case . . . he'd rather milk cows on his father's farm. "Roosevelt is going to win anyway, so what's the worry?" he whispered to himself. "Hattie will just have to live with it." The only problem was that with 35 days left before the November election, Landon led FDR by a margin of 2-1 in New York, Pennsylvania, New Jersey and Maine in the most recent Literary Digest Poll.

Jerome could not decide if the Capitol Building looked more impressive from the front or the back. The approach to it, walking up Pennsylvania Avenue, was more than impressive. It was memorable. It was a sweeping picture of history kept alive by the legislators of the New Deal. Whatever shape the country was taking to rise from the ashes of The Great Depression were getting the final touches and preliminary stamp of approval right up until the time the news bills were signed into law under the signature of Franklin Delano Roosevelt . . . 31st President of the United States. All of his thirty predecessors, from George Washington to Herbert Hoover, signed bills into law from partisan Congresses of varying degrees and Jerome knew that one could not work without the other. But it was not until he got to the back side of Capitol Hill, where he could no longer see the White House but was closer to the United States Supreme Court building than he'd ever dreamed of, did he get the full impact of a government at work. Ideas were sent back and forth from the Congress to the White House until they took the form of a bill ready for the president's signature. Whether it was good or bad law would eventually be decided by the Supreme Court. It was a constant flow of ideas, bills, laws and decisions moving amongst them all in a triangle of democracy that had been going on since the time of George Washington, John Adams and Thomas Jefferson. Jerome was tempted to the edge to go over to the Supreme Court Building for the day, but realized that he'd look like a fool in Professor Lucien's office tomorrow morning if he was unprepared. Reluctantly, he strode over to the Library of Congress situated next to the Supreme Court on the same side of the street. One place for the knowledge to be written down . . . the other a place for it to be stored. Jerome was going in to uncover some knowledge.

The law library was on the third floor, but he could hardly drag himself out of the main reading room. This was a library the likes of which he had never seen. The cathedral-like vaulted ceiling with its dome cover and overall rotunda shape was unmatched by any research facility he'd been in before. A phalanx of librarians stationed at certain points around the inside periphery of the circulation desk looked to be the ready dispensers of what to look for and where to find it. A quiet humming buzz and the mild flipping of book pages were the only sounds that echoed up to the dome of the room. The discovery of knowledge through the ages reverberated through the room. It made the preparation for his meeting tomorrow seem all the more imperative to Jerome. He approached one of the stationed, waiting librarians and asked if the law library was open and if, in fact that would be the best place to locate information about the third degree. The librarian quietly responded in the affirmative to both questions and directed Jerome to the hallway leading to the back of the main reading room where he would find the elevators.

The librarian at the circulation desk in the law library was equally as helpful. "We have a good deal of information on the third degree" he offered nicely. "Are you interested in something in particular?"

"I'd like to start off with some general background information ... something to give myself a basic idea of its history" replied Jerome.

The librarian pointed to the second floor of the law library. "If you'll go up there and make your way to the third aisle down the first row, I think you'll find what you are looking for on the fourth shelf from the top of the stacks. If you need any more help, don't be afraid to ask." The small black metal nameplate affixed to his suit jacket lapel said "Mr. Ross" and Jerome thanked him appropriately.

Mr. Ross was correct. There was a whole shelf full of material on the third degree. Jerome was not sure where to begin. He did not exactly have to start writing his paper today and knew that deep research might be futile until Lucien gave him the green light on the subject. He fingered and thumbed his way through some of the volumes for awhile until he happened upon one he found more interesting than the others. "Eliminating the Third Degree: A New Plan to Obtain Evidence" by Professor Raymond B. Motley. The introduction of the book explained that Motley was a professor of Public Law at Columbia Law School in New York City.

"Perfect" smiled Jerome to himself. "The whole first chapter is a history of the third degree ... Columbia, too ... I'll bet that Lucien knows him ... at least they were on the same faculty ... what a stroke of luck." More Reed luck ... just when he needed it. Jerome read through the chapter carefully and made plenty of notes. He was surprised to learn that Motley could trace the beginnings of the third degree as far back as 1664 when magistrates in England used wily methods to obtain confessions from suspected criminals. Jerome liked the idea of combining the history of the practice with the modem day cases of outright brutality employed by police to literally beat confessions out of suspects. The level of brutality had become so offensive to the public that in some states an outcry for its prohibition had become an issue for voters to decide at the election booths.

One of the volumes that Jerome had stacked at his table recounted a case in 1932 where a New Jersey woman had taken her life and that of her five year old daughter because, as her suicide note read, the police had relentlessly harassed her and her husband, a shell-shocked war veteran, about an auto accident in which a small child had been run over and killed. "They tried to put the blame on us and I warned them about my husband's condition but they continued to put us through the third degree." The woman's body was found in a locked automobile in a tightly closed garage at the rear of their home. The 30-year old mother and her daughter died from carbon monoxide fumes from the idling engine of her automobile. The stress of the police's third degree tactics caused the woman's husband to repeatedly disappear leaving her with no income or means of support and so she decided to end her life and take her daughter with her.

A different chapter laid out the execution of a North Carolina convict . . . a 22- year old Negro who died in the gas chamber in early 1936 taking only twelve and one-half minutes to succumb to the deadly, poisonous gases. He had been tried and convicted of murdering an 18-year old co-ed. The foundation of the prosecutor's case was the young man's confession which he apparently offered up after two merciless days of the Asheville police's third degree. For nearly a month the murder had baffled police and was only laid to rest after they had the confession in hand. Right up until the time the executioner closed the door of the gas chamber behind him, the convict continued his repudiation of his confession saying that it had been beat out of him.

Legitimately guilty or honestly innocent both of these lives had been snuffed out because of a heavy element involving the third degree. Jerome spent the next two hours pouring over similar cases, filling half a notebook in the process. He stopped when he felt he had more than enough information to carry him through what he thought would probably be the no more than fifteen minutes Lucien might give him to state his case for a paper on the third degree. He returned the volumes to the shelf and went back down to the circulation desk to ask Mr. Ross one more question. He had one more case he wanted to read about.

"Excuse me" he said "but does the library keep back copies of *The Washington Post?*"

"Yes we do" replied Mr. Ross. "How far back did you need to go?"

"I was wondering if I could get copies for the whole week of July 2, 1902."

"1902" said Ross plaintively. "I'm pretty sure we have them that far back . . . but you wouldn't be able to get them today. I'd have to check first and if we have them, I'd have to request them from storage. Newspapers that old are not housed on the premises. How soon did you need to look at them?"

"Well . . . not right away, of course. Do you think it would take more than a week?"

"I'm sure we can get them before then. Why don't you write your name and telephone number down on this piece of paper and if I can get them, I'll call you to let you know they're here . . . that was the whole week's worth you were interested in?"

"Yes, please" said Jerome politely. "The week of July 2, 1902."

Mr. Ross took the paper from Jerome and looked at it. "Very well, Mr. Reed . . . if I can get them, I'll call you straight away."

"Thank you." Jerome walked away and decided to take the stairs out to the street.

THE GRAYLOCK

Chapter Nineteen

The slow walk back to The Graylock in the mid-day afternoon sun was a treat for Jerome. He felt wonderful. He stopped in Lafayette Square again and sat for awhile to read his notes from the library. He had been thinking about his research all the way home and he decided exactly how he would present it to Professor Lucien. There was no question in Jerome's mind that Lucien would like the idea. Jerome, himself, had already decided that it was a good topic and once he set his mind on something . . . that was it. It was his well-hewn, steely Reed determination that vaulted him into a singular frame of mind. He enjoyed the research because he liked learning new things. He had an active mind that needed to be stimulated by a constant flow of new information. The law would be a good feeding ground for him.

As he closed the garden's back gate behind him after walking up the alleyway, Jerome saw a young man . . . perhaps close to his own age . . . sitting near the ivy patch in the back corner of the garden. Jerome knew instantly that it must be James Parrish because he was in a wheelchair. He was surprised because for some odd reason he expected Mr. Parrish to be a much older man . . . at least that's how he sounded when Jerome took his reservation. But, at first sight, he didn't look to be any more than 22 or 23 years old. He was a handsome, strawberry blond with a strong jaw and an upper body and arms that were in compassionate contrast with the spindly legs that kept him bound to the wheelchair. Jerome walked over and introduced himself as the fellow who took his reservation last night. James' handshake was like an iron vice coming from deceptively gentle looking hands.

"Nice to meet you, Jerome" was the pleasant response. "Thanks for taking my reservation at the last minute . . . I was really in a spot. Not a lot of hotels were willing to book me after I told them that I was in a wheelchair. I think that they assumed I'd be too much bother . . . or risk. But I am pretty adept at getting around on my own as much as I can."

"It's not a bother at all here. I hope the room's alright."

"Everything's just fine. Your friend at the desk, Tim, was a terrific help getting me settled." Jerome smiled at the thought of Tim being at his most charming best. "Tim's a good man to have around" said Jerome ". . . that's for sure." Jerome heard the screen door slam and watched Polly round the corner wall with a small tray in her hand. She motioned for Jerome and James to come closer to one of the outdoor tables Hattie had in the garden. "Y'all boys come on down here now!" she shouted. James began to move the wheels of his chair with his hands and Jerome asked if he could help. "Nope . . . thanks anyway . . . I'm pretty used to doing this!"

Polly set the tray on the table while James wheeled himself into place. "Mr. Parrish . . . the Mrs. wanted you to have just a bite to eat seeins that you might be tuckered out from yo' travels an' all . . . it's jes a little sandwich I fixed up in my kitchen an' some nice iced tea. I hope you like it."

"How could he help but like it if you fixed it?!" said Jerome as he leapt over the ivy and geranium swirl at the base of the Georgia pine tree. "Hi ya, Polly" he beamed as he grabbed a seat next to James.

"Where you been all this day, Jerome? I ain't seen yo' handsome face since long gone yesterday . . . you been over at the law school all this time?" Polly asked. She was in her genuinely good mood.

"I was up at the Library of Congress looking a few things up for a meeting I have tomorrow with one of my professors."

"An' on an empty stomach again, I bet" replied Polly as she shook her head ". . . I 'spect you'll be needin' a sandwich too."

Jerome was about to take Polly up on her offer when James interrupted. "You can have half of mine if you like . . . I actually had a little snack that I ate in my room before Tim brought me out into the garden . . . I don't mind sharing." James put half of the ham sandwich into a napkin and gave it to Jerome.

"That's real nice of you, Mr. Parrish" said Polly. "If you need anythin' at all you jes tell ol' Polly here an' I'll git it for you . . . if half a sandwich don't fill you up . . . you jes say so an' I kin make another."

"Thanks very much" said James "and please thank Mrs. Crickmore for me, too."

"You can thank her yourself, if you want too . . . the Mrs. says she very much would like you to have dinner with her tonight, if you is free, that is."

"Sure . . . that's fine with me . . . it's not like I'll be roaming around town or anything!" James joked. Polly was not sure how to receive the humor but it cracked Jerome up. He laughed and said James might be sorry no matter how hungry he was tonight. "I hope you're a Republican!" James shook his head. Like most young men his age or Jerome's or Tim's . . . he was for FDR. "Should be a fun night for you then . . . sorry I'm going to miss it."

"Mr. Jerome . . . don't you go makin' no jokes bout the Mrs. and her dinners. . . . 'sides . . . you ain't gone ta miss nothin' anyhow."

"What do you mean . . . I'm not on duty tonight!" Jerome

protested.

"You is now, Mr. Jerome" Polly chortled with the last laugh. "You sho' is now! The Mrs. done invited that Mr. Lewis and Mr. Parrish here fo' supper an' she wants both you and Tim downstairs to help."

"Who's Mr. Lewis?" asked James.

"Oh, God . . . not him!" said Jerome.

"Now Mr. Jerome don't go makin' fun o' no guests 'round here . . . it ain't nice . . . 'sides Mr. Lewis been comin' here for a long time now an' . . . ." Jerome interrupted her. "But, Polly . . . the guy is a little strange."

"Don't make no nevermind nohow . . . the Mrs. done invited him to join y'all an' that's that!"

"I don't see why Tim can't handle it . . . where is he anyway?"

Just then a window flew open from the third floor and Tim was hanging halfway out flailing his arms about and making faces. "Polly . . . Polly help me. . . . I think I'm going to fall!!" Jerome busted up with laughter at the sight of his friend faking a fall to the garden below.

Polly threw her hand on her ample hips and shouted up at him. "Mr. Timothy . . . you best git yo'self inside o' that window fast fo' I gives you what for! Why you hangin' outta there like some jackass hollerin' in a field? I asked you ta bring towels up to Mr. Lewis' room an' git back down here quick . . . I didn't tell you nothin' bout' foolin' 'round in no window!!! I'm gone ta beat you with my broom when you git down here . . . that's what!!!"

"I don't know what I'm gone ta do with the eithers of yous young boys" she said to Jerome as she retied her apron. "I jes don't know."

Tim yelled again . . . this time to Jerome. "Hey . . . Jerome did you get . . . ." Polly cut him right off. "I jes done told you Mr. Timothy, you ain't got no business hollerin' like yous out in a field somewheres!!!"

"Yeah . . . but I have to find out if Jerome . . . ." She cut Tim off again.

"Mr. Timothy . . . don't you worry nothin' 'bout Mr. Jerome . . . an' if I hears you one mo' time tryin' to bring him into yo' troubles, I'm gone ta beat you blue . . . that's what!! Now you git yo'self inside o' that window an' downstairs right now!!" Polly turned and made her way back to the side door, but not before she noticed one thing. "Jerome, go on up into the ivy patch an' pick up those dead geraniums in the corner there for ol' Polly, will you . . . the Mrs. don't like to see nothin' but live flowers about."

Jerome excused himself from James' table for a moment and walked up to the ivy patch. They must be the geraniums he and Tim saw Hattie picking last night at midnight he thought. He stepped over the iron posts at the edge of the patch and gathered up the few that he saw. He was just about to walk over and toss them into the garbage shed when he noticed a few more that had fallen deeper into the patch a few feet away. He stepped carefully so as not to crush too much of the ivy under his feet and bent over to pick up the few remaining stems. In doing so, he felt his fingers brush against what seemed like a flat stone that had been covered up. He picked up the last geranium and curiously moved some of the ivy aside. It was larger than an ordinary garden stone. He pushed the ivy further aside and saw that it was a single flat slab embedded in the dirt. He bent further down and nearly stopped breathing when he saw an inscription on the dark gray slab: "My Edmund 1864-1902".

He took two leaping steps and hopped out of the ivy patch nearly falling backwards in the process. "Good god" he gasped. "Has Hattie got her husband buried out here in the back of the hotel!"

He tried to mask his astonishment at this discovery so as not to alert James and quickly turned towards the shed to throw the geraniums in the garbage.

When he lifted James into the side entrance of the hotel, Tim greeted them both at the entrance of the tool room. "Can I give you guys a hand?" he asked cheerily. James responded graciously to the offer and wondered if it would be too much trouble to be brought back to his room until it was time for dinner. Jerome easily maneuvered the front stair case with James in his wheelchair and after he got him comfortably settled in Room 205 again, excused himself with the reminder for James to ring the switchboard when he was ready to come down again. When he closed the door behind him, he flew down the front stairs and practically assaulted Tim, who was answering an outside call, with a wild motion for him to meet Jerome in the kitchen when he was finished.

"I have something important to tell you!" he mouthed to his friend. "Something very important!!"

Chapter Twenty

While Jerome waited for Tim in the kitchen he noticed that he had efficiently already set up the three dinner trays for Hattie, Mr. Lewis and James Parrish. He heard Tim shout from the switchboard "Jerome . . . come give me a hand here . . . this thing is going crazy!"

It was unusual for Tim not to be able to handle all calls on the switchboard with ease. "Can you take this for awhile?" Tim asked.

"Yeah . . . but listen, I have to tell you . . . ."

"Can it wait?" Tim seemed more excited than agitated. He pulled a set of keys out his pants pocket and jingled them in front of Jerome. "These, my friend, are the keys to the house across the street . . . Hattie wants me to turn the lights on since Maneray's not here . . . I volunteered gladly as I'm sure you can guess . . . I can't wait to see what I find over there!"

"Tim" replied Jerome ". . . you're not going to find anything like I found . . . ." Tim interrupted him again. "Like what you found in the library on the third degree . . . c'mon Jerome . . . tell me later . . . I want to get over there and back before she gets up from her nap . . . take over for me here, will you?" Without waiting, Tim skirted around the front desk still jingling the keys.

Jerome watched him dash across the street and disappear

inside the townhouse.

"Unless there's another body buried over there, whatever he finds is going to pale in comparison to that graveyard in the back." He saw the white light come on over Room 205 on the switchboard and hoped that James did not want to come back down so soon. He didn't want to leave the switchboard unattended while Tim was on his treasure hunt in the townhouse.

"Hi, James. This is Jerome. Everything alright up there?"

"No problems. Thanks" said James, but he paused for a moment.

"You sure?" asked Jerome.

"Yeah . . . I'm fine. But, do you think Mrs. Crickmore will mind if I don't have dinner with her and that other fellow tonight? I'm feeling a little tired and I want to turn in early, but I have a lot to organize before I got over to the White House tomorrow morning."

"The White House!" exclaimed Jerome "you're going to the White House . . . what for?"

"It's kind of a long story . . . but I'm supposed to be there bright and early and I don't want to get stuck in the dining room all night . . . Tim told me earlier that her dinners can go on and on sometimes."

"He's right . . . they sure can. Don't worry about it . . . I'll square it with Hattie for you. It's probably best that she doesn't know you're going to see the President anyway . . . she has a tendency to get a little heavy handed when she talks about him. Tell you what . . . one of us will bring the dinner up to you after we get her settled . . . no need for you to miss one of Polly's specialties . . . we can run it up the back stairs . . . courtesy of the house."

"Thanks . . . you sure she won't mind?"

"She'll never know about it . . . wouldn't mind even if she did. Is seven o'clock too late for you to eat'?"

"Nope . . . that's fine . . . whenever you get a chance." Jerome disconnected the line and looked through one of the front windows to see any sign of a returning Tim. There was none. He started to look through his notes again to make sure he had a good grasp of everything he wanted to say to Lucien tomorrow morning.

The incessant ringing of the switchboard stopped and Jerome thought this was a perfect time to try and call home again. He had calmed down a bit since seeing the slab in the ivy patch and preferred to think that it was a memorial to Hattie's husband that had been grown over with the passing decades . . . rather than his burial plot. The operator put him through and he grinned when he heard his father's voice.

"Hi dad!! . . . It's me . . . Jerome!"

"Well, hello there stranger! How are you? Your mother and I were beginning to think we put the wrong address on our letter. Did you get it?"

Jerome wanted to be careful not to actually lie to his father, but did not want to let on about the strange goings on at The Graylock either. "Oh, I got it alright, dad . . . there was just some mix-up in the mail delivery, but I did eventually get it . . . I got Stevie's letter, too. How is he doing?

"Oh, much, much better. The doctors took his stitches out two days ago and there's hardly even a trace of a scar . . . it's so little. But, it was a close one there for a bit . . . we were afraid we were going to lose him."

"It was that bad?" Jerome was feeling an overwhelming surge of homesickness. For the first time since he arrived in Washington, he actually felt like he would rather be in Buttermilk Falls.

"It was pretty bad, son. He should never have been in the barn and he knew it . . . but you know how stubborn he can be . . . worse than you."

"What was he doing in there?" asked Jerome with a worry in

his voice.

"Well, he was trying to help out after you left . . . I told him not to mind . . . but he went in there one afternoon after school when I was out in the fields . . . Gail found him in a heap on the barn floor wheezing his last breaths right there. She dragged him out of the barn and started giving him a resuscitation right on the ground. Your mother saw them both from the upstairs bedroom window and ran out fast as she could . . . they put Stevie in the car and drove like hell to the hospital. I didn't know anything about it until I came in from the fields a couple of hours later. I called out to your mother in the house and nobody answered and then I saw a bit of a mess on the stairs and couldn't find Stevie or Gail in the house. I couldn't figure out what was going on myself especially since I saw the car was gone. Thank God the phone rang in the living room not too long after I got inside. I don't mind telling you I was getting a little worried. But everything's alright now . . . back to normal."

Jerome was shaken at his father's recounting of the experience. It was not the whitewashing his mother had given the tale in her letter, but he realized now that she probably did not want to have him worry over something he could do nothing about. "Are you sure everything's ok, dad?" asked Jerome needing the paternal reassurance.

"Everything's fine, Jerome. How are things down there. You're first letter didn't say too much." The first letter was written three days after Jerome arrived in Washington. His father would not believe what had happen since then.

"School's going great . . . most of it is pretty interesting and it's not as hard as I thought it would be . . . it's just a lot a work . . . mostly a lot of reading. I'm really doing especially well in my criminal law class."

"Now I wonder why that does not surprise me at all!" his

father teased. "Are you managing ok with that hotel setup? Can you handle both at once . . . work and school?" Jerome wanted to sidestep this question entirely . . . and he was saved by the bell . . . several bell's in fact . . . three incoming calls at once.

"I'm learning to balance it ok . . . listen dad, I have to go. I'm on the switchboard right now and there are a few calls coming in. Give mom my love and say hi to the kids for me. Tell Stevie I got his letter, ok?! I'll try to write him back this week."

"Ok, son. You take care of yourself, now. We miss you terribly."

"I miss you, too. Bye."

"So long"

Jerome put two of the incoming calls on hold and answered the first. Took a reservation from the second. It was Maneray on the third line. Jerome was barely civil to him. "Tell Mrs. Crickmore that I've had some car trouble and I won't be back until Monday now" was all he said before he hung the phone up in Jerome's ear. Miffed, he continued to speak as though Maneray were still on the line. "Then I guess we'll just have to settle our score on Monday, won't we Mr. Maneray?"

Jerome watched the lights go on in the townhouse and assumed he'd see Tim returning right thereafter. He watched for a bit but saw no sign of Tim. "He's poking around in there . . . I just know it." He wanted to tell him what he saw in the garden. Maybe it was no big deal. People put shrines and memorials up to deceased loved ones all the time . . . and they weren't always in the cemetery. But something just struck Jerome in an odd way about Hattie's memorial to "My Edmund" and he wanted to see if Tim saw it the same way. She never, ever spoke about her husband. In fact she never spoke about having been married. If Polly didn't consistently refer to Hattie as the "Mrs." neither of the boys would be reminded that she ever had a husband. He wanted to think nothing of it . . . all of his wondering was nothing more than mere speculation at this point, but his keen Reed instincts told him that something was amiss.

His wandering speculations were cut short when he heard Tim come in the front door. He had a blank look on his face which gave no indication that he'd uncovered anything but dust over there. Tim walked through the front lobby, passed Hattie's room and tapped the front desk a couple of times motioning to Jerome to follow him into the kitchen.

"What did you find?"

Tim ran his fingers through his hair and now had a fully bemused look on his face. "You wouldn't believe it. It's a fully furnished house . . . all four stories. All the bedrooms are fully made up . . . towels, linens . . . the works. There's a library stacked with books . . . the living room on the second floor had a huge piano in it . . . there's wood next to the fireplace. The dining room table is laid out for eight and there's silver candelabras everywhere. There's some of those bizarre oil portraits of God only knows who, like she has in the lobby, all over the place. But as full of stuff as it is the place has this empty feel all around it . . . and there's not a photograph of a single soul anywhere. There's three fancy picture frames on the floor next to the couch in the living room, but no photographs in them. The kitchen is full of pots and pans and dishes.

"Nothing's covered up? No sheets or anything over the furniture?"

"Nope . . . you could move in tomorrow. It needs a good cleaning, though."

Jerome was just about to share his discovery in the ivy patch when the switchboard started to ring again. "Don't go anywhere" he said to Tim. "I have something I have to tell you."

The call was for him. It was Mr. Ross from the Library of

Congress. "Mr. Jerome Reed, please" he said.

"This is Jerome."

"Mr. Reed . . . this is Mr. Ross from the Library of Congress. I have located your newspapers from 1902."

"Wonderful" replied Jerome. "That was fast work."

"Thank you. It really was nothing more than a couple of telephone calls. The good news is that, if you like, you can look at them tomorrow. There's a delivery being made from the storage house and they've put your papers on it."

"Tomorrow . . . that's great." Jerome wanted to see them as soon as possible, but knew that he has his meeting with Professor Lucien after class and he had to be on duty at the switchboard at three o'clock. "On second thought, Mr. Ross, tomorrow's going to be a busy day for me. I won't be able to get up to the library. Are you open on Saturday?"

"Yes we are . . . but only until three in the afternoon. Can you make it up here by then?"

"Yes, I can. Saturday will be a much better day for me."

"Fine then. We open at ten in the morning. Like I said I'll be here at the front desk until three o'clock. Just ask for me."

"Thanks Mr. Ross . . . see you then."

Jerome went back into the kitchen to hear the rest of Tim's story . . . and anxious to tell him about the secret in the garden.

"Listen . . . you'll never guess what I saw in the garden this afternoon." Tim was distracted. His mind still fumbling through what he saw in the townhouse. "You know, Jerome . . . Duffy was suppose to go over and switch those lights on instead of me. But he was in another of his usual rushes to get out of here today. Polly said that he and Hattie had some words after breakfast, but didn't know what it was about."

"Do you think she knew and just wasn't saying anything?'

"No . . . she's too pure to tell a fib. But Duffy was acting pretty strange when I got here at three o'clock . . . not his usual kind of strange either. It was like he definitely did not want to go across the street no matter what Hattie said."

Jerome said nothing for a minute trying to make some sense of it all. "I don't understand" he finally said. "Something's not adding up here . . . especially since I think that ivy patch out there is really . . . ."

"Boys! Boys . . . where are you? . . . there's no one at the front desk." Hattie was up. It was more like she was resurrected. "Don't let on like we think there's anything wrong, Jerome. We don't have anything concrete yet."

"Wait a minute!" Jerome protested. "You haven't heard my story yet."

Too late. The estimable Mrs. Crickmore opened the kitchen door and stood in the doorway smiling broadly at the two. "There you boys are again . . . huddled in the kitchen . . . and looking too suspicious for your own good! What is this big pow-pow about?!" she joked.

Hattie looked like she had been transformed . . . or at least transformed back to her old self. She was a far cry from the somnambulant geranium picker they spotted in the garden last night at midnight. She was in high spirits and looked wonderful. Her hair was perfectly set and she was dressed as though she were about to take in a night out on the town. The sparkle was back in her eyes and the color back in her face. She was ready to entertain.

Tim jumped in to deflect any further questions about their "pow-pow" in the kitchen. "Hattie" he said with an honest surprise. "You look great . . . you must be feeling better."

"I feel wonderful, Timothy. Thank you. Whatever I had is gone now and I'm back. I hope Polly has made us a feast for tonight. I think my stomach is ready for it!" She squeezed both the boys on their shoulders. "How are you boys doing? I'm glad you're both here."

"Well, since you asked Hattie . . . Jerome and I were trying to figure out a way to avoid Mr. Freethinker tonight!!" said Tim. He knew she didn't really want to know why they were talking in the kitchen and he was taking advantage of the moment to switch to Hattie's favorite topic . . . The Graylock and its guests.

"Oh now don't be silly, Tim . . . Mr. Lewis is a fairly harmless man . . . a little eccentric . . . but then that's his right to be that way if he chooses. We all have our oddities, don't you think?"

Jerome looked at Tim not knowing what to say. "Jerome, dear . . . you have a much too serious look on your face. I hope you're not getting burdened down with your studies . . . you must leave some time for fun in your life."

As they suspected, Jerome and Tim did not hear a word about last night. Hattie showed no sign of the "miseries" today and there was no indication that she had "words" with Mr. Duffy earlier. She was in another of her classic good moods and was going to spread it infectiously.

"Jerome, take your mind off your worries and go out into the garden and clip me a few of those pretty roses, will you? I want to decorate the dining room tables with them." She pointed out the kitchen window to the rose beds, but Jerome could not tell if she cast her eyes towards the ivy patch. "I just love to have pretty flowers around . . . it lifts everyone's spirits so."

Jerome grabbed the clipper from the tool room and wondered if the roses, too, would find their way into the ivy patch after Hattie used them for decoration.

"Timmy, my dear . . . set me up a drink tray. Mr. Lewis and Mr. Parrish will be down soon and I'm in the mood to entertain!"

THE GRAYLOCK

Chapter Twenty-One

Jerome just finished clipping a half dozen roses when he saw Hattie waltz into the garden. She was humming an unrecognizable tune and Jerome did his best to avert his eyes from an unintended glance towards the ivy patch. "Oh, those are beautiful Jerome" she said pointing at the roses in his hand. "How about clipping a few of the forsythia branches up there . . . the yellow will compliment the roses beautifully." When he was done he walked towards her. "What's on your mind, Jerome. You don't look happy . . . not homesick are you?" Jerome did not want to let on.

"No" he replied not looking at her directly. She'd be able to tell if she looked too closely . . . everyone always could. Jerome was not good at hiding things. "I've just got this important meeting with my criminal law professor tomorrow after class and I guess I'm a little preoccupied."

"Not in trouble at school, I hope!" she teased. "You struck me from the beginning as one who would be the best in the class."

Jerome smiled at the compliment. "No . . . it's nothing like that. I have a paper to write and I want to make sure that I present the research properly . . . that's all."

She took the cut flowers from him and took a short whiff. "I'm sure you'll do wonderfully. What topic have you decided to impress this professor what's-his-name with?"

"His name's Lucien . . . Professor Lucien and I'm going to write a paper on the tactic of using the third degree in obtaining confessions from criminal suspects." Hattie squinted her eyes and looked up at the tall pine tree. "What's the matter . . . too sunny out here?"

"No . . ." she said without too much thought "that name, though, has a familiar ring to it." She took another whiff of the flowers. "No matter . . . when you've checked as many people into this hotel as I have a lot of names begin to sound the same . . . Let's go back inside and put these flowers in some water."

Hattie took Jerome's arm and they headed towards the screen door. "Oh, by the way, James Parrish . . . the guy in the wheelchair . . . isn't coming down for dinner. He hoped you wouldn't mind. He going over the White House tomorrow morning for something . . . I don't know what . . . he didn't say . . . but he wants to turn in early."

"The White House! My goodness . . . I wonder why he's going over there?" Jerome shrugged. "I told him we'd bring a dinner tray up to him instead . . . if that's alright with you."

"Of course! Give it to him whenever he wants. I can't wait to find out what that son of a bitch Roosevelt has to say to him."

Jerome just rolled his eyes. "Hattie . . . did you ever think that maybe he's going to see Eleanor?"

"He'd be a damn sight better off if that were the case. There's a woman to be proud of."

"Well, she married the President didn't she?"

"Everybody makes mistakes, Jerome. Everybody makes mistakes. You shouldn't have to pay your whole life for them! Too bad Eleanor's was Franklin."

Jerome said nothing. He only wondered if Hattie's mistake was Edmund. He hoped his mistake would not be living at The Graylock.

Mr. Lewis, the freethinker, showed up on the dot of eight o'clock in as lively a mood as Hattie. He still had his scraggly blue suit on but this time adorned it with a memorably ugly lime colored dress shirt with ruffles on the front and a fuchsia tie that was thrown over his shoulder like a scarf, but would have been too thin if he had worn it . . . like a nonfreethinker. He "wanted to show off his ruffles" was his unrequested explanation to Tim about his untied necktie. Nevertheless, he proved an amiable dinner companion for Hattie. They both sipped bourbon and chatted the night away. If he was not laughing at her derogatory references to FDR's presidency, she was chortling, equally amused, at his tirade against the Catholic Church.

"Mr. Lewis, you are a wonder" she quipped during dinner. "How do you truly expect to win a lawsuit against the pope . . . he's a very powerful man."

"Powerful nothing . . . why he's just a bother that's all . . . a real pain in the ass. He's rich though, I'll bet you that. That's why I had to hurry up and sue him . . . he won't be very powerful after he's dead!"

"Is the pope dying?" Hattie asked without any real interest. "I hadn't read anything about it in the newspapers."

"Oh the poor man" said Lewis scornfully "they say he has varicose veins now . . . he may never walk again. 'Irregular heart action' is the latest diagnosis. What do they expect? He's 79 years old! If you ask me he's suffering from the infirmities of old age. And now nobody can get in to see him because he's depressed, the poor bastard . . . except that Cardinal Pacelli, who's probably trying on the pope's robes when His Holiness isn't looking."

Tim heard Mr. Lewis prattling on from the front desk and thought if anybody should be trying on some new clothes it should be Mr. Lewis. He was just as happy when Hattie voiced no objection to his not joining them for dinner. He begged off with the excuse that he wanted to study at the front desk and after he helped Jerome fix a dinner tray for James Parrish, he did just that. He eavesdropped on their dinner conversation only as a distraction from his cases on Civil Procedure.

The conversation went on for another hour or so. Church and State . . . State and Church . . . Roosevelt and the pope . . . power and politics . . . the pope and politics . . . Roosevelt and power . . . Roosevelt and everything. "We need a new president more than we need a new pope" was how Hattie brought the evening to a close. Mr. Lewis thanked her for the dinner and the "stimulating conversation" as he put it. "I always consider you a freethinker, Mrs. Crickmore even if I can't get you to join my organization."

She walked him past the front desk where Tim was studying. "I don't join organizations anymore, Mr. Lewis. I learned early on in life that you're better off on your own. Good Night. It was nice to see you again." She and Lewis parted company and Hattie knew that'd he be back again someday to file another law suit . . . probably wearing the same blue suit. For all his freethinking ideas, Hattie found Mr. Lewis rather predictable . . . always had.

"Everything ok with you, Tim?" she asked standing at the door to her room. Tim nodded. "You were kind of quiet tonight . . . both you boys have been quiet. Where's Jerome?"

"Upstairs . . . We have a lot of case reading to do right now."

"Ok . . . I'm not trying to pry . . . just want to make sure everything's alright with my boys!" Tim smiled back. Maybe all this weirdness is just an exaggerated sense of eccentricity after all, he thought. She can be so nice sometimes.

"Listen, Tim . . . that young man in Room 205 . . . Mr. Parrish?"

"Yes, that's him . . . James Parrish . . . the one in the wheelchair."

"Right . . . Jerome told me that he is scheduled for an early morning meeting at the White House tomorrow. Can one of you boys get up early and see that he gets down the stairs and out to his car alright?"

"I'll do it" volunteered Tim.

"Thanks, dear. I'll see you boys tomorrow. Sleep tight." She went into her room and closed the pope, Mr. Lewis, James Parrish, the President and all the world behind her for another day. Tim hoped that Hattie would sleep tight, too. No midnight strolls in the garden tonight he hoped.

It was just past eleven when Tim knocked on Jerome's door.

"Hi . . . how was dinner with the freethinker?"

"I stayed away . . . sat at the front desk most of the night. They seemed to be having a good time, though. Nobody got out of control. Hattie was in rare form with Roosevelt! I can't figure out why she dislikes him so . . . it's a real passion with her" said Tim as he flopped onto Jerome's bed. "What are you doing'?"

Jerome pushed himself away from the desk and threw his legs up onto it. "Just finished re-reading my notes for the big meeting tomorrow . . . I am ready!" he shouted. "Writing this paper will be easy after this meeting."

Tim rubbed his eyes under his glasses and yawned. "You look beat . . . I thought you said the shift went by easily" remarked Jerome.

"It was alright . . . been worse nights, believe me. It's that house across the street that's bugging me. It's like Hattie is completely unaware of it except to want the lights on every night. You know she didn't even bother to ask me what I thought of the house . . . I think she knew that I was over there to flip the lights on."

"I thought you said she wanted Duffy to do it . . . maybe she still thinks he did."

"No, I doubt it. When he dashed out of here this afternoon, he told me where the keys were . . . I'm pretty sure she heard him.

Do you know what he said? He said 'I can't stand going over there . . . it makes me sick with bad memories.' That's as much as I have ever heard Mr. Duffy ever say in a personal way. And, believe me, the look on his face made it pretty clear that there was no way he was going over to that house. I never saw him like that."

"The way you described the inside seemed pretty innocuous though . . . except for the fact that it's fully furnished and no one lives there . . . that's the odd part."

"I think there's something more . . . there was a study and another room all the way in the back of the house on the first floor that I didn't get a good look at. I think I'll try again tomorrow."

Jerome dropped his legs flat on the floor and leaned towards Tim. "I can't believe I let you get me so far off track sometimes . . . ."

"Jerome . . . you are just as interested in this as me . . . admit it."

"That's not my point. No matter what you find snooping around over there . . . you can't match what I stumbled on by accident this afternoon out in the garden!"

"What?"

"Well, I can't for sure . . . but I think Hattie's husband might be buried in the ivy patch in the back corner of the garden."

Tim did not move a muscle. He barely took a breath. He stared at Jerome as though his friend were about to drive a stake through his heart. He could not speak. "Tim . . . did you hear me?" asked Jerome. Tim adjusted his glasses and sat upright on the bed. "Have you flipped?" he asked Jerome ". . . are you trying to tell me you think she's got a honest-to-goodness body buried out there?" He reached over and closed the bedroom door tightly . . . as though Hattie might be able to hear them four floors above her own bedroom. "I know things are weird around here . . . but maybe you're letting it get to you."

Jerome shook his head. "Nope. I know what I saw" he said with conviction. "I can't say for certain that's it a burial plot . . . but there's a big gray slab of granite or something covered up by the thick ivy in the corner there."

Tim was listening . . . simply bug-eyed. "Is there anything on it?"

"My Edmund 1864-1902" said Jerome. "And I practically jumped out of the ivy patch when it hit me that I might be standing on somebody's grave."

"Wait a minute . . . who's Edmund?"

"Aren't you listening to me?" balked Jerome. "Edmund is Hattie's husband!!"

"How do you know that?"

"I asked Polly a couple of weeks ago . . . just in passing. She told me his name was Edmund Crickmore."

"Jesus . . . I can't believe what I'm hearing . . . it's starting to make sense now."

Jerome agreed. "All those midnight strolls when she's had too much bourbon . . . she must be out there talking to her husband!"

"How did you find this out? I mean . . . what were you doing up in that ivy patch anyway?"

"Polly asked me to pick up some dead geraniums off the ivy . . . she said Hattie doesn't like to see any thing but live flowers around. I'm sure what I picked up were the geraniums we saw her picking around midnight. It looked like she just threw then into the patch and hoped they land near the gravestone?"

"Jesus Jerome . . . this is awful . . . do you really think it's a gravestone?"

"It sure looked like one to me" shrugged Jerome. "Is it against the law to bury somebody in your backyard? I mean who says everybody has to get buried in a cemetery?"

"I think you're skipping the big picture, here. He died in 1902, right? Washington was hardly the wild west . . . even then. I'm sure a cemetery plot was at least conventional . . . I wonder how he died?"

"I don't know . . . but I think it sheds a little light on that tirade she pulled when she threw all those people out of the hotel."

"Right!" said Tim as he snapped his finger. "She was a little drunk and kept calling King Edward VIII 'Edmund' by mistake . . . and I found her crying in the garden . . . all dirty. I'll bet she was up in that ivy patch when I was in the kitchen doing the dishes!"

"Didn't you ever wonder why she never talks about her husband?"

"I do now!" said Tim ". . . but when I put two and two together here, I still come up with three . . . something's missing and I'll bet it's in that house across the street . . . and I know for sure now that I'm going to find that Life Extension place on Saturday. Are you still coming with me?"

"I can't now . . . some material I asked for up at the Library of Congress has arrived . . . I have to go up on Saturday and look at it."

"No matter . . . I'll find it myself. I'll wait for you back here. Duffy's taking the whole morning, afternoon and night shift. We don't have to spell him at all. Are you going to be back here around dark tomorrow?" Jerome nodded. "Why?"

"I need you to cover the switchboard for me while I go back over to the house . . . I want to check those two back rooms out . . . if Maneray is coming back on Sunday, tomorrow will be my only day to do it. I'll never get back in there once he returns."

"Oh . . . that reminds me. He called this afternoon . . . he's not coming back until Monday . . . said he had car trouble."

"Fine with me . . . I hope he never comes back . . . but I'd better check those rooms out tomorrow anyway." Tim got up from the bed and opened the door. "I'm going to bed. I'm beat. God, I hope I don't see Hattie out in that garden tonight."

"'Night Tim. See you tomorrow."

The first thing Tim did when he got into his own room was to look out the back window. He did not see Hattie prowling about. There was no movement in the garden below. But he cast his eyes on the ivy patch . . . almost tempted to go down with a flashlight and see the granite slab for himself. He thought better of the idea and layed down in bed. He pulled his journal out from the small cabinet between the two beds and began to write.

"Dear Sam" he began to write. "I hope you're still watching over me because there are some strange people and some very strange things going on down here. Jerome doesn't look too worried, but I am. Keep a close eye out for me . . . ok?"

Tim closed the journal and tried to get some sleep.

THE GRAYLOCK

Chapter Twenty-Two

When Jerome opened his door to head for the shower early Friday morning, he found a breakfast tray outside his door. The cover was still warm and the coffee was hot. There was an inside section of the early edition of The Washington Post with a handwritten note along the top . . . "Good luck with your meeting this morning . . . don't take it on an empty stomach! Love, Hattie."

He picked the tray up and placed it on his desk. He poured himself a bit of Polly's delicious coffee and sat down to soak in the thoughtfulness of Hattie's gesture. He began to feel somewhat sneaky about his plans to snoop around Hattie's past with Tim. "Maybe it's none of our business" he mused while sipping another taste of the coffee. He picked up the phone to connect with the switchboard. Maybe Tim sent the tray up as one of his jokes . . . he was embarrassed with the possibility that Polly trekked up four flights of stairs to leave the tray at his door.

"Good morning, Mr. Reed. How are you this fine morning?" It was Hattie. She was working the switchboard at 7:20 in the morning. "The world must have started spinning in the opposite direction while I was asleep" joked Jerome. "Why are you up so early?"

"I felt like it" chuckled Hattie. "You know years ago I used to practically do everything myself here . . . except cook the breakfasts. This is just like old times for me this morning."

"Thanks so much for the breakfast tray . . . I could have come down for it. You didn't have to have Polly walk all the way up."

"She didn't!" quipped Hattie. "Mr. Duffy and I brought them up. One for you and one for Tim . . . by the way in case you're interested in the morning headlines . . . Tim got the front section of the newspaper. I know how you like the local flavor so I gave you Section Two." Jerome laughed at Hattie's none too subtle reference to his remark the night she dined with Mildred Pack.

"You enjoy your breakfast now and don't worry about us down here. We have everything under control."

Jerome capped the tray to keep the food warm and wrapped a towel around himself and went to take a shower. He saw a tray outside Tim's door as well, but he could tell that the food had already been eaten . . . a sure sign that Tim was already awake and well fed. Jerome knocked on the door and stuck his head inside.

"Hey . . . 'morning . . . breakfast in bed! Not bad, huh?" said Tim. He was already showered, fully dressed and sitting at his desk reading the front section of the newspaper. "Any more of this pampering and I'd likely forget that I still have to do a little checking around across the street!"

"Yeah . . . Tim . . . about that. I was thinking" he pause a second and wondered how he was going to say this. "I was thinking that maybe whatever it is, it might not be any of our business . . . maybe we'd better back off."

"Yeah . . . I thought about that too for just a moment before I got off duty last night. . . . and again this morning with the delivered breakfast and all, but I'm going ahead with it anyway. If there's nothing really wrong going on then we just keep our mouths shut and live with the weird behavior around here. If there is something fishy happening, then we have a right to know. We are more than guests here . . . Hattie has always wanted us to feel at home here . . . if there's something wrong in my home I want to know."

"Why can't we just ask her?"

"Great idea" snapped Tim. "Why don't you do that on your way to class this morning?" Jerome hung his head a bit and Tim felt a little guilty about being so abrupt. "Look, Jerome . . . she has a pattern of not answering questions that she doesn't want to . . . she's said herself that she doesn't like to deal with unpleasantness. Look how she reacted to our complaints about Maneray. Nothing is resolved and he's coming back in four days. She isn't going to tell us anything she does not want us to know. We have to find out for ourselves."

"I was just having some second thoughts about it. You said yourself that she can awfully nice sometimes . . . I mean . . . she's pretty good to us when you think about it."

"No denying it . . . I actually like her quite a bit . . . but I don't want to get blindsided by any more bizarre behavior. So . . . I'm going to poke around a little more this afternoon after you get back . . . if nothing's up then we'll close the book on it and just live with her eccentricities. Ok?"

"Ok . . . it's a deal. I'm going to get cleaned up and finish breakfast. I'll see you later this afternoon."

Jerome carried his notes on the third degree with him to class, but he knew he'd only have to look at them if Professor Lucien wanted specific reference sources named. Otherwise, he was completely prepared with his presentation. He sat in class and mostly listened to Lucien lecture on cases and elements of assault and battery. Jerome recited one case, just to make his presence known, but spent the rest of the time taking extra careful notes for Tim who was skipping class to help James Parrish get ready for his White House visit. Tim knew that if he could rely on anyone's notes from criminal law class it was Jerome's.

The wait in Lucien's office after class was so much longer than expected that Jerome began to wonder if the professor had forgotten about their meeting. Jerome tried in vain not to be too conspicuous a presence as he watched Mrs. Falk, Lucien's secretary, busy herself with the daily mail. He wondered what it was like to be around a man like Lucien all day long. Mrs. Falk was nice enough but did not seem overwhelmed at the idea of being so close to what Jerome regarded as a real role model. She looked as though she performed her tasks dutifully and went home. If she were reassigned to another of the school's professors, it might have suited her just the same.

"You look a little anxious, Mr. Reed" she said.

Jerome did not respond with either a "yes" or a "no". He wasn't sure if he was anxious or not. He knew he wanted to get the meeting over with and didn't understand the reason for the delay.

"Then professor shouldn't be too much longer now. He's been trying to contact the proper local authorities to make a report about an automobile accident he was in last night."

"I guess he wasn't hurt" replied Jerome. "He seemed fine in class this morning. Was anyone injured?"

"I don't believe so. The professor was alone in his car and from what I understand the other driver sped off into the night" informed Mrs. Falk. "Can you imagine? Some people are so irresponsible." She looked like she was ready to carry on some more about the incident when her intercom buzzer interrupted her.

"Yes Professor Lucien. What can I do for you?" she said in the most polite tone. "Send Mr. Reed in please, Mrs. Falk."

"You can go in now, Mr. Reed." Mrs. Falk made a motion towards the office door with her hand but did not get up. Jerome showed himself in.

"How are you Jerome? Sorry to have kept you waiting. I've had a devil of a time trying to get some straight answers from the local police. Please sit down. If you don't mind I have one brief call to make and then I'll be with you directly."

Jerome glanced about the office while Professor Lucien tried to contact his insurance agent. The office was not the ostentatious warren of legal acumen Jerome would have expected from a former Columbia Law School Professor. It was modestly furnished and more orderly than he thought it might be. Jerome had expected more of a professorial clutter. Papers were stacked neatly in the corner of his desk. The book shelves were filled with cases and materials on criminal law as Jerome expected they'd be. But, there was hardly any sign of Lucien's life of practicing law. There were no photographs or mementos reflective of his years in the courtrooms of New York City. Jerome thought that perhaps they were of such a personal nature they might be displayed in Lucien's home. His desk was not grand by any means, just serviceable. Lucien filled the chair behind it comfortably. Jerome thought he looked more approachable in the office than when he stood in front of the class lecturing. His dominance on display in the classroom took on a gentler guise of distinction as he sat in his desk chair. The opportunity to connect with him was now palpable whereas in the classroom it was distant. His Gallic features were handsome up close and not so formidable as they appeared from the desks in Lecture Hall #1. He was personable in this more intimate setting . . . not so much the personality that the lectern graced him in. Jerome wondered only in passing what color Lucien's hair might have been before it turned so snowy white . . . who pressed the neat white shirt under his gray suit now that his wife was dead . . . what he did in his spare time. He wondered what it must be like to know so much about criminal law. He wondered what it was like to be Professor David Lucien looking across the desk at Jerome Evans Reed. His wonderings were cut short when Lucien firmly placed the telephone receiver back into it's cradle.

"Well, I think I'm covered for that accident" he said to Jerome ". . . but insurance adjusters can be quite the wily characters sometimes!"

Jerome shifted in his chair and tried to relax. He nodded in agreement and added "Mrs. Falk told me you had an auto accident last night."

Lucien pushed his glasses onto his forehead and scratched the side of his whiskerless face. "It was the damnedest thing. Someone came speeding from out of nowhere and forced me right off the road. Whoever did it was in some big hurry, I can tell you that."

"Did you get a look at the other car?" Jerome asked.

"Not really. It was coming onto eleven o'clock so, of course, it was too dark to see anything clearly and the idiot didn't have the headlights on the car to boot. There's a mighty big scrape of green paint on the side of my own car, though. But that won't help the police much. I hardly think there's only one green automobile in the Washington, D.C. area." Jerome decided to see what kind of mood the professor was really in.

"You're assuming, of course, professor that the driver was from the Washington, D.C. area. Might it not have been someone from out of town?" Lucien smiled. "Perhaps, Jerome . . . but who from out of town would drive all the way here to run me off the road?" Jerome floated another balloon. "How do you know it was intentional? So far, you seem to be treating it like, well . . . like an accident."

Lucien laughed. "And so I should continue to do so, shouldn't I? At least until I get some elemental proof of a crime. Very good. You are thinking like a lawyer. Don't assume something is wrong until you have some evidence to support your suspicions!" He continued to smile as he pulled himself closer to the desk. "Now let me take myself off the hot seat and put you on it . . . what have you decided to write your paper on?" The meeting had begun.

By the time it was over Jerome and Professor Lucien had discussed more than just the impact of the third degree on confessions, trials and the judicial system. Nearly a half an hour had passed . . . twice the time Jerome initially thought the professor might grant him. Lucien thought Jerome's approach to a paper on the third degree was well thought out and if properly written would make interesting reading. He made the suggestion that Jerome try to find some convictions that were overturned on appeal because the police had literally beaten a confession out of an innocent man. "Play those cases against the ones where the third degree actually worked . . . find the ones where thorough investigations succeeded in the place of the rubber hoses. It's in those cases that you'll see how to strike a proper balance between law enforcement and judicial equity. Then law and order will begin to mean something to you." It was the only suggestion he made but it was enough for Jerome. He had made a connection with the man . . . not the professor. He saw a glint of what it was like to have been a warrior for justice for a lifetime. The end product of sheer dedication and passion for the law was sitting across the desk from him.

Lucien's friendly advice on how not to let the system get the better of you was even more valuable for Jerome. Lucien asked him why he decided so early on to make criminal law his area of expertise. Jerome responded with the tale of his grandfather, Judge Ward, and how important an influence he had been in his life.

"When did he die?" asked Lucien

"1928" answered Jerome. "He was murdered actually . . . no one knows why . . . no one was ever arrested. My father found him one morning in the back of the barn. He'd already been dead for several hours. No weapon was ever found, but it look as though he'd been beaten to death with a pipe or some heavy metal object of that sort."

"He was a circuit judge, you say?" Jerome nodded. "What was his name?"

"Judge Ward - Hugh Ward" Jerome replied wistfully. Lucien said he remembered vaguely reading something about his death in the New York City newspapers. "I'm sorry for your family's loss. Your grandfather was an important man to you no doubt."

"He is the reason I want to be a lawyer . . . he's the reason I am going into criminal law." Lucien looked at his student with pride . . . proud of his eager mind and enthusiasm . . . he knew that the years would transform those attributes into knowledge and wisdom. He added cautiously though "I hope you're not going through all this law school just to avenge your grandfather's death."

"My grandfather is the primary motivation for me wanting to be a lawyer . . . he meant the world to me . . . he still does. His murder is just something my family has to live with."

"Good . . . because revenge is a bad motive for anything. You can never really get back at somebody for doing something to you . . . negativity only breeds more negativity. You'll stand yourself in good stead if you use your grandfather's life . . . not his death . . . as the cornerstone for your career."

Jerome stayed in the school's library for several hours after his meeting with Lucien was over. He was so pleased with the way it had gone that he couldn't help but think that things were falling so well into place for him . . . at least in law school. Anything else was clearly of secondary importance to him. He had to remember that. On the way back to the hotel he reflected again on his fate to be attending law school in Washington. He concluded that it was a better deal than playing the waiting game with Cornell Law School. He would not be doing research in the Library of Congress if he was enrolled in Cornell. He would never have seen the Capitol Building or the Supreme Court either. He'd be living on the farm and driving over to classes every day. As much as he sorely missed his family, he knew that this was a great time for him to grow . . . a chance to see things he might never see. Only time would tell if he eventually stayed in Washington, but for now he knew he was where he was suppose to be . . . even if it meant living at The Graylock.

THE GRAYLOCK

Chapter Twenty-Three

James Parrish was sitting alone at the round table in the garden. He was staring up at the sky when Jerome entered through the back gate. The overcast sky was an accurate reflection of the state of mind James was in and he did not notice Jerome approaching. Jerome could tell that all was not well as the optimistic disposition of the young man in the wheelchair was replaced with a solemn look of dejection. Jerome did not disguise his own sound feelings but did not force them upon James either. He walked quietly over to where James was sitting.

"Hi" he said, saying nothing more. James forced a smile and lifted his right hand slightly off the arm of his wheelchair as if to wave hello. Jerome placed his notepad and books on the table and asked "Mind if I sit down here with you for a minute?'

James gestured as politely as he could for Jerome to join him but the forlorn motion gave no guaranty of the kind of company he'd be. "Did you make it over to the White House ok?" James nodded and took a deep, heavy breath . . . more like a sigh, but clearly not one of relief.

"Yeah . . . I did . . . Tim was nice to help out . . . it always makes things easier on my companion when he doesn't have to do all the lugging me around by himself." James bit his lower lip and shifted uncomfortably in his chair. Jerome let a moment pass before saying anything else. Finally he asked "So how did it go?" James arched his back and let his neck stretch. He put both of his sturdy arms behind his head and clasped his strong hands together. He might have almost smiled if the sad look in his eyes had not spelled out resignation . . . not defeat . . . but definitely resignation.

"Horrible . . . if you really want to know." He let his long arms fail to the side of the wheelchair. "It was a disaster."

"Sorry" said Jerome honestly "what happened?"

"Well . . . it's kind of a long story, but the end result was the President didn't have the time to see me. If I had been told that when I was granted this appointment, I wouldn't have come in all the way from Philadelphia. If seeing another man in a wheelchair upsets him, then his Chief of Staff should never have made the appointment with me."

"That's what they told you?" queried Jerome ". . . that seeing someone else in a wheelchair would upset the President? . . . How can that be?"

"I could hardly believe it myself . . . but that's the implication they gave me. I think they must have thought that I'd show up on crutches or something like somebody who was fighting back from polio."

"Aren't you?"

"No!" shouted James. "I've never had polio. What difference does it make anyway? Am I suppose to have a debilitating virus so that the President of the United States will feel better about looking at me? I can't walk . . . so what! Neither can he . . . except half the country has no idea that the man sitting behind the desk in the Oval Office is sitting in a wheelchair! He refuses to be photographed in a wheelchair . . . what a joke!"

Jerome never really thought about it before, but come to think of it he had never seen a picture of FDR in his wheelchair. He was always photographed behind a lectern or sitting in a regular chair. It gave the impression that he had recovered from his attack of polio when in fact the real truth was that the President of the United States could not walk on his own and never again would be able to. He still could not understand why he would not meet with James. "Are you sure that was the reason the President couldn't see you? Maybe some pressing matter came up?"

"Believe me Jerome, I know when people are getting the willies around anybody in a wheelchair. I've been dealing with it my entire life. I can feel it in the air" James declared soundly.

"I don't get what you mean."

"I can't walk. I've never been able to walk and I never will be able to walk. I don't have polio and don't pretend to. I've spent almost my whole life in a wheelchair. I'm not ashamed of it. People can stare all they like and they can keep their sorrowful looks to themselves . . . they're lost on me. I'm not someone to feel sorry for. I got infantile paralysis when I was three months old . . . I was barely learning to crawl. I've never stood upright on my own . . . ever. I have no idea at all what it is like to be able to walk."

James was not on a tirade. He was simply stating the facts . . . in a way that Jerome had never heard them before. He understood that most people felt sorry for anybody in a wheelchair . . . and he was one of them. As much as Jerome like to run and walk, he couldn't help but feel sorry for anyone who couldn't. He was never condescending . . . more compassionate than anything else. But James recognized the "I'm at a loss for words" look on Jerome's face . . . it was one he had been seeing for years. He tried to explain.

"Jerome, do you miss flying?" James asked. Jerome had a puzzled look on his face and he laughed a little bit at the question. "What do you mean 'do I miss flying' . . . I can't fly."

"So . . . do you miss it is what I'm asking you?"

Jerome smiles at the hint of what James was getting at. "You're being silly . . . I can't fly . . . nobody can."

THE GRAYLOCK

"Then you don't really miss it do you? I mean . . . it probably seems like it might be a nice thing to be able to do . . . wouldn't you agree?"

"Well . . . yeah . . . I suppose so, but I don't give it any thought . . . like I said . . . I can't fly . . . only birds can fly."

"Are you sorry for yourself because you can't fly?" persisted James.

"James, you are being ridiculous. I'm never going to be able to fly, so what's the point?" He looked at James and now he was smiling . . . like the James of yesterday afternoon.

"My point, counselor" he teased ". . . is exactly that. Flying seems nice to you. So what? You can't fly . . . never will be able to. Big deal. It's the same with me and walking. I'm not stupid . . . I see that everybody around me can walk. Looks nice . . . so what? You can't miss something you never had. People who have been crippled because of polio used to be able to walk . . . and they probably miss it. That's not the case with me. I have no idea what walking is like . . . I can only imagine . . . sort of like flying for you. But you know damn well that you are never going to be able to fly, so why waste your time wishing that you could? I don't miss being able to walk and I can assure you that I probably spent a whole lot less time wishing I could walk than you spend wishing you could fly. I have better, more important things to do with my life than worry about something I'll never have . . . and don't miss anyway." He took a breath. "Do you get my point now?"

Jerome smiled almost sheepishly. "Yes I do . . . you're quite amazing . . . the one I feel sorry for now is the President . . . sorry that he passed up the chance to meet you . . . his loss is our gain here at The Graylock!" Now James was beaming. "Let me tell you Jerome . . . there were two men at the White House in wheelchairs this morning, but only one of them was crippled and it sure as hell wasn't me. There's nothing wrong with me!"

"Yeah . . . I'll say! Do you mind me asking what you were going down there for anyway?"

"I was seeking the President's support in my efforts to get a crazy 1932 ruling by International Gymnastic Federation reversed" explained James.

"Why . . . what did Roosevelt have to do with it?"

"Nothing, really . . . but he's in a wheelchair and the nine of us were all in wheelchairs at the time of the ruling . . . I thought he might want to lend us a hand."

Jerome did not exactly understand the connection. "What do you mean by the "nine of us"?

"Oh, I don't suppose you remember anything about it . . . although it was widely picked up by the newspapers back then. It was out in Los Angeles a few days before the start of the '32 Olympics."

"You were in the Olympic Games?"

"Should have been" said James matter-of-factly. "I had the best shot of any of the gymnasts in my event of winning the gold medal."

"Doing what?"

"Rope climbing . . . I was the best on the team, but the night of the qualifying finals the International Gymnastic Federation ruled that all gymnasts with physical imperfections would be barred on the ground that our "defect" gave us an undue advantage over the guys who were physically sound . . . can you tell me where the logic is in that? I have infantile paralysis and therefore I have an undue advantage over a walking upright gymnast?"

Jerome reflected quickly on his high school gym class and the fact that all the boys had to be able to climb the rope to the top of the gym and get back down again or else fail the class. It was torture. You had to have nearly arms of steel to get up and down that rope. Now he knew how James got his upper body in the perfect physical condition it was in. He was an Olympic athlete. "How could they say that you had an advantage. It doesn't make sense?"

"Doesn't make sense" is only the half of it! shrieked James "... those bastards stole away our dreams . . . we were the best gymnastic rope climbers in the United States . . . probably the world . . . we worked like donkeys to get ourselves in Olympic shape. I started training myself right after the 1928 Olympics. I lifted weights . . . climbed ropes for hours and hours. I used to pull myself up a ladder to the top of our house in Philadelphia and let myself down rung by rung until my hands bled. I did enough push-ups to cover a whole battalion of Marines. Soon enough I started winning some local and state competitions. I started getting a lot of press . . . so did the others. That Federation knew we were coming to the Olympic Games . . . they knew it for over two years. None of us could believe what they did to us on the very night of the qualifying finals. It felt like somebody had cut our hearts out while we were still living. It was the most horrible thing anyone had ever done to me."

Jerome was stunned and speechless. All he could say was "What happened?"

"Nothing happened . . . that's what . . . they told us we were out and that was all there was to it . . . Poof . . . they were running the show and they told us to get out . . . it was no better than saying to our faces 'Go away little boys with spindly legs . . . you're not good enough and we don't want you here. Go home now and stay indoors.'" Jerome could see the tears begin to well up in the corners of James' eyes. He watched silently as James wiped one of his eyes. "The real truth was that we were the very best this country had to offer . . . the very best. We would have swept the medals. We were so excited about showing people that we weren't cripples that . . . ." He was getting too chocked up to say anymore.

Jerome sat completely numb in his chair and completely filled with respect for James Parrish . . . this man in a wheelchair. James composed himself and continued.

"We begged for a hearing . . . something where we could maybe talk it out, but all we got was a brief meeting in a cheap hotel room with one of the staff members of the Federation who told us the decision was irreversible. I was so disgusted and angry that I whipped the Olympic rule book at the simpering bastard." James laughed at the thought of himself four years ago. "Christ . . . you should have seen me . . . I was out of control. I backed the guy right into a corner with my chair and kept screaming . . . I mean really screaming in a rage to him. 'Fuck you!!' I said over and over. 'You tell those cowardly bastards that if there's anybody with a defect it's them. You tell those bastards that.' Then I reached up and I grabbed him by his collar with one arm and tossed him on the hotel bed. I think he must have thought I was going to kill him. I was probably angry enough to and then I saw how scared . . . really scared he was and I backed right off. I mean he was only the messenger. I wheeled backed and told him to tell the Federation that I'd be back. I told him to tell them that I was not a cripple and would not allow anybody to treat me like one . . . and then I left. He probably didn't tell them a thing."

"Who won . . . the medal I mean?" said Jerome.

"Don't know . . . it wasn't the United States that's for sure. The three gymnasts who eventually competed in rope climbing were all from the U.S. Naval Academy but the Federation's action swept away from the slate any possibility of us getting a medal in rope climbing. Besides . . . that wasn't even the point. The point was that they should have let us compete and let the best athlete take home the medals. The real sense of competition does not exists if the best aren't there to challenge you."

"What do you do now?"

"Continue to fight for another four years. I want to make the Federation reverse the ruling so that anyone like me who wants to can compete in the 1940 Olympics . . . there's nothing to be afraid of . . . real athletes welcome competition . . . it brings out the best in you. The medals, after all is said and done, usually wind up on a shelf somewhere anyway." Jerome heard Tim yell from the kitchen window. "Hey . . . James . . . .your car's out front."

"Time to go" said James. "I'll walk you out front" said Jerome.

As he pulled the iron gate on the side of the hotel closed, Jerome could see James' companion placing the luggage in the trunk of the car. "It sure was nice meeting you James. I hope you come back someday."

"Thanks for all your help, Jerome. Say goodbye to Tim for me. You've both been a great help. Kind of an interesting little place you live in here." Jerome laughed and offered no explanation. There was no explaining The Graylock anyway. He watched James companion lift him into the front seat of the car and put the wheelchair in the back. He waved as they drove down N Street.

When he walked through the front door of the hotel he saw Hattie standing at the front window watching James' car drive off. "Nice guy wasn't he Hattie . . . . I told him he should come back soon."

"Good" she replied ". . . yes he was a fine boy. I hope he does come back. I'd like to have dinner with him. Did he tell you what that son of a bitch at the White House did to him this morning?'

"Yeah . . . he told me" said Jerome.

"I hope that son of a bitch never gets re-elected" she huffed. "I'm going into my room now . . . I'll be out later." She turned and grabbed Jerome dead set in the sights of her darting blue eyes. "Don't ever, ever let anybody steal your dreams away, Jerome. You hold on to them like they are your life . . . because that's exactly what they are. You let somebody steal your dreams and you've let them steal your life."

She closed the door to her room firmly behind her.

THE GRAYLOCK

Chapter Twenty-Four

Tim called the switchboard at six o'clock sharp. "Is she still in her room?" he asked Jerome. "Yes" he replied. "No sound from her." Tim knew that this would be the best time to back into the townhouse across the street and finish his erstwhile investigation. "Ok . . . I'll be down in a minute." In his heart Jerome wanted the strange matters at The Graylock sifted out but was just as glad that Tim was the one who was willing to do the snooping. He just didn't feel right about doing it himself. By the time Tim got down to the lobby, Jerome had taken a reservation from Hattie's friend, Virginia Claypool Meredith . . . she would be arriving very late this evening. Her visit was a couple of weeks overdue but she told Jerome that she had not been feeling all that well and had to cancel alot of her engagements. Hattie will be glad to see her, thought Jerome. He remembered how excited Hattie was the first night he started on the switchboard and he took Mrs. Meredith's reservation. "My dear, dear Virginia" Hattie called her. Now she was finally coming back to The Graylock.

Tim picked the keys to the townhouse from the top desk drawer in Hattie's office. "Hey" he said to Jerome "I forgot to tell you . . . I found out where that Life Extension place is . . . it's up on Connecticut Avenue . . . about a mile or so north of here."

"Are you still going up there tomorrow?" asked Jerome

"Yep . . . maybe I'll run into Mr. Duffy!"

"Did you see him today?"

"Yes . . . and he acted like nothing ever happened . . . he was right back to his 'stylish' old self . . . I'm going across the street now . . . it's starting to get a little dark . . . time enough to get the lights on . . . look around and get back here before Hattie gets up . . . did you check to see what's for dinner?"

"No" said Jerome. "I haven't been in the kitchen yet . . . are you staying in tonight?" Tim nodded. "I think I'll catch up on a little casework . . . see you in a bit." He walked with purpose through the hotel lobby and out the door. Jerome watched him open the front door to the townhouse and disappear into the past.

Tim flicked the outside lights on as soon as he got into the front vestibule. It was still just barely light enough for him to make his way to the back room without having to turn the room lights on. He did not want to draw undue attention to himself if he could avoid it. The first room was stashed full of old boxes and some tattered furniture. The second room . . . the one closer to the back door of the townhouse was the startling one. It looked like a doctor's office. There was an examining table tipped to its side along the left wall. There were view boxes to read x-rays along the right wall. Tim pulled one of the cabinet drawers open and found rusted clamps, hemostats and scalpels inside. He opened another of the cabinet drawers and found broken syringes and gauze pads. Could Hattie's husband, Edmund, have been a doctor wondered Tim. It was odd, he thought, that these were the only two rooms in the whole house that were in a state of complete disarray. It looked as though someone had tried purposefully to turn them into storage areas. Unlike the rooms upstairs, there was dust and dirt everywhere. The boxes were not neatly stacked and some were plainly overstuffed and carelessly tied together with twine. It was a bungled packing job . . . whoever did it.

Tim bent over to see what he might find in the lower cabinets. It was beginning to get dark and there was little light coming through the windows of the back door. He briefly looked around to see if there was a light switch in the room but did not see one. It would be hard for him to make an excuse to Hattie why he needed to be in her townhouse during the light of day so he needed to move fast now and find out what he could while there was still a little light left. He open one of the cabinet doors and pushed some old newspapers aside. There were three smallish boxes in the rear of the cabinet. He reached all the way back with his left arm and pulled two of them forward. He began to rub his nose from all the dust he was raising. Just then he heard a noise coming from right outside the back door . . . in the small fenced in yard. He pulled himself up from the floor and accidentally bumped his head against one of the cabinet drawers he mistakenly left open. "Ow!!" he shouted out and rubbed his head. The sound was heard in the back yard. Tim simultaneously lifted his head and clearly saw the source of the noise in the back yard. It was Maneray. He was dropping something behind the wood pile in the corner of the yard. Tim immediately dropped to the floor to hide himself. Maneray!! What is he doing in the back yard? He's not supposed to be back until Monday anyway. How did he get back there? Tim laid as close to the cabinet as he could so as to be out of Maneray's line of vision. It was too late. He saw the door knob twist back and forth . . . back and forth.

"Owlster . . . you're in there . . . I know you are . . . I know you saw me" Maneray said wickedly. "Don't try to hide little lawyer boy . . . I know you're in there." Tap . . . tap . . . tap. It was the sound of some metal object knocking against the window pane. "Owlster . . . did you run away from me?" Tap . . . tap . . . tap. "It's getting dark out here Owlster . . . I might not be able to see straight when I shoot." Tap . . . tap . . . tap. It was the sound of

Maneray's pistol against the window. Tim did not move a muscle. He was practically too scared to breathe. "Owlster . . . are you still listening to me?" The tone of Maneray's voice was vindictive and scornful. Tim laid motionless on the floor with his head pressed against the boxes he had pulled forward only moments ago. "Owlster . . . if I were you I would pretend that you never saw me back here . . . I wouldn't want to have to hurt you . . . and believe me I can." Tap . . . tap . . . tap. And he was gone.

Tim waited a few moments before he pulled himself into a crouched position. His face was covered with sweat. He carefully looked up and saw that Maneray was gone . . . at least nowhere in sight. He didn't know what to do. He started to push the boxes back so he could close the cabinet doors when he noticed some faded writing on the side of one of them. It said "Life Extension". Nothing more. Still shaken from the sight of Maneray, Tim lifted the box onto the counter and untied the twine.

The first things he saw were some old photographs . . . several different sizes . . . all of Hattie as a young woman . . . very young. Tim was at first struck at how pretty she was. He noted her dazzling eyes that seemed to dare the camera to capture her whirlwind personality in still frame. There was another photograph of Hattie and an older man . . . a man stiffly postured in a wooden chair with his hands clasped and a monocle dangling from his vest into his suitcoat pocket. Hattie was seated on the arm of the chair smiling gently in a floor length, long sleeved dress. Tim thought perhaps the man was Edmund Crickmore, but saw no indication on the back of the photo that would identify him or the year of the photo. Both the man and Hattie wore wedding rings. "This must be Edmund" he mouthed to himself. He appeared to be at least a dozen years Hattie's senior . . . maybe more. It was hard to tell from the photos. He flipped through several more photos . . . some of them group shots. The only person he recognized in any of the photos was Hattie. He wondered who the other people were. Hattie never spoke of having brothers or sisters . . . never spoke of her own family for that matter . . . least of all her deceased husband.

Tim set the stack of photos aside and pulled out a dusty, small book entitled "Cryonic Engineering" and another called "Laboratory Principles of Liquefied Air". Underneath the books was a sizable stack of papers bound with a narrow ribbon. The typewritten cover page was named "Experiments in the Separation of Gaseous Mixtures". The author was Edmund Crickmore, M.D., Ph.D . . . it was dated November 11, 1901. Tim reached in the box and grabbed another stack of scientific papers. They were all authored by Hattie's husband . . . "The Structure of Matter at the Molecular Level," "Extending the Human Life Span", "The Concept of Cryonics", "What Happens at Low Temperatures" and "Molecular Shifts through Electron Transfers".

Tim was baffled. He did not understand what these papers were about. He did not have a real sense for medicine or science. But he made the connection to Duffy's pamphlet on the Life Extension Institute. "What was Dr. Crickmore practicing back here?" he wondered. He delved into the box one more time and grabbed a tiny pile of old newspaper clippings. Worse than being threatened by Maneray, he could not believe what he read. He had uncovered Hattie's past.

The clippings were yellow and dry . . . almost fragile. They were from *The Washington Post*. The date looked like it might be July 1902, but it was clipped so closely that the date and page were badly faded. The headline was not faded. It clearly read: "Socialite Suspected in Husband's Suspicious Death". The under-headline was just as shocking: "Nine Arrested as Police Bust Secret Society". Secret Society? There were no photographs that accompanied the story, but the words were enough for Tim.

Hattie was arrested when police believed that her husband died under suspicious circumstances. She was taken into custody from the townhouse and the account named the eight others who were also arrested. Among them was, as the newspaper put it, "Walter Duffy, 18 years old . . . a runaway from a reform school in Culpepper, Virginia who had been living under a false name in Washington, D.C. for two years. The story claimed that Dr. Edmund Crickmore, who had been banned from practicing medicine only a year earlier, was the misguided leader of a group of miscreant citizens who were devoted to the prohibited practice of life extension through cryonic surgery. Dr. Crickmore was censured by the local medical board when they learned be had been conducting illegal cryonic experiments in his office at 1743 N Street in the fashionable Northwest section of Washington. The background of the story told of how liquefied air, first produced in Paris by a Dr. Caillete 18 years earlier, had been smuggled into the country by Dr. Crickmore so that he could experiment with it in lowering terminally ill patients' body temperatures . . . hopefully to prevent their deaths until suitable medical procedures could be implemented to extend their lives.

Dr. Crickmore, terminally ill himself, apparently instructed his young wife of nine months, former Washington socialite Miss Hattie Matthews, how to perform intramuscular injections of liquefied air with a syringe. The paper said the doctor's inexperienced wife failed in her procedures one night and Dr. Crickmore met with a ghastly and immediate death in his own office. The ambulance attendant was quoted as saying "It was the most horrible sight I'd ever seen. There was blood spewed everywhere . . . it was like the guy's heart exploded out of his throat." Mrs. Crickmore, 27, and Walter Duffy, 18, were arrested on the spot . . . covered in blood.

Tim let the clippings limply fall from his hand into the box.

He felt like all the blood had been drained from his body. Duffy and Hattie arrested in the murder of Dr. Crickmore? Something else must have happened. There must have been a trial. He looked in the box but could see no more news clippings. If they were murderers, they'd have spent time in jail but he knew that Duffy's been working this hotel switchboard since he was 18 years old. There's a link missing here ... he knew it ... and he was going to find out exactly what it was up at the Life Extension Institute tomorrow morning.

He replaced all the scientific papers, books and photographs in the box and put it back in the cabinet where he found it. His hands were shaking. He was more than nervous. He was scared. Between Maneray's threat to kill him and the fact that Hattie and Duffy may have killed Dr. Crickmore, Tim did not know where to turn. He closed the doors to the two rooms and made his way through the small receiving room at the foot of the stairs leading to the living quarters. He took one look behind him at a place he wished he had never gone into. He slammed the front door forcefully and started to walk across the street to the hotel. With his head bowed down he whispered "Please Sam ... please ... if you're listening ... don't let anything happen to me ... I think I've taken our adventure too far ... get me out of this one safely 'cause I'm starting to get scared."

THE GRAYLOCK

Chapter Twenty-Five

Jerome intercepted Tim just as he came in the front door. The ashen look on his face was grayer than the dust the front of his shirt and pants were covered with.

"Geezus Tim, you look like you've been rolling around on the floor over there."

"I practically was" was Tim's sullen response. "Jerome . . . I think it's a whole lot weirder than we thought. I've got to sit down and tell you this." Jerome was surprised at Tim's demeanor. He had lost all his bounce and flair and he looked awful. Jerome grabbed him by his arm and led him to the front staircase.

"You can't sit down anywhere looking like you do . . . Hattie's going to know that something's up" he whispered.

"You mean she's up already?"

"Yes . . . that's exactly what I mean . . . keep your voice down . . . she's in the kitchen . . . she's starting to plan for that Mrs. Meredith's arrival later tonight. You can't let her see you like this . . . you're a mess. Go upstairs and change . . . get cleaned up. She's looking for you anyway . . . I'll tell her you went upstairs to take a shower before dinner."

Tim stood there looking around the lobby empty-eyed. "Good grief, Tim . . . what did you find over there?" Tim did not know where to start.

"He's back, Jerome" he winced to his friend. It was a clear look of worry on his face and Jerome recognized it. "What do you mean? Who's back?"

"Maneray."

"Yeah . . . on Monday . . . I told you that already."

Tim shook his head. "No . . . he's back now. I saw him from the room all the way in the back of the townhouse. He was stuffing something behind the wood pile. . . . I think we're in some deep trouble here, Jerome . . . I know he saw me in that room through the door window . . . he warned me not to tell anybody that I saw him."

"Tim . . . he's not back here . . . at the hotel . . . there's no sign of him."

"I'm telling you, Jerome, Maneray is back in town . . . maybe he never left!!" Jerome was perplexed. He could not figure this out and didn't have the time to right now. "Listen Tim . . . you have got to get upstairs . . . out of Hattie's sight." Tim went up to the fourth floor and Jerome went to distract Hattie in the kitchen.

He found her puttering through the cabinets. "I wish I could remember where I put that good china" she muttered to herself.

"What are you looking for Hattie?" asked Jerome.

"I'm trying to find my good set of china. I want to make sure Polly has it all cleaned up for dinner with Mrs. Meredith tomorrow night. She'll be way too tired for a big meal when she gets in tonight, but I'm putting out all the best china and silver for her tomorrow. I think I'll call my pilot friend, Louise McPhetridge and ask her if she can join us . . . you know she won the Bendix race . . . I told you that, didn't I?"

"Yes . . . I think you did mention it . . . she beat Amelia Earhart, didn't she?"

Hattie clapped her hands in the air. "Just like I said she would!! She beat them all! I hope she's free tomorrow. I want her to meet my dear Virginia." She paused to think a moment. "Oh, Jerome... I know tomorrow is Saturday and both you boys have off, but could I ask a special favor of you both?"

"Sure" said Jerome.

"Would both of you mind being on hand tomorrow evening to help out? I don't think Mr. Duffy is too good with setting up nice trays and serving food. I know that Polly won't be able to stay. She goes to church services on Saturday evening... never misses them and I don't want to impose on her where her worship is concerned."

"I can be here. I'll be gone most of the day... but I can be back in time to help get the drinks and dinner going."

"Oh... thanks dear. I want to make sure Virginia has a nice time... I'm so excited to see her again. I hope Tim can be here. Where is he anyway? I'll ring his room once to see if he's in."

Jerome stopped her at the kitchen door. "Oh he's here, Hattie ... he's taking a shower... he wanted to get cleaned up a bit before dinner."

"Well, you boys help yourselves whenever you want... I'm going to take a little tray into my room. I'm going to spend a little time getting myself ready for Virginia's arrival... my, it just seems like ages since she was here last. This will be such a treat!"

Jerome left Hattie merrily puttering in the kitchen and thought that it was nice to see her legitimately happy that a friend was coming to stay at her hotel. It was nice to see her in buoyant spirits. He rang Tim's room with the coded three rings so Tim would know who it was... no answer. He must still be in the shower concluded Jerome. He heard Hattie come 'round the corridor corner humming another unrecognizable tune.

"Say Jerome... would you be a dear and go check Room 11 ... just to see if it's all ready. Virginia loves that room. It has such a lovely view of the garden. I'm sure Polly has fixed it up just right

". . . but I want to be extra sure that we have everything in order. . . . you don't mind do you?"

"No . . . of course not. I'll do it now."

"And then dear . . . you go out and get me a half dozen roses and a half dozen of the irises from our garden. I'm going to make a pretty arrangement for Virginia's room. I have just the right vase stored away in my room somewhere. I'll have to go look for it now."

"Hattie, you sure are excited about seeing Mrs. Meredith" said Jerome.

Hattie clasped her hands in front of her and smiled brightly. "She's just my dearest friend in the whole world. She's been such an inspiration to me . . . in my darkest hours Virginia has always been by my side. My heart simply soars when I know she's on her way back to The Graylock to see me."

Jerome went off to double check on Room 11 and Hattie went into her room to search for her special flower vase. The view of the back garden was truly lovely from the room. It was also one of the prettiest rooms in the hotel. It did not look as though it had been furnished at a yard sale. One of the two large bedroom windows looked straight out at first floor level into the ivy patch. "I wonder if Mrs. Meredith knows what's out there" said Jerome to no one. "I wonder if she's ever seen Hattie on one of her midnight strolls." He could see that there were plenty of roses and irises in bloom right now and he would have no problem getting a bunch together for Hattie. He looked up at the sky and though he'd better get at it right away.

He could see there was a heavy storm brewing.

Chapter Twenty-Six

Hattie peered through the heavy red drapes on the front window of the hotel's lobby. "Rain" she said with dejection in her voice. "Just my luck . . . oh well . . . at least it's good for the flowers." She sighed and turned around to bring the flower vase she found in her room into the kitchen. There she found Tim sitting on the counter with his feet propped up on one of the cabinets. He was eating a bowl of cereal and staring out the window into the garden.

"Well, my stars . . . if it isn't the handsome Timothy Owlster!" she teased him. Tim did not respond in his usual way. He simply said hello and continued to stare into the garden. Hattie could tell something was wrong. She always could with Tim.

"You know Tim, I'm pretty sure there's plenty to eat in the refrigerator if you want a snack . . . you don't have to eat cereal."

"It's all I care for now. Thank you" was his response. Hattie wondered what was bothering him. "Are you alright dear?" she asked sincerely. Tim look at her oddly. He could not see Hattie Crickmore the present owner of The Graylock. He could only see the former Hattie Matthews, 27 year old Washington socialite, widow of Dr. Edmund Crickmore . . . covered in her dead husband's blood.

"Tim?" she said moving closer to him. "Are you feeling

alright?"

Tim snapped out of his ghastly vision and said "My stomach's a little upset, that's all." Hattie felt better now that she had an answer . . . even if it wasn't the truth. Jerome came into the kitchen with a very healthy looking bunch of flowers. He was surprised to see Tim sitting on the counter. He was even more surprised at how Tim looked. He was dressed simply in a white crew-neck T-shirt and blue work pants . . . no socks and a pair of old loafers to cover his feet. He was obviously freshly clean from a shower . . . his hair was still wet and brushed straight back. But there was a noticeable lack of color in his lips and the usual red blush in his cheeks had disappeared. Except for the change of clothes and a shower, Tim looked every bit as bad a he did when he came back from the townhouse.

Jerome tried to cover for him the best he could. It was diversionary conversation he used on his parents when he was trying to cover for his twin brothers, Jimmy and Alan, when he knew they were in trouble. He glanced at Tim to try and get his attention, but he was still staring out the window.

"Boy, I can't imagine what Polly would say if she saw Tim with his feet on the counter like that!" he said to Hattie. She was rinsing out her vase and filling it with water. She heard Jerome but did not look up. "Oh . . . we can let him slip by just this once. Timmy's not feeling too well. We always like to make allowances here at The Graylock!" she said cheerily. Good, thought Jerome. She's not really paying him any mind. He laid the roses and irises next to Hattie near the sink. He positioned himself in between Hattie and Tim with his back to her. "Say . . . Tim, if your not feeling too hot . . . why don't you go prop your feet up in the dining room. Nobody's in there. I'm going to start setting up dinner trays in here in a minute . . . I don't want to be clanging things around in your ear." Tim got the message and slowly walked around the far end of the kitchen and into the dining room.

"I've never seen him so sullen" said Hattie. "He looks terrible."

"Aw . . . it's probably just one of those stomach viruses" volunteered Jerome. "He'll be good as new by tomorrow."

"I hope so" responded Hattie. "There!" she added with pride. "How do they look?" Jerome could tell that Hattie had a way with arranging flowers. She had turned his bunch of cut flowers into a lovely bouquet. "Will you take these, Jerome, and put them on the dressing table across from the bed in Virginia's room . . . it's the table that's next to the window."

"Sure . . . I'll be right back."

Hattie then walked softly into the dining room and saw Tim still munching on his cereal and mindlessly flipping through an old issue of "The Breeder's Gazette." Hattie stopped and looked at him carefully before saying anything. Tim did not notice her presence until she spoke.

"Mrs. Meredith would be very proud to see one of my boys reading her magazine" she said mildly.

"Oh . . . I was just paging through" he said without emphasis "she'll be in later on tonight I hear" he added blandly.

"Yes! . . . she will" replied Hattie. "I want both you and Jerome to meet her . . . maybe you'd like to join us for dinner tomorrow evening? It'd be fun!"

"I'll see how I feel."

Hattie uncomfortably rubbed her lower lip with her index finger. She walked three steps closer to Tim who was still paging through the magazine. She bent over slightly and kissed him on the crown of his head. "I hope you're feeling better, Timothy." She left to return to her room and Tim managed to mumble a weak "thank you" as she turned.

Jerome returned from setting the flowers in Room 11 and

assumed Hattie was back in her room as he did not see her milling about. He saw Tim sitting very still in the dining room. "Tim" he said directly "you are starting to worry me a bit. What happened over there?"

By the time Tim finished his scary tale in detail Jerome looked just as pale. They were both sitting at the table awash in what still seemed to Jerome to be a mystery. "So there was no trial?"

"I don't know . . . I didn't see any news clipping about one. There were a couple of boxes next to the one marked 'Life Extension' but I didn't look closely at them."

"And you're sure it said 'Walter Duffy' in the paper?"

"Absolutely sure. It had to be him. The paper said he was 18 years old . . . he was a runaway who'd been living in Washington under a false name for two years."

"Sounds like Mr. Duffy, but if he's been working here since he was 18, like he claims that would start him working here the same year as Hattie's husband died . . . 1902."

"According to Hattie . . . that's the year she started running the hotel. It was just about that time that Polly started cooking here, too."

"Did you see her name anywhere in the clippings."

"Nope . . . the only two names I recognized were Hattie's and Duffy's."

"That stone out there in the ivy patch says Dr. Crickmore died in 1902. Maybe he really is buried out there."

Tim sighed with a heavy air of exhaustion. "I've already convinced myself that the garden is his big gravesite. But if the scandal took place in July 1902 and that was the same year that she started running this place . . . that doesn't really allow for any jail time . . . hardly enough time to put a trial together. I wish there were more papers. Something is missing here."

Jerome thought seriously for a minute. "Ok Tim . . . let's just assume that we are living with some strange creatures here. It doesn't necessarily make them criminals. It looks like, even from a purely logistical standpoint, that there was no trial and no jail time for either Hattie or Duffy. So some information must have come the prosecutor's way that would have made him decide not to press charges. If that was the case, then it would make sense that Hattie could have opened the hotel sometime in 1902 . . . buried Edmund in the back and hired Duffy to start working the front desk."

"That would be ok if that's what happened . . . but I think there's something more to it . . . I think you're probably right about the jail time . . . it hardly seems likely that there could have been any . . . probably no trial either. But there had to be something big for the prosecutor to drop the charges. The news clippings let on like this was a huge scandal . . . remember this was 1902 as well. It was not usual for socialites to be arrested as suspects in their husband's death. This was hot news . . . I wonder how they got off scott free."

"Maybe they didn't . . . we don't really know that. Maybe they had to agree not to experiment in that scientific cryonic crap . . . or whatever it was. That might explain Hattie's big blow-up when she saw that pamphlet on the Life Extension Institute."

"35 years after the fact . . . to have a reaction as severe as that!?" cried Tim. "I think it was something more than that . . . something bigger set her off.

"I don't know . . . morals were pretty strident back then and Hattie's always been a little unconventional. They probably thought she was some kind of a wanton woman back then . . . experimenting with odd types of life extension and all. Maybe they threatened her with jail unless she agreed to disband that society or whatever it was and forget about continuing with Edmund's experiments."

"I don't know . . . still seems to me that something's missing" offered Tim. "But I don't suppose either Hattie or Duffy is a danger or threat to either of us. It's just so weird to think of them doing stuff like that years and years ago."

"I don't know what to make of it to tell you the truth, Tim. But not a whole lot has made sense to me since I got to this hotel anyway. This is just stranger than all the rest of the stuff."

Tim rubbed his hands through his hair and shrugged. "What are we going to do about Maneray? I mean this is a serious problem."

"Do you want to call the police?"

"What do I tell Hattie when they get here . . . I'll have to tell her that I saw him when I was snooping around over in her townhouse. God only knows what her reaction might be . . . she might toss me out of her. It's clear from those two rooms that she has definitely buried that part of her past and doesn't want anybody to know about it. I'm screwed if I tell the police and screwed if I don't."

"Well we can't prevent him from getting into the hotel. He's got a key to the front door and can come in anytime he wants. And you're right . . . if you tell the police . . . Hattie's going to find out that you were digging around over in her house. She's not going to like that one bit no matter how fond she is of you. Besides . . . he can always say that he works here and was looking for something in the back yard. His menacing threats will only be his word against yours . . . those are bad odds. I say we keep watch out for him and deck him the first chance we get. I'm still pissed that he threw my mother's letter away . . . and Stevie's, too."

"I think he had a gun, Jerome. He kept tapping something against the window pane and it didn't sound like his fingernails."

"We'll just have to keep a careful eye out that's all. I don't know what else we can do. We can tell Ali that if he sees Maneray come in the hotel anytime at night before Monday to ring either of us in our rooms immediately."

"Yeah . . . I suppose that's all we can do until he shows up for work . . . you know I thought I'd feel a whole lot better after I knew why Hattie acted so strange sometimes . . . now I wish I didn't know anything."

"We still don't know everything. . . . maybe it actually gets better!"

"Not likely if The Graylock is involved. Let's gets something to eat. I'm hungry again."

THE GRAYLOCK

Chapter Twenty-Seven

The fitful night's sleep Jerome had was finally ended with the knock on his door early in the morning. He had been tossing and turning most of the night wondering how all the odd pieces fit together in the puzzle of The Graylock. He was subliminally trying to listen for the creek of the old iron gate on the side of the hotel. It would mean that Oliver Maneray had returned . . . probably in his usual drunken stupor making an unannounced entrance through the tool room. Unannounced to all but Ali, the night switchboard operator. He saw everything because he never slept on his shift and Jerome asked him to keep an eye out for Maneray. Ali gladly agreed . . . he knew there was trouble in the air.

Jerome heard the knock again but was barely out of his half sleep. The door opened anyway and Tim walked in. "Jerome . . . are you awake?" Jerome rubbed his eyes and shook his head, still buried in his pillows, as if to say no. Tim shook him by the shoulders. "Wake up" he said not too loudly.

"What time is it?" mumbled Jerome.

"Almost a quarter to eight" replied Tim "c'mon farm boy" he teased "the day's practically half over."

Jerome propped himself up on his elbows and looked at Tim. He was showered, shaved, probably fed and dressed to go outside.

"Where are you going so early?" questioned Jerome. "It's Saturday . . . no classes . . . no work . . . where are you off to?"

"I'm going up to that Life Extension place up on Connecticut Avenue." Jerome fell back into his pillows. "Tim . . . haven't you had enough of playing detective for awhile? Maybe you should back off for a bit. Maneray's the big problem now . . . not Hattie and her dead husband."

"No . . . I've been thinking about this all night. Maybe Maneray's involved in this somehow. If I find something out up there that has anything to do with him . . . then I'll have a real reason to call the police." Jerome sat up in his bed and folded his arms around his knees. "Tim . . . be careful up there. I don't think you know what you're getting into."

"Don't worry about it . . . ok? If it looks a little dicey . . . I'll just leave. I have to be over at Carolyn's later anyway. What time are we supposed to be back here to help out with that Meredith lady?"

"I don't know . . . Hattie didn't say. I guess five or six o'clock. Have you been downstairs yet . . . did she check in last night?"

"Yeah . . . I had breakfast already . . . she's here . . . Ali checked her in after we came upstairs. Hattie's up . . . Duffy's here . . . Polly's already starting to get things out for the big dinner. I think you're the only one in the hotel who's still in bed!"

"What's the mood like down there?"

"Except for the torrential downpour outside, it's like all's well with the world . . . I steered clear of Hattie and Duffy, but Polly told me she hasn't seen Hattie in such good spirits in a long time . . . all because Mrs. Meredith is here . . . what time are you going up to the Library of Congress?"

"Round ten, I guess . . . I'll be back long before five o'clock."

"Ok . . . I'll meet you back here then. Bye." Tim walked out and closed the door and before Jerome good take a good stretch to make himself fully awake his telephone rang. It was probably Hattie wanting some help with something downstairs he thought.

"Hello" he said clearing his throat.

"Hello Jerome, my boy. It's Everett Roberts here. How are you this morning?" Jerome smiled at the sound of Everett's voice.

"Hi Everett! I'm fine, thanks. I thought you weren't coming back until next Wednesday."

"So I thought myself, but the president's had a lot of re-scheduling lately and I'm to meet with him again this evening."

Jerome rubbed his face to make himself more awake. "Sounds pretty exciting."

"I hope I didn't wake you . . . I realize it's a bit early in the day."

Jerome was almost embarrassed that this man a half a century his senior was already up ready for the day and Jerome knew that if Tim hadn't woke him up, he still be sleeping. "No" he said meekly. "I'm awake . . . I'm getting ready to go up to the Library of Congress this morning to do some research."

"If I'm correct the Library doesn't open until ten on Saturdays. How would you like to meet me for breakfast this morning . . . my treat, of course. It seems we've had difficulty crossing paths of late and I do believe that after my meeting with the President tonight, I'll be off to Maine for a couple of weeks. If you're not busy perhaps you can join me this morning?"

"That's a great idea, Everett. Thanks. Where would you like to meet?"

"Why don't you come down here to the Hay-Adams? They have a very nice breakfast in the Empire Room. Let's see . . . it's almost eight o'clock now . . . can you make it in a half an hour?"

"No problem at all. I'll see you then."

"Wonderful . . . I look forward to it."

Jerome showered, shaved and dressed in fifteen minutes. He was genuinely excited about seeing Everett again . . . it would be the first time since they met on the train almost seven weeks ago. He decided to throw a tie on at the last minute . . . more out of respect for Everett than anything else . . . but he was not sure if the Hay-Adams would have some sort of a dress code. It was, after all, not like having breakfast at The Graylock. He grabbed his notebook and pen and dashed down the four flights of stairs only to see Polly standing at the foot of the staircase.

"Now where you goin' all flyin' every which way, Jerome? You can't go nowheres now anyway . . . jes look at that hawbil rain comin' down an' you ain't even got no umbrella . . . an' I know fo' a fact you ain't had no breakfast!"

Caught in the act. Jerome scooted past Polly and looked out the front window. It was teeming outside . . . a real Fall thunderstorm complete with morning lightning. One of the things Jerome did not own was an umbrella. "I have to get over to the Hay-Adams Hotel, Polly. Do we have a spare umbrella anywhere?"

"Now what you gone ta do over at that fancy place anyway at this hour of the morning?" Without thinking, he told her. "I'm meeting a friend of mine for breakfast." Polly had a look of real rejection on her face. "Why you got to go over to that fancy place fo' yo' breakfast. Ain't my cookin' good 'nuf fo' you anymore, Jerome?"

"No . . . no . . . Polly. That's not it at all. I love you . . . I love your cooking, but my friend is staying at the Hay-Adams. It's a lot easier for me to run over there than it is for him to run over here . . . he's 73 years old." Jerome hoped that Polly bought the explanation. "I mean look at it . . . it's pouring rain out there!" he added.

"Well . . . I 'spect that explains it enough. But you an' Mr. Timothy both seems in such hurries to get out o' here this morning that I was thinkin' yous boys was up to somethin'."

"Naw . . . nothin like that" he said, hardly believing it himself. "I have to go up to the Library of Congress after breakfast and Tim just had some early morning errands he had to do."

"Well, I 'spect both of yous boys will be plenty hungry by dinner time" Polly beamed. "An' I am makin' one of my finest special ham dinners for the Mrs. and her friend Mrs. Meredith. I know yous boys have been invited, so I'm makin' a extra lot of food!"

"Your the best Polly. I'll be plenty hungry by the time I get back . . . now do you know where I can get an umbrella?" Polly directed him to the tool room where he found one left behind by a guest from who knows what year. Hattie heard him rummaging around in the tool room and brought him in the dining room for a quick introduction to Virginia Claypool Meredith . . . the Queen of American Agriculture . . . as Hattie introduced her. Jerome could see that Hattie was nothing less than delighted to have her friend visiting at The Graylock. They were both sitting at Hattie's round table in the dining room enjoying a leisurely breakfast and chatting like old friends. Jerome made brief small talk about his family farm in Buttermilk Falls and promised they'd chat more about it over dinner. He excused himself by explaining that he did not want to be late to meet his friend at the Hay-Adams. "Bring him in for dinner tonight!" exclaimed Hattie. Jerome almost let it slip that Everett would be meeting with President Roosevelt tonight, but didn't want to start her off on politics at twenty minutes past eight in the morning.

He had but ten minutes to get over to the Hay-Adams. Under better weather conditions the short distance would be easy to make in that time. But this was a rain storm the likes of which Jerome had not seen in awhile . . . certainly not since he got to Washington. No time for a cab . . . he couldn't afford it anyway. He ran most of the way with his notebook stuffed underneath his shirt and sweater. He made it down to the hotel in eleven minutes

. . . not entirely soaking wet by the time he got there . . . but certainly not looking like he would have wished Everett to see him for the first time since they met. He looked like he had been caught in a bad rainstorm.

The concierge in the hotel lobby directed Jerome to the Empire Room and the maître d' eyed Jerome suspiciously when he asked to be taken to Mr. Roberts' table. Luckily, Everett notice him speaking with the maître d' and waived him over to his table.

"Jerome . . . good to see you again!" said Everett as he extended his hand. Jerome shook it firmly . . . honestly glad to see him. He apologized for the way he looked. "Nonsense . . . you're just a little wet that's all." Everett turned to the maître d' "Charles . . . would you be kind enough to bring my young lawyer friend here a towel so he can dry off a bit?"

"Certainly, Mr. Roberts. I'd be glad to."

Jerome laughed at Everett's reference to his being a "young lawyer" and said it was jumping the gun a bit. "You should get used to people calling you a lawyer, Jerome. . . . you'll be one before you know it . . . time passes quickly!" Charles, the maître d' returned with a towel and Jerome began to feel a little more human the more he dried off. Everett took the liberty of ordering breakfast before Jerome arrived. "I figured you to be a pretty hearty eater, Jerome. I hope you don't mind." Jerome dried his hair a little more in the back and shook his head. "Whatever you decided, Everett . . . fine with me." When the waiter brought in the steak and scrambled eggs along with a tall stack of buttered wheat toast a pitcher of freshly squeezed orange juice and a pot of hot coffee, Jerome thought Everett must have been reading his mind. It was a delicious breakfast and the Empire Room was simply elegant. Jerome was as relaxed as he had been in weeks and hardly gave The Graylock a thought. He described without much detail to Everett what it was like to live there. He was more interested in what FDR was like in person. He wanted to hear more of Everett's old war stories. Everett, in turn, was sincerely interested in how Jerome found his law studies in the early going. Jerome wanted to jog Everett's memory about the murder of Teddy Roosevelt's aide, Nathaniel Farley.

"I remember you said on the train that the local police and the White House Pinkertons gave the suspect a real grilling, with the third degree, when they finally had him in custody."

"That's right" said Everett. "It was a long time ago, but I remember that they got a confession out of him after a couple of days."

"Well . . . I'm writing this paper on the history and use of the third degree for my criminal law class. I'm collecting interesting cases on how the tactic itself has produced confessions over the years. You see, a confession obviates the need for a trial. As I see it, the courtroom trial is the place for someone to be found guilty or not guilty . . . not the back room of some police station. If police beat a confession out of someone, who just can't take the severity of the third degree any longer, that person never gets an opportunity to confront the accusers and to be judged by a jury. No one ever gets to see the presentation of real evidence . . . no one gets to hear the real facts of the case. The accused never gets a proper defense and the prosecutor never gets to represent the people as the law requires. The constitution is dismissed entirely and somebody who crumbled under duress is hauled off to jail . . . perhaps someone who is actually innocent of any wrong doing."

Everett listened closely and observed carefully. "I had a notion on the train that you'd make a good lawyer, Jerome. I have no doubt of it now. But, I think you'll find that in the case of Mr. Farley . . . the police caught the right man. How are you going to check this out anyway?"

"I've ordered the back issues of *The Washington Post* from the

Library of Congress. That's where I'm headed today. I want to read the press accounts . . . since there was no trial there's no information on it in the casebooks."

"He was quite guilty, I can assure you of that."

"Probably so . . . but the point I'm trying to make in my paper is that the third degree is not always a reliable weapon in the cause of justice. Sometimes it works . . . but I have some cases to prove that sometimes it doesn't work. My argument is that it has the potential for abuse in small backwater towns where the press doesn't bother to cover . . . or it can exist in the highest office of the government. Just suppose the police nabbed the wrong guy for the murder of Mr. Farley. It would have been bigger news than the murder itself . . . but when an innocent man or woman succumbs to the third degree from some nowhere place hundreds and hundreds of miles from the White House who is there to pick up the gauntlet?"

"So your paper is going to focus on the press coverage of criminal trials?" inquired Everett.

"No . . . not at all. It's going to focus on the constitutional principal that we are all supposed to have equal justice under the law. That's the inscription on the U.S. Supreme Court Building . . . and we cannot guarantee ourselves that if we allow potentially abusive measures like the third degree to have the blessing, full force and effect of the law. It's unconstitutional."

"I'd certainly like to read it when you're finished. It sounds quite interesting."

"Oh sure . . . I'd love to get your opinion on it . . . after all . . . you started me thinking about it with your story about Teddy Roosevelt and Nathaniel Farley . . . my criminal law professor thinks it'll make an interesting paper, too . . . except I didn't tell him about including a third degree from the White House . . . that'll be the surprise."

Everett took his last sip of coffee and looked admiringly at his young friend. "Jerome . . . I do believe that you love the law . . . and law school to boot . . . it shows in your face. You clearly enjoy what you are doing. There's no feeling like that. I've had it my whole life. I'm happy for you."

Jerome took the compliment in stride. "Nice of you to say, Everett . . . I'm sure I've picked the right career for myself . . . and you're right . . . it's a very comfortable feeling."

"Speaking of comfortable feelings . . . I'm getting way too comfortable in the seat. I always feel that way after a good breakfast. I've got to get up and move around" said Everett.

Jerome looked at his watch. "Yikes . . . I've got to get a move on, too. It's way past ten and I've got to get all the way up to Capitol Hill in the bad weather."

"Let me get you a cab" offered Everett. "No charge, of course, the driver can come back and get me after he drops you off. I have a few errands to run before I settle in and make the final preparations for my meeting with President Roosevelt tonight."

Jerome was slightly embarrassed at not having enough money for a cab himself and he dreaded the thought of getting soaked again on his way to the library. "Everett, you've been generous enough as it is . . . ."

Mr. Roberts cut him off without being rude. "Don't be foolish . . . it's my pleasure. I was struggling at something I loved to do once myself, if you can believe it. When you are as old as me I'm sure you'll return the favor to some enthusiastic young lawyer."

Everett walked Jerome to the front of the hotel and one of the waiting cabs. He instructed the driver to take Jerome to the library and return to the Hay-Adams for another round of stops. They shook hands warmly and Jerome thanked Everett again for the breakfast, his company and all his generosity. He wished him well with his meeting at the White House and Everett promised to call the next time he was in town. Jerome glided into the back seat and closed the door. As the cab pulled away from the hotel onto 16th Street, he turned around to wave good-bye again but Everett had already stepped back inside the hotel to get out of the rain.

Jerome could think of nothing but how lucky he was to know Everett and how well things were going to turn out for him in law school.

Chapter Twenty-Eight

By the time Tim returned to The Graylock it was a bit past two o'clock. The relentless downpour had not stopped since early morning and he was soaked through to his skin. Before he changed clothes he lit a small fire in his fireplace and called Carolyn to cancel their plans to visit George Washington's home at Mt. Vernon. She suggested next Saturday and Tim readily agreed. They both assumed Mother Nature's torrents would have run their course in a week's time and they'd be able to enjoy the museum as well as the grounds by then. Tim was just as happy to have the afternoon to himself . . . he had some things to think about from his trip up to the Life Extension Institute.

It took him awhile to find the place. The address listed in the telephone book was old . . . it was no longer on Connecticut Avenue. Tim wound up taking the bus way up behind American University . . . well over the top of Wisconsin Avenue. He found it at the very end of a small, winding street called simply Franklin Lane. There was no address on the outside of the building, but when he called the Institute with the new telephone number he got from the operator, their receptionist gave no further instructions other than he could "find us at the end of Franklin Lane . . . near American University." And so he did.

The "Institute" looked more like an unkempt tenement. The

receptionist, Sally Marie, as she introduced herself, was nearly 70 years old and was very curious how a young man like Tim found out about the "Institute". Fishing for information, Tim took a wild stab in the dark and said that he knew a couple of the members so he decided to check the place out for himself. Sally Marie said that the membership of the Institute had fallen off considerably in recent years and was now quite small. "Who is it, of our members, that you know?" she asked.

Tim tried to solve a mystery right away. "Oh, I know Mr. Maneray pretty well . . . Oliver Maneray. Do you know him?" Sally Marie shook her head instantly. "No . . . I know every one of our members by name and face . . . we have no Oliver Maneray at the Institute."

Damn, thought Tim. Nice try. "Oh . . . well . . . I'm not sure that he's actually a member . . . maybe he's just curious." He let the Maneray lie drop right away. "Umm . . . I think the one who is actually a member here that I've spoken with is Mr. Duffy . . . Walter Duffy. I'm sure you must know who he is." Tim said hoping his second stab in the dark would pay off. Almost before he finished his sentence, Sally Marie's wrinkled face lit up with a smile of recognition. "Oh Walter . . . of course I know Walter!!" She wanted to know if Mr. Duffy had sent Tim up to the Institute. "Oh . . . umm . . . not really" he said stumbling for a legitimate response. "I just sort of found myself interested one night and thought I might just come up myself and have a look-see." Sally Marie stood up from behind her desk and pointed Tim towards a table of brochures in the next room. "Why don't you browse through some of these for awhile and I'll check to see if Dr. Harpez, the President of the Institute, is able to have a chat with you right this very day!!" She pulled Tim into the next room and from a few feet away he recognized the pamphlet that Mr. Duffy dropped in the hotel. It was stacked on the table along with other materials extolling the virtues of the Life Extension Institute. Sally Marie was hanging onto Tim like she needed help standing up. She was making him very uncomfortable.

"We don't believe in dying here, you know that don't you?"

Tim was not prepared for this. "Well . . . I just wasn't too sure what you were all about up here." Sally Marie squeezed his arm a little harder and tried to produce a coy look from underneath her layers of wrinkles. "No . . . no indeed. We do not believe in dying at all here at the Institute" she declared with vigor. "Why just look at you . . . you're a young man . . . wouldn't you like to live forever?!"

He wanted to say "Not if I wound up looking like you" but knew that insults would not get him the information he wanted. "Well . . . I don't know about that" was his vocalized response.

Sally Marie tugged at his bicep a little harder and smacked Tim on the chest. "What do you mean you don't know!? Think about it! What can you do when you're dead?" Tim tried to distance himself from her, but Sally Marie had a tight grip. "Well, nothing . . . I suppose . . . but you know . . . when it's time for you to go . . . ."

"Who says when it's time for you to go? Who? Tell me." She was right in Tim's face and he was not prepared for the hard sell.

"Oh . . . I'll tell you what you need. Yes sir . . . I'll tell you exactly what you need right now!" She let go of his arm and almost danced back to her desk. Tim was just relieved to be set free from Sally Marie, the part-time preying mantis. "You need to have an appointment with Dr. Harpez . . . that's what!! You need to see Dr. Harpez right away! And I'm going to call him right now."

In a few seconds Tim picked up eight brochures and pamphlets from the table and followed Sally Marie into the front room. "Listen . . . I don't think I can stay . . . really . . . I just wanted to come by and get some information. You don't have to call Dr.

Harpez . . . really . . . I have to go."

"Well don't rush off before I give you a schedule of our meetings." The meetings. Tim knew now for sure that the "meetings" that Mr. Duffy was always running off to had to be up here at the Institute. Tim tried another stab at some more information. "Umm . . . those meetings . . . Mr. Duffy can probably fill me in on those, don't you think? . . . I mean . . . he comes to a lot of your meetings doesn't he?"

Sally Marie poked the air with her crooked index finger "Almost never misses one . . . he's a regular. But come to think of it now, I haven't seen Walter in a couple of weeks. I hope he's alright." Tim suspected what Sally Marie could never dream of . . . Hattie probably forbade Duffy from coming to any more of these "meetings" after she took the pamphlet in a huff that night . . . almost two weeks ago.

Tim decided to take a shower and get into some dry clothes. Jerome would be home in a couple of hours and then he'd replay his odd encounter with Sally Marie. He removed the damp pamphlets and brochures from his back pocket and laid them on his desk near the fireplace. He read them on the bus ride back to the hotel and looked at them again briefly as he got ready to shower. They were as confusing to him as they were strange. "Beyond Creation: Immortality for You"; "Into the Years with Cell Repair" and "Tomorrow with Everyone: Plans to Live Forever" were three that he simply did not understand . . . and therefore could not take seriously. The pamphlet that Mr. Duffy dropped . . . the one that caused such a stir with Hattie was the one with general background information. It explained that the Life Extension Institute was operated by individuals who were grounded in the belief that medical science could extend anyone's life well beyond what was presently considered a normal life span. It advocated experimental cryonic surgery, organ transplants and reanimation. The basic tenant of belief for the Institute's members was that living life was such a gift that it should never have to end . . . never have to be taken away. Tim re-read that particular pamphlet a couple of time on the way home, but still didn't really understand it. The concept of living forever was foreign to him. It was not something he ever thought of. It didn't particularly interest him.

What was still very curious to him was Hattie's past, and Mr. Duffy's apparently on-going involvement with such an off-beat organization. He could not imagine why Mr. Duffy associated himself with the Institute, why Hattie ever did and why she got so steamed when she saw that pamphlet. Polly mentioned that Hattie and Duffy "had words" that next day and Tim was more interested in what those words were than the words in the strange brochures from the Institute. He'd talk it over with Jerome later.

Right now he wanted to take a shower and warm his bones up a bit.

Mr. Duffy did not hear the shower running as he climbed the fourth flight of stairs. He was bringing the fresh towels up to Jerome and Tim's rooms. He offered to do it for Polly who was still in the kitchen making grand preparations for this evening's dinner for Mrs. Meredith. The hotel was deadly quiet and Duffy knew his absence from the front desk and switchboard would not be a problem. Polly had already made up the rooms earlier in the day, but did not have the towels ready and Duffy volunteered to help her out. He knocked on Jerome's door and opened it when he got no response. He quickly placed the clean towels on his desk and left. He repeated the procedure when he got to Tim's room. When he opened the door, he could see the wood burning in the fireplace and wondered where Tim was. He notice how homey the room seemed with the fire lit and was glad that at least Tim was out of the rain. He walked over to Tim's desk to place the towels there and saw the materials from the Life Extension

Institute. He stopped . . . dead still . . . with the towels in his hand. Dropping them onto the chair, he picked up one of the pamphlets off the desk . . . the one about the background of the Institute . . . the same one that has fallen out of his cape. He picked them all up and knew instantly where they had come from. He got very nervous . . . more so than usual when Tim burst through the door whistling. Duffy jumped and Tim was shocked to see him in the room. He looked at him dumbfounded and clasped the towel around his waist. As soon as he saw Duffy, he saw the pamphlets in his hand. Neither he nor Duffy knew what to say.

"I was bringing you some clean towels . . . Polly didn't have them ready earlier" said Duffy with a quiver in his voice. Still, Tim was at a loss for words. "Where did you get these?" was all Mr. Duffy could think to say next.

"Mr. Duffy . . . I'm sure you know where I got those" said Tim pointedly. He stepped behind the closet door to quickly put on his dry clothes.

"What were you doing up there? I mean . . . why would you be interested in anything this stuff has to say?" Duffy put the pamphlets back on Tim's desk. His hands were trembling. He was not angry . . . just unsure how to react to the exposure. Tim had pierced into his private life . . . what little he had of it outside of The Graylock. Duffy did not want to explain his interests. He wanted to be left alone . . . to do as he pleased.

Tim threw his old plaid shirt on and hurriedly brushed his wet hair back with his fingers. He could see that the discovery of the pamphlets on his desk made Mr. Duffy very uneasy to say the least. "I was concerned . . . Jerome and I both . . . well, we thought it was a little strange that Hattie would have such a fierce reaction to the pamphlet from the Institute you dropped from your cape a couple of weeks ago. So . . . I decided to investigate a little."

"Tim . . . please . . . you shouldn't be poking around. You don't know what you'll find. You don't know about this place" Duffy replied . . . still quivering. Tim knew he had to tell him. Otherwise he'd never get his answers. He decided to go for broke.

"I already know more than you think."

Duffy raised his hand to cover his mouth . . . not to muffle a scream . . . more like to hide his embarrassment. He was otherwise still . . . almost frozen in time. Finally he whispered "What?"

Tim walked a little closer to him and pleaded directly for an answer. "Mr. Duffy . . . what happened the night Dr. Crickmore died?" Duffy turned his back and stared vacantly into the fire.

Tim moved closer. "You were there, Mr. Duffy . . . I know you were. Jerome knows, too. I've seen the rooms across the street . . . the ones that look like a doctor's office . . . I saw the clippings from the newspaper. It said you and Hattie were arrested. What happened?"

Duffy turned clumsily in a half circle and moved to leave the room. He kept his face turned away from Tim's. Tim gently moved his arm out to arrest Duffy's escape.

"Mr. Duffy . . . you have to tell me" he implored. "What is going on around here!?"

Duffy raised his head. His pince-nez spectacles had fallen off and were dangling at the side of his jacket. His lips were dry and the hollowness of his cheeks was more prominent than ever. He did not rail against Tim's outstretched arm, but instead lowered himself slowly into the easy chair facing the fireplace. It was a gentle descent intended to ease his fragile frame into a position of safety . . . a position comfortable enough to unburden a tale hidden for 35 years.

"It was awful" he began softly "the worst thing I'd ever seen." He carefully rubbed his hand against his greying sideburn and place his spectacles firmly on the bridge of his nose.

"It all happened so quickly, it seems . . . there was this air of desperation and Hattie was screaming so. Dr. Crickmore was lying on the examining table with his shirt sleeve rolled up. He had been teaching me how to give him his injections . . . I told him I didn't want to learn . . . I didn't like the notion of sticking anyone with a needle . . . or anything for that matter. But he was a very persuasive man . . . Dr. Crickmore. I was barely eighteen years old . . . still scared of being caught."

"Caught with what?" asked Tim gently.

"I was a runaway, Tim. Two years before Dr. Crickmore died I ran away from this place I was put in . . . they called it a reform school back then, but it was more like a jail . . . that's what it seemed like to me. It was a horrible place to live . . . so I ran away from it . . . escaped was more like it. It was way down in Virginia . . . closer to the borders of Tennessee and Kentucky than anything else. I didn't stop running 'till I got to Washington . . . took me almost two weeks. I knew if I was caught, they'd send me back to that place. I would rather have been dead than spent another night there. But, I made it here . . . I was sixteen years old and nearly half starved to death . . . but I was free of that place and the bullies in it."

"Did Dr. Crickmore know this?"

Mr. Duffy nodded his head ever so slightly. "They both knew . . . I saw him walking down Connecticut Avenue one afternoon. I asked him for some pennies to get something to eat. I had been stealing from the outdoor market and I knew they were looking to nab me at it. Dr. Crickmore had a kind looking face and I thought I could get a couple of pennies from him. He told me that he'd give me some money if I came back with him and cleaned out his back yard a little. That's the first time I met Hattie . . . that afternoon. She was quite a sight. She brought me some food after I cleaned that little yard up some and we started talking. I told them the truth about my running away . . . and if I had to, I'd keep running

"... all the way to Canada, if that's what it took. I told them I was never going back to that hell house."

"Mr. Duffy ... that doesn't explain how you came to be in the examining room that night. Why were you giving Dr. Crickmore injections?"

Duffy slumped further into the chair. He took an uneasy breath and scratched his forehead. "After that day I first met them both, I kind of had the feeling that they were ok ... if you take my meaning ... you know ... I got the sense that they were not going to turn me in. So, a couple of days later, I went back to the house and asked if there was anything I could do for them ... sort of like an odd job or some errands ... something like that ... so I could have a few more pennies. Hattie was great. She made this big long list of stuff for me to do ... I didn't mind working and I worked hard, too. I was glad to be off the street. I saw Dr. Crickmore in his office ... he looked very busy ... but I never saw any patients. Hattie told me he was a research type of doctor. I didn't pay it any mind. All I knew was that I was getting some food and a few cents. At the end of the day, Hattie asked me where I was going. I told her flat out that I had been sleeping in Rock Creek Park. I didn't bother anybody and nobody bothered me. She said she wouldn't hear of that and told me I could stay in the small room up at the top of the house. No strings attached. She said if I wanted to light out the next morning ... I was free to do so."

"That night I before I went to sleep and I tried to remember the last time I felt like I was sleeping under a friendly roof ... and I just couldn't. Certainly never in that reform school. ... never with my own parents ... their house was almost as bad as the reform school. I thought I had forgotten how to close my eyes peacefully. Hattie and Dr. Crickmore gave that back to me when I needed it most. They treated me like a was a real person."

Tim pulled the empty desk chair around . . . closer to him . . . straddled it and rested his arms on its back to listen to the rest of Mr. Duffy's tale. "Did you wind up working for them?"

"Almost full time . . . they had a lot of friends and I would do odd jobs and the like for their friends. I got to be quite busy after awhile. Dr. Crickmore gave me a key to the door and told me I could come and go as I pleased. I could spend the evenings with them or I could go off on my own . . . however I chose. Sometimes I was with them and then again . . . you know . . . I started to make a few friends of my own. It was a wonderful time. They were as kind to me as two people ever have been. Like I said . . . everything was great . . . until that night."

"So . . . what happened?"

"Well . . . Dr. Crickmore took sick about a year before that night. He wasn't doing so much research anymore . . . he was so tired all the time. If you read those newsclippings you have some idea of what kind of research he was involved in and . . . ."

Tim interrupted. "It said he was in a secret society . . . you were part of it and Hattie and some others."

Duffy smiled a crooked smile at the recollection of it. "There's was really no society to speak of . . . nothing really secret about it either. They just had meetings that's all. They were all interested in the idea of being able to live longer . . . using medicine to live longer . . . just a plan to extend life for those who loved living. I didn't have any official formal education but I'd listen to them some nights and I was taken with the notion of living a long life. It was mostly the same people at the meetings all the time . . . so some ambitious reporter wrote that we were a secret society."

"Nothing illegal going on?"

"Not to my way of thinking. Dr. Crickmore ordered by mail from this doctor in Paris who was doing some real experiments in that area . . . you know . . . he had the special medical tools and information . . . that sort of stuff . . . and Dr. Crickmore wanted to buy the instruments and what not from this Paris doctor. The local medical board found out about it and bounced him out of the profession faster than who knows what. They accused him of trying to import illegal medical supplies. Just because they didn't make those instruments in the United States didn't make them illegal . . . they knew that. They couldn't really charge him with breaking any laws . . . but they had made such a stink about it that they decided to stop him from practicing medicine. It was terrible to watch him under such stress that way . . . they made his life miserable . . . he was trying to defend himself and they were calling him some kind of witch doctor. They were powerful and he was not . . . that's what it came down to. So they crushed him like a bug. He was never the same after that. It seemed like he was just plain sad all the time. Either me or Hattie would try to cheer him up . . . but it would never last. I still think today that those doctors from the medical board brought the sickness on him."

"What was he sick with?"

"I really don't know, Tim. To this very day, I'm not sure. If a man can die of sadness, I think Dr. Crickmore did."

"But what was in the injections?"

"I never asked . . . I probably would not have understood it anyway. But after awhile he got so weak that he needed help with them. That's what I did at first . . . just helped him out . . . you know . . . with the rubber tourniquet. I'd steady his arm and such. When Hattie wasn't there . . . I'd be the one to help."

"Where was she?"

"Still finishing up law school . . . and having her own troubles there, let me tell you . . . a young pretty woman in law school in 1902 was not something those men were used to . . . and smart to boot. Hattie was as sharp as tack . . . still is, if you ask me. But she never complained about her troubles to Dr. Crickmore. She didn't want to make his health worse. She always unloaded on me . . . I listened, too. I knew all too well what it was like to feel put upon and I could see that those fellows in the law school were giving Hattie more than her share of a hard time. She found it hard to study and take care of Dr. Crickmore, so I told him that whenever he needed some help . . . he should just call for me. I felt like I owed him at least that much. So . . . I learned how to give him his injections. The syringe was always filled before he called me in and I would just find the vein and shoot it in."

"How many times did you do this."

"Towards the end it was almost every day. I could practically do it with my eyes closed."

"And the night he died . . . ?"

"Well, like I said earlier . . . it all happened so quickly." Mr. Duffy stopped talking and bowed forward in the easy chair. He propped his elbows on his knees and rubbed the back of his neck to ease his recollection. "It was an awful sight. I know it wasn't more than a little past nine o'clock because I was going out that night to see a friend of mine. I was ready to get going and Dr. Crickmore asked me if I'd give him a shot because Hattie was in the study preparing for exams and he didn't want to disturb her. I thought nothing of it. I was ready to go but I told him I'd wait. He said he'd hurry. I just hung around in the vestibule until he called me into the examining room. When I went in he was prostrate on the table. Sometimes he was in the chair, but this time he was on the table. I only noticed that he was looked awfully tired that night and I told him so. I said he should rest more. He said he'd get plenty of rest soon enough. Like I said . . . I didn't think anything of it. I gave him his shot and pulled the needle out . . . turned around to the sink to drop it in some sterile water when I heard the most awful sound . . . like a terrible gasp or something. I whipped around and I saw Dr. Crickmore tearing at the rubber tourniquet . . . he was half sitting up and then he fell back onto the table. He was trying to stick his free hand inside his shirt . . . grabbing at his heart. I saw the look on his face and I got scared to death. I started screaming for Hattie to come down right away. I tried to pull him off the table and into the chair . . . I don't know why, but I did and he fell on top of me. I got out from under him and I was still screaming for Hattie. I tried to prop him up some, but he was a heavy man and . . . and . . . and he had this look of horror on his face and he couldn't talk . . . I knew he was trying to say something . . . but he could hardly gasp for air."

 Mr. Duffy buried his face in his hands at the telling of his own tale. He rubbed a glistening from his eye before he started again.

 "I didn't know what was happening . . . I gave him the shot just like I always had done . . . but this time he was dying . . . I knew it by the look on his face. He grabbed me by my shirt so hard that he ripped it and coughed so hard that he whole body started to convulse . . . his legs were shaking and then he spit out this awful amount of blood on me. He couldn't stop coughing up blood. When Hattie ran into the room she saw both of us on the floor . . . covered in blood. She started screaming "Edmund . . . Edmund!" She bent down right over him. She looked right to me and asked me what had I done? I was starting to cry . . . I was so scared. I didn't know what to say. Hattie ripped open his shirt and put her head right onto his heart. He stopped coughing and his whole body stiffened up. She started yelling at him "Edmund . . . breathe . . . Edmund . . . breathe!!" He grabbed her hair and coughed more blood up . . . all over her face. She didn't care . . . she kept yelling "Edmund . . . don't die!! . . . please, please Edmund . . . don't die!!" I sat there just shaking his shoulder and crying. But I saw him look at her for the last time . . . I have never forgotten it. I've never seen anybody look at another living being with so much love . . . he tried to hug her but all he could do was cough one more time . . . more blood on her face. Then he collapsed back into my lap. Dead. Gone forever."

Duffy sat back into the chair and nervously rubbed the palms of his hands against his pant legs. He did not look at Tim . . . did not look at the fire . . . only looked back into the past.

"We both sat there . . . Hattie and I . . . stunned and speechless . . . but she didn't cry. We tried to lift him off the floor back onto the table, but we couldn't. She eased his head onto the tile floor and helped me up. I was shaking like a leaf. She rubbed her hands on her dress and called for an ambulance. I think she knew the police would be there, too. She told me to say nothing . . . absolutely nothing or they'd probably send me to jail . . . worse probably back to that reform school. I pleaded with her not to let them take me. And she didn't . . . she took the blame for everything."

"What?" said Tim incredulously.

"She told the police it was all her fault . . . that she had been helping to medicate her husband for some months now and something went accidentally amiss. The coroner said it was an air bubble in the syringe that got into his bloodstream and burst his heart right open like a geyser."

"You didn't check the syringe before you injected him!?"

"No" said Duffy sadly. "I thought he always did that. I just gave him the shot . . . I killed her husband and she saved my life."

"Mr. Duffy . . . you didn't kill Dr. Crickmore" said Tim, trying to comfort him. "You obviously weren't trained to look for air bubbles in the syringe. It was an accident . . . that's all . . . just a horrible accident."

That did not seem to ease Mr. Duffy's mind much. "She told me we'd probably be arrested . . . but to stick to the story no matter what or I'd be a goner . . . they took us down to the police station . . . put us in separate rooms and gave us the third degree . . . a real going over, let me tell you. But I was so afraid that they'd send me back that I stuck to the story no matter how much they yelled at me . . . accused me of all sorts of stuff . . . you know what I mean. I just couldn't go back there."

"You mean to the reform school?"

"Yes . . . that's what I mean. It was inhuman for me. Some judge and my parents got me committed there because they thought I was trouble. I wasn't trouble to anybody. I was sixteen years old . . . spent most of my days trying to protect myself from being pushed around by boys bigger than me and every night just . . . just trying to . . . to get through them, that's all."

Tim shrugged his shoulders and said "I don't get it."

Duffy wrung his hands tightly. "Every night they would . . . just . . . you know . . . they just would start . . . ." He looked up towards the window that looked out onto the garden. He let his hands fall to his sides. "Every night they would force themselves upon me. Do you know what I mean?"

Tim sat still. He looked at Mr. Duffy with an understanding and compassion that said yes . . . now he understood. "You know what I mean, don't you?" Tim finally nodded.

"Every night . . . every single night. It was all the bigger boys. The rough ones . . . and there was not a single, solitary thing I could do about it. It was an unbearable humiliation for me . . . and all they did was laugh at me . . . every single night."

"I'm sorry Mr. Duffy. I'm really so sorry."

Mr. Duffy exhaled a breath of relief that was 35 years old. He turned to Tim opened his eyes a little wider. "Well . . . it wasn't you anyway . . . it was them. I know you and Jerome, big as you both are, would never humiliate anyone like that. There's nothing for you to be sorry for."

"I mean I'm sorry for prying around . . . I'm sorry I made you talk about something you didn't want to talk about."

"You didn't make me do anything, Tim. I could have left this room . . . I know you wouldn't have stopped me. You wouldn't have hurt me . . . No . . . I guess it was good to get it out . . . to tell somebody else . . . one of the reasons I took to Dr. Crickmore's notion, if you will, about living a very long life was that I wanted to outlive all those boys in the school who hurt me so . . . I wanted to know that one day the world would be a place where they no longer lived . . . but I still did. That would have made me feel safe . . . finally. When I realized after many years that I was wasting my time thinking like that . . . I mean . . . I could have died any minute and they'd still be alive . . . all I did after I realized that was to want to live long enough to forget those nights. I don't think I ever will, though you know. I guess there just always going to be part of my past . . . just like Dr. Crickmore . . . except he was a good part."

"Umm . . . Mr. Duffy . . . could I ask you one more thing?"

"Sure" said Duffy "why not? . . . I mean . . . what don't you know now?"

"Is that really Dr. Crickmore buried out in the garden?" asked Tim.

"Oh . . . yes" he said without batting an eye "that's him. That's her Edmund." Duffy rose from the chair and straightened his jacket. Tim rose as well . . . out of respect . . . but was not sure what to do. "I have to get back to work" said Mr. Duffy and he headed towards the door. "Mr. Duffy?' Tim said politely.

"Yes?"

"I can come down later and help you, if you need me to."

Duffy smiled and thrust one hand into his pocket. "You can call me Wallace . . . you know . . . I mean if you want to."

"Wallace?" said Tim

"Yes . . . that's my real name. I changed it when I ran away."

Tim laughed just a little bit. "You changed your name from Wallace Duffy to Walter Duffy?"

"Yes... seems a little silly... you'd think I'd have made a bigger change, but I've never had much of an imagination... just a lot of spunk." He closed the door behind him and Tim sat at his desk... thinking for a moment. He took the brochures and pamphlets from The Life Extension Institute and tossed them into his fireplace. He didn't bother to read them again. He knew all he wanted to know. He'd tell Jerome all about it later.

When Tim finally came downstairs, he heard Hattie and Polly fussing about in the kitchen and he went in to say hello.

"Why Timothy!" said Hattie. "There you are... I was wondering if you had gotten swept away in the rainstorm. How are you, dear?"

Tim looked at Hattie quite differently now... after learning what he had from Mr. Duffy. She was no longer just an amusing woman who owned The Graylock. He saw her as a woman of strength and compassion... great compassion. She was a woman of intellect and high interest in her fellow travelers through life... and she was still very amusing.

"I'm doing alright Hattie... how about you?" he replied.

Hattie threw her small shoulders back a bit and squinted at him. "Timothy... why are you standing there with that charming smile oozing all over your face? What's got you in such fine fettle on this rainy day?" she teased.

"Just you, Hattie... just you" he said in his most complimentary fashion.

Hattie walked over from the oven and stood right next to Tim and poked him in the shoulder. "Just me? Good... then this a great time for me to ask you to go back out into that deluge out there and get us some groceries for breakfast tomorrow morning. We're all out of eggs and we could use another pound of bacon."

"Don't forget the milk... an' we kin use some mo' wheat bread, too" chirped in Polly. "Mr. Timothy, you best write this down 'cause if yous forgits anything . . . I ain't gone ta give you none of my fine goose I got cookin' fo' the special dinner tonight!"

Tim scooted around Hattie over towards the oven where Polly was shifting pots on the stove. "Goose nothin'" he teased knowing he get a good rise out of his favorite cook. "I'll bet you've never even cooked a goose . . . I'll bet there's nothing but some dried old meatloaf in that oven. That's what it smells like to me!!"

"You ain't gone ta smell nothin' if I punches you in yo' nose!" she yelled. Tim put his hand daringly on the oven door handle. "Mr. Timothy . . . don't you go openin' that oven door. I'll git my broom an' hit you. . . . that's what!" He bent over and opened the door . . . giving Polly her favorite target. "Mr. Timothy . . . I ain't even gone ta git my broom . . . it's too far away . . . I'm gone ta hit you with this ol' fryin pan . . . that's what I'm gone ta do!!"

Tim shut the oven door as quickly as he opened it and stood up even faster. "It is a goose!! Polly . . . are you cooking that big old goose just for me?"

"I ain't cookin' nothin' fo' you . . . you is bad and that's all. I'm cookin' this goose for the Mrs. an' her friend . . . that nice Mrs. Meredith and whoever the Mrs. invites to dinner . . . an' I hopes it ain't you."

"Aw . . . Polly . . . c'mon now . . . Hattie invited Jerome to dinner . . . she has to invite me!"

"Don't you go talkin' 'bout Mr. Jerome, now . . . you is always tryin' to bring him into yo' troubles . . . now you go on now an' git to the store like the Mrs. asked you . . . an' don't you forgit nothin' or I don't know what I'm gone ta do to you."

Tim walked a half circle around the heart and soul of The Graylock's kitchen and gave her a huge bear hug from behind. "You're the best, Polly . . . just the best cook in the whole world."

Polly liked it and Tim knew that she liked it. She could yell at him from now until the end of law school and he knew he would never mind it. "Alright Mr. Timothy . . . you let go o' me now" she said with a huge grin. "Git off to the store and hurry back fo' you catches yo death out there in the rain. I'll fix you a nice sandwich fo' when you git back here . . . go on now . . . I got me plenty of work to do." Tim released her from his arms and walked into the dining room.

"Ok Mr. Charm . . . here's the grocery list and the money. Where's your umbrella? Mercy . . . the rain's hardly let up a drop since this morning. You don't really mind doing this, do you Tim?" Hattie asked sincerely.

Tim shook his head. "No, of course not, Hattie . . . anything for you." He reached over and took the list and money and place a quick kiss on her head. "I won't be too long."

Hattie adjusted her earring and wondered what had gotten into Tim. "You don't have a jacket either, Tim. Don't go out into this storm without a jacket."

Tim pulled an umbrella from the pile in the tool room. "Damn . . . my jacket's all the way upstairs." Then he had an idea. "Hey Mr. . . . umm . . . I mean Wallace" he shouted towards the front desk. "Can I wear your cape to the store?"

Mr. Duffy was trying to hide his smile, but it was creaking through his tiny face. "Oh yes . . . I suppose you can . . . I mean . . . it's alright with me. Try not to get it muddy, though . . . it's my only one."

"I'll be careful" promised Tim as he took the black cape off the wall hook and swung it around his broad shoulders. Polly walked out of the kitchen and saw Tim waltzing around like a toreador.

"Mr. Timothy . . . ain't you gone yet? Why you dancin' around in Mr. Duffy's clothes . . . that thing don't even fit you right nohow."

"I think I look pretty good in this! I think I look quite stylish!"

Polly walked past Tim into the dining room and just shook her head in wonderment. "I don't know whats got into you this day, Mr. Timothy. You sho' has got some funny bizness in you today . . . that's what I thinks . . . some kind o' funny bizness."

Tim left through the side door and Hattie watched him carefully as he pranced in the pouring rain through her garden . . . in Mr. Duffy's cape. She got up from her chair and told Polly she was going back into her room now until dinner time. She made one stop at the front desk to say something to Mr. Duffy.

"He called you Wallace just then. Not Walter . . . Wallace. How did he know that?"

Mr. Duffy stopped fidgeting with the registration book and said directly to her. "He knows everything, Hattie."

She shifted from one leg to the other without emotion on her face. "Everything?"

Duffy nodded. "He found most of it in the rooms across the street. He was up at the Institute this morning, too. He and Jerome have been piecing things together."

"Jerome knows, too?" she asked.

"Most everything. They were concerned that something awful was going on . . . so I just told Tim the truth . . . he seemed fine with it."

"Everything?" she said again. Duffy affirmed. "They're good boys, Hattie . . . nothing to worry about with them. I think I did the right thing by telling Tim the truth."

Hattie walked very slowly to the door of her room. She turned back a bit towards Mr. Duffy and said "Yes . . . I guess you did Wallace. No harm done by it, I suppose." She walked into her room and let the door close behind her. It was the first time she called Mr. Duffy by his real name in 35 years.

Chapter Twenty-Nine

Jerome had been waiting for over two hours by the time Mr. Ross arrived at the law library. He apologized profusely upon his arrival and explained that the terrible rainstorm had put his car right out of commission. Public transportation into the city from his home in Silver Spring, Maryland was nearly terminated because of the weather conditions. Lightning struck trees falling on power lines made distance travel almost an impossibility.

"I'm terribly sorry Mr. Reed . . . for the delay. Please accept my apology. I was fully determined to be the first to arrive this morning . . . until Mother Nature stepped in and changed my plans. I had a devil of a time getting into the city."

"No need to apologize, Mr. Ross. I've had plenty of reading material here to keep me busy . . . got a chance to dry off a bit myself" said Jerome in earnest.

"Well, when I left last night, I locked your newspapers in my desk so they'd be right here first thing in the morning for you. I suppose I could have left them down in the storage racks, but then you might have had to wait for them to be retrieved . . . and now look what happened . . . you been waiting as it is since I'm the only one with a key to my desk drawers. Oh . . . you know what they say about 'good intentions.'" Mr. Ross was trying to dry himself off and get organized at the same time. Jerome could see that he was succeeding at neither. "Look, Mr. Ross" he offered "I'm still reading some background material up there in the stacks. I have enough to keep me busy until you get settled. Why don't I just come back down in awhile after you get squared away?"

"You sure you don't mind? . . . I suppose I am a little discombobulated right now" admitted the old librarian.

"Not at all" stated Jerome. "You just do what you have to do and I'll come back later . . . I have all afternoon." Jerome returned to his solitary desk in the stacks and began to read additional cases on the third degree. No more than fifteen minutes had passed when he laid his head down on the desk to rest and promptly fell fast asleep. When he awoke, *The Washington Post* newspapers for the week of July 2, 1902 were on the corner of his desk. Jerome did not notice that Mr. Ross brought the papers up himself when he realized some time had passed and Jerome had not come to claim them. He got up from the chair still in a bit of a sleepy daze and walked over to the railing. He looked down at the librarian's desk to wave a sign of thanks. He caught Mr. Ross' eye and he returned the wave. He also pointed to the clock on the wall to let Jerome know that the library would be closing soon as it was nearly three o'clock. Jerome nodded an acknowledgement and realized that it was unlikely that he'd get through the week's worth of newspapers in twelve minutes. He'd been asleep at the desk for over an hour. He decided to ask Mr. Ross to keep the papers locked in his desk until Monday. For the few remaining minutes, however, he wanted to briefly scan the back issues to see if he could find what he was looking for. He started with the headlines. He didn't have to go any further. More than what he wanted to know was on the front page. What he needed to know, he found under the headlines and they hit him in the face like a hammer.

The first two issues said, nothing about the missing Mr. Nathaniel Farley. The third one, dated July 2, 1902, blasted his absence from his White House duties and consequent murder all over the front page. There was a picture of the crime scene underneath the banner headline. It showed an angry Teddy Roosevelt who resolutely informed the inquiring press that "I will have the man who did this found. I will bring him to justice. On my honor as President and on young Mr. Farley's soul, I vow to you all that I will have this done." The paper described the condition of Mr. Farley's body very much the same as Everett had to Jerome on the train ride. The additional pieces written all described the outrage of the locals, especially the President, over the horrid nature of the crime. The relentless search was on for the killer. Jerome was trying to read quickly. He knew he'd be able to pour through these articles with more care on Monday, but he was curious nonetheless. He could hear the rustling of people leaving the library below and noticed the lights in the back of the library were being shut off. It was three o'clock. Closing time.

His perusal of the July 3rd issue's front page provided follow up stories without conclusions. It merely read "Suspect Arrested in Murder of White House Aide". Nothing more.

But, the issue dated July 4th wrapped Jerome in a fear so intense it seemed as though he were frozen in time. He wanted to move. He wanted to move quickly, but what he saw held him in his seat . . . fixated . . . praying for God to grant him another breath.

The headline burned into his eyes like a wrangler's brand. Stunned and shocked, Jerome wanted to get away from it, but it held him there . . . burning the answer to his mystery in his mind forever. "Vagabond Confesses to Murder" read the edge to edge banner in three inch deadly black letters. "Prosecutor Succeeds With Third Degree" read the smaller inch and a half headline leading into the front page story. Jerome could not focus his eyes on the reporter's account. He sat alone with his fingers pressed to the photograph on the left hand side of the front page. It was a picture of the serious looking, young local prosecutor watching as two more serious looking police officers led the confessed killer into the paddy wagon. The description underneath the photograph frightened Jerome to his bones. "Local prosecutor, David Lucien, watches as police return confessed killer, Oliver Maneray, to D.C. jailhouse."

Jerome tried to mouth Maneray's name to himself and could only make a murmuring sound. Maneray. He could not say the name. He looked at the picture again. There was no mistaking what the paper said. It was a picture of a 27 year old murderer. It was a picture of a man who was now 62 years old and living in The Graylock . . . two floors below Jerome and Tim. One floor above Hattie. Four blocks from the man responsible for sending him to prison for 35 years . . . Professor David Lucien. Jerome tried to control a normal breathing pattern but failed when he tried to piece the facts together.

Tim said Maneray was back . . . with a gun. Tim believed that Maneray never left. Professor Lucien was run off the road three days ago in the dark of night. Maneray's "return" to the hotel was being delayed by car trouble. Jerome knew now that it was more likely car repair. He was probably having the paint from Professor Lucien's car removed from his own. It was not an accident like Lucien assumed. Maneray was back to take his revenge on Lucien. He was going to kill again.

When Mr. Ross tapped Jerome on the shoulder, he whipped around so fast . . . so defensively that Ross stepped back two feet. Jerome looked like a deer caught in the headlights of an oncoming car. He felt like he was strapped to the tracks of an oncoming train.

"Mr. Reed . . . it's closing time. Everyone's gone . . . we'd like to lock up now" said Mr. Ross in a measured tone. "I'll need to take your papers back." Jerome looked at the front page photograph again . . . then back at Mr. Ross.

"I have to take this with me" he said bluntly . . . clutching onto the July 4th issue like a precious grail.

"I'm sorry Mr. Reed" responded the librarian "but those newspapers are part of the library archives. They can't be checked out."

Jerome shook his head vigorously and leaned forward. "But . . . but you don't understand. I . . . I have to show . . . to show this to . . . ."

"Again . . . I must emphasize that these papers are not part of the circulation library. As I explained . . . they are archives. You have there our only copies of those issues" Mr. Ross said with polite determination. "Goodness knows what would happen if I allowed you to take them out . . . especially in this weather. Just look at that rain pouring down outside . . . No . . . I'll be happy to hold them for you in my desk again until Monday . . . if you'd like to come back then."

Jerome could hardly hear Mr. Ross' reasonable explanation. All he could see was that photograph of Lucien watching Maneray being led away to prison. He feared for the professor's life. He feared for the life of everyone at The Graylock. For the first time ever, he feared for his own life. "Is there a public telephone I can use here?" he asked Mr. Ross.

"There's a booth in the main corridor on the first floor. If you hurry, you might get there before they close it off."

"Thank you" Jerome said hurriedly. He snatched his coat and started to dash away. "Mr. Reed" the librarian called out after him "you forgot your umbrella." Jerome turned back quickly and took it from Mr. Ross' outstretched hand. "Mr. Reed . . ." he called again "would you like me to save these papers for you until Monday?"

"Yes . . . please . . . save them. I'll be back!" said Jerome with-

THE GRAYLOCK

out looking back. Mr. Ross watched Jerome nearly leap down the three flights of stairs to the main floor and sprint out the door of the law library wondering what could have gotten into him. He collected the newspapers and walked back to his desk to lock them up for safekeeping.

Jerome did not wait for the elevator to carry him to the main floor of the library. He sped down the stairs only to find a burly security guard stationed at the doorway to the main corridor. "Sorry . . . the library is closed. You'll have to leave by the side door."

"I have to use the telephone" snapped Jerome. The guard shook his head. "Sorry . . . the library is closed" he repeated. "But this is an emergency" pleaded Jerome with real urgency. "I can't let you through. Rules . . . you know" he said steadfastly and pointed towards the side door. "I think there's a booth on the corner. Try there." Jerome had no choice but to exit by the side door as instructed. He stepped back into the teaming rain and opened his umbrella. He could not see a telephone booth in the distance . . . but with the rain coming down as so hard, it was difficult to see much of anything more than a few feet away. He began to walk swiftly up the street and look for a place to make a call. The one booth he did see was being used. He was trying not to panic. He knew that if he remained calm, he would be able to handle the situation. He did not see any stores open. He had but one choice . . . head for The Graylock as fast as he could . . . maybe he'd see a telephone booth in the way. He started to break into a run, not knowing how long he could keep it up. The hotel was a good two miles away and he was in his dress shoes . . . in the pouring rain. But he could focus on one thing and one thing only . . . get back to the hotel and warn Hattie about Maneray and then call Professor Lucien. The faster he ran the more his ankles hurt from running in hard shoes. But every time he thought of stopping, he thought of that murderer returning to The Graylock. He thought of Maneray running Lucien off the road in the middle of the night. He thought of Maneray threatening Tim with a gun . . . and then he ran faster and faster and faster.

He was several long blocks away from Capitol Hill when he tried to beat a traffic light at F Street. He thought he had the right of way, but all he could hear was the blaring horn from the taxi turning the corner and swerving sharply to the right to avoid hitting him. Jerome skidded and slipped on the wet pavement and landed on his stomach next to a parked car. He dropped his umbrella and his notebook trying to break his fall and looked up just in time to watch the wind blow the umbrella down the street. He saw his notebook underneath the rear wheel of the car. He heard the taxi door slam as he was getting back on his feet.

"Jesus H. . . . I'm sorry, mister. I had my wipers on . . . but I didn't see you running there. Jesus . . . are you all right? . . . Let me help you up." The driver took Jerome's arm and helped him to his feet. Jerome was slightly dazed, but more concerned with getting back on track to the hotel. He and the driver stood in the rain and Jerome looked at him a second time.

"Jake?" he said.

"Yeah . . . that's me . . . Jake Milden. Are you alright?" Jerome nodded. "Yeah . . . I'm ok . . . just soaked" answered Jerome.

"Do you remember me?" he asked the driver. "You gave me my first taxi ride in D.C. back in early September. Remember? I was going to The Graylock . . . you wouldn't drive me down N Street . . . do you remember?"

"Yeah . . . Yeah . . . now I remember . . . you was goin' to law school right?!" recollected Jake ". . . goin' to live at that nut house hotel?"

"That's right" shouted Jerome "and that's exactly where you are going to take me now! Back to The Graylock. C'mon . . . let's go . . . I am in one big hurry! Don't ask for directions . . . you know where it is." Jerome trotted over to Jake's cab and dove into the back seat. Jake followed quickly on his heels and started the taxi. "What are you doin' out in this rain?" he asked without looking back at Jerome.

"Jake . . . I'm in terrible hurry. I have to get back to the hotel as fast as you can drive. I don't have any money with me . . . I can pay you when I get there. Just hurry, please!"

"I ain't goin' in to that place . . . I'll wait for you outside . . . but I ain't goin' in there!!"

"Alright!! Alright!! Jake . . . please . . . just get me back there . . . fast!"

Jake made pretty good time on the road considering the weather. Jerome was trying to think of the best way to tell Hattie that she hired a convicted murderer four months ago. "Maybe I should just call the police and let them handle it" he thought to himself "I mean I have reason to believe that he ran Professor Lucien off the road . . . he threatened Tim. But I don't know where he is. How can I get him apprehended before he tries to come back to The Graylock?" Jerome kept rubbing his wet hair trying to figure it all out. The simpler he tried to make it, the more complicated it became. He did not know how to untie a knot he had nothing to do with in the first place. He wanted his grandfather with him to help him figure this out. "How did this get to be such a mess!" he whispered "I've only been here two months." He realized he could not get despondent. He did not have the time. Jake was rounding the corner of New Hampshire Avenue to Connecticut Avenue. Jerome could see that the traffic light at the corner of Connecticut Avenue and 17th Street was red. But as Jake pulled up to the traffic light . . . the same place he let Jerome off at eights weeks ago . . . even from the back seat of the taxi, Jerome could see that there was too much red for one traffic light. His instincts turned upside down. Something was wrong. Something was very wrong. Jerome rolled the window down in the back seat and look through the driving rain a half a block down N Street to the outside of the hotel. There were flashing red lights everywhere . . . from the ambulance . . . from the police cars . . . from the fire engine.

"Oh my God . . . I'm too late!!!" yelled Jerome. He leapt out of the taxi and ran like lightning towards the hotel. He saw a rain soaked, forlorn Mr. Duffy standing just underneath the red awning . . . he got closer and he could see that the hotel's front door was propped wide open. Several police officers blocked Jerome from getting any closer to the hotel's entrance. Just as they said "You can't go in there, sir" Jerome saw two ambulance attendants leave the hotel . . . each at the opposite end of a stretcher . . . laden with a body . . . completely covered over in a white sheet. A dead body.

Jerome tried to bust through the police line and they grabbed him tightly by both arms. He tried to shake them loose, but to no avail. He screamed out "Mr. Duffy!!! Mr. Duffy!!!" He tried to tell the officers that he lived in the hotel. He yelled again to Duffy . . . this time he heard him. He motioned to the police to let him go and beckoned Jerome forward just in time for him to watch the ambulance pull away . . . off to the morgue. "You'd better come inside, Jerome" said Duffy with no more cadence than a pall bearer. Jerome stepped inside the lobby while one of the officers began to question Mr. Duffy. Jerome eyes darted all over the lobby. Nothing seemed out of order. He could see no damage. All he saw was Polly standing in the corner near the front window. She was crying as she watched the ambulance drive down N Street.

"Polly . . . what happened here!?" he blurted out. She turned to him. It was the saddest he'd ever seen her look. "Oh . . . Jerome

". . . this heres a bad day fo' the hotel" she said through her tears "a very bad day fo' all of us."

Jerome wiped the rain from his face and walked over to Polly. "What happened?" he said barely above a whisper.

"She wanted to be up an' dressed at four . . . so she told us to ring her . . . in time for her to git herself ready on account o' she said she had things she wanted to do 'fore dinner. An' so when Mr. Duffy done rang her room an' there was no answer . . . he told me I should jes go an' knock an' remind her that it was time fo' her to git up. So I did, Mr. Jerome . . . I did an' I open the door jes a little to let her know I could git her whatever she wanted . . . an' then I saw her . . . I saw her there . . . jes lyin' there." Polly broke down an' wept utterly. Jerome tried to comfort her. "It was jes awful" she continued. "I went screamin' fo' the Mrs. . . ."

"What did you say?" said Jerome "You went screaming for who?"

"The Mrs. . . . ain't you been lisnin' to me, Jerome? I was scared so I went to find the Mrs. an' tell her!" Polly was heaving she was crying so hard.

"That wasn't Hattie they just carried out of here on a stretcher?"

"No!! No . . . Jerome what you talkin' 'bout?" cried Polly. "That there was po' Mrs. Meredith them doctors done carried on outa here, that's who! Mrs. Meredith done died in her sleep right up there in Room 11. She passed on durin' her afternoon nap!"

Jerome's brain was about to explode from confusion. "Mrs. Meredith died? I just saw her this morning. She looked fine."

"That's what I'm tellin you Jerome . . . she died while she was takin' a nap . . . not mo' 'n twenty or thirty minutes ago . . . God took her . . . jes like that. Oh . . . this is a bad day fo' us here."

"Where's Hattie'?"

"She's in the back . . . grievin' somethin' awful. She loved Mrs.

Meredith so . . . better 'n she was her own sister . . . always lookin' foward to her visits . . . and now she done died right her in the Mrs.' hotel. I'm gone ta pray fo' the both o' them, that's what I'm gone ta do." Polly wiped her tears away with her apron. Jerome touched her softly on the shoulder. "You rest now, Polly. Try to relax some . . . everything's going to be all right."

"Thank you, Jerome. I sho' is glad yous back now . . . an' Mr. Timothy should be here by an' by."

"Where'd he go?" asked Jerome.

"The Mrs. done sent him to the store fo' some breakfast foods. He's out in that rain now, but he'll be back by an' by." Jerome turned away and walked towards the dining room. He saw Hattie staring at her nail polish . . . motionless.

"Hattie . . . may I come in?"

She looked up at him with sorrowful eyes and motioned for him to sit down at her table. "It's a dark day for us, Jerome . . . a dark day."

"I'm sorry about Mrs. Meredith, Hattie" he said quietly. Hattie tilted her head towards the door and mindlessly rubbed her palm. She looked like her world was crashing but she was not crying. Somehow she found the strength to retain her composure.

"She was the Queen of American Agriculture . . . did I ever tell you that?" she said poignantly. "Yes m'am . . . you did" said Jerome.

"She was my closest friend in the whole world . . . my dearest confidant. I suppose it was right that she pass on when she was close to me. It seems only fitting. Not right, you know . . . just fitting. Life doesn't always turn out right." She sat up a little straighter in her chair. "She was only 87 years old. That doesn't seem very old to me." She patted Jerome's hand. "Does that seem old to you, dear?"

Jerome shrugged uncomfortably. "I don't really know . . . I

suppose not . . . I mean some people live longer."

"And some don't" replied Hattie "you just never know . . . try as you may . . . you just never know. It's best to live your life fully while you have it."

Mr. Duffy stood at the entrance to the dining room. "Hattie . . . the coroner said he'd call tomorrow . . . he'll have some paper work for you to look at . . . if that's ok."

"Certainly . . . that will be fine, thank you Mr. Duffy" she said looking at him most kindly. "You've been a wonderful help. Thank you, Mr. Duffy." He nodded briefly and left to return to the front desk.

"Hattie" said Jerome softly. "I don't want to upset you . . . perhaps this might not be the best time . . . but I have to talk to you about something I found out. It's very important."

She rubbed her forehead with her small fingers and turned the corner of her mouth up into the faintest remnant of a smile that she could manage.

"You and Tim have been finding out a lot of things lately, haven't you?" Jerome did not follow up. "I know you boys . . . well, shall I say 'stumbled' across certain information in my house across the street."

Jerome had no time to be shy now. "Yes, Hattie . . . we . . . we did find out a few things . . . but this . . . what I'm about to tell you is different. It's not about . . . you know . . . it's not about the stuff across the street."

"What then?" she asked mildly. "What is so important that you have to tell me now. What could make this day any darker than it is already?"

Chapter Thirty

Tim waited inside a coffee shop next to the grocery store for what seemed like an eternity to him for the rain to let up. After what was really only forty-five minutes, he decided that whatever protection his umbrella could afford him in the torrents would have to do. He could dry off sufficiently, for the second time in a day, after he got back to the hotel. The rain would not ruin the breakfast foods, although he was not too sure how well the paper bags would hold up. Managing the three large bags of groceries and the umbrella, with no cooperation from the wind, was a balancing act that he was losing the longer he was out in the rain. When he finally reached the back alleyway, he only hoped the bottoms of the paper bags would hold out until he made it to the garden gate. He felt like taking Mr. Duffy's cape off and bundling all the groceries into it and hauling them over his shoulder . . . but he did not want to hurt Mr. Duffy's feelings by using his precious cape as a tarp for hotel groceries. So, he carried on . . . forward with the umbrella held in front of him to ward off some of the driving wind and rain. It blocked his view partially and several yards into the alleyway he did not see the man to the side of one of the garages . . . waiting for him. Tim stopped when he saw the man's feet move into the middle of the alley.

"Trying to hide underneath that cape, little lawyer boy?" the man snarled. Tim lifted the umbrella away from his face . . . over his head. He could smell the alcohol when he stared into the man's face. It was Maneray.

"I warned you" he said as he shoved Tim backwards. "What the fuck do you want!" yelled Tim trying to gain his balance.

"Your ass, little lawyer boy. Your ass." Before Tim could think to drop the groceries and protect himself, the first hammering blow from Maneray's huge fist landed across Tim's jaw and sent him sprawling backwards onto the brick pavement. The groceries spilled everywhere. Tim knocked his head against the bricks and laid there . . . stunned. Maneray leaned over and grabbed him by his shirt collar. The second blow landed on the side of Tim's head and knocked his glasses off. "I hate you and everybody like you!" Maneray growled as he brought the third brutal blow directly down into Tim's nose . . . breaking it . . . spurting blood and cartilage on Maneray's shirt. Tim heaved and rolled over on his side. He tried to get his hands up to his face but they were trapped and covered in Mr. Duffy's cape. Maneray watched Tim struggle on the ground and then reeled his boot back and threw a swift, solid kick into Tim's ribs . . . cracking two. Maneray sneered at his victim and wiped his face . . . and disappeared into the rain. Unable to see without his glasses, barely able to breathe through a broken nose and unable to move because of cracked ribs Tim's body collapsed and he lost consciousness.

Polly stayed in the kitchen long after she was supposed to have left for the day. Saddened by the death of Mrs. Meredith and worried that Hattie might need her help, she told Mr. Duffy that she was going to tidy up and stick around for awhile. She began to put the best hotel dishes back in the cabinets. There would be no celebratory dinner tonight. She removed the roasting goose from the oven to let it cool. She could store most everything in the refrigerator for a few days . . . what was perishable she dumped into the kitchen garbage pail. Noticing that it was full, Polly wrapped the bag tightly and decided to bring it out to the back shed herself. She looked out the kitchen window into the garden and saw that the rain had just begun to let up considerably. The sky was still dark and foreboding and she could hear thunder claps in the distance. She walked out to the tool room and overheard Mr. Duffy tell Hattie that the coroner would be back tomorrow with some papers for her to sign. Jerome was seated beside her ready to impart his grave knowledge about Maneray's past.

As she unbolted the door, she heard Hattie ask "Polly . . . you're not leaving are you?" Polly walked to the door jam of the dining room and said reassuringly. "No m'am . . . I'm jes takin' this gawbage out to the shed . . . I'll be right back." Hattie had a relieved look on her face. She did not speak . . . did not have to . . . Polly knew that Hattie appreciated her staying. Hattie turned to Jerome to let him begin his tale, but she watched Polly walk in the misty rain through the garden to the shed as she listened.

The strong winds had blown the back gate open and it was swinging back and forth on its hinges . . . open and shut. Polly unlatched the shed door to throw the garbage into the big cans when two stray dogs appeared at the gate.

"Go on now dogs!" Polly yelled and waved her arm to shoo them off. "Git . . . ain't nothin' fo' you here!" She set the garbage down to close the back gate and keep the mongrels out. The gate had swung wide and she stepped into the alley to grab its handle. "You done heard me now . . . I said git!" She tried to shoo them away again with her free arm and she pulled the gate closed with the other. "Go on, I said! . . . git on up there with them other dogs!" She pointed fiercely up the alley to where a group of stray dogs were pawing at garbage . . . spilled into the alleyway. Polly looked up at the strays growling over spoiling food. "Ain't that awful . . . people lettin' gawbage set out there like that . . . think didn't nobody have a broom' round here 'cept me" she said to herself. "I got half a mind to go clean that up myself . . . it ain't right havin' them dogs runnin' all 'round back here carryin' sickness an' all." She looked again at the pack of scavengers and shook her head in disgust. She looked one more time as she pulled the gate to a close. This time she did not see the dogs. She released her grasp on the gate and it swung wide open again. Polly stepped fully into the alley . . . took a few steps closer to the dogs that were not more than twenty yards away. She stepped quickly a few more feet closer and covered her mouth in horror . . . in disbelief. In the middle of the alley she looked up towards the body and back again at the hotel. She ran a few more feet and came to a dead stop. The strays were lapping up what they could off the pavement . . . and off the body. Wanting to scream . . . unable to make a whimper . . . her vocal chords knotted too tightly to cry out for help, Polly turned and broke into a frightened and hysterical run back to the hotel.

Hattie saw her in a state of real distress running towards the side door. She stood up . . . alarmed. "Something's wrong, Jerome. Something's wrong with Polly."

Polly busted through the side door and screamed wildly for Jerome. "Jerome! Jerome! You got ta help!! Mr. Jerome . . . you got ta help!!"

All three . . . Hattie, Jerome and Mr. Duffy . . . ran into the tool room. "Polly . . . what is it? What's wrong?" asked Hattie. She did not answer. She grabbed Jerome's shirt and pulled him out the door. "Mr. Jerome. . . . you got to git out there!!" She kept pushing him. "Polly . . . Polly, dear calm down" said Hattie "what is out there?"

Polly wanted to break into tears, but she was too frightened. She grabbed ahold of Jerome's arm and pointed him to the gate. "It's Tim . . . it's Tim . . . he's lyin' out there in the alley!!! I think he's dead!!" Jerome was gone in a flash.

Polly turned to Mr. Duffy. "Call an ambulance!! Git some doctors here!" Hattie remained calm. She looked at Duffy and motioned him inside. "Go . . . Wallace . . . call the ambulance . . . and get the police back here." She took Polly's hand. "Polly . . . you bring me out there . . . show me what you saw." The two women rushed hand in hand up the garden steps, out the back gate and into the alley. Hattie could see Jerome already on his knees . . . bending over Tim's body. She began to run towards him. He heard her running and yelled back to her. "Get an ambulance here fast . . . he's still alive!" Hattie turned swiftly to Polly and told her to go back into the hotel and make sure Mr. Duffy had the police and an ambulance on the way. "Then go into the storage space underneath the front stairs and bring as many blankets as you can carry . . . hurry!!"

Hattie stood over Jerome as he gently tried to move Tim. He was bruised and bloody. His right eye was swollen shut and the break in his noise was painfully apparent. His clothes were soaked through from the rain. He tried to part his lips to speak. Hattie lowered herself carefully to the pavement and brushed his matted soaked hair away from his forehead revealing two huge lumps from hitting the bricks. "Don't talk, Tim dear. Don't try to talk . . . we have an ambulance coming right away. Everything's going to be alright. We're here now . . . everything's going to be fine. We'll take care of you." She saw his glasses on the ground about three feet away and reached to pick them up.

Jerome saw Polly rushing up the alley with an armful of blankets and he got up to meet her. He pulled two blankets from her pile and draped them closely around Tim's arms and legs. Polly dropped herself to the pavement near Tim's head. She rolled one of the blankets up into a pillow, gently lifted Tim's head and placed it underneath. "Mr. Timothy . . . this is ol' Polly here now

... we gone ta take good care o' you ... don't you worry none 'bout that" she said in a teary whisper "jes don't you worry, you hear ... you gone ta be fine in no time." She rubbed his shoulder, but had to close her eyes at the sight of his battered face. Hattie placed another blanket over his chest.

Jerome bent closer to Tim and placed his hand on Tim's shoulder. "Tim ... Tim ... this is Jerome" he said looking straight at him. "You don't have to talk, but just nod if you can understand me."

Tim moved his head in slight nod. "Good ..." Jerome said to him "that's real good ... listen to me Tim ... there's an ambulance right on its way and we'll get you to the hospital as fast as we can. I'll stay with you the whole way ... ok?" Tim nodded again and tried to move his lips to speak. Hattie looked quickly down the alley to see for any sign of the arriving ambulance.

"Tim ... I have to ask you right now ... just nod yes or no ... ok?" Jerome placed his hand on the side of Tim's swollen face. "Did he do this to you, Tim? Did Maneray beat you up?" Polly looked at Jerome. "Mr. Jerome ... what you talkin' 'bout?" she said in a confused hush. Hattie also looked at Jerome, but Jerome kept his eyes on Tim while he nodded "yes." Only then did Jerome raise his eyes and look at Hattie.

"What have I done?" she whispered. "What in heaven's name have I done?" She kneeled over in complete contrition and held his head lovingly in her hands. "Oh God ... what have I done? Timothy ... Timothy, can you hear me? It's Hattie, dear. Oh ... my dear I am so terribly sorry. Please forgive me." She looked up at Jerome. "Please forgive me" she repeated ... lost in the horrible misery of the moment.

Jerome jumped up when he saw Mr. Duffy lead the ambulance attendants carrying a stretcher through the garden gate into the alley way. "Up here!!" he yelled to him. "Hurry!" The attendants broke into a run. They took one look at Tim and did not speak. They firmly took hold of Hattie and moved her out of the way so they could lay the stretcher on the ground next to Tim. Polly stood up and moved away from Tim's head. "Don't you go hurtin' him none now, you understand?" she snapped. "Don't you hurt this po' sweet boy no more n' he been hurt already. I'm watchin' you!"

Mr. Duffy stood a few feet away and could not believe his eyes. He said nothing. Jerome walked over to him and spoke very directly. "Mr. Duffy . . . Mr. Duffy . . . listen to me. I am going to the hospital with Tim. You have to do some things for me while I'm gone . . . ok? . . . Mr. Duffy? Are you listening to me?" Duffy kept his eyes on the ambulance attendants as they lifted Tim onto the stretcher and readjusted the blankets. "Mr. Duffy" repeated Jerome "walk with me back to the hotel. I'll tell you what I want you do." They all followed the stretcher back into the garden, down the side of the hotel and out to the front to the waiting ambulance. Jerome instructed Duffy to find Professor Lucien's telephone number in the directory and call him immediately. Duffy was to explain that he was calling for Jerome and that it was a grave emergency . . . that the professor's life was in danger and that he should get a police guard to his home right away. "Tell him that Oliver Maneray is out and means to do him harm. Tell him that I will explain everything when I get back from the hospital. Can you do that?" pleaded Jerome.

"Maneray??" said Duffy. "What does that creature have to do with this?"

"Maneray did this to Tim, Mr. Duffy" Jerome replied flatly. "Make sure the police get a full description of him when they get here and have them post a guard at the back gate, the side entrance and the front door. Under no circumstances let him into the hotel. Do you understand?"

THE GRAYLOCK

Mr. Duffy looked at Tim in the back of the ambulance. "If that bullying bastard ever shows his face at this hotel again, I'll kill him myself" he declared. Hattie took his hand and held it tightly. "Wallace . . . we'll let the police take care of this." Two squad cars were just pulling onto N Street as she spoke. "Jerome, call us from the hospital as soon as the doctors see Tim."

"Alright, Hattie . . . I'll call you as soon as I can" he stepped into the back of the ambulance. "Make sure the police post guards at the hotel." The ambulance driver slammed the open door turned on the siren and sped off to the emergency room. Hattie stepped up to speak to the officers and all of them . . . Hattie, Mr. Duffy, Polly and the police went into The Graylock.

It was past nine o'clock by the time Jerome returned to the hotel. When Mr. Duffy saw him come through the front door he jumped up from his seat at the front desk and shouted "They got him, Jerome. They caught the bastard!" As weary and tired as he was, Jerome wanted to hear all the details. When he called from the hospital he learned that Hattie had already given the police a full description of Maneray and that a hunt was on. "They found the creature . . . drunk in a bar about six blocks up on Connecticut Avenue!!" said Duffy triumphantly. Same as when he killed Nathaniel Farley 35 years ago thought Jerome. "They've got him downtown . . . locked up like the animal he is!" Duffy told Jerome. "I hope he rots there" he added.

"Oh I don't think you'll have to worry any, Mr. Duffy. Maneray's not getting out this time."

"This time" asked Duffy. "What do you mean this time?" Jerome was too tired for another long tale telling. "I can explain it to you later . . . ok? Where's Hattie?" Duffy pointed to the dining room. "How's Tim?" Jerome smiled a bit. "He'll be ok . . . the doctors just want to watch him for a bit . . . he should be home in a week…maybe less."

He walked into the dining room and saw an exhausted Hattie nervously sitting at her table. He pulled out the chair next to her and sat.

"Hi" he said. "You alright?" She nodded.

"Sure" she replied unconvincingly. "How is Timothy? What do the doctors say?"

"They are going to keep him there for a few days . . . he was pretty beat up, Hattie. They've set his broken nose ok, but he's got two badly cracked ribs. Maneray must have kicked him while he was on the ground. There's nothing wrong with his eye though . . . except for the swelling. They said that'll take a week at least for it to go down. They x-rayed his head and didn't see any skull fractures, but they were a little worried. Apparently he hit the brick pavement awfully hard. He's got a nice sized lump in the back of his head and he had a small concussion . . . the doctors said that's probably what made him pass out like he did. The ribs didn't puncture his lungs, but they're watching to see that he doesn't develop any pneumonia from having laid out there in the rain."

Hattie buried her face in her hands. When she looked up she asked. "Did you talk to him?"

"Yeah . . . but not for very long. He's awfully uncomfortable as you can imagine. He said Maneray caught him by surprise near one of the garages out back." Hattie rubbed her cheek. "They've got him, you know." He nodded. "Mr. Duffy told me. Tim also said that Mr. Duffy told him everything about the night your husband died."

"Yes . . . I know that. I suppose Mr. Duffy told as much as he knows."

"What do you mean?"

"Mr. Duffy doesn't know everything . . . only I know everything about that night."

"Did you know that Maneray was arrested that same night for the murder of a White House aide to Teddy Roosevelt?"

"I do now. I've had a long chat on the telephone with your Professor Lucien. You mentioned his name to me awhile back . . . I thought then that it sounded familiar to me. Now I remember why."

"He was the one who got the confession out of Maneray for the murder."

"Yes . . . of course . . . that, too. But more importantly, at least for me, he was the one who let us go . . . decided not to press any charges against me or Mr. Duffy. It was that night I knew I'd never practice law . . . I had to agree to it."

"I don't understand" said Jerome.

"Well, you see . . . my husband was very sick. He was quite ill when we married, but I knew that . . . he told me so when we started to court. But, I didn't care. I fell in love with him . . . he was the kindest man I knew. He was very good to me, too. He treated me with great respect . . . he was a very thoughtful man. Neither of us knew how long he would live when we got married."

"What was wrong with him?"

"Cancer . . . a little bit at first, but it spread quickly. He was always looking into new ideas and theories how to ward it off . . . medically . . . spiritually . . . philosophically . . . he didn't care and neither did I. I just wanted him to live as long as he could. That's how he got involved with that Life Extension Institute. They had all kinds of schemes on how to extend your life and Edmund was interested . . . and anything that was going to extend his life, I became interested in, as well. I never saw anything wrong with it . . . but his so-called doctor friends did . . . and they drummed him out of the profession . . . called him a 'quack'. His health deteriorated on a daily basis from that day forward. It was awful to watch him die slowly. When the pain got to be too much, he started giving himself morphine injections. I couldn't bear to do it and when he got too weak he taught Mr. Duffy the procedure. It wasn't against the law for me, as his wife to help with the injections . . . but Wallace was not a member of the family . . . strictly speaking . . . although Edmund and I treated him as though he were.

"What has this got to do with Maneray and Professor Lucien?"

"David Lucien and I went to law school together. He was already in his third year when I first started. He was the only student in his class to wish me well. I was the only woman in the whole law school. I didn't see much of him that first year . . . every so often in the library . . . things like that. He graduated at the top of the class and took a job in the prosecutor's office. Every so often over the next two years his name would be in the newspapers for winning some case or another. He was very ambitious. A lot of people thought he'd run for District Attorney. The night Edmund died and they brought Wallace and myself down to the station house for questioning, David was there . . . standing watch over the manhunt for Mr. Maneray. Needless to say . . . he was shocked to see me there. I lied when I told him that I gave Edmund the injection . . . but I just knew that he'd put poor Wallace in jail if I told the truth . . . Wallace was a runaway teenager, you know. They'd have shipped him back to that reform school in Virginia where I know he would have killed himself or have been killed. He's . . . well he's . . . at least back then he just wasn't all that strong enough to defend himself and he'd been horribly abused in the school. Edmund was already dead . . . nothing I could do to bring him back. I couldn't bear the thought of Wallace dying, too. So I lied because I knew they . . . wouldn't do anything to me."

"So they let you go?"

"Yes . . . after a while. After the police grilled me like a common criminal. They did the same to Wallace. They let us go after a couple of hours . . . accused us of all sorts of sordid goings on and none of it true. But before I left, David took me in a room privately and let me know I was going to be in big trouble with the bar examination committee as far as my fitness and moral character were concerned. They were very strict in those days . . . if there was anything suspicious about you at all, you would never get admitted to the bar."

"That's why you never practiced law?"

Hattie shook her head. "I knew David was right. Because of the arrest, I'd never get through the character committee. They'd start adding this and that up and conclude that I was not fit to be a lawyer. They'd look at my socialite days . . . the fact I married an older and wealthy, not to mention, dying man. They'd look into the Life Extension Institute and see everything wrong instead of everything that was right with it. They'd probably even try to portray Edmund as a morphine addict who was expelled from the medical profession. I didn't want that to happen. I loved him and I didn't want to see his name dragged through the mud by people who knew nothing about him."

"You never thought of trying to fight them?"

"I suppose if things had not gotten worse when I got home that night, I might have given it some thought at another time. But, that's not what happened."

"What do you mean?"

"I returned home and told Wallace to go stay with some of our friends over on P Street for the night. I wanted to be alone . . . and there was that mess to clean up in Edmund's office. I guess the shock of the evening began to wear off a few hours later and the reality of losing my husband and my career began to sink in. I got very upset and emotional and I had not been feeling all that well of late anyway. I was always worried about Edmund and my final exams were coming up that semester and I was four months pregnant.

"You had a baby?"

"No, Jerome" said Hattie frankly. "I had a miscarriage . . . I lost my babies that night in the hospital. I had just become way too upset with the horror of the evening and I knew something was wrong when I finally laid into bed. I was in such pain I could barely move. I got to the telephone to call for help. I crawled outside the front door, but that was as far as I got. By the time they got me to the hospital, it was too late to do anything. I lost them."

"Them . . . ?"

"Twins . . . my boys. Gone to heaven the same night as their father. My life has never been the same since. Nothing has been able to replace them . . . until you and Tim came along . . . and now this . . . ."

"Jesus . . . Hattie, I'm sorry . . . my God . . . why didn't you say anything??"

"I just don't know why, Jerome. I guess I have tried with all my might to forget about it, but when I saw Timothy lying out there in the alley in such a state . . . it came back . . . that feeling of overwhelming loss. I didn't want to go through that again . . . I couldn't . . . and I've been sitting here for hours just praying that he'd be alright and come back here . . . I've been praying that neither of you would leave . . . you won't leave will you?" Hattie dabbed the corner of her eye to hold back the tear . . . trying to pretend it was not there, but Jerome saw it.

"Hattie" he said softly "nobody's leaving you . . . I'm not going anywhere. Tim's staying. It's all over now. Everything's going to be fine. Maneray's locked up and he's going to stay that way for a long time . . . don't worry about that. We're here to stay. Mr. Duffy's here . . . Polly's here. Now we can start to have some fun. Ok?"

Hattie stood up gracefully and cleared her throat. "You're a godsend to me . . . the both of you. She walked over to the side door of the dining room an opened it. A cool breeze came immediately through the screen. "The rain seems to have taken the mugginess away . . . I'm going out to the garden for a bit." She turned towards Jerome who had a worried look on his face. Hattie paused for a second. "I guess you know now why I go out there sometimes at night."

"Yes . . . I do . . . I understand now. Don't stay too long . . . it's gotten a little cool out."

"I'll be back in directly, Jerome. Why don't you have Polly fix you something to eat? I won't be long." She pushed the screen door open. "Jerome . . . ?"

"Yes m'am?" he said.

"I thought you might like to know . . . my boys are out there, too . . . a little further back in the corner . . . it's a smaller stone."

Jerome smiled at her. "That's nice . . . it's pretty out there."

Hattie folded her arms close to her and walked with her head up back to the ivy patch all the while letting the soft evening breeze dry her tears. She sat on the brick wall in between the iron posts nearest Edmund's grave and moved her hand across the top of the damp ivy.

"Hello, Edmund dear . . . boys" she said blowing a kiss into the corner. "Guess what?"

THE END

Made in the
USA
Columbia, SC